MELISSA DE LA CRUZ

Summer On EAST END

Includes *TRIPLE MOON* and *DOUBLE ECLIPSE*

speak

ALSO BY MELISSA DE LA CRUZ

TRIPLE MOON

SPEAK

An imprint of Penguin Random House LLC

375 Hudson Street

New York, New York 10014

First published in the United States of America by G. P. Putnam's Sons,
an imprint of Penguin Random House LLC, 2015
Published by Speak, an imprint of Penguin Random House LLC, 2016
This omnibus edition published by Speak, an imprint of Penguin Random House LLC, 2018

THE LIBRARY OF CONGRESS HAS CATALOGED THE G. P. PUTNAM'S SONS EDITION AS FOLLOWS:
Names: De la Cruz, Melissa, 1971–
Title: Triple moon : a Summer on East End novel / Melissa de la Cruz.
Description: New York, NY : G. P. Putnam's Sons, an imprint of Penguin Group (USA), [2015]
| Series: Summer on East End ; book 1 | Summary: Twin witches (and Norse goddesses) Molly
and Mardi Overbrook are sent to North Hampton for the summer where they must learn to
control their powers before the White Council exiles them to Limbo.
Identifiers: LCCN 2015020238 | ISBN 9780399173554 (hardcover : alk. paper)
Subjects: | CYAC: Sisters—Fiction. | Twins—Fiction. | Witches—Fiction. | Magic—Fiction. |
Goddesses, Norse—Fiction. | Mythology, Norse—Fiction. | Hamptons (N.Y.)—Fiction.
Classification: LCC PZ7.D36967 Tr 2015 | DDC [Fic]—dc23
2015020238

Speak ISBN 9780147515384
This omnibus edition ISBN 9781984835567

Printed in the United States of America
Design by Richard Amari.

1 3 5 7 9 10 8 6 4 2

For Mike and Mattie, always

And my Witches of East End family
WitchEEs forever!

With thanks to Jennifer Besser and
everyone at Penguin for making a new home
for a little white magic

I was too young that time to value her,

But now I know her. If she be a traitor,

Why, so am I. We still have slept together,

Rose at an instant, learn'd, play'd, eat together,

And wheresoe'er we went, like Juno's swans,

Still we went coupled and inseparable.

—William Shakespeare, As You Like It

* C *

FADE TO BLACK

*E*ven by Manhattan private school standards, Bret Farley's party was unforgettable. It wasn't just the bottomless flow of top-shelf liquor or the mounds of gleaming caviar, the world-class sculpture collection and the spectacular views of the city from the Park Avenue penthouse, or the rumors of a hidden elevator down to a clandestine indoor lap pool of black marble. It wasn't the designer drugs or the thousand-dollar stilettos. It wasn't all the fooling around in gilt bathrooms and between silky Italian sheets.

The night of Bret Farley's party was unforgettable because, by the end of it, two of the guests were dead.

The prime suspects behind this tragic turn of events, the Overbrook twins, Molly and Mardi, had arrived at Bret's penthouse a little after ten, bewitchingly identical in their dark features and lush black hair, but oh so different in style. Molly was the height of chic, Mardi the essence of rebellion. Equally gorgeous and equally brilliant.

So why, only moments after taking their first drinks from a caterer's silver tray, did both goddesses start to feel undone?

Molly was sipping champagne, Mardi a very dry Manhattan. This they both remembered. They also remembered that blue-eyed, ultra-suave Bret had flirted with both of them, telling Molly the vintage bubbles and caviar were all for her benefit, then leading Mardi by the hand among the bronze legs of the enormous Louise Bourgeois spider, the crown jewel of his family's collection. The only other of that size graced the lobby of the Tate Modern in London. The twins recalled the body of the spider looming in the apartment's vast entryway, beautiful and malicious.

Each sister had been glaringly jealous of Bret's attentions to her twin. But neither one could begin to remember where those attentions had led.

There was an obscene swirl of luxury: reflective surfaces, sparkling views, high art, thumping music, and shiny beautiful rich kids who were striking poses for their Insta accounts, gossiping, drinking from priceless crystal, and falling down wasted onto one another.

The Overbrook girls were very much a part of this ruling scene, but they were apart from it as well. Because Molly and Mardi weren't simply pretty and privileged; they were supernatural.

With supernatural instincts.

The twins could tell that something was up that

night, something more than just Upper East Side private school mischief, but they found themselves too spellbound to investigate. Was it in their drinks? Or a deep corruption in the atmosphere? If you'd asked them at the party if they thought it would end in carnage, they would have laughed, but not wholeheartedly. They would have let out tinkling, nervous laughs. Laughs that admitted suspicion. But suspicion of what? Of whom?

The last thing Molly remembered, before blacking out, was the sound of Bret's sexy whisper in her ear. "This is all for you, Molly," he was saying, "every flower petal, every flute, every ivory caviar spoon."

Only she didn't want to believe him because she had just seen him with her twin, probably telling Mardi the same thing.

The last thing Mardi recalled was the bronze underbelly of the giant spider. Bret was telling her it was called *Maman*, because the artist believed that spiders were protective and benevolent. "You're the only girl here who could possibly get the reference," he whispered. His arm rested on her shoulder. "You love spiders, don't you, Mardi?" She managed to say, "Yeah, spiders are cool," and then her memory went blank.

The next morning, the legendary Overbrook twins stared at each other across their kitchen table through raccoon eyes. Neither one had taken off her mascara. They were still in their rumpled party clothes. Molly in her cocktail dress, Mardi in her torn black jeans. Somehow they had managed to order coffee and eggs online from the diner down the street.

They were too spent to start their usual argument about whose fault it was that the eggs were over easy instead of sunny-side up and who had been stupid enough to order whole wheat toast instead of sourdough. Somehow, there was no energy for fighting.

When they finally managed to speak, they sighed, in unison, "What happened last night? What the—?"

Then they sank silently into their breakfast, each straining to remember the previous night.

It was several hours before they got the news.

*

PART ONE

HOT FUN
IN THE
SUMMERTIME

*

THRIFT SHOP

Mardi Overbrook shifted into fourth gear on the Montauk Highway, gunning to pass what had to be yet another banker's kid in a brand-new black Ferrari. She belted along to Macklemore, singing about the twenty dollars in her pocket, her car vibrating to the powerful beat as it dusted the ultimate Hamptons douchemobile. Sucker had probably paid extra for automatic because he never learned to drive stick.

Her own car was a Ferrari too, but it was far from new—a 1972 red convertible Daytona that had lived many lives. It didn't look anything like Banker Boy's car, and she didn't look anything like his preppie girl-friend either. Mardi had a rainbow tattoo that circled her neck like a python and an emerald-studded barbell through the tip of her tongue, which she stuck out at the astonished driver as she blurred by him, screaming along to her favorite song.

At the light, she glanced down at her phone, which

was sitting faceup on the ebony leather passenger seat. Her social media feed was flowing in a steady stream, showing the streets and interiors of the city she was leaving behind. Unlike the majority of the stuck-up kids at her stupid prep school, she wasn't getting the posts of sunsets in Mustique or cocktail parties in Nantucket. No, her feed was full of the real stuff from after-hours clubs all over the five boroughs of New York City, places without names or defined locations, places that appeared and disappeared in water towers and in abandoned fleabag motels, places she called home because she traveled there in a manic rebel pack that she called family. The pictures were of passed-out teens, teens staggering out into the daylight like disoriented moths, teens in various states of undress. She smiled down as they migrated across her phone screen. Her tribe.

She adjusted the strap of her vintage leopard-skin push-up bathing-suit bra, which she was wearing with a pair of threadbare rhinestone-encrusted denim shorts. The outfit had been left decades ago in the back of a closet by one of Dad's girlfriends from his Studio 54 days. There was great stuff to be pillaged from Dad's past in the Overbrook loft in Greenpoint—if you knew where to look.

Mardi grabbed the phone, puckered her lips, and took a quick close-up, posting it for all her friends back in the city with a tagline: "Don't you dare forget me while I'm gone."

Why in the Underworld was she leaving her life behind? Could someone please remind her?

Oh, yeah—she was leaving her life behind to spend the summer babysitting in a sleepy town lost somewhere on the East End of Long Island. With her princess of a twin sister, Molly, no less.

It was a fate worse than being badly dressed.

As she drove farther out from civilization, the landscape grew more pastoral and the salt smell in the air grew more pronounced, irritating her eyes so that she started to tear up. She was not one to cry, but this summer stretching ahead of her, an endless ribbon of small-town boredom, was a depressing prospect. She hadn't even arrived in North Hampton, and she already felt trapped.

Mardi Overbrook hated feeling trapped.

She gritted her teeth, shifted into fifth gear, and turned the music up, determined not to admit defeat. If she was going to live for the summer in North Hampton, then she was going to make North Hampton worth living in.

A post popped onto her phone, which she instantly knew was from her twin. Not only because it was a phony artistic shot of some sand dune, complete with endangered shrubs and a pensive-looking seagull, that Molly had surely stopped to capture along her route—typical pretentious Molly—but because of the pink gold ring rolling over the image, undulating like soft taffy across the screen.

This was what young witches did lately to wink at one another through cyberspace. They overlaid their static posts with moving images visible only to their kind. Everyone had a symbol, like a living emoji. There were waxing and waning moons, twinkling stars, beating hearts, all sorts of romping mythical creatures. It was a tribal thing. And tribes were the whole point of social networking, right?

Molly and Mardi always had the rose gold ring, subtly carved with a diamondback pattern, floating through their posts, but only the two of them could see it. They had other images for sharing with the general witch population. Mardi used a vaulting rainbow, Molly a galloping thoroughbred horse. Only to each other did they make the golden ring visible. They'd never talked about it. But that's how it was.

So, when Mardi sent the image of her red lips out into the world, Molly alone would notice the symbol of their sisterhood floating across the screen, while the rest of Midgard's witches saw a snaking rainbow and the general population saw nothing but a cherry-red pout and a hint of leopard and lace.

Normally, this notion that she shared something unique with Molly wouldn't faze Mardi. It was no big deal, a stupid twin thing. But today she had to admit that she found it just a little bit comforting that, as she left the known world, there was someone—even if that someone was *the most irritating person in the universe*—who was truly on her wavelength.

The phone rang, and her father's handsome face filled the screen. She turned the music down and instinctively slowed, as if he could see her, although she was still twenty miles over the limit.

"S'up?"

"How about 'hello, Dad'?" Troy Overbrook asked.

"S'up?"

"Are you almost there, my sweet?"

"Honestly, I have no idea. The GPS is acting weird."

"Well, can't your sister navigate for you? I told you it was tricky."

Mardi looked at the empty seat beside her. "Molly's right here, but I'm afraid she's fully occupied painting her nails a lovely shade of lavender and simply cannot be bothered to come to my aid, Your Majesty. So sorry, Your Highness. At your service, My Lord. Deferentially yours, Master. Is that what you want to hear?"

Troy sighed. "Well, at least you girls are together. And what I want to hear is that you are both going to take this summer with Ingrid seriously. She's an old, dear friend of mine, and I'm afraid she may be our last hope. Show her some respect. Take good care of her children. I'm asking you to try. For your own good."

"I still can't believe you're making us do this—for the whole summer!"

"Do it you will. You have no idea how ugly things will get if you blow it."

"Life is an ugly thing, Dad."

"Not as ugly as Hell, my sweet."

A flashing red light appeared in Mardi's rearview mirror.

"Dad, gotta go. I'm being pulled over."

"What?" There was a groan on the other end. "Okay, but I want you to promise me that there will be no funny business. Take it like a mortal. A mortal who deserves a speeding ticket. I'll pay the fine. You have *got* to learn some self-control."

"Okay, promise, Dad. I swear. Okay. Bye."

She hurled the phone onto the floor and downshifted to a perfect stop. Before the police officer could open his door, she had already appeared between the exhaust pipes of her ridiculously powerful cherry-red car.

Her hair was jet black and knotty. Her eyes were dark and defiant, her makeup artfully smudged. Her legs were endless, sprouting pale and willowy from a pair of gladiator sandals covered in bronze spikes. The effect, with her studded shorts and pointy leopard bra, was quite unnerving. Her stomach was so defined and her arms so ripped that she looked hard to the touch, both wildly attractive and severely off-putting at the same time. The green glow emanating from the precious stone studding her tongue gave her the hypnotic quality of a cobra.

"Young lady," said the cop as he stumbled from his car door, "you should remain in your vehicle."

"Noted for next time." She laughed, squinting at him

until he stumbled again. "Next time, I will remain in my vehicle. Promise." Control her powers? Seriously, Dad, what were powers *for*?

"Next time?" he slurred. Then, making a super-human effort to get ahold of himself, he said, "License and registration, please."

"Say 'pretty please.'"

"Pretty ple—wait a second, you're not old enough to be driving a car like this!"

"I'm sixteen. Last time I checked that was the legal driving age."

"License and registration," he repeated, making his syllables yawn in slow motion. Then he said it again, way too fast, three times over, in a high, squeaky car-toon chipmunk voice: "License and registration! License and registration! License and registration!"

"Officer"—she grinned and took a step toward him—"are you harassing me?"

He looked down at his shiny black beetle shoes and clenched his fists, attempting one last time to get a grip on himself in the presence of her overwhelming magic.

"Miss, you were going over ninety miles an hour in a fifty-mile-per-hour zone. License and registration." This time his voice sounded as though he were underwater.

Gleefully, Mardi watched him close his mouth for fear he would start blowing bubbles. This was one of her favorite tricks to play on authority figures: to fill their mouths with so much saliva that they became terrified of becoming human soap-bubble wands.

"My speedometer told me I was right at the limit, Officer," she said sweetly.

He made a sound, but his lips wouldn't part to form words.

She laughed and hopped effortlessly back into her car.

"I'm afraid," she said as she revved the engine, "that you and I are going to have to agree to disagree, Officer."

She left him standing stock-still by the side of the road. She had made sure he wouldn't move a muscle for five minutes and that his memory of the encounter would be as fuzzy as a fading dream.

Sorry, Dad.

Why be mortally weak when she was immortally gifted?

She was the daughter of Thor, after all.

FANCY

As she made out with Leo Fairbanks in the back of an Uber limousine, Molly Overbrook not so surreptitiously checked her phone over his muscular shoulder. Her feed was flying with the jet-set frenzy that always marked the beginning of the summer season. Her friends were posting from private seaplanes as they hopped between St. Maarten and St. Barths, from yachts in Newport and from villas on Lake Como and the Côte d'Azur. Each image sent a current of jealousy coursing through Molly's gorgeous frame. She hated her "friends."

Molly was not headed anywhere remotely cool. Quite the contrary, she was on her way to the sleepiest town on the Eastern Seaboard. *To babysit.* And to get lectured by some old lady friend of Daddy's named Ingrid Beauchamp about how not to abuse her magic.

Whatever. She had never felt quite this indignant before. Life was totally unfair.

The most galling picture on her feed showed a clique

of bikini-clad vampires from Duchesne, a rival Upper East Side prep school to Headingley, where she and Mardi had just finished a disastrous but wickedly amusing sophomore year. The Duchesne vamps were arrayed on a white-sand Caribbean beach, brandishing exotic cocktails, each of their bodies a gleaming perfection. Vampires could eat whatever they wanted and not put on an ounce. The famous Blue Blood metabolism. A bunch of social X-rays. Not so with witches. A witch could get as flabby as a mortal if she let herself go. There was no justice on this Earth.

Molly unlocked her glossy lips from Leo's mouth and sighed.

"What?" Leo pulled a few inches away and looked into her dark eyes. He was the hottest guy of a certain set in all of New York City, on his way to his summer home in East Hampton.

When she and Mardi had a fight this morning about Mardi's insisting on driving to North Hampton in that ridiculous old car, which had no trunk—i.e., no room for Molly's three giant Louis Vuitton suitcases—Molly went into one of her huffs and tapped out an order for an Uber limo. After, she texted Leo and offered to drop him off at his house on Lily Pond Lane en route, ostensibly so he wouldn't have to take the train but mostly because the idea of being alone with her thoughts in a car for three hours was unbearable.

Of course, Leo, varsity tennis champion at Headingley, jumped at the chance. With her luxuriant dark mane, mesmerizing dark eyes, willowy curves, vertiginous cleavage, and impeccable style, no one could resist her. And she and Leo had been dating on and off all spring, although her interest was waning pretty hard.

Boys were like shoes. Once you owned them and had worn them out once or twice so that all your friends had seen them and done their oohing and aahing, the high was pretty much over. Leo was smoking cute, but he was last season's catch. You might hold on to a guy like him for a while just because he was high quality. But, once the thrill of the conquest was gone, it was time to go shopping again. You're never that psyched about a pair of scuffed shoes, now, are you?

At this image of worn-out shoes, Molly crinkled her upturned button nose. She would never understand how her sister wore those ratty, smelly used clothes. What was Mardi trying to prove?

As if summoned by the negative thought, a post from Mardi popped onto Molly's screen, a shot of Mardi's pucker in that cherry-red lipstick she liked, along with a strap of that leopard-print bra she'd filched from some skanky old flame of Dad's. So gross. Mardi had written a whiny comment asking her low-life crowd not to forget her over the summer. Pathetic. By the end of the summer, most of Mardi's so-called friends would have overdosed or been shipped off to rehab. There would be no one left to remember her anyway.

Despite her irritation, Molly couldn't help but feel a little bit comforted by the sight of the phantom rose gold ring drifting over her sister's mouth, the ring that she alone could see. The twins shared a secret language that might come in handy in the boonies of the East End. At some point, they just might need to shore each other up.

She fiddled with the ring on her finger, the physical model for the image that drifted secretly across the twins' posts. The ring was warm and luminous, its diamond-shaped grooves pleasantly worn, like a kind old woman's face. She and Mardi passed the ring back and forth between the middle fingers of their right hands. The exchange was almost unconscious and totally peaceful. In every other aspect of their lives, from who got the most cereal in her breakfast bowl to who got to control the playlist at a party to which girl got more of Daddy's attention, the twins were viciously competitive. "It's not fair!" was their constant refrain. But when it came to the ring, which they had shared for as long as they could remember, there was simply no issue. It drifted between them. And they had a tacit understanding that one of them would keep it at all times.

Frustrated with Molly's distraction, Leo checked out her phone too. "Wow," he said. "Is that Mardi? She looks hot!"

Spiked with jealousy, Molly pulled him closer and kissed him harder.

"Whoa." He laughed, enjoying her passion after such a tepid make-out session earlier. "I've never seen you take anything so personally."

Molly refrained from replying, locking him in a rage-infused kiss instead. She jammed her tongue down his throat and kept it there until the limo pulled up in front of his family's ten-million-dollar vine-covered house.

Feeling confident that she had erased any impression her sister might have made on *her* boyfriend, Molly waved him off. He stumbled onto his vast lawn, racket bag slung over his shoulder, and in an instant, he crumpled under the bag's weight. She watched, cackling to herself as he squirmed in a helpless puddle, gradually going still. Someone would find him in a few hours and assume he was wickedly hungover. He would remember nothing.

Causing silly boys to black out was a favorite sport of Molly's.

As the limo glided back toward the Montauk Highway, she put her headphones on and scrolled through for her go-to song. Over the blasting music, she yelled to the driver that she hoped he knew where they were going, because she herself had no idea of East End geography. All she had was an address.

He said the GPS wasn't showing him the place exactly, but he was sure they would find it.

She shrugged. She wasn't in any hurry to greet her oppressive fate.

Why was Daddy doing this to them? Why was he so intimidated by the White Council? If the Council wanted to punish her and Mardi, they would have done so already. But Daddy was convinced that, this time, after the havoc they had wreaked on Headingley Prep and the wild accusations flying in all directions, things would be different. If Molly and Mardi didn't shape up and start to use their magic "responsibly"— yawn—Daddy feared they would be hurled into Limbo or some such ridiculous thing. But he was wasting his time worrying. And, worse, he was wasting their precious summer by banishing them to North Hampton, because she and her sister were never going to change their ways. No one could make them. There was no point in trying.

Molly belted along with Iggy Azalea as the green of the Montauk Highway started to give way to the gold of undulating sand dunes. She scrolled down her posts, looking to see if anyone had "liked" the photo she had taken earlier, when it had occurred to her that she should put up something tragic and artistic about her upcoming fate, a tableau of nature to be followed by radio silence. Make them wonder.

She'd told the driver to pull over for a minute, teetered out onto a dune in her stilettos and snapped a shot of a seagull. She hoped Bret Farley would be intrigued, but so far there was no indication he had seen it—no "likes" no "favorites."

Why did she care whether or not Bret saw her post? She repressed an image of his ice-blond hair, blue eyes, and sharp cheekbones, wanting to banish him from her mind like last year's platform shoes. But his memory was haunting her—perhaps because he was the one that got away? Bretland Farley was the ultimate pair of designer stilettos that were all sold out in her size.

For a while she pouted in silence. Then she put her headphones back on.

As the limo eased into a sudden bank of fog, the bright day grew misty and strange, and Molly grew uneasy about what lay before her.

"Are we almost there?" she whined.

She couldn't hear the answer to her question because her ears were suddenly ringing with a full orchestral sound. It was a total rush. She recognized it as the theme music for some famous movie that Daddy was into. *Apocalypse* something. While the orchestra galloped forward, louder and louder, she envisioned helicopters and exploding bombs. She was carried away from the moment in a thrilling fever vision.

Then it was if her soul had been deposited on the other side of a dream. The sky was bright again, everything was calm, and Iggy was rapping again, boasting about how fabulous she was. Molly knew the feeling.

"We made it," the driver chirped with palpable relief as they passed a WELCOME TO NORTH HAMPTON sign.

They drove through peaceful fields of corn and potatoes, a peach orchard. There were quaint farmhouses that probably weren't air-conditioned, a shabby bar called the North Inn, and some beachside restaurants advertising local fare on chalkboards. There was no frozen yogurt, no Starbucks. Molly looked desperately along the road for any brand names she might recognize. At this point, she would have settled for a Duane Reade pharmacy. But there was nothing. She was going to wither and die here.

Her feed had stopped. It was just as Ingrid had warned in her email: North Hampton was not wired for social networking—no Facebook, no Tumblr, no Twitter, no Snapchat, nada. You could text and email here, but that was about it. When you came to North Hampton, your whole being was immersed in the actual place, rather than scattered throughout cyberspace. "In some ways," Ingrid had written, "North Hampton is outside of time. It is the perfect place to reflect."

At the very moment that Molly's limo pulled up to a beachfront colonial house, freshly painted robin's egg blue, with a saltbox roof and white gables, Mardi's idiotic Ferrari screeched to halt in the unpaved driveway. Molly waited for the dust to settle before she nodded to her driver to open her door. She didn't want to ruin her Prada shift. She couldn't imagine that this town boasted a decent dry cleaner.

Molly surveyed the front yard: a swing set, a dome-shaped jungle gym, and a huge vegetable patch. Then she turned her eyes to her sister.

The twins emerged tentatively from their respective vehicles.

"Nice ride," they sneered at each other in unison.

✳ 3 ✳

AMERICAN PIE

Something about the little family that rushed out of the pretty gabled house in welcome made Mardi wistful, but only for a second. She quickly remembered she had no desire to be here, and no desire to like these people she was stuck with.

She recognized Ingrid, a.k.a. Erda, from old pictures of Dad's, since witches don't age unless they choose to (they had that on the vampires at least). She was fair and slender in a flour-dusted red apron tied over a blue eyelet sundress. Her blond hair was swooped into a loose bun.

Ingrid's daughter, who looked just like her except for two missing front teeth, was also wearing a red apron. In her case, though, the flour was everywhere. The poor kid's hair was practically white.

The mortal next to Ingrid had to be her husband, Matt Noble. He was very fit, handsome, with salt-and-pepper hair and chin stubble. He held a squirming towheaded baby who was wearing nothing but an unbleached diaper. When the baby started to fuss, Matt began to curl him up and down like a barbell, eliciting delighted squeals.

Mardi forced a smile. Playing house with a mortal might be fun for a few years. But eventually, Ingrid was going to watch him age, drool, and die, Mardi said to herself, with the wicked sensation she derived from seeing insects splatter on her windshield. Beneath her evil glee she felt an undercurrent of sadness.

"Welcome to the East End!" Ingrid hugged each girl, while Matt stopped his antics with the kid long enough to reach out and shake their hands.

"I bet you can tell that Jo and I have been baking." Ingrid gestured happily to the little girl's flour-covered hair. "We've just put two pies in the oven. I hope you like pie."

Mardi nodded slowly. "Sure, I like pie." She had never met anyone who actually baked. Or cooked for themselves, for that matter.

Ingrid seemed to know what the girl was thinking.

"You probably don't get to do a lot of cooking with your father in New York, what with all the restaurants he likes to go to."

"I don't think Dad knows how to turn on the stove in our kitchen. We either go out, eat cereal, or get takeout."

"You won't find any takeout in this house," Matt

chimed in. "My mother-in-law, Joanna Beauchamp, who is still in charge of the place even from beyond the grave, wouldn't hear of it."

Ingrid laughed and squeezed his arm. "My mother equated eating takeout with being depressed," she said, quickly adding, "But, of course, everyone has a different perspective—and different circumstances." Obviously, she didn't want to seem critical of the twins' bachelor lifestyle right off the bat. "Come in. Come in."

The house was more spacious and hip inside than one would expect. Walls had been knocked down to create an open kitchen and living space. The wide-planked wooden floors were painted white. The furniture was midcentury modern mixed in with some Italian leather pieces and a smattering of well-chosen antiques. Windows had been enlarged to create great pools of light.

Mardi, who had been envisioning an overstuffed French Provençal nightmare, was palpably relieved. Glancing at Molly, she could tell her twin felt the same.

Matt noticed them looking appreciatively around and explained that his architect brother had helped them remodel the place when they moved in ten years ago.

"And the spirit of Joanna Beauchamp didn't mind all the changes?" Mardi quipped.

Not at all, Matt said. Joanna herself had been a compulsive remodeler and redecorator. She believed houses were alive and should always be evolving. It was only where home cooking was concerned that she was a deep traditionalist.

Speaking of which, thought Mardi, the pies were starting to smell amazing.

Matt offered to take Jo and Henry on a walk to give Ingrid and the girls some time to get to know one another.

As soon as he and the kids were gone, Ingrid shifted her tone slightly, becoming more serious, piercing almost. Before the twins knew it, they were sitting side by side on a white leather sectional, holding glasses of herbal iced tea full of lemon wedges. Ingrid faced them, ramrod straight, on a chocolate-brown ottoman.

"Girls," Ingrid began, "your father sent you to me because he is worried about you. Thor—I mean Troy—is one of my oldest friends, we've known each other for years, give or take a century here and there—and I've promised him I would try to help you learn to use your magic."

Molly interrupted her, "What I don't get is why Daddy doesn't want to deal with us himself. What's he doing that's so important that he has to, literally, farm us out? Commercial real estate deals in Brooklyn?"

Mardi glared at Molly, willing her to shut up. It would be so much smarter in this situation to fly under the radar than to be confrontational. This wasn't some mortal moron they were dealing with. This witch was as powerful as they were, if not more.

Ingrid seemed unfazed by the interruption. "Troy tells me you are completely out of control, that you are hexing and wreaking havoc out in the open all over New York City, and that there was even a certain fatal situation among your classmates. I understand the White Council is threatening to send you to the Underworld, pending the results of the mortal police investigation. If anything like the Salem witch trials occurs in Midgard again, we could all be punished." She let that sink in. Mardi squirmed and felt Molly doing the same next to her.

Mardi didn't want to think about what had happened just a few weeks ago. The accident on the night of that half-remembered party at Bret's. The fatal one that Ingrid had just mentioned.

"Listen, the Council could reimpose the Restriction of Magical Powers that we suffered under for centuries before it was lifted only ten years ago. Every one of us could be condemned to a life in the shadows. And you two could be banished forever to the Kingdom of the Dead. Am I making my point?"

The girls looked at her blankly.

Ingrid sighed. "Your father warned me that none of this seems to trouble either of you. Can one of you at least tell me what's been going on? What happened with those kids who fell onto the subway tracks? Please tell me that wasn't you."

"Of course not!" cried Mardi.

"It wasn't our fault!" whined Molly.

"Molly, let me explain!"

"No, wait, Mardi, I'm talking!"

"Girls"—Ingrid remained calm—"may I remind you that you are sixteen years old? You're bickering like toddlers."

Molly smirked. "Point taken. Mardi, why don't you do the honors?"

Mardi was suddenly furious. As soon as Molly didn't want to be the one explaining, then neither did she. She realized she had been tricked, left holding the burning potato.

"Fine, whatever," Mardi snapped. "It's true we maybe have a little too much fun with our powers sometimes. But we had nothing to do with what happened to Parker and Sam. We were at the same party on the Upper East Side, at Bret Farley's, but . . ."

The problem was that, while both twins clamored instinctively to have the last word, neither one of them could remember what actually happened the night Parker Fales and Samantha Hill fell onto the tracks in front of an oncoming 6 train.

"We mess with people. But we don't *kill* them." Even as she was sure she was telling the truth, Mardi was nervous because she intuited that they had been involved at the scene of the crime somehow. She wished she could remember that night with any kind of clarity, but there was a gray fog around her memory.

Mardi looked to her sister for help, but Molly appeared as confused and uncomfortable as she did. She was fiddling anxiously with the rose gold ring on her right hand. She slipped it off and handed it to Mardi, who put it on her own hand without missing a beat.

Ingrid, sensing the girls' discomfort, softened her tone. "Listen, don't worry about the sequence of events right now. We have all summer to get the bottom of it. Let's just establish some practical boundaries for the time being, okay?"

"Okay," said Mardi, relieved to be off the hook but also dreading the rules that were about to be laid down.

"First of all, my family. Matt, as you must know, is mortal, and he's the chief of police. He knows I'm a witch and that I use my magic primarily to help people in town with medical and emotional issues, but we have an understanding that there is no magic in the house. We try to keep things as normal as possible. When the Restriction was lifted, the deal was that we witches could practice magic, *as long as we didn't draw too much attention to our supernatural abilities.* Matt"—she cracked a smile—"is a rules guy."

"What about the kids?" asked Mardi.

Ingrid explained that Jo had definitely inherited her powers but that they weren't sure about Henry yet. He certainly seemed to emerge unscathed from some pretty hairy situations, but maybe he was simply a lucky boy. Matt was hoping his son would take after him, but for now, only time would tell.

"So, keep it on the down low, here in the house and in town as well. What we are going to work on, girls, is using your magic for good. And using it with subtlety, which," she said as she smiled at their brash and contrasting outfits, "doesn't appear to be a strength yet."

4

ROYALS

*Y*ou little . . . ! You spilled raspberry fruit goo on my Alexander McQueen top! This was one of that last pieces he designed before he killed himself!" Molly looked desperately down at the large spot spreading over her neckline and glared at Henry. "This piece," she said, her voice trembling with indignation, "is a treasure . . . or at least it *was* a treasure."

Molly recoiled to a safe distance from the boy's filthy hands. He squealed with delight at her distress, the organic red sludge dribbling down his chin. At least he was contained in his high chair and couldn't come after her to do more damage.

Matt, Ingrid, Jo, and Mardi all milled around the kitchen island as if nothing had happened, making macaroni and cheese ("homemade, never from a box!") and nibbling on the remains of the otherworldly delicious strawberry rhubarb pies that Ingrid and Jo had baked to welcome the twins into their home. Nobody seemed remotely concerned that this devil in diapers had just ruined a priceless top, one of the linchpins of Molly's wardrobe, a classic in cream-and-black-striped silk with a built-in corset. McQueen had designed it expressly for his muse Annabelle Neilson. There were only three in existence, Annabelle's, Giselle's, and Molly's.

Molly was in shock. And the "no magic in the house" rule meant that she couldn't do anything to lift the stain until she got outside, by which time it would probably be too late for her powers to save the situation.

Matt and Ingrid were going to a party that night at Fair Haven, which they described as a glorious historic mansion on its own private island facing the town. Gardiners Island it was called, after the Gardiner family, the oldest and wealthiest of North Hampton's clans. Supposedly the house had just undergone a fabulous renovation and this party was to be the unveiling. There were at least three hundred people invited. Matt and Ingrid hoped the girls wouldn't mind if they went out on the night of their arrival, but they couldn't resist the chance to see what the Gardiners had done with the place.

Molly couldn't believe she was going to have to sit at home with these kids while there was a party going on where she actually might be able to show off some of her wardrobe and have a bit of fun. After only a few hours in this godforsaken place, she was already feeling totally deprived.

Affecting dignity in the face of her tragic situation,

she announced that she was going upstairs to her room to change into something more appropriate for the evening at home. But as she started toward the staircase, she was struck by a brilliant, if obvious, idea.

"Hey," she said. "Ingrid, Matt, you really don't need *both* of us to babysit, do you? I mean, I'm sure Mardi could handle it. She's *great* with kids. She tells *awesome* stories. You don't mind if I come with you, right? Meet some people? It's not like I'm going to hang out at that skanky North Inn bar."

"The North Inn is where my sister Freya works," said Ingrid matter-of-factly.

Molly felt Mardi's hard black eyes on her, scornful and victorious. Mardi loved it when Molly made a fool of herself. Needless to say, it was mutual.

"Well, I'm sure it's a cool bar." Molly tried to back-pedal. "I mean, how can it not be? All I'm saying is that I would love to check out Fair Haven and meet some people." She was already thinking about what she would wear. She could see that Ingrid and Matt weren't going to mind. It all hinged on her sister now.

Ingrid stirred a big lump of butter into some whole-wheat penne with grated cheddar and poured the mixture into an earthenware baking dish. "Well, I suppose it's fine with us, right, Matt?" He nodded, sprinkling bread crumbs, freshly crushed from a day-old baguette, onto his wife's pasta mixture.

They really were a team, thought Molly. Bummer that it would only last a few decades. What was Ingrid thinking? Mortals were to be played with, but not married. Hadn't Ingrid gotten the memo? Wasn't she supposed to be the smart one here?

"Do you mind if I go, Mardi?" Molly asked testily.

"You think I want to go to some silly Gatsby-style party?" Mardi made the finger-down-throat gag-me sign.

"Okay! Thanks! I'll go get dressed." Phew.

"But you owe me one!" Mardi's voice followed her up the stairs.

Molly decided on a buttery suede miniskirt that zipped up front and back, purchased this past spring during a long weekend in Paris. Daddy had taken her along on a business trip but of course had had no time for her and had given her his credit card to assuage his guilt. Such an easy target, her father, so much guilt for never spending any time with them. She paired the skirt with a simple blush-colored silk top and silver mules that her personal shopper had sourced for her from an image she'd seen in Italian *Vogue*.

As Molly, Ingrid, and Matt crossed the bridge to Gardiners Island in the family's maroon Subaru wagon, Molly's spirits lifted. The dunes surrounding the mansion of Fair Haven were lit up to a fiery gold with giant torches. The house itself burned bright and beckoning. This might not be such a lame summer after all.

After a valet whisked their car into the twilight,

they started up a blazing path bordered with iridescent white peony bushes in full bloom. The crowd, Molly noticed immediately, was well-dressed for the most part, in a clubby, preppy sort of way. Not too shabby. This was more like it.

Through large picture windows, she could see what looked like a ballroom hung with baroque chandeliers, alight with wax candles. Somewhere out of view, a band softly tuned its strings. A rogue flute trilled and then went silent.

As a waiter handed Molly a flute of champagne and she waved away a tray of hors d'oeuvres, she felt a pair of eyes gazing upon her with startling intensity. She blushed inside. Before she knew it, a graceful hand had whisked away her glass and handed her another. Its champagne had fewer bubbles than the first. The color was darker, more like honey than wine.

"Try this instead," came a suave voice. "It's vintage. You are much too beautiful tonight to be drinking brut."

"Too beautiful *tonight*?" Molly's flirting instinct surged. She flipped back her silky curtain of blue-black hair to look squarely at her interlocutor. "Why only tonight?"

"Not *only* tonight. But *especially* tonight." The voice belonged to a stunning young man of about seventeen. He was olive skinned with jet-black hair and chiseled cheekbones. His blue eyes twinkled in striking contrast to his dark features. He wore a navy blazer over a be- spoke shirt of white linen with a discreet monogram on its cuff: the initials TG in delicate silk of the deepest red. Could he be one of the Gardiner brothers who owned Fair Haven?

As if reading her thoughts, he introduced himself. "Welcome to Fair Haven. I'm Trystan Gardiner. Call me Tris."

"Molly Overbrook." She held out her hand for him to shake. She was surprised to find herself a tad nervous. Usually, she was the one who intimidated all the boys. But Tris was utterly cool, calm, and gracious, while she had butterflies in her stomach. He was so formal, yet so familiar. As she clinked her champagne flute with his, her hand trembled ever so slightly. "Beautiful house," she managed.

"Yes, it's wonderful to come back to. My family was away from it for ages. Until about ten years ago, Fair Haven was a relic. There was no one on this island except the ospreys who nested all over our beaches. They still do make their home here, of course."

He was in boarding school in England, and his older brothers had overseen a complete restoration of the house and grounds. They were off again, traveling the world, and he lived in the house with their stepmother. He gestured a few feet farther up the torch-lit path to an immaculately groomed older woman wearing a summery Chanel suit and two-toned pumps, who was deep in conversation with Ingrid and Matt, most likely about finishes and light fixtures.

"So," Molly asked, "how are you dealing in North Hampton? Is there anything to do here?"

He looked her over appreciatively, her glittering blue-black eyes, cascading hair, calf muscles taut in her silver mules. It was as if he were sculpting a masterpiece with his sharp blue gaze.

Molly had never felt quite so beautiful, and that was saying something.

"Hm." He repeated her question: "Is there anything to do here?" His smile was both wicked and winning. "Well, there certainly is now that I've met you, Molly Overbrook."

* 5 *

RESCUE ME

*O*nce the grown-ups had pulled out of the driveway, Mardi took Jo and Henry to the beach in front of the house. She tossed a blanket over the silver sand, and they sat down and watched the sunset with Fair Haven lit up on Gardiners Island across the bay.

Henry had a bucket that he filled with little fistfuls of sand. He dumped it out over and over, with no signs of boredom or slowing down. Kids were so weird. Mardi supposed she was going to have to give him a bath after this to get the sand off his body before putting him to bed, and she shuddered at the drudgery of it all. She was never having children.

Jo kept running her finger over Mardi's rainbow tattoo, murmuring, "It's so, so, so pretty!" It was all Mardi could do not to swat the little girl away from her neck.

Finally, she pulled herself to standing and suggested they go put their feet in the water.

"Sure," said Jo. "But will you tell me why you have a rainbow bridge on your neck?"

Startled, Mardi inhaled sharply. "Why did you call it a bridge?"

Without answering, Jo demanded, "Tell me the story of the rainbow bridge! Molly promised you tell good stories!"

Frigging Molly, thought Mardi with a grimace. Molly was across Gardiner Bay, probably sipping champagne and nibbling caviar toasts and smoked salmon, while she was stuck babysitting.

Obviously, Jo wasn't going to leave Mardi alone until she talked about her tattoo. She might as well get it over with. It was a story their father had told them when they were young, when they asked the usual questions about their family and where they came from.

"I'm surprised your mom hasn't told you! You see, my rainbow bridge, like you called it, is actually the Bofrir Bridge, a magical bridge built by the king of the gods so that all the other gods could travel from Middle Earth, which is the ordinary world where we all live now, to their palace in heaven, a castle called Valhalla, which was built using the labor of dragons."

"Neat!"

Phew, the kid seemed satisfied. Mardi had always liked that story about Asgard, she thought as she twisted the ring on her finger.

Suddenly, she felt a brush of soft fur on her ankle.

She looked down to see Jo scooping up a black kitten.

"Midnight!" Jo cried out in delight. "Midnight, where have you been?"

Mardi understood immediately that Midnight and Jo had a magical bond. "Is Midnight your familiar?" she asked wistfully.

"Yes. Are you a witch too?" Jo's question was completely without guile.

"Yes, I am." There was no point in lying.

"And your sister?"

"Yes."

"So, then, where are your familiars? Why didn't they come to live here with you?"

"Our dad made us board them for the summer." Mardi felt a pang for her Siamese cat, Killer, who was stuck in an overpriced pet hotel in SoHo. She missed Killer's steady companionship, her knowing gaze, and deep purr.

Killer had an archenemy in Molly's Fury, a small Löwchen dog, with the typical long feathery hair in front, smooth hindquarters, and upturned fluffy tail. Of course Molly would be shadowed by a specimen of one of the priciest dog breeds on the planet, and one that required heaps of grooming to maintain its absurd hairstyle.

For the most part, the two animals despised one another. Fury yapped at Killer. Killer hissed at Fury. They sometimes even peed in one another's water bowls. But every once in a while, for no apparent reason, they would curl up together and nap, their eyelids fluttering in unison as if to the same dream.

"Henry!" Jo screamed out to sea, shattering Mardi's reverie. "Oh, no!"

Mardi followed the little witch's anxious gaze to discover that the baby boy had somehow managed to launch himself in an orange kayak and was drifting off into the twilight at an alarming rate.

"No!" Mardi screamed, yanking off her sandals. "Jo, stay right here! Don't move! I'll get him!"

As she ran into the water, Mardi watched in horror while the kid stood up, wobbled, spread his arms, and jumped out of the kayak as if he thought he could fly. Then Henry disappeared under the water.

Mardi swam faster than she ever had in her life, knifing through the darkening sea toward the spot where she had seen Henry disappear. Her heart was pounding. Her arms and legs tensed with the muscle memory of the thousands of laps she had swum this past year as a way to calm her anxiety and steady her racing pulse. She had to remind herself to breathe.

She reached the kayak and began diving around it, waving through the water with her arms and legs in the desperate hope of touching a little limb. Nothing.

Then she heard the distinct chime of baby laughter. Miraculously, Henry's chubby fingers were grasping the front tip of the kayak. He was hanging there, feet dangling in the sea, cackling to himself. She grabbed him and held him close.

"Henry, why on earth did you do that?"

By way of answer, he stuck his thumb in her mouth to touch her emerald tongue stud. "Wowie," he squealed. As far as Mardi could tell, his vocabulary consisted of four words: *Mama, Dada, more,* and *wowie.*

The rush of gratitude she felt toward the universe was intense. She burst into tears, then realized she should wave to reassure Jo, who was standing motionless in the surf. Had Jo used magic to rescue her brother? Or was he simply really lucky and really coordinated? Or was it something else?

Mardi lifted him into the seat, grabbed the back of the kayak, and kicked her legs like an outboard motor, propelling it to shore. As she pulled it up onto the wet sand and let Henry scamper out, vowing never to take her eyes off him again when he was in her charge, a gorgeous dark-haired figure appeared on the beach.

Mardi was not easily impressed by physical beauty, but this woman was a total fox. Her hair was dark with red-gold highlights. She was small, more petite than the long, lanky Mardi, and much curvier. She was barefoot in skinny jeans of an iridescent, opaline black that perfectly cinched her tiny waist, along with a silver and bronze silk bustier that would have been cool in any decade over the past thousand years. Her breasts were mesmerizing, perfectly full and high. They should have seemed disproportionate to her tiny frame, but they looked as right and natural as full blossoms on a slender stalk. Her cheekbones popped, and her large green up-slanting eyes twinkled in the light of the rising moon. She didn't look remotely troubled by the fact that the baby had just been pulled from the jaws of the sea.

Mardi recognized this creature instantly as one of her tribe, a goddess from Asgard stuck in Midgard, or Middle Earth, for all eternity after the bridge connecting the two worlds was destroyed centuries ago. Here in Midgard, the gods lived among humans as witches and warlocks. Molly and Mardi's own father, Troy Overbrook, was once known as Thor, god of thunder. And this gorgeous woman on the beach, exuding ripeness and sexuality, had to be Ingrid's sister, Freya, goddess of love. She had reached her eternal age of about twenty-five and would not grow physically older until the end of time, unless of course she chose to.

As if to confirm Mardi's hunch, the young woman held out her pretty hand, smiled blinding white, and said, "Hi, I'm Freya Beauchamp. You must be one of Troy's girls. Ingrid told me you guys were here this summer. Welcome!"

"Thanks. I'm Mardi."

"Nice to meet you. That was an impressive rescue just now. You're a good swimmer."

"I spend a lot of time in the pool back home." Mardi was still wearing her leopard bra and short shorts, which were soaked now. The black dye from the leopard spots was running, streaking her six-pack. This was one of the problems she ran into, wearing clothes of dubious origin.

As if reading Mardi's thoughts, Freya said, "Let's get you guys into some dry clothes. You're shivering, and it looks like Henry's diaper has absorbed half of the water in Gardiner Bay. It's sagging down to his knees. Poor kid."

Inside the house, Mardi toweled Henry off, put him in a dry diaper, then asked if Freya would keep an eye on the kids while she ran upstairs to change.

"Wait a second, are you the only one here? Did they all leave you with Jo and Henry to go to the party on Gardiners Island? That is so uncool. I was stopping by so that we could all head out together."

"No big deal. I didn't want to go anyway. Preppy is not my scene."

Freya let out a silvery laugh.

"Honey, preppy is only the surface of it. You have no idea. I cannot tell you how much fun I've had through the years at Fair Haven. The Gardiner men are something else. Killian and Bran are out of town right now. You might say they're both on hiatus from me. But there's some fresh Gardiner blood in town. Now, get yourself dressed to go out."

"But what about Ingrid's kids?"

Freya was tapping out a number on her phone. "I've got that covered. Ingrid's housekeeper lives down the street, and she loves Henry and Jo. I don't understand why Ingrid didn't call her to come in the first place."

"I think," said Mardi, "that Dad told her to give me and Molly some responsibility. He has this idea that he's going to make good little witches out of us here." •

"As if Troy was ever a good boy himself!" Freya gave an ironic smile. "Give me a break."

"I don't want Graciella to put me to bed!" Jo shrieked. "I want Mardi to stay! I want more rainbow stories! Auntie Freya, don't go!"

"Don't be like that, Jo," said Freya firmly. "There's nothing less attractive than a little self-witch. Mardi is going to be here all summer. You'll get plenty of stories. Now, let's take her to the attic and show her our dress-up clothes, shall we? Let's get her ready for the ball."

As they walked up to the attic, with Henry and Midnight crawling up the stairs at their heels, Freya explained that when her mother and father "died," her mother left Ingrid the house because it was obvious that Ingrid was going to have a family. Freya liked children fine, but not half as much as she loved her freedom. Since Matt was moving in with Ingrid, Freya bought his bachelor pad from him. It was a little ways out of town on an isolated strip of beach, a sleek all-glass house that was a peaceful refuge from her busy social job at the North Inn bar. It was perfect for her, except for one thing: there wasn't enough storage space to accommodate the overflow from her epoch-spanning wardrobe.

She had filled every closet. And all the shelves and surfaces were piled with her clothes. It was enough to make minimalist Matt wince whenever he paid a visit to his old home. All this to say that she still used the attic at the Beauchamp homestead as a backup closet, and she was sure they would find something here that Mardi would approve of.

As they opened the house's uppermost door, Mardi gasped. Freya wasn't kidding about quantity. This was a treasure chest of the sexiest fashions from the past hundred years or so, with a focus on the 1920s, '60s, and '70s, and a few throwbacks to much earlier times when undergarments could be spectacular. There were dozens of tiny beaded flapper dresses, suede fringe skirts and tops, rhinestone encrusted micro-minis, corsets and garters, all hanging on bars that went around the four walls of the large room. The space was illuminated by skylights through which the moon poured its glow, so that the pearls, beads, rhinestones, and sequins glimmered like stars. There were rows and rows of shoes, mostly heels, arranged around the room by color. It was as if the attic were encircled by some exotic, multistriped snake.

"What's your pleasure?" asked Freya.

For the first time in her life, Mardi had no idea what she wanted to wear. Her mother had disappeared when they were young, and her sister had a totally different aesthetic, so she'd never had anyone to help her pick out clothes. She had always relied on her innate sense of eclectic thrift-shop style. But this was too much for her to process.

"I'm having total sensory overload," she said with unaccustomed shyness. "You're gonna have to pick something out for me."

"Are you serious?" Freya clapped with glee.

Mardi nodded her coal-dark head.

"Awesome! Jo, help me out here. This is going to be so much fun."

"Nothing pretty, though," Mardi hastened to specify. "I don't do pretty."

"Don't worry, we've got it covered."

In no time, Mardi was outfitted in a pair of denim hot pants with a silky Bengal tiger appliqué across the butt, tall patent boots, a cutoff Lou Reed T-shirt, a light-weight black pigskin vest from back in Freya's New York City days, and an arm's length of black rubber bangles.

Graciella arrived and swept the kids under her wing. Freya declared that the Ferrari was a way cooler ride than her Mini, and the witches screeched off into the night.

✳ 6 ✳

I KNEW YOU WERE TROUBLE, PART ONE

$\mathcal{M}$olly sat cross-legged on one of the deep-red velvet poufs strewn throughout the immense candlelit ballroom of Fair Haven in order to receive the weary bodies of its dancing guests. There was an ethereal band playing salsas, tangos, and merengues. She and Tris had been twirling across the floor for seven numbers, and she had sent him to get her another drink as she sank into the plush cushion and let the breeze from the open windows waft over her. The scent of lilacs from the lavish bushes just outside filled her senses. She was deeply content. For about five minutes.

Where the Hell was he? Okay, so he had made a cute comment about needing some extra time to track down another bottle of vintage champagne. But there was no excuse to leave her alone for this long. It *was* his house, wasn't it? Shouldn't he have unfettered access to the best of the booze and a direct line to the staff? If he wasn't back soon, she was going to leave the room, and he would have to search for her if he wanted to see her again this evening. No one kept Molly Overbrook waiting.

She looked around her at the swirling couples and began to feel a familiar itch to perform one of her signature party tricks, like slipping potions into drinks to remove all inhibitions or breaking spaghetti straps with the force of her gaze so that cocktail dresses fell to the floor. She especially liked to undo the work of Botox over the course of a few minutes so that dozens of women, unbeknownst to themselves, would erupt in wrinkles, creases, and worry lines. Each one of them would start smugly thinking how all of her "friends" had suddenly aged, and each would feel great about herself, until she got home, looked in the mirror, and screamed. By the morning after the party, the spell would have worn off, the offending wrinkles would be frozen again, and the whole thing would feel like a distant nightmare. But it sure was fun while it lasted.

Molly, of course, would never need Botox. She and Mardi would remain fresh-faced ever after. Daddy was forever just shy of fifty. And Ingrid would always present between twenty-seven and thirty-two. Molly wondered, though, about the half-mortal kids. Would they go one way or the other? It was a complicated question, and Molly was not one to enjoy thinking too hard, especially when she was alone. Where was that Tris Gardiner? If there was one thing she hated, it was being taken for granted.

A waiter kneeled in front of her pouf, proffering a silver tray with a full caviar service, a generous mound of shining black beluga surrounded by blinis, sour cream, minced red onions, and finely diced hard-boiled eggs. He handed Molly a china plate, and she went about delicately assembling two perfect blinis, trying to stave off the sting of rejection.

As the rich salty burst of flavor swirled through her mouth, a fresh vision from the past rose up inside her, vivid and urgent. There had been an obscene amount of caviar that crazy night in New York at Bret Farley's. The luxurious taste, along with the plush feel of velvet on her skin, sparked her senses, giving rise to whole new layer of memory. As the music and dancers blurred around her, she began to recall more of the buried details of that fateful party. That cool April night, the first buds out on the trees lining Park Avenue, came flooding back to her.

Both Molly and Mardi suspected that Bret was one of them. A warlock. There was something supernatural about his charm. But he hadn't given them any clear indication, and so they all three danced around the possibility.

The twins had never been attracted to the same guy

before, and Molly couldn't imagine that Mardi would be interested in someone as mainstream rich as Bret. But he seemed to know how to engage Mardi, and Molly didn't like this fact one bit.

That mysterious night, searching to ground herself with a familiar sensation, she had felt her right hand for her ring. It wasn't there. Had she passed it to Mardi without noticing? This had happened before, of course, since the ring slid so automatically between them. But she was positive she had been the one wearing it when they left for Bret's party, and she had no recollection of coming close to Mardi since they arrived. Certainly not close enough to slip a ring on her finger. Weird. She must have drunk that first champagne too fast.

She tried to steal a look at Mardi's hand through the doorway, but Bret and Mardi were now talking to a couple of juniors from Headingley. Parker and Sam, she thought their names were. They were a freshly minted couple, hanging all over each other. Their conjoined bodies blocked Molly's view of her sister.

After this, her mental image of the party grew fuzzy again. Her vision began to ebb. The last things she felt with any clarity were her frustration at not being able to check Mardi's hand to make sure she had the ring, and her insane jealousy of Bret's attention to her twin.

Later, of course, Parker and Sam would end up dead, crushed by a subway train in the early hours of Sunday morning, and Molly and Mardi, infamous for their pranks at school, would be prime suspects. But

Molly knew she and her twin had nothing against either Parker or Sam, and she had no memory of the accident. Her sole lingering sensation was one of strange powerlessness.

Emerging from her vision in the middle of the ball at Fair Haven, Molly looked down at her empty plate. In the throes of her involuntary memory, she had eaten all of her beluga. All around her, the Fair Haven ballroom came back into focus. The candles, the velvet, the dancers, the sparkling drinks, the scent of lilacs through the open windows. It was all perfection. Except for one thing. Tris Gardiner was still not back at her side. Annoying!

Like her sister, Molly had a quick temper. She looked around the ballroom for a suitable object on which to take out her rage. She envisioned shattering the lead plate windows that had been the most expensive aspect of the renovation, according to Tris. Or she could send one of the brand-new Swarovski crystal chandeliers crashing down amid the dancers. Or she could pierce the giant silver punch bowl on the buffet table with a hundred tiny holes, turning it into a strainer so that the bloodred liquid would flood out all over the freshly finished ebony floors. Perhaps she could set that sweet-smelling lilac bush outside aflame. That would be kinda fun.

But then another idea occurred to her, an idea so

good it simply took over and became stronger than she was. Before she could stop herself, everyone dancing at the party—and there were at least a dozen of them—grabbed their stomachs and started to heave violently, turning the dance floor into a slick of vomit. The band clanged to a stop amid mass screaming. "It's the oysters!" "It's the scallops!" "It's the shrimp!" "Somebody call an ambulance!"

Molly surveyed the ensuing chaos with the calm of one who had given expression to a violent impulse and no longer felt any pressure building inside. Her pent-up anger released, the world felt light again. Nothing could touch her. Certainly not some vain, ridiculous boy.

Breezily, Molly rose from her velvet cushion and sauntered among the black-clad staff rushing to the scene with mops, buckets, and towels. The guests, bewildered, were looking down at their ruined dresses and shoes. Molly chuckled to herself. It wasn't everyone who could cause sudden stomach flu.

"What do you think you're doing, young lady?" Ingrid was blocking Molly's path, shaking her head so hard the blond strands were falling from her bun, giving her an ironic beauty in the midst of her anger.

"What are you talking about?" Molly twirled her thick gold chain and batted her dark eyes in a parody of innocence.

"I may be many things, Molly, but I'm not stupid. I know that was you," Ingrid whispered furiously, taking Molly by the arm and leading her firmly into the garden, out of earshot of the traumatized party guests.

Quelle buzzkill.

Molly realized there was no point in trying to lie to Ingrid. So she took a different tack: "Okay, look, I'm sorry. I can't always control myself. I was dealing with some negative feelings just now. Some really tough stuff with Daddy that I have to work through. Sometimes the magic just flows, you know."

"Actually, kid, there is really no excuse for making people vomit in unison. None whatsoever. I don't care how miserable you are."

"Obviously, you have no sense of what it's like to be raised by a single parent."

"In truth, dear, I do. But that's another story. And it's not what we're talking about here. We're talking about the fact that you need to learn how to control your magic. We can't have vicious spells erupting from you girls every time you get bored at a party."

Eye roll.

"I can imagine that Troy isn't always the most present father, although I know he loves you very much. You girls are going through something difficult, with that investigation in New York and the Council on your backs. Which is why it is all the more important that you stop acting so frivolous right now and get a grip on your powers. Am I making myself clear?"

"Sure." Molly wanted out of this conversation pronto.

She was no fan of lectures. "Fine, I promise, no more magic for the rest of the party."

"The rest of the party?" Ingrid flared. "As far as we're concerned, this party's over."

"But we've only been here for about an hour! Look, I swear, I'll be good. You and Matt can't be ready to leave already."

"Actually, Matt has a headache. He'll be glad for an excuse to go."

"A headache. Really? God, it must suck to be mortal."

Ingrid simply glared at her, refusing to dignify her comment with a response.

Molly started to squirm. "You're really going to drag me home like some little kid?"

"We're going to treat you like a little kid until you stop acting like one."

7

EVERYBODY EATS WHEN
THEY COME TO MY HOUSE

$\mathcal{A}$s a wildly impressed valet whisked the Ferrari off to the large clearing in the dunes that served as a parking lot for the Fair Haven party, Mardi looked up the torch-lit path toward the spectacular old mansion. Night had fallen, and the lush grounds were mostly in shadow so that the trees and bushes appeared as dark figures, like spirits hovering in the gloaming. Mardi got a strong vibe from this place, not spooky exactly, but charged. Gardiners Island was definitely a place that spanned two worlds.

As she and Freya started up the path, all eyes on their stunning figures, Mardi was startled to see Molly, Matt, and Ingrid heading toward her with hanging heads.

"Hey, guys!"

They looked up, startled. "Freya! Mardi! What are you doing here?" Ingrid was trying to look pleased by the surprise but was obviously confused. "Who's watching the kids?"

Matt's expression of alarm perfectly mimicked his wife's. It was as if they spoke as one, Mardi thought with a twitch of sadness that she quickly squelched. Ingrid had made her own bed by marrying a mortal man. Why did Mardi keep feeling sorry for her?

"I called Graciella," Freya explained. "I stopped by to see if we could head to the party together and found poor Mardi stuck at home. It didn't seem fair."

"I guess you're right," said Ingrid. "We should have left both of them home."

Whoa, Mardi thought, noting that her sister had a "busted" look all over her face. *What did she do?* Mardi was dying to know. A pleasure in party tricks was something the sisters actually shared.

"They obviously aren't ready to handle adult situations yet," Ingrid fumed.

"Lighten up, Ingrid," said Freya. "If you and Matt are tired and want to head out, I can chaperone both of them."

"No, we'll take Molly," Ingrid said decidedly. Then she remembered her manners. "Oh, Molly, this is my sister, Freya."

"Cool skirt," said Freya, holding out her hand. She had finished her skinny jean and metallic bustier outfit with six-inch python heels and a python belt, and she looked even more stunning than she had back on the beach.

"Thanks. Cool shoes!" said Molly, clasping Freya's fingers as if they could somehow hold her back and save her from the ride of shame home in the family Subaru.

"Time to go, Molly," said Ingrid. "You girls can continue your lovefest some other time. I'm sure Freya's closet is big is enough for all of you."

Molly cast Freya a thanks-for-trying look as she sulked off behind her captors.

Mardi couldn't help but feel a tad gratified at her sister's misfortune. There was some relief at having this beautiful summer evening all to herself. With her twin gone, Mardi didn't have to compete all night. Now she could relax into her own skin and really check this crazy place out.

"Don't mind Molly," she said to Freya. "She's spoiled selfish."

"You really think you're that different from her?" Freya asked.

"Totally!" Mardi shot back. She was caught completely off guard by the question.

Freya frowned thoughtfully. "Ingrid and I might be very different, but we're the best of friends. One day you'll be glad you have a sister who has your back." She grabbed them each a glass of champagne from a passing tray.

Biting her tongue, Mardi accepted the champagne

gladly. While she was normally utterly unconcerned with what others thought of her, she found that she really wanted Freya to like her. Freya was so cosmically cool.

They clinked glasses in the moonlight as a band somewhere inside Fair Haven struck up a waltz. The music swayed out through the enormous open windows of what looked like a chandeliered ballroom. Notes poured over the vast front lawn, enticing the crowd to come inside and dance. Freya and Mardi were carried on the tide toward the house.

As they walked up the path, they reached out to one another and clinked glasses again.

"Champagne really isn't my thing," said Mardi. "It's more Molly's style, as you can probably figure. But this stuff isn't so bad."

"Don't worry," Freya stage-whispered, "I know where they stash the tequila around here."

"Awesome," said Mardi. "You're a bartender, right?"

"That's right. I'm the queen of the North Inn. My drinks are known as love potions. I've created a menu of drinks: Infatuation, Irresistible, Unrequited, Forever . . ." Her mouth shaped the cocktail names as if they were juicy pieces of fruit bursting on her tongue.

Mardi was equally attracted to—and equally wary of—both sexes. Her dad, who was rabidly heterosexual, couldn't understand how she could flow so freely in her appetites. Couldn't she go definitively one way or the other? Mardi looked down at her boots and snarled just thinking about how binary he was. How limited. Freya was probably the sexiest girl she'd ever met, but she was also sort of like an aunt, or an older sister, so that was, um, weird.

"Love potions, huh?" she asked.

"Mardi, the trick to being a—quote unquote—good witch, here on Middle Earth, is to twist your sense of mischief to spreading the love."

"I'm not so sure that spreading love is in my nature. Rage is more like it."

"You'll see." Freya winked a feline eye and turned to say hello to a conservatively dressed middle-aged couple.

Mardi took a step toward the front door. There was an odor of roasting meat wafting from the house. Her nostrils flared. She realized she was starving.

But as she took a step toward Fair Haven's luminous entryway, with its promise of dinner, she was immediately stopped by a silken male voice. "You must be Mardi Overbrook." Someone was blocking her way.

She couldn't stand it when people, men in particular, messed with her freedom of movement. It made her blood boil. "Yeah," she said, pushing around him. "That's me."

"What's the hurry?"

She looked up, annoyed. He was about seventeen, in ripped jeans, a T-shirt, and a beat-up leather jacket. His hair and skin were dark like hers, but his eyes were as brilliant blue as hers were deepest brown. She could see his lean form through his thin T-shirt. His arm muscles rippled in the moonlight; he must be a swimmer like her.

She was taken. But to his face, she said, with all the coldness she could muster, "If you must know, I'm headed to the buffet."

"Do you want me to show you the fastest way?"

In spite of herself, she cracked a smile. "I'm sure I can find it. I know how to take care of myself."

"That," he said, "is perfectly obvious. Just think of me as a means to an end. Your support staff. I know where the kitchen is, and I have friends here on the inside."

"Do you work here or something?"

"I live here. Or I could live here if I felt like it. It's my house. I mean, my brothers are the ones who brought it back to life for the family, and my stepmother is really into it now. She gives garden tours and stuff."

"So how come you don't live here if it's your family's house?"

"I like my brother's boat better. It's a fishing yacht called the *Dragon*. I spend most of my nights there, on the water. I'm Trent Gardiner, by the way."

"Hi, Trent," she said.

"Hi, Mardi."

"How do you know who I am?"

"Freya told me about you and Molly coming to town for the summer."

"You're tight with Freya?"

"She's close to my older brothers, Killian and Bran. Close to both of them, if you know what I mean. She's got a lot of love to go around."

"So I gather."

As they talked, he guided her into the house with a hand on the small of her back. Normally, this would have driven her crazy with the urge to hex him, to web his hands into duck feet or make his gums bleed profusely, but somehow she didn't mind. There was nothing condescending or controlling in his touch, it was firm, gentle, protective.

The buffet in the crystalline ballroom, with its huge windows open onto fragrant gardens, was lush and bountiful. Jaded as she was from Manhattan excess, Mardi still couldn't help but be impressed. She wasn't so much struck by the cost of the food—she knew well from her private school world that there was no limit to what people could spend—as she was touched by the loving attention to detail. There was a suckling pig turning on a spit over an open flame, a perfectly rare prime rib and a glimmering lacquered duck breast. There were duck-fat potatoes; truffle risotto; green beans tossed in an almond pesto; a salad of local tomatoes, grilled peaches, and feta, sprinkled with basil from the Fair Haven garden; and another salad of shaved fennel and fresh fava beans. Even though she knew it had been expensively catered, Mardi could tell that someone had given this meal a lot of thought.

"Is your stepmother a foodie?" she asked over the music as she filled her plate.

Trent laughed. "My stepmother lives on saltines, gin, and Fresca. I'm the foodie. This is my menu," he gestured to the spread. "What do you think?"

"I'll let you know when I've tasted it."

"Make sure you get some of the risotto. I stirred it myself."

"You cook?" She nearly spit out the champagne she was swallowing.

"Why so surprised?" His eyes twinkled mischievously.

She thought about it. "I shouldn't be. Everyone watches the Food Channel these days."

"Ah, so now I'm just like everyone?"

"No you're not, actually. I know lots of people who watch cooking shows, I don't know anyone who really cooks."

"Follow me," he commanded softly.

Instead of bristling, she happily trailed him, sensing that he was taking her somewhere she would have chosen to go on her own. Balancing their laden plates, she and Trent meandered through a labyrinth of passageways and down a pine staircase into a vast basement kitchen with large French doors framing a sunken herb garden. There were so many copper pots hanging from the ceiling that Mardi had the urge to take a soft mallet and play them like gongs.

The staff smiled at Trent fondly. No one skipped a

beat when he opened a double-wide Sub-Zero—another part of the renovation, he explained—and pulled out a stash of foie gras terrine. He said he had made it himself. "And you have to have some of this cherry compote with the foie gras. I did it with cherries from our orchard."

Was this gorgeous boy really talking to her about compote? About how he didn't use a cherry pitter because he preferred the sensation of pitting the cherries with his fingers?

"Why are you looking at me funny?" he finally asked.

"I've never met a domestic person before." She almost added, *especially one who looks like you*, but she figured he could read this aside in her eyes if he was paying attention.

"North Hampton will do that to you," he replied. "I wasn't into this stuff when I got here either. I always liked good food, but I thought you bought it. I guess there's some kind of connection to nature here. Or to the past. It's kind of a wormhole that way. You know, Freya's an awesome cook."

"Really?" It was hard to picture Freya in an apron. "I can't see Freya over a hot stove. But her sister, Ingrid, makes great strawberry rhubarb pie. Too bad she's so uptight."

Trent walked Mardi through the herb garden around the side of the mansion to a restored eighteenth-century greenhouse. He unlatched the door and led her inside, where he gave her a quick tour of the twisting palm trees, *Agave ferox*, African violets, Swiss cheese plants with bright lacy fronds. There was a reflecting pool where pink and white water lilies floated in harmony. Interspersed with the larger plants were the herbs Freya used for her potions at the North Inn: damiana, burdock, feverfew, valerian, catnip, and angelica root, to name a few. Trent told Mardi that his brother Killian had planted them for Freya. "Ten years ago, this place was a ruin. Killian brought it back to life for her."

They sat on a bench, and Mardi attacked her plate.

He watched her and smiled, amused. "You don't eat like a girl, do you? I'm sorry, was that sexist?"

"Sort of," she said, "but I agree. I hate the way most girls eat. Like my sister, for example. It's either tiny bites of caviar and sips of champagne or nonfat frozen yogurt and Diet Coke. The only time she actually eats is when she sees I have something I really like and she insists on taking 'her' half just so I don't get it all."

"Sounds like you guys have a really healthy relationship." He grinned. "Do you want 'your' half of my foie gras?"

Without waiting for her to say yes, he popped a piece of brioche toast, slivered over with foie gras and drizzled with cherry compote, into her mouth. From someone else, it could have been a forceful, annoying gesture. But it was exactly what she wanted from Trent.

"Wow. Thanks for sharing. And by the way, you said Freya had told you about Molly and me coming to North

Hampton. But how did you know which sister I was when you saw me?"

Trent searched her face with his sea-deep eyes. "Freya had the lowdown on you both from your dad. She said you were the cool one."

Without giving her time to respond, he leapt to his feet and pulled a metal box out from among the stalks of some long green plant whose leaves were clamped shut like smirking mouths. He opened the box, pulled out a pair of long metal tweezers, extracted a writhing worm, and held it up to one of the bulbous leaves. The tight green lips suddenly parted wide. Trent dropped the worm into the heart of it, and the leaves snapped shut on its prey.

"Venus flytrap," he said. "We're not the only carnivores around here. I promised Killian I would feed them while he's gone."

"Can I have one of those to take home?" Mardi asked breathlessly, fantasizing about how much fun it would be to feed Molly to it piece by piece, first her fingers, then her toes, then her wicked tongue, all the way down to her black, black heart.

"Sorry to interrupt, guys, but I'm low on catnip for the bar," Freya said, appearing in the moonlight carrying a small wicker basket and pair of gardening scissors.

As Freya kneeled to clip, Mardi saw that she was not only a glamorous goddess but a nurturing one. If Mardi hadn't happened to like Freya so much, she would have hated her for being so perfect.

"As long as I'm here, I'm also going to grab a little angelica root."

"Go nuts," said Trent. "It's your greenhouse."

Once Freya had gathered her ingredients, she told Mardi they should probably take off. "We don't want Ingrid on our case," she said.

Trent walked them to their car and gave them each a good-night kiss on the cheek. His faint stubble set Mardi's skin aglow. He squeezed her hand, pressing her ring softly into his palm.

"See you around?" she asked.

"It's a small town," he replied with a smile.

As Mardi shifted the old Ferrari from first gear into second, heading away from Fair Haven toward the bridge to the mainland, she checked her rearview mirror to see Trent's strong dark figure silhouetted against the starlit sky. He was smoldering, yes, with those soul-melting eyes and that hard body, but he was also sweet. Something about him felt like home. A home she had never had.

✳ 8 ✳

YOU BETTER WORK, B✳TCH

"*W*hy on Earth do I have to get a job, Daddy?"

"Because it's character building."

"I have plenty of character already."

"Touché, Miss Molly, but you're still getting a summer job. There's got to be something to amuse you in North Hampton. What else are you going to do all day? Shop?"

"Do you realize that doing menial labor for two and a half months will barely net me enough for a new handbag this coming fall?"

"I realize that, yes. But many wealthy families who give their kids everything still have them do low-paying jobs as teenagers. These jobs are a part of their education. They teach the value of work."

"So you admit that it's a total pretense."

"Sweetheart, if you and your sister don't learn to integrate better, you are going to spark a modern-day Salem witch trial. Did you read the papers after those kids were killed? Did you watch the news? You have got to start 'pretending,' if that's what you want to call it. We need all the pretense we can get right now."

"But, Daddy, I'm a goddess. Goddesses don't have paper routes. They don't waitress. Or pump gas."

"You're a goddess who is cut off from her natural world. You can only use your powers if you assimilate into this one. Look at the Beauchamp sisters. Ingrid is a librarian. Freya bartends. They inhabit a disorienting space where nobody quite notices that they never age."

"Are you suggesting that I live here in this backwater forever to keep the mortals off my trail? Are you banishing me? That is a fate worse than death, Daddy. You must know that."

"Relax, relax. New York City is a plenty disorienting enough space for you to spend eternity in without anyone batting an eye. I'm not worried about geography. I'm worried about the human authorities accusing and convicting you so that our own higher authorities banish you to the Underworld. I don't want to lose my babies for all eternity. Can you blame me?"

"Okay, okay, okay, fine, I'll get a job, but can we make it fun? Can I be a sleazy, jet-setting, sleight-of-hand real estate tycoon like you?"

"Molly, you're sixteen." Troy sighed. "And I'm not that sleazy, am I?" he asked, sounding wounded.

"No, of course not. You're awesome Daddy, you know that. Look, I can dress way older. Totally pass for twenty. And you should see the inventory out here. All these places with fabulous bones screaming to be fixed up. And so, so undervalued. And the land, Daddy, utterly wasted on potato farms and fruit trees. It's scandalous."

"Molly—"

"Just listen! I could be the force behind the development and marketing of the next Hampton. We just need to put this place on the map, take down that stupid force field that old Joanna Beauchamp put up a few centuries ago, give North Hampton a train station and a Jitney stop, and we're golden. We're the new gem of the East End."

"Can you try to understand, Molly, that the point of this summer exercise is for us not to draw attention to ourselves? To fly under the radar? To be normal?"

"You call disappearing from the face of social media normal?"

"Please, will you just get a job? The kind of basic job that kids your age do during the summer? As we've established, even trust-fund kids do it. It's the American way."

"Maybe."

"That's my girl. I knew you'd see reason. Tell your sister I said hi, doll face. I've got to run. I have to make a call."

"What else is new?"

"Don't sass me, kid. And take care of yourself, okay? Have some chowder for me. Manhattan clam chowder. The tomato-based kind. I swear it's not fattening."

Molly put her phone down on her bedside table,

opened her window, and leaned out into the bright morning. Her room faced the water. There were sand toys scattered on the beach below, and a couple of kayaks. Matt was out on his paddleboard, moving swiftly across the bay. She supposed he was trying to stay fit as long as he could for his immortal wife, poor guy. Good luck with that.

Molly could see Gardiners Island in the distance, with Fair Haven stately in its lush green grounds, ringed with golden dunes. Somewhere on that island was Tris Gardiner.

Why had she blown it at the party the night before last? She had such power and such strength, yet she had so little control over it. Was it possible that Daddy and Ingrid were right? Did she really need to learn some discipline? She shuddered at the thought.

She supposed she should get ready for the day. She stepped into her small en suite bathroom. It had a Scandinavian feel to it, blond wood, white tile, a single skylight. She showered and dressed in a fitted white sundress and a pair of wraparound cork platform sandals. She wanted something fresh yet beguiling for her job search. She kept her makeup light and chose a pale lipstick.

Downstairs, she found Mardi in an oversized Sigur Rós T-shirt, slumped at the kitchen island over a pile of three steaming blueberry pancakes. Next to Mardi, Jo sat dreamily staring at her rainbow tattoo. The little girl had already finished eating and was absently running a finger in circles through the maple syrup puddled on her plate, lifting it to her mouth and licking it. There was evidence of Henry's breakfast smeared all over his high chair, but he was thankfully absent. For now, the white dress was safe.

"Pancakes?" Ingrid chirped, handing Molly a plate of two.

Molly didn't really want to be eating pancakes, but she couldn't keep herself from blurting out, "Wait a second. Why does Mardi get more than me? I only have two. She has three."

"Four actually." Mardi yawned. "I already ate one."

"Sorry," said Ingrid. "I'm afraid that's the last of the batter."

"You snooze, you lose," Mardi said.

If no one else had been in the room, Molly would have snatched a pancake from her sister. But since she had an audience, she made a show of sitting up very straight on her barstool to contrast her posture favorably with Mardi's slovenly slouch.

After breakfast, she announced that she was going to cycle to town to look for a job. Could she please borrow Ingrid's bike?

Ingrid had a three-speed painted a cheerful red, with an oversized wicker basket hanging from the handlebars, "for trips to the farmers' market." As Molly pedaled it through bucolic North Hampton toward the Main Street, she wondered how much trouble she would get into if she used her fake ID to gain employment at Ocean Vines, the high-end wine store next to the town's old-fashioned, third-run movie theater. At least that way she would learn something about wine to add to her culture and patina.

She imagined that Tris Gardiner was a frequent patron of Ocean Vines. He certainly seemed like a connoisseur. She pictured him coming in for advice on the perfect white Burgundy to accompany a romantic sunset picnic with a certain girl on the beach. She would play along, pretending he was referring to someone else, until the last minute, when he would break into a sexy laugh and tell her he would be picking her up at six.

Why couldn't she get him out of her mind? It was driving her crazy. She squeezed down hard on her handlebars in frustration and felt the press of the gold ring on the middle finger of her right hand. Last night after family dinner at the local fish-'n'-chips place, while they watched television with Ingrid and Matt after the kids were in bed, Mardi had slipped Molly the ring in a barely perceptible moment of sisterly bonding. Ingrid and Matt had not noticed a thing. They had been cuddling, which was sickening to watch. Old people should not do PDA as far as Molly was concerned.

Molly sighed as she rode past Ocean Vines, but she was immediately distracted by the charming, gingham-framed picture window of a gourmet shop two doors down called the Cheesemonger. Her eye was caught in particular by a display of a red-lined picnic basket with leather straps and big brass buckles. There were pretty metal plates, with a floral design that mimicked fine china, and pearl-handled cutlery. Inside the basket was an array of gourmet foods: wild boar sausage, cloth-wrapped aged Cheddar, veiny Roquefort, artisanal crackers, a tin of shortbread, a farm-stand pie, a bottle of local sparkling cider. It made her want to lie on a blanket and hear opera under the stars. And she didn't even like opera.

At least, Molly thought as she leaned her bike against a tree, *I will feel civilized in a place like this.*

It never occurred to her that there might not be a job for her at the Cheesemonger, and it certainly never occurred to her that she might not be a suitable hire.

If she'd been honest with herself, she would have had to admit that this twee, "charming" sort of shop was not at all up her alley. She usually made fun of any person, place, or thing that tried to appear homespun. While she knew this deep inside, she didn't want to acknowledge it. She didn't want to question the fact that, for some inexplicable reason, the Cheesemonger was pulling her inside with a magnetic force.

As she entered the narrow store, a bell tinkled behind the counter and a pretty, long-lashed elfin boy with huge cornflower blue eyes popped out from behind a door that presumably led to a storage room.

"Well, hello," he said with a cheerful goofiness. "How can I help you?"

Molly smiled, sweet and blinding. This was going to be easy. She decided to give herself the "challenge" of getting herself employed on the strength of her charms alone, without resorting to magic. Although of course she would do whatever it took. She was not one to follow rules too closely, not even her own.

"Actually," she said, "I was hoping *I* could help *you*."

"I—I'm sorry?" He began to fiddle nervously with a cheese knife in his right hand. He had sandy hair and mild, pleasant features.

She reached across the old-fashioned register and steadied his hand with hers. "Don't worry, I won't bite you," she said. "I thought you could probably use some help around here. I'm sure you're expecting a huge influx of customers over the summer, and I have great retail experience." She neglected to mention that all of this retail experience was on the consumer side, and not in sales. It hardly mattered. She knew what people liked.

"Oh, I get it now. You're looking for a job?"

She nodded, bouncing her dark hair seductively against her slender neck. "I'm spending the summer in North Hampton, and I'd like to do something productive with my time. I'm very interested in a restaurant or boutique hotel career. I'm exploring my options. And I would like to deepen my understanding of the gourmet food business. I'm thinking my ideal hours would be from eleven to six or seven, during the part of the day when one doesn't want to get too much sun." She laughed. "That's probably your busiest time anyway," she added, gesturing around the empty shop.

"A-actually," he stammered, "I'd love to hire you, but—"

"But what?" She withdrew her hand.

"Well, it's actually my mom's store, and she's left me to work here for a few months. She didn't really give me the authority to make this kind of decision."

"That doesn't make much sense, now, does it? I mean she left you in charge, didn't she?"

"I suppose she did, but I'm not sure we have the budget to—"

Molly was beginning to itch with impatience. She figured that if she worked on him long enough, she could get what she wanted the "normal" way. But Molly Overbrook was not known for happily biding her time. And with such powerful forms of persuasion at her disposal, why subject herself to this silly back and forth, when she knew the end result would be the same no matter what?

Before she had time to consider what she was doing, she had whispered an incantation that had him handing her a neatly pressed blue-and-white-striped apron to match his, with the Cheesemonger logo, a mouse with a beret and curled mustache, embroidered on the front.

He invited her behind the counter in order to show her how the displays were organized. "The cheeses are by country. From left to right, we have France, Spain, Italy, and the US. The meats are over here by France. The prosciutto, salami, and roast beef are all from local farmers. Do you know how to use a meat slicer?"

"Of course," she lied.

"And, in this case, we feature a few salads that I source and make myself, along with a daily quiche. I also make muffins and scones. And over there are the pies and cakes I buy from a wonderful woman down on Dune Road. People sometimes come and stay for lunch." He gestured to two wrought-iron tables, each with two chairs, at the back of the store. "Finally, the breads and other baked goods are in these square baskets back here."

He seemed to gain confidence as he moved through his familiar little universe. He took visible pride in his wares. Within his limited sphere, she remarked with a certain degree of appreciation, he appeared almost passionate. It was sort of attractive, she had to admit.

Suddenly he stopped talking and flushed. "I'm so sorry!" he exclaimed. "I have no idea how we've come this far without an introduction. Marshall Brighton." He looked down at his Converse high-tops as if her beauty was too dazzling to look at.

"Nice to meet you, Cheeseboy, I'm Molly Overbrook. And I start tomorrow."

✳ 9 ✳

THE DOCK OF THE BAY

𝓜y mommy is a librarian, and my daddy is a police-man," Jo practically sang as she spoke. She and Mardi were curled up on the couch, with Midnight napping between them. "So, what job are you going to get, Mardi? Mommy says you need to get a job."

"I think I'm going to work on a fishing boat," said Mardi. She had been racking her brain to find some way to escape Ingrid's controlling gaze. It had to be physical work, work that would numb her frustration and tame her anger. She pictured herself hauling nets full of stripers across wave-swept decks, diving with a harpoon to spear swordfish and tuna. She would be one of the guys, in her short yellow slicker and high rubber boots, going out for beers at the North Inn after a hard day's work.

"How fun to be a fisherman!" Jo closed her pretty eyes. "You'll be like a silver mermaid on the prow of the ship. The fish will see the shiny green light from your mouth and the pretty rainbow on your neck, and they will be under your spell. They will come flying out of the water onto your fishing boat just to be your friends. And by the time the sun rises, you will have so many fish on the boat that all the other fishermen will love you and crown you their queen."

"You're a great storyteller." Mardi smirked. However, her face fell as her mind snagged on six little words from Jo's vision: *by the time the sun rises*. What an idiot Mardi was. Fishing boats went out before dawn. Mardi hated the morning. Unless, of course, she was seeing the sunrise after a night of clubbing, in which case the morning might as well be the evening, since she was heading straight to bed. The notion of vigorous exercise in the ocean spray was a whole lot less appealing when she had to consider setting her alarm for some ungodly hour. Never mind. She had to think of something else physically punishing enough to expend her energy.

"So, what do you know about potato farming?" she asked Jo.

Before Jo could answer, Ingrid came in and suggested that Mardi help clear the breakfast dishes.

Man, did Mardi miss her online delivery services. But she bit her tongue, rinsed the plates, cups, and silverware, and loaded them into the dishwasher. Although she hated to admit it, dishwashing actually wasn't that bad. She felt a simple satisfaction in the domestic chore. The running water on her hands was hypnotic. As she worked, she noticed that her ring finger was bare. She faintly remembered slipping the ring over to her twin while they were watching TV with Ingrid and Matt, but she could no longer picture the actual moment of the exchange. She and Molly could recall their ring exchanges for a little while, the way you hold on to a vivid dream, but eventually the images would fade.

"So Jo tells me you're considering a fishing career?" Ingrid smiled as she gathered her things to go to work at the library. Since the children had been born, she went only part-time, three afternoons a week, during which time Graciella, the housekeeper, watched Jo and Henry.

"Yeah, I was considering doing fishing. Until it occurred to me that I would have to get up at some crazy hour. So I've scratched that career path. But it would be cool to find something to do with water." As she spoke, she realized how drawn she was to the sea. "And I guess that if I'm going to work on controlling things in myself, I need to be pretty active. Otherwise, if I don't, you know, move my body a lot, stuff builds up inside me, and it all starts busting loose."

"Sounds like you've been doing a bit of thinking," said Ingrid with barely concealed delight. "Funny how that happens when life slows down."

Mardi smarted a bit at Ingrid's self-congratulatory tone. "Well, I guess I'm off to the docks to see if I can find a job that'll keep Dad off my case and keep me from killing someone this summer."

With that, she went up to her room, pulled on a 1965

black-and-white-striped minidress, and slipped into a pair of dark gray Vans that she had illustrated herself in black Sharpie, with an intricate pattern of skulls and bones. She waited to go downstairs until she heard Ingrid's car start and then fade into the distance. She had had enough advice for one morning.

As Mardi pulled out of the driveway, she was terrified by the thump of little Henry landing in the passenger seat beside her, as though he had dropped out of the sky.

"What the—!"

She slammed on the brakes and looked up to see that he must have fallen from the branch of the oak tree above the car. How had he gotten up there? And how had he chosen this very moment to let go, when she happened to be passing under to break his fall?

She didn't want to know, and she certainly didn't want to deal with explaining what had just happened. She didn't need people accusing her of recklessly endangering a child right now. She turned off the car, scooped him up, and carried him back to the house.

She knocked on the front door and handed him to Graciella. "I found him wandering in the driveway," Mardi claimed.

Not waiting for a reply, she rushed away with the distinct sensation of Henry's silent gaze tracking her every movement from the safety of Graciella's arms.

Without looking back, she sped to the North Hampton harbor, where the Ferrari drew curious and appreciative looks. She parked and began to walk along the docks, not quite sure what she was looking for but somehow certain that she was in the right place.

"Hey," came a familiar voice, "fancy meeting you here."

"Trent!"

His hair was wet, and his thick lashes sparkled with tiny crystals of salt. He must have been fresh from the water. He had on deep green board shorts, flip-flops, and a worn blue T-shirt with the words THE ONE THAT GOT AWAY in faded lettering across the chest.

"Who's the one that got away?" she asked.

"It's the name of a local fish place. A friend of mine runs it. It's awesome. Best bluefish I ever had. They do it with fennel, olives, and orange rind. Maybe we can go sometime."

How could he look so studly and be talking about fennel and not seem totally ridiculous?

"Yeah, sure. I do bluefish sometimes."

"Cool . . . So, it's good to run into you here. Want to see my boat?"

"Oh, that's right. You live on a boat here. Now I remember. The *Dragon*, right? Your brother's boat?"

"You got it. Come check it out."

When Trent took her hand in order to lead her to his mooring, she didn't snatch it away as she normally would with a virtual stranger. In fact, she liked the feel of his sun-kissed skin. He played with her hand. "You have a ring tan right there," he said, amused at the white skin around her fourth finger.

"Yeah, my sister has the ring on now. If I'm not wearing it, you can be sure she is, and vice versa. That ring is basically the only thing we know how to share."

Trent gave a sunny laugh as they approached a long sleek white boat with a high mast and gleaming teak decks. With childlike delight, he explained that the *Dragon* was considered a midsized sport fishing boat, that it had twenty-foot outriggers and a seventeen-foot high beam, and that it could cruise at up to forty-four knots at 2,330 rpm.

He started Mardi's tour up top, on the exterior gallery with its mezzanine-style cockpit replete with tackle, coolers, and a fridge full of beer.

"What are you doing here anyway?" he asked.

"Looking for a job," she said.

He nodded. "Want a cold one?"

"Sure."

He popped the tops off two icy pale ales and handed her one as they headed down a flight to the second tier, the flybridge and peninsula style console. There was starboard and forward seating, with bright orange-and-white-striped cushions.

"And finally, down here," Trent announced, opening a solid teak door onto steps leading to the interior gallery, "is where I lurk." Belowdecks, the walls, cabinetry, and built-in beds were all of cherry wood. The counters were black granite. The upholstery was leather, chocolate with cream piping.

Mardi looked around for a few minutes, then whistled. "No offense," she said, "but I didn't picture you living somewhere quite so . . . well . . . fancy. I got the impression you were escaping all that by hiding out on the *Dragon*. But this here is pretty flash."

"It's not my boat, remember. This is all Killian's doing. And Killian was all about impressing Freya when he bought it. I'm nothing but a squatter on the *Dragon*." He took her hand again. This time, he did not let go. "But a squatter has squatter's rights." He winked. "Which means I'm entitled to visitors whenever I want."

She turned around so he wouldn't see her blush. Then she made her way back up the stairs.

Back in the daylight, she told him more about her job search, that she wanted something physical, on or near the water, but that there was no way she was getting up early to work on a fishing boat. Did he have any ideas?

"I'm sure we can think of something," he said. "But why the urgency to get a job? Can't you relax for the summer?"

"I'm sort of in trouble," she blurted out, not sure why she was trusting him with this information but unable to hold back. "Molly and I both are kind of screwed, actually. And we have to make a show of cleaning up our acts and pretending to be normal so that the authorities will leave us alone."

"What happened?"

"I don't really want to talk about it," she said.

"Fair enough," said Trent. "But I'm all ears whenever you're ready." He led her back to the deck, where they looked out to the sea through a forest of masts and billowing sails.

"Thanks," she said.

"So, about a job," he said calmly. "You look pretty strong to me. How do you feel about loading and unloading cargo?"

✳ *10* ✳

C IS FOR COOKIE

Once Freya found out that Molly was working at the Cheesemonger, she made a habit of stopping by on the way to her shift at the North Inn for her favorite sandwich of cave-aged Gruyère, salted butter, and cornichons on a crusty baguette, always followed by a brownie studded with walnuts and pecans.

"I've inherited my mom's sweet tooth," Freya complained. "Ever since she left this world, it's as if I've taken on her curse. I can't go a day without chocolate. It's a good thing I'm running off my feet for eight hours a night."

Molly looked across the tiny round café table at Freya. The brownies didn't appear to be doing her an ounce of harm. She was flawless in a tight black jumpsuit with a scooped back, her tiny waist cinched by a gold rope elaborately knotted at her navel. Her toenails glimmered a wicked purple in peeky-toe heels. Her lips were impossibly glossy, and her cheeks glinted as if by the light of their own private moon. She exuded magic from every pore of her body. *How*, wondered Molly, *did she keep it in check?*

"You should stop by the bar sometime, Molly," Freya suggested. Then she turned to Marshall, who was behind the counter, dicing cucumbers for a Greek salad. "You too, Marsh. I won't card you guys if you don't tell."

Marshall graced Freya and Molly with a shy but knowing smile. Molly had to admit that there was something endearing about him. As he loosened up around her, he was beginning to banter and make jokes. His cracks were often self-deprecating and amusing without being mean.

He liked to make up little songs while he worked. Her favorite was "Mangoes on My Mind," to the tune of "Singing in the Rain," which he sang as he prepped the mango salsa for the crab cakes.

Marshall was cute, but she was much too impressed with Tris Gardiner, who loomed large in her mind's eye from the Fair Haven party, to give Cheeseboy any serious consideration. It might be fun to have him follow her around like a puppy, but he was nothing compared to Tris.

"Tell me"—she leaned in close to Freya—"what do you know about the youngest Gardiner brother? Is he really bad news? Or do we sort of like him?"

"Well, well, well." Freya raised her eyebrows playfully. "So we've met young Trystan, have we?"

"Maybe. And maybe he's been texting me."

"Really?" Freya asked, raising an eyebrow. "But I thought . . ." She frowned.

"Why? Is that so hard to believe?" Molly asked, annoyed.

"No. I guess I just had him pegged wrong, then," Freya said.

"What do you mean?"

"Nothing. Forget I said anything."

"Anyway, he's pretty hot," Molly admitted. "I mean, he's certainly a catch in this town. But it's not like there's fierce competition."

She stole a glance at Marshall and saw that he had stopped chopping.

"Molly," he said softly, running his hand nervously through his fine sand-colored hair, "can you mind the store for a few minutes? I forgot to pick up my heirloom tomatoes at Jasper Farms. I'm going to ride my bike over right now. I'll be back soon."

"No problem," she said, standing up, retying her apron and making a show of going to stand behind the counter.

Freya gestured to Marshall with her chin. "I think you might have hurt his feelings. I think he likes you."

Molly rolled her eyes. "Does it look like I care?" But she felt a small, unfamiliar twinge of regret for her harsh words.

She got up and manned the counter. It was close to July, business was picking up, and Molly found she enjoyed the ritual of entertaining the Cheesemonger's customers. There was a certain elegance to the activity of slicing, wrapping, and serving beautiful foodstuffs in pretty packages and charging a lot of money for them. She enjoyed the feel of the register keys on her fingertips. The job was like playacting, and she was quite good at it. It was even fun, until someone was rude, impatient, or, God forbid, belligerent. Unsavory customers would often find their picnics infested with red ants, their cars covered in seagull droppings, or their sunglasses mysteriously shattered in their cases.

For the moment, though, the Cheesemonger was empty, except for Molly and Freya, who was sipping a double espresso with the last of her brownie. Molly seized the opportunity to ask the question that was really on her mind.

"The Gardiners are warlocks, aren't they? Tell me I'm right. I get the impression that they are divine, like us. I got such a magical vibe the other night. Am I onto something?"

"There's no point in trying to tell you otherwise if you already sense it," answered Freya, serious all of a sudden. "Yes, they are like us. Fair Haven sits on the seam between two of the nine worlds of the Known Universe: Midgard, where we are destined to live out our days, and the Land of the Dead. It's the joining of the living and the twilight words. Somewhere inside that mansion is a crucial entry point into the skeleton of the universe. I used to know where it was, but the refurbishment has obscured all that. It's a mystery again."

"Wow." Molly's eyes widened. She was not easily impressed, but this was intense.

Freya continued. "Our mother, Joanna, placed a powerful containment spell on the house centuries ago. Ingrid and I are the spell's guardians now. Believe me, you don't want to be messing with those boundaries, especially in your delicate situation. You really don't want to be rocking the boat at this point."

This was getting too heavy for Molly. It was time to bring it down a notch. "All I want to know is whether or not you think fooling around with a Gardiner brother is a good idea."

"Fooling around, my dear, is always a good idea, especially if his last name is Gardiner." Freya laughed, appearing relieved to change the subject and to leave the spooky territory of the gloaming behind in favor of happier concerns. "You don't need my approval for that!"

"That's great news because I did actually text him back and—"

At that moment, the bell to the store's entrance tinkled, and in walked Mardi, wearing a pair of cutoff OshKosh overalls over an electric yellow tube top.

Molly gave Freya a meaningful look and put a finger to her lips. She did *not* want her sister in her business.

"Hey, guys," she said. "What's good today? I'm ravenous. I've been lifting crates of sardines all day."

Molly sniffed the air, crinkling her tiny nose. "I can tell."

"Hey, I showered after work."

"Where? In the public bathroom?"

"If you must know, I showered on a yacht."

"Which yacht?"

"None of your business."

Freya burst out laughing. "I thought Ingrid and I were bad when we bickered. You girls put us to shame. If you don't watch out, you'll scare away all of Marshall's customers." She downed the final sip of her espresso, gave each twin a kiss on the cheek, and drove off in her pumpkin-colored Mini Cooper to begin her night of charmed mixology at the North Inn.

"Freya invited me to come to her bar sometime. She's not going to card me," Molly boasted once she and Mardi were alone.

"I'm sure she won't card me either. No one ever cards me."

"That's because you cheat with your magic."

"And you don't?"

"You got me there," sighed Molly. There was a shift inside her, something about the way her sister's rainbow tattoo caught the afternoon light as it slanted in through the Cheesemonger's picture window, which made Molly want to let up and enjoy this moment. She found that she didn't feel like fighting anymore. "I'll admit that I use my magic on bouncers, bartenders, and door guys all the time too. So we're even. Truce? Want a sandwich?"

"Sure."

"Roast beef? It's rare like you like it. And we have this gorgeous purple mustard. It's purple because it's made from the must of wine grapes."

"*Gorgeous* mustard?" Mardi teased, but with no sting in her voice. Molly could tell Mardi's heart wasn't in it, and so she didn't take offense.

"For once, can you please trust me? Try it."

As Molly sliced focaccia, spread the purple mustard, layered the meat with crumbles of Gorgonzola and arugula leaves, a question began to form in her mind. She didn't know exactly what the question was, but she knew it had to do with that fateful night back in April, with the party at Bret's house, the lost hours, the tragedy. It wasn't until she handed Mardi her sandwich with a bottle of high-end root beer that the words came out fully formed: "Did you have the ring on that night?"

Mardi, of course, knew exactly what night Molly was referring to. The twins were symbiotic. This was the precise reason why they were also the bitterest of rivals. Intuition is not always an easy thing to share. But there were moments like this when they both relaxed their guard and searched for common ground. Together, they were circling the idea that maybe their ring was more than just a private symbol between the two of them. It had some kind of power. After all, it was the only thing they had left of their mother.

"I don't think so. No, I didn't have it on at Bret's. I did wake up wearing it, weirdly. But I didn't have it when I was checking out that awesome spider sculpture with him. I remember feeling for it and thinking you must have had it."

"But I didn't," said Molly, instinctively checking her right hand to make sure the ring was still there now. "I remember thinking *you* must have had it."

"Well, one of us has to be wrong. The ring never disappeared, obviously, because it was still there in the morning."

Molly bristled. The brief interlude of sisterly bonding was so over. "Well, it's obviously not me who's wrong!"

"Are you implying that it's me?" Mardi tore into her roast beef furiously. "Because it can't be me. There's no way. I am so much higher functioning than you."

"Oh, so I'm supposed to be the ditzy one?"

"Well, since I'm *not* the ditzy one, it goes without saying that you must be."

"You're the one who was wearing it the morning after! I think that proves that *you* spaced, not me!"

The girls were interrupted by Marshall, returning with a small wooden crate of green, yellow, and orange tomatoes in all kinds of funky, nonengineered shapes. He'd obviously recovered his spirits and was all freckled smiles from behind his colorful heap of summer bounty.

"Have I stumbled on an epic battle?" He grinned.

"Sort of," Molly and Mardi answered as one, starting to laugh in spite of themselves.

"Great," Marshall said, putting his vegetable crate

down on top of the cheese case, "because deflating massive conflict happens to be my specialty. Did you ladies know that I have ten-year-old identical-twin half brothers? Whenever I go to visit them in Philly, they make me wear a cape with a capital *P* sewn on the back. *P* stands for Peacemaker. That's my superhero identity."

"Where is this going?" Molly asked, cracking a reluctant smile.

"You'll see. Now, I don't have my cape here, so you'll have to use your imaginations. You've got to picture me flying over the counter, like so." In an agile leap, he cleared the counter to land right in front of the cookie basket. He took an oatmeal chocolate chip cookie—both sisters' favorite—laid it on a small plate with a knife, and put the plate on the counter. "Here's the twin challenge," he said, somehow maintaining eye contact with both of them. "One of you gets to cut the cookie in half. The other one gets to pick her half first."

"This is my store," Molly said immediately. "I work here. So, I get to decide. And I want to cut the cookie," she insisted.

"Okay, that works out great," Mardi quipped, "because I want to choose my half first."

"Wait a second, never mind. You can cut. I'm picking! It's my store, remember?" Molly knew they were bickering like children. It was even worse here in North Hampton than back in the city. It felt like someone had hexed them with a curse of discord. Why did they have no control of themselves?

"That is so unfair!" Mardi grabbed the knife. But instead of turning it on the oatmeal chocolate chip cookie, she pointed it at Molly's face.

Molly laughed. "Marshall, as you are my witness, my own sister is threatening me with a knife."

"A butter knife, I might add," Marshall said, totally deadpan. "Ladies, would you like to witness my earth-shattering peacemaking skills in action?"

Mardi lowered the knife, and they both stared at him in disbelief as he began to eat the disputed cookie himself.

He began to sing a song from *Sesame Street*: "*C* is for cookie. That's good enough for me—"

"Are you channeling the Cookie Monster right now?" Molly couldn't help but smile at Marshall. She was melting inside.

"Scrumptious," he sighed, by way of an answer. "My mom's secret recipe. I'm the only soul on Earth she will ever trust with it." He took a long, languorous bite, then he took two more cookies from the basket and handed one to each girl. "The moral of this story is all you ever have to do in life is realize there is *always* enough to go around. That full basket has been there this whole time."

The girls chewed in silent contemplation. *He was sort of right,* Molly thought. And sort of adorable. And he baked killer cookies.

"Would you girls like some strawberry lemonade?"
They nodded.

Marshall poured three tall glasses, stirred in fresh mint leaves, and handed them around. "Ladies, I would like to propose a toast to Peace. With a capital *P*."

In unison, they raised their lemonade. "Peace!"

Molly gave this happy new state of affairs about five minutes. But she supposed it would be sweet while it lasted.

11

REHAB

*A*my Winehouse was singing about not wanting to go to rehab, and Mardi was singing right along with her. She hated anything that smacked of an intervention, and this scene had all the elements.

She and Molly were sitting side by side on the couch in the living room of Freya's spare modern house, the one she had taken over from Matt when he got married, piling it high with her excess clothes. In this glass and steel setting, the clothes, stacked by color, looked like abstract expressionist art rather than clutter.

Presumably, this out-of-the-way location, with its unfettered views of empty beach and open sea, was a neutral spot, the exact sort of place where interventions were staged.

Mardi trailed off a lyric in the face of Ingrid's admonishing glare. Even Freya looked dead serious beside her sister. For once, her neckline gave no hint of cleavage. The two women sat cross-legged on a sleek leather-upholstered bench.

Most ominous of all was the dapper older man whose lanky frame was folded into a camel-colored Eames chair. He appeared every bit the Upper East Side shrink in a bespoke gray suit complete with a red pocket square. He had a faint mustache and goatee. His bald brown head was shiny under the light.

"Girls," Ingrid began, "this is our dear friend Jean-Baptiste Mésomier. He has been very helpful to us through the centuries. The most recent time he came to our aid was about ten years ago when we had our last crises of memory threatening the community. In order to speak to you, he has kindly agreed to travel up from New Orleans back into our midst."

"Jean-Baptiste," Freya chimed in, "Molly and Mardi Overbrook, Troy's girls."

"It's a pleasure to meet you both," said the old man in a light French accent. "Now, how may I help you?"

This sounded suspiciously like the kind of open-ended therapy question Mardi despised. "Could you start by telling us what exactly we're doing here?" she retorted.

"Mardi!" Ingrid looked mortified. "Please be respectful. You are speaking to the god of memory himself."

"He's come to help you with your amnesia," Freya added helpfully. "We're starting to think that someone has been messing with your memories. There's no reason for you both to be so vague about what happened the night those kids were killed in Manhattan. We suspect foul play."

"You mean we didn't just black out because we were wasted?" Mardi was in the depths of a dark sarcastic mood. "Why do you guys have to tease everything out to make it so *meaningful*? Why can't we just be ordinary kids who do ordinary stupid things at parties?" She knew she was being disingenuous, but she couldn't stop.

"But, Mardi," Molly interjected, "we can't be ordinary." She pronounced the word *ordinary* as if it were toxic. "We're extraordinary by nature. We're not like other kids. We're—we're . . ."

"We're legendary!" exclaimed Mardi, intending to be sarcastic, but realizing as she pronounced the words that they were absolutely true. Her father was the god of thunder. The mortals had named Thursday after him. That was her family heritage: the days of the week were named after her forebears. Who else could claim that?

"Yes," the old man purred, "indeed we are legendary. We are all myths and legends. Powerful ones, I might add. And, as my great friend and countryman Voltaire once said, 'With great power comes great responsibility.'"

"I thought that was Spider-Man," said Mardi, genuinely perplexed.

"Actually I think it was Thomas Jefferson," Molly chimed.

"Regardless of who said it, it pertains to the two of you," said Jean-Baptiste.

"Girls," Ingrid sighed, "this is serious. Please pay attention and try to focus. Here's the problem as we see it. You two have been creating quite a stir in and around your high school in New York. You are wanton with your spells and hexes—making girls' hair fall out in clumps, causing sworn enemies to make out with one another in broad daylight, rewriting test questions to make them—quote, unquote—less dry, inducing temporary paralysis in your rivals, and the list goes on."

"Way to go, girls!" Freya interrupted with irrepressible glee. "I turned a teacher's eyebrows purple once because she told me I wasn't trying hard enough in geometry, and once, I made my elementary school principal loudly declare his undying love for our class's pet lizard. He got down on his knees to propose and everything. I can't remember what lifetime that was, but it was a good one."

"Awesome," cried Mardi, high-fiving Freya.

"Cool," Molly echoed.

"Come on, Freya," Ingrid chided. "You're not helping our cause here. You and I live in North Hampton, a disorienting space that doesn't exist on any map and is protected by strong spells. It would take a heck of a lot for us to be persecuted here in this day and age.

"But you twins, on the other hand," she continued, looking squarely at Mardi and Molly, "have been living large in the public eye. Granted, New York City can absorb massive amounts of weirdness. Which is all the more reason that we have to hand it to you. It's quite a feat on your part to have the mortals who live there actually beginning to suspect witchcraft and enchantment. It's saying a lot in today's skeptical, electronic age . . ."

Ingrid seemed to lose her train of thought for the moment. Freya took up the slack: "The rumor about that young couple who died is that the two of you somehow put a spell on them and used your powers to force them onto the tracks in front of an oncoming train. If that rumor turns into a formal legal accusation, we're in big trouble. The one thing the White Council has forbidden is another witch hunt. They won't tolerate any more trials or convictions. So, if it's not true that you killed them, you've got to cooperate with us to help us figure out what really happened. You have to let Jean-Baptiste help you to retrieve that night."

"What do you mean, 'if it's not true'?" Mardi's blood rose. "Of course we didn't kill them. We barely even knew them. We ran in totally different crowds. But that's beside the point. We would never kill *anyone*. I've never even killed a roach with my magic." She paused to gather her thoughts. "Okay, maybe we express a little uncontrolled anger here and there. But mostly, we have fun with our powers. Believe me, we don't murder people. We don't even really hurt people. We sometimes toy with them is all."

"Yeah, mostly we just embarrass them," Molly added.

"Molly, Mardi." Jean-Baptiste rolled their names off his tongue with calm authority. "Or, rather, I should call you Mooi and Magdi, for those are your true given names, Thor's daughters, twin goddesses of strength and rage: you will both grow serious now, if you please. And you will both please close your eyes."

Before she had time to raise an objection, Mardi's lids dropped thick and leaden over her eyes. Instantly, the cubic beach house was blacked out. She no longer felt she was sitting in the light, airy living room on stilts over the beach. Gone were the pale wood, the brushed steel, and the glassy views of the gray green sea. Instead, she saw a swirl of lush, garish colors: bloodred, royal blue, burnished gold, all tinseled over with sprays of silver. She sank into a decadent and disturbing dream.

There was water here too, but it was not at all the vibrant water of the ocean. It was the overheated water of an interior lap pool encased in black marble. She was swimming in somebody's private pool, in a dimly mood-lit room. Along the shining black rim of the deck were half-empty glasses of alcohol in varying shades. The drinks were sloshed everywhere. For all she knew, what looked like the white flakes of a snow globe, swirling around the filter, were the remains of spilled cocaine. The water was too warm to actually move in, and the pool was much too small for real laps. One flip turn and you would be halfway across it. Mardi felt herself stewing, like a lobster in a pot over a flame, slowly losing her will to live.

As her senses grew more acute and the picture of the pool in its luxurious setting came more sharply into focus, she realized that she wasn't alone in the water. Molly was there too. And Molly wasn't wearing a swimsuit. Mardi looked down at her own body. Neither was she.

They were skinny-dipping. And there was a boy with them. He was chasing them in a half-playful, half hostile game. There was much splashing and flirting, but also a bit of fear. Was it Bret? He had Bret's sharp features and platinum hair, but she couldn't be sure. She couldn't remember.

Molly seemed to be teasing the boy, whoever he was. "It's so, so powerful. You know you want it! But the ring is ours. You can't have it. And you can't have us."

Mardi's every intuition told her they should get out of this water and run. But her body was lulled by the warmth, and it was all she could do to dodge Bret-not-Bret's unwelcome caresses as he dove after her and her sister. When was this farce going to end?

Then the boy was shouting at them. Except his voice was different from Bret's, higher-pitched and whinier, but oddly familiar. She knew she had heard this voice recently, but in the confusion of her fugue state she could not match it to a face.

Finally, Mardi's frustration boiled over. Tapping into the anger at her core, she was able to break through whatever curse was blurring her mind.

"Get away!" she screamed. The desperation in his movements made her feel physically sick. Fitfully, he grasped for the girls' limbs in the dark water of his private Manhattan pool. "You bitches are going to burn in Hell!"

Mardi despised him as she had never despised anyone before. "Leave us alone! Don't touch me! Don't touch my sister! You can never have our ring!"

The power of her own voice brought her back to her senses. She opened her eyes to find herself back on the couch in Freya's stark modern living room, surrounded by kindly, curious, and concerned faces. She looked at Molly, who was also blinking and who appeared deeply confused. Molly was shaking, pale, and drained.

Mardi had the urge to take Molly into her arms and cling to her. What was it that they had been through together? Who was that weird guy in the pool with them? Why did he want their ring? What was so powerful about it?

"I think," said Jean-Baptiste from the depths of his leather seat, giving Freya and Ingrid a meaningful look, "that that we have certainly done enough work for one afternoon."

After they were released from their session, Mardi and Molly stood together on the empty beach in front of the house, catching their breath and comparing visions. They found that they had been in the same black marble pool, taunted by the same creepy guy with the bizarre whining voice. He had wanted their ring, and they had been trying desperately to keep it away from him.

"Did you see whether or not he finally got it?" Mardi asked.

Molly shook her head. "I'm not even sure which one of us had it that night."

"It must have been you because you woke up with it, right?"

"I guess. It's all so vague . . . But I remember clearly from the vision that it was really important to us to keep the ring away from him. I remember sensing that it was super powerful."

"Yeah, I remember that too . . . Maybe the ring is more than we've always thought."

"You mean more than just something between the two of us?" Molly lifted her finger. The rose gold caught the soft light of the setting sun. The diamondback pattern shimmered.

"Yeah, Molly, it's definitely bigger than we are." Mardi took a thick platinum box chain off from around her neck. "Maybe we should wear it around our necks for a while? That way we'll be more aware of it, and of who has it, instead of slipping it on and off our fingers without always remembering. It'll be safer. Here, take this chain."

Molly didn't argue. She took the chain, unclasped it, slipped the ring onto it, and put it on. The ring hit her just below her clavicle.

As Mardi looked at her twin with the rose gold gleaming against her chest, she had the distinct impression that she was gazing into a mirror at her own dark features, her own black hair, and her own uncertain future.

* 12 *

RUNNING WITH THE DEVIL

What are you doing tonight?

With a surreptitious glance at the phone in her bag, since she was supposed to be minding the kids, Molly read Tris's text yet again. She appreciated his restraint in not using abbreviations. Nothing was more of a turn-off than being referred to as "u." Tris was obviously a product of good breeding. She approved.

She started to compose an answer in her head. This was no easy task. She wanted to see him again, but she didn't want to seem overly available.

"Jo," she asked, "if you want someone to want to be your friend in kindergarten, what do you do?"

Molly was walking the children to the lunchtime story hour at the North Hampton Public Library, pushing Henry in his all-terrain stroller while Jo skipped beside her. The plan was for Molly to drop them off and then head to her afternoon and evening shift at the Cheesemonger.

The library was about a mile from the house, on a

leafy green square with a stunning view of the water. When it had almost been torn down a few years ago to make way for condos, Ingrid had spearheaded the effort to have it landmarked, thwarting developers in order to preserve the character and integrity of the town. She still talked a lot about that battle, about getting the mayor on her side, the petitions and the fund-raisers. Ingrid, Molly thought, faintly baffled, was one of these people who actually took pride in bettering the world around her. Was Ingrid a different species of witch from Mardi and her? Molly couldn't imagine herself ever taking in two obnoxious teenagers for a whole summer out of the kindness of her heart. Come to think of it, *was* there any kindness in her heart?

There had to be, didn't there?

"If I like someone and I want them to like me back, then I ask Mommy to help me bake some brownies to give them," Jo said matter-of-factly. "We always bake our brownies from my grandma Joanna's recipe. I never got to meet my grandma, but Mommy says she still loves me and that her magic is still in the house, and that's what makes all our sweets taste so good."

This answer cut Molly to the quick. She had no idea who her own mother was; their father never talked about her—he was too sad—and no one had ever baked with her in her life.

Hating to feel sorry for herself, she scrambled to find the humor in the situation.

"I don't think," she smirked, "that brownies are the fastest way to his heart."

"To whose heart?" asked Jo.

But Molly didn't answer. She had veered into strategy mode. The trick to hooking Tris, she decided after several false mental starts, was to blame the fact that she was free tonight on the dullness of North Hampton. She should imply that, had Tris tried texting her back in the city, he would have had to get in a long, long line . . . Now that she had her message, she had to come up with the actual words to convey it.

Having handed Henry and Jo off to their mother, Molly went another mile to the Cheesemonger. Her crisp white bandeau-top sundress would easily transition into night if she were to meet Tris for a late dinner. She was wearing flats but had heels in her tote. Since Mardi had given her a ride home last evening from work, Ingrid's bike was still parked behind the shop. Molly had aligned her stars so that nothing could get in her way. Getting what she wanted was a specialty of hers, she thought with pride, having completely recovered her confidence after her unexpected moment of doubt on the street with Jo, that sweet little witch.

Inside the Cheesemonger, Marshall was singing a song about the runner beans he was busy trimming. He waved a handful of beans at her and belted out a song about running with the devil.

It was the head-banging Van Halen song that Daddy still liked to blast through the house when he was feeling spry. It was so incongruous with Marshall's boy-next-door looks that she burst out laughing.

"What?" He smiled. "What's so funny?"

"It's just that you don't look like you could run with the devil for a second."

"Looks can be deceiving." He shrugged his shoulders playfully. "Take, for instance, these very runner beans. They look pretty misshapen, and they have a few brown spots. Their color isn't uniform. If you were looking for perfection in a gleaming supermarket, you might turn up your nose at these particular beans. But these particular beans are actually fantastic, bursting with flavor. All of their color and beauty is on the in-side. So you have to know them in order to love them. Do you want to try one?"

"Sure. Can I eat it raw?"

"Absolutely," he said.

Molly suddenly felt shy as she took a bean from his outstretched hand. He had been keeping his eyes mostly on his work, and this was the first time he was really looking at her. "Um," he said, watching her face for signs of appreciation as she chewed. "You look pretty today. I mean, you look especially pretty today. Because you look pretty every day." He grew flustered and looked down at the floor, where he obviously latched on to the first thing that caught his eye. "I like your shoes."

"Thanks. I like your beans. You're right, they taste way better than they look. I guess this is another one of your life lessons, right?"

He shrugged. "Do you want to help me slice them? It would be good to get ahead on prep work before people start coming in for dinner stuff on their way home from the beach."

"Good thinking. Sure I'll help you. Why not?"

Because Marshall assumed Molly wanted to be helpful, she found she actually did. It was like he drew a sweet shape for her to step into. She found herself in a cheerful role she had never quite imagined before.

As he was showing her how to slice the runner beans, humming the Van Halen song again, he placed his right hand on top of hers over the paring knife. "Try to do it diagonally, like this," he said gently.

"Okay . . . So you think I'm pretty, huh?" she asked with a wicked smile.

Under normal circumstances, she would have tortured and humiliated a guy who tried to flirt with her like this when he should have known he had zero chance. But either she was starting to lose her edge, or she kinda liked him, because she was definitely flirting back.

The doorbell tinkled with the beginning of the late-afternoon rush. For the next few hours, she and Marshall worked together, side by side, until about seven, when business started to taper, since everyone in town knew that the shop closed at eight.

At one point around five o'clock, she stole into the bathroom, pulled out her phone, and finally answered Tris. To be honest, I'm not quite sure what I'm doing tonight. The possibilities are so endless in this town that I don't know where to begin. Any advice?

After that, she checked her phone between customers and sometimes even in the middle of preparing an order. Why wasn't he texting her back? Who did this guy think he was?

The irritation she had felt back at the party over a week ago overtook her again. If anyone in the shop even thought about messing with her, if anyone asked for their turkey sliced a bit thinner or for light dressing on their line-caught tuna salad, she was afraid of what she might do to them. But the evening customers didn't cross any lines, and Marshall stayed buoyant throughout. Molly found no excuse to blow her top, which made the waiting all that much harder.

Finally, as she was hanging up her apron and Marshall was starting to switch off the lights, a message flashed on her phone.

Have you finished your shift at the Cheesemonger?

How did Tris even know she was working there? They hadn't seen each other since the party, and she hadn't mentioned her job in any of her texts to him. He must be watching her from afar. Spying. How sexy.

Yes, she typed. She certainly was finished with the shop for today. Assuming he would now offer to pick her up and take her somewhere for the evening, she started fishing in her giant bag for her heels.

"Hey, Marshall," she said, "do you mind leaving the lights on for another minute or two? I'm going to pop into the bathroom and freshen up."

"Of course. I'll wait for you. You have Ingrid's bike here, right?"

"I do."

"I—well—I have my bike too. And I was wondering, wondering . . . wondering if you wanted to take a ride together over to the North Inn. You know, the bar where Freya works?"

Marshall was seriously getting ahead of himself. He was nice and all, but she would have to put him in his place. The rush of haughtiness that filled her soul reminded her of who she really was. She was Molly Overbrook, and she was unattainable by ordinary means. She had been playing at being sweet to this cute, but very ordinary boy. But no more.

"Some other time, Cheeseboy. Sorry, I have a date tonight."

"Oh. Okay."

Although he looked disappointed, he was not as crestfallen as she would have liked, which meant he might try to ask her out again. She was coming up with something else to say when her phone beeped.

It must be Tris saying he was on his way. She felt a rush of victory. Marshall became the last thing on her mind.

She darted into the bathroom, pulled out her makeup bag and began to curl her eyelashes. The lighting was terrible, overbright, so she did a little dimming incantation. "That's much better," she sighed to herself. When she had finished with her lashes, she took a look at her phone to see where she should wait for him and was miffed to read that he wasn't actually coming for her.

Can I expect you at Fair Haven within the hour?

What, was he *summoning* her? How cosmically conceited of him! It was all she could do not to crack the bathroom mirror.

Somehow, she steeled herself and managed to walk out of the shop and hop onto her bicycle without wreaking any havoc.

"Well," said Marshall, locking the door to the shop, "good night, Molly. I look forward to seeing you tomorrow."

She waited for him to pedal off before she started riding in the direction of home. Because there was no way she was heading to Fair Haven and giving Tris the satisfaction of answering his booty call.

Or was there?

Was there, perhaps, more than one way to look at this situation? Molly could, of course, decide that Trystan Gardiner was an arrogant bastard who didn't deserve a moment of her attention. But, following her own logic earlier about how lame this town was, she could make the case that an invitation to Fair Haven was as good as it got. He was offering her a private tour of his mansion, without any of the hangers-on who had been clamoring to check out the latest renovation at the big party last week. He was letting her in on an exclusive basis. As his date. Considered in this light, his invitation grew quite appealing. Besides, she was lonely. She wasn't used to going this long without male attention. And Cheeseboy didn't count.

Slowly, Molly turned around. Instead of going home, she steered her red bicycle toward the bridge to Gardiners Island.

Summoned, indeed.

13

MEMORY MOTEL

$\mathcal{M}$ardi hadn't even kissed him yet. She and Trent had come close a couple of times on the *Dragon*, within fractions of an inch, but their lips had never touched.

He had given her keys to the *Dragon*'s cabin so that she could shower at the end of the day or grab a drink during a break from her hard physical work. Often she would bump into him on his deck or on the docks, where he was helping a friend renovate a clam shack into a farm-to-table restaurant. They always had charged exchanges. And, without being pushy, Trent made it quite clear with his body language that he would be open to more than just talking. But he hadn't made a move.

Usually, Mardi hated nothing more than to feel pressured, so she was grateful for Trent's restraint, but she was growing frustrated too. She was going to have to make the first move. Again. When she actually liked someone, she always did. Probably because she was so intimidating with her tongue stud and her tattoo that boys didn't want to blow it. But she could tell Trent wasn't cowed by her. She hadn't been this intrigued by a boy in a long, long time.

She had been beside Trent most of the day, unloading lumber for the new restaurant, and her body was aching for him. Wasn't it time now to give him the signal to pull her into his arms and down into the *Dragon*? It wouldn't take much.

He was only an inch away, sitting beside her on the dock, dangling his bare feet next to hers. There was a now-familiar hint of salt on his skin catching the late-afternoon light. In order not to stare at him, she looked out to sea.

"Do you have any plans tonight, Mardi?" His voice was insistently sexy, yet gentle.

There. He'd made his move.

But all of a sudden she was terrified.

She turned to face him and immediately felt herself swimming in the beauty of his bottomless blue eyes. She could drown in them. Lose herself.

It was tempting. Too tempting. She was able to hold his gaze for only a few seconds before she had to look away again. It was as though she were being sucked into a riptide. She had to protect herself from her own attraction. "Thanks, Trent, but I have a date with Freya at the North Inn."

As soon as she said it, she felt a sting of regret. Along with a huge sense of relief. She liked this guy too much to get close.

"That's cool." He sighed, crinkling those gorgeous eyes into the sunset. "Well, maybe some other time."

"Yeah, some other time."

Now that she had pushed him away, Mardi was able to look at Trent again and take in the full picture of what she was denying herself: the broad shoulders and ropy arms, the strong hands, the high cheekbones and full lips, and the deep eyes sparkling now with something like sadness. What was wrong with her?

"You'll like the North Inn," he said. "It's a cool place, and Freya really lights it up. Maybe we can go together sometime soon?"

"Sure. Maybe."

He flashed a smile. "I'm going to go out on a limb and take that as a yes, Mardi Overbrook."

"Maybe it is."

As Mardi left him behind on the dock, she felt her body being pulled back in his direction with a magnetic force. It was all she could do to rip herself away and run to her car. Man, did she need a strong drink to distract her right now.

Freya had more than once hinted at the possibility of tequila shots. And she'd said she thought Mardi would dig the rock-'n'-roll vibe of the North Inn. Too bad Mardi wasn't wearing something with more of a '70s feel tonight. Her black denim cutoffs and vintage Black Sabbath T-shirt were pretty basic, but she was going to give the place a try. Freya would be happy to see her. And Freya would probably also have some advice for her on how to loosen up around Trent.

As she was figuring out which way to turn to get to the North Inn, Mardi's headlights suddenly illuminated a red bicycle pedaled by none other than her sister. Who else but Molly would be riding a bike through a beach town in four-inch stilettos?

Mardi pulled the convertible over and waited for Molly to ride up to her.

"Where are you going in those shoes?" Mardi asked.

Ignoring the question, Molly asked, "Where are *you* going?" She appeared flushed and distracted.

"To check out Freya's bar. Wanna come?"

"Thanks, but I'm on my way to Fair Haven."

"What for?" Mardi's curiosity was instantly piqued.

Molly answered with nothing but a smug smile.

"Well, if you're going all the way to Gardiners Island, you really should have a light on your bike." Ever since the session with Jean-Baptiste, Mardi had been feeling protective of her twin.

"Don't worry." Molly laughed. "I have reflectors on my tires, and, more importantly, I've put up a repellent shield against drunk-driving lowlifes as well as blind old ladies who shouldn't be allowed behind the wheel. So don't sweat it, sis. I'm not going to end up as a splotch on the road tonight."

"You should still be careful . . . You can't tell me who you are going to see at Fair Haven?"

"I can. But I won't."

With that, Molly pedaled off into the night.

Mardi gritted her teeth all the way to the North Inn. Why did her sister have to act like such a brat at a time when they should be sticking together? It was so frustrating that they couldn't get along right now. The friction was even stronger than usual. A real curse.

And why was Molly being so secretive about Fair Haven? The only person of interest who had anything to do with Fair Haven was Trent. But Trent was never at the house, so it couldn't possibly be Trent that Mardi was going to see, besides which, Trent would never look at Molly, and Molly would never look at Trent. So what the Hell was Mardi stressing about?

She parked the Ferrari in between a pickup truck and a Volvo in the North Inn parking lot. This was probably going to suck.

But once she was inside the bar, Mardi was pleasantly surprised. The jukebox was playing "Memory Motel" by the Rolling Stones, another of Dad's favorites that she had unconsciously learned by heart.

Mardi wasn't the only one familiar with the song. Half the patrons were singing along as they drank. There was even a couple slow-dancing. The place, which was totally unpretentious, its wooden booths carved with years' worth of names and messages, managed to be mellow and relaxed while at the same time giving off a charged party vibe. It was as if the North Inn orbited its own interior sun. And that sun's name was Freya.

Freya was warm, brilliant, and life-giving. Even when her customers weren't looking directly at her, they were inspired by her presence. Mardi wasn't the only one who was half in love with her. Freya was wonderfully steady, and yet she was always in motion, vibrantly shaking and mixing drinks, calling everyone by name, cranking the tunes.

This feeling of entering a private universe when she came into the bar was instantly familiar to Mardi from her endless nights and early mornings at after-hours clubs. Even if the people here were older and a thousand times less hip than her crowd back in the city, they formed a similar pocket of belonging.

"Mardi, great to see you!" Freya handed Mardi a drink right away. As soon as she tasted it, Mardi realized it was exactly what she wanted, mescal with pomegranate, jalapeño, and some other unidentifiable flavors that Mardi imagined came from herbs out of the greenhouse at Fair Haven, where she and Trent had shared their dinner. The memory felt distant already. How long exactly had she been in North Hampton? Time here was freaky.

"How did you know I would love this drink, Freya? Do you read minds?"

"I do where matters of the heart are concerned."

"That must get pretty weird on occasion."

"Mmm-hmm. It can be a little TMI sometimes."

"Still, it must also be cool to see into people's hearts."

"*You* could see into people's hearts too, Mardi, if you chose to focus. You have a seer's gift. I sense it. If you quieted down, you could see everything I see."

"Really, I feel like I can't see anything right now. I feel like the blindest kid in town." She took a long appreciative drink, licking the peppery rim of her glass to get the full intensity of its flavor. "What do you call this drink?"

"The Omnivore. I mixed it just for you. And I'll never pour it for another."

Mardi smiled. Freya was too awesome. "Freya, what do you think of Trent?"

"You mean Trent Gardiner?" Freya's green eyes came into sharp focus.

"Yeah, the guy we were hanging with in the greenhouse at Fair Haven the other night."

"What about him?" Freya asked. "He's great. One of my favorite people. He's basically like a brother to us. We sort of adopted him since he's all alone this summer."

"Cool."

"Have you mentioned him to your sister yet?" Freya asked.

Mardi shrugged. "No. Why should I? She's being such a pain lately."

Freya looked as if she wanted to say something more but had decided against it.

14

KISS

$\mathcal{A}$s Molly rode across the bridge to Gardiners Island, her excitement was tinged with a slight foreboding. The house was not nearly as well lit as it had been the night of the party. Only two windows, one upstairs, one down, shone out into the night. The rest of the mansion appeared as a dark mass against a moonless sky. She could not help but recall Freya's words about the place being built over a seam between this world and the Land of the Dead. She began to feel vulnerable on Ingrid's bicycle, with black water on either side of her. Her protection spell would work against stupid human drivers, but would do nothing to save her from being swallowed up into the deep, were she to fall off the bridge and through some portal into a parallel world. Suddenly Daddy's warnings about Limbo didn't seem quite so frivolous. Maybe she should turn back?

Yet despite her fears, she was pulled toward the

island, with its promise of Tris, as if by soul-attracting magnet. She *had* to go; she had to see him again.

Once she was safely across the water and looking for a spot on the grassy dunes to lay her bike, a light rose at her back, illuminating the sand in front of her in a large glittering circle. For a second, she felt like an escaped convict who had just been caught at the climax of a dramatic manhunt. But, after a beat, she decided she appeared more like a pop star in the limelight, with her killer heels and freshly applied lipstick. Or at least that's how she should play it. After all, she wasn't sneaking around. She had been invited here.

She turned to the source of the light beam to see Tris holding a brass lantern above his head in order to spotlight her to maximum effect.

"Molly." His voice was deeply welcoming, an intimate stage whisper that carried across the dunes. "I'm so glad you came."

"I was curious to see the house without all those random locals crowding around."

"Fair enough." He took a step toward her. He was wearing crisp white jeans and a white linen shirt with his TG monogram in gold thread, gleaming rich and subtle on the cuffs. His bare bronzed feet rested comfortably in the sand. He was every bit the young lord of that manor in casual attire.

"Anything else you're curious about?" He smiled as he took her hand. "Aren't you a vision," he said as he took her waist and spun her so that the skirt of her white dress flared out into the night. "Come to the house. I'll mix you a drink. I can already tell we have much to celebrate."

This guy was too much. Yet Molly couldn't call him on it, and she allowed herself to be guided up the misty path to Fair Haven.

Molly was not accustomed to being spellbound. She was supposed to be the spell*binder*. This passive walking like a clueless bride being led to the altar was absurd. She had to get ahold of herself. However, she simply didn't feel like taking her accustomed control of the situation. Not quite yet.

Tris brought her into a small, mahogany-paneled library that she had not seen on her first visit. One wall was composed of floor-to-ceiling shelves of leather-bound, gold-lettered volumes. Between the wood panels on the other walls was hand-painted wallpaper in a striking William Morris floral design. Molly recognized it from an internship she had done last spring with a world-class interior decorator. The internship had started out well, as Molly had "a good eye," according to her employer, but ended abruptly when said employer asked Molly to pick up her dry cleaning one too many times and her boss arrived at a client meeting to find all her fabric samples in shreds, smelling distinctly of fried garlic.

"What are you smiling about?" Tris asked, ambling over to a gleaming bar cart.

"Just recalling a little prank I played a few months ago."

"Oh, yeah? I like pranks." He raised his eyebrows, so startlingly black over his bright blue eyes that she caught her breath. "Tell me about it," he said.

"It's not the sort of thing a girl like me is supposed to share." Buried in her refusal was the hint of a question. She was testing this young warlock. She could tell he knew she was a witch. And she was pretty sure he was aware that she was onto him too. But she wasn't going to be the first one to drop the façade.

"After one of my dirty martinis, you won't be able to keep it from me. In fact, you won't be able to keep anything from me."

"Dirty martinis are so housewife," she snorted.

"Is that so? Well, if you're after something with lychees or muddled mangoes, you've come to the wrong establishment. No toothpick umbrellas at Fair Haven, I'm afraid."

"I'm not even going to respond to that. I like my martinis without brine. Brine makes me think of mud. And I don't want to drink mud. Do you have any St-Germain?"

"I think I can manage a little elderflower."

"Good." She watched with pleasure as he began to do her bidding. "So, what're you doing in North Hampton?" she asked.

"I could ask you the same question."

"But you won't," she retorted, unstrapping her delicate sandals and letting them fall to the floor as she folded her smooth legs underneath her on the soft leather seat of the armchair.

"Okay, I won't. I pretty much do anything a beautiful girl tells me to do." For the first time, Tris lost his cockiness, and she felt herself truly vulnerable to his charms. Trying to resist his flattery was like swimming against a current. She knew there was no point in tackling it head-on. When you are caught in rip, Mardi always told her, you want to go at an angle.

"I'm still waiting for my answer," she deadpanned.

"Cheers first?" He handed her a golden martini and then raised his own "dirty" glass to hers. "Please, Molly Overbrook?" he asked, almost anxiously, as though he was worried she might disappear were he to say the wrong thing. "Drink with me?"

She had been prepared for the arrogance and the charm, but this vulnerability was potentially disarming. She wanted to give in, but she knew she shouldn't.

"Okay. I'll take one sip, if you'll tell me what you're really doing hiding here in East End instead of living out in the world," she said.

"Deal."

As they clinked glasses and drank deeply, he settled himself with feline grace on the arm of her chair, his toes grazing her bare thighs.

"I'm on Gardiners Island because I'm in a little bit of

trouble, I'm afraid. I think you might know what I'm talking about. We're the same, you and I."

She nodded. "Are you being punished by the Council too?"

He bristled just perceptibly. "Not exactly punished. But I need to lie low for a while."

Molly felt a thrill of recognition. She and Tris were prisoners of the same fate.

"Trystan Gardiner"—she locked eyes with him—"if this is an act, it's awfully convincing."

"Molly Overbrook, you are the most amazing and beautiful witch I've ever met. Not to mention one of the smartest. If this were an act, you would see right through it. Now, kiss me."

Molly wanted to understand more of her newly revealed soul mate, but she also wanted to stop thinking and to simply succumb to his embrace. The evening's riptide was suddenly taking her exactly where she wanted to go. Resistance was no longer necessary. She saw nothing but his deep blue eyes, his strong chin, and his muscular arms as he leaned in toward her and pressed his mouth against hers.

* 15 *

WILD HORSES

$\mathcal{B}$ack at the North Inn, Freya's delicious, spicy cocktail gave Mardi a brief sense of belonging. She downed it fast and instantly craved another. But as she started in on the second one, the drink began to take its true effect, and she surged inside with a deep longing for Trent. She looked across the bar at Freya, who shot her a quick smile and a complicit wink as if to say, *My mixology never fails to unveil my customers' true desires. Now, go out and find that boy of yours.*

"Thanks, Freya," Mardi whispered. With her second cocktail unfinished, she left a twenty-dollar tip under her glass and stepped out into the fresh air. Behind her the jukebox was blaring the Rolling Stones' "Wild Horses."

Slipping into the Ferrari, she opened her bag to fish for her keys and found the twenty she thought she had left on the bar. It was origami-folded into the shape of a heart.

"Freya, you are a keeper," she exclaimed into the salty night air as she revved the engine and took off for the docks.

Pulsing with expectation, Mardi approached the *Dragon* sometime after midnight. Her mind was alive with visions of Trent emerging sweetly from sleep at her touch, his bare muscular chest outlined in a soft white sheet. She pictured his eyes opening, his gaze alighting on her face, his arms outstretched in a wordless embrace. This was as corny and romantic as she had ever felt. She blamed Freya and her love potion, even if she wanted this boy as never before.

She walked up to the boat, but the *Dragon* was locked and empty. Trent had told her that whenever he was on board, he left the cabin door open. He didn't like the idea of shutting himself in. Of course it was just another way to say, *Come see me anytime—I'll be waiting*. Well, she was here now.

Except he was nowhere to be found. Had she missed her chance? Had she put him off for too long? Had he given up on her? Was he in bed with someone else at the very moment she wanted to be with him?

She sat on the dock and let the night hours roll over her, and her mind drifted back to the shaky memories of that awful night at Bret's house with the giant bronze tarantula, the "crown jewel" of the family's priceless sculpture collection. Had she and Molly really been na-ked in that slick black indoor pool, with the Valkyries singing opera on a giant flat screen while some creepy guy chased her and Molly through the water? Or had that ancient Creole memory god slipped them some peyote the other day in Freya's living room?

Through the predawn darkness, Mardi heard a rush of bicycle wheels coming off the Gardiners Island Bridge and guessed that Molly was racing back to Ingrid and Matt's house in time to make a show of being there in the morning. In spite of herself, she began to harbor a paranoid vision of Molly and Trent together. It seemed impossible, but then again, he wasn't here on his boat, and Molly had just spent the night at Fair Haven. Okay, so Trent wasn't exactly Molly's style of guy. She didn't go in for rough around the edges. But then again, he was a gorgeous, rich heir, no matter how he dressed.

Mardi winced into the breaking dawn. Her mind was racing. Molly *was* her identical twin. If Trent couldn't have Mardi, would he go for Molly? Would Molly be all in? Her sister wasn't known for her scru-ples where other people's crushes were concerned. Could this be their idea of a sick joke? Mardi tried to stop herself from thinking about it, but her skin crawled with suspicion.

The horizon started to a burn a faint rose gold. The first glimmer of dawn found Mardi dangling her feet over the side of the dock beside the empty *Dragon*. There was no sound except for the gentle lapping of the water against the sides of the boat. She felt her anger rise along with the sun.

She didn't exactly know what her dad expected her to take away from this summer of exile, but she feared that whatever his hopes were, they were going to be dashed. She was as dark, mad, and frustrated inside as ever.

One thing that happened when you entered a new microcosm, especially one as limited as North Hampton, was this: no matter how petty and lame you thought its social hierarchies were, you found yourself caring where you fit into them and whether or not you were having as good a time as everyone else. It was more than a competitive instinct; it was a desire to belong. Even in the lamest, preppiest, stupidest, most backward town on the planet, you didn't want to be alone.

Mardi stretched, took a final look at the vacant *Dragon*, and stood up. It was time to go home, put in a couple hours of sleep, and stop freaking out about her sister hooking up with her crush. Suddenly, she was exhausted. She craved the guest bed back at Ingrid and Matt's. In a few hours, a big load of kitchen equipment for the restaurant would arrive, and she would need some energy to get through the day. She figured it would be good for her to work blindingly hard. It would help numb her frustration.

As she was getting to her feet, two familiar voices approached her. She recognized Jean-Baptiste's gravelly French accent. It was as if she had conjured him with her thoughts about her and Molly's vision. And Jean-Baptiste was talking to none other than . . . Trent Gardiner.

"Lovely to see you again, young man."

"I'm glad we talked, Jean-Baptiste. Thank you," Trent said softly, as if to respect the sacred quiet of the dawn. Mardi realized as he spoke that she would know his melodic voice anywhere. It had burrowed deep inside her and lodged like a secret treasure. She hoped beyond hope that he hadn't been hooking up with her twin.

The men betrayed some surprise when they came upon Mardi stretching next to the *Dragon*, but neither one of them lost his composure.

"Why, Mardi!" Jean-Baptiste, dapper in an off-white linen suit, made her name sound like trickling notes of music. "How lovely to see you here, and how unexpected." It was impossible to know whether he was truly pleased, shocked, or annoyed. He was as unreadable as any good shrink.

Mardi didn't know whether she was more stunned to run into Jean-Baptiste on the docks at five-thirty in the morning or to realize that he was on such friendly terms with Trent, who was standing comfortably beside him in the green board shorts she liked so much, sipping coffee from a metal thermos. The coffee smelled like heaven.

Reading her mind, Trent held the thermos out to her. "You look like you need this as much as I do. This gentleman here does not know the meaning of rest. We've been talking all night."

"You have?" She tried not to sound too happy. "You've been with Jean-Baptiste all night?"

"Yep." He grinned. "All night."

She took his coffee gratefully, inhaled its steam, and felt her head clear so quickly that she looked at him with a start. This was no ordinary brew. Trent was no ordinary guy. And here he was hanging out with the god of memory. He *had* to be one of them. That would explain so much. But she wasn't quite ready to ask him openly what his divine status was. Their dance was not far enough along yet.

"I see that you two are acquainted," Trent said, looking from Mardi to Jean-Baptiste.

"Yes, thanks to my lovely young friends Ingrid and Freya Beauchamp. They have convinced me to spend the summer here, to escape the New Orleans heat and to help Mardi and her twin sister, Molly, with a project they have."

"A project?" Trent looked mischievous. How much, Mardi wondered, did he know?

Mardi took a deep breath and began to explain without really explaining. "You see, Jean-Baptiste is part of the doomed effort to reform Molly and me. You should know, Trent, that the two of us, the terrible twins, have been sent here by our father, who fears we are out of control. Dad thinks a summer in the town that time forgot, with normal jobs, life in a stable family that doesn't live on takeout, and sessions with Dr. Mésomier here will somehow set us straight." She was trying to be sarcastic, but her words had no barb. She was too happy to see Trent and profoundly relieved to see he wasn't with any other girl, let alone her twin.

"Well," said Jean-Baptiste, "I'd best be getting back to the Rose Cottage, my charming if overstuffed, overchintzed bed-and-breakfast. My hostess, Mrs. Ashley Green, is a lovely woman, but she does tend to worry about her guests. Besides, I'm rather spent after an evening keeping up with this one." He gestured to Trent.

"You look less tired than either of us," Trent said. It was true. After a presumably sleepless night, Jean-Baptiste was as crisp and bright as his violet pocket square, while Mardi and Trent were both yawning as they passed the coffee back and forth.

"Nevertheless, I shall leave you two," Jean-Baptiste said with a quiet, knowing smile. Mardi and Trent locked eyes for a moment, and by the time they looked around again, the old man had evaporated.

"This coffee is fantastic," Mardi said, enjoying his intense gaze on her as she drank.

"Have you been here long?" he asked.

"I was at the North Inn for a while, hanging out with Freya, and I thought I'd stop by the *Dragon* on my way home—even though it's not really on my way home—and see what you were up to."

He nodded.

She noticed his eyes drawn to the rainbow snake around her neck. He looked at it with such interest that she shimmered inside. No one had ever taken her in so fully before. Yet she still hadn't opened up about who she really was. And neither had he.

"Look, the sun is coming up," she said, looking out at the first rays.

He came up behind her, wrapped her in his arms and nestled his chin on her shoulder. "It's so peaceful, isn't it?" he whispered in her ear.

"Mmmm." She leaned back into him.

"Mardi, I don't want to push you, but I want you to understand that I really care about you, and I can tell you're in some kind of trouble. Jean-Baptiste didn't tell me much. He feels he can't. But he gives me the impression that your struggle is more than a simple discipline problem. You're not just some spoiled brat from the big city. I want you to know. . . ." He trailed off.

"Know what?"

"That I'm just like you," he whispered, and she knew exactly what he meant.

"I thought so" was all she could manage.

"You're not the only one who's exiled here," he continued. "I need Jean-Baptiste's help as much as you do."

She turned around to face him. There was hardly a

breath of space between them. For a few beats, she simply looked into his eyes. Then, because her feelings for him were, yet again, too powerful for her to understand, she pulled away. "I should go," she said.

Gently he took her hands in his. "Wild horses can't drag me away," he said, as if he had read her mind earlier. But he released her and turned toward his beautiful boat while she wandered back to her red convertible, her heart full of hope and confusion.

*

PART TWO

Summer Nights

*

16

WE ARE FAMILY

*A*lthough it was profoundly bucolic, North Hampton was not devoid of progress. The once decrepit, faintly sleazy motel on the outskirts of town had recently been gussied up into a boutique establishment, complete with vintage photographs in burnished frames and Jonathan Adler throw pillows in nautical colors. Not to mention the historic estate of Fair Haven, which, as the whole town knew, had just been renovated with central air, induction stoves, and radiant heat in its bathroom floors. Among the local clam shacks and candy stores, a traveler could now also find some of the same gourmet food that was flooding the rest of the Hamptons.

The Cheesemonger carried several brands of handcrafted crackers at ten dollars a box. An ambitious young local named Joshua Goose was opening a restaurant whose menu would explain the provenance of every beet green and beef cheek without a trace of irony.

But these were superficial changes. They gave North Hampton the illusion of keeping up with the times when, in fact, it was shrouded for eternity in a spell of timelessness. How else could its inhabitants fail to notice that the Beauchamp sisters, Freya and Ingrid, never aged? No one had ever noticed as their mother, Joanna, felt her wrinkles go smooth, her gray hair go brown, and her belly swell in order to give birth to them again all those years ago. North Hampton, despite its nod to the occasional trend, was a place of oblivion.

It was also a place that prided itself on its traditions, one of which was Manhattan clam chowder, made with clams from the bay and chunks of potato, onion, and tomato from surrounding farms. So when Marshall suggested that they try making and selling New England clam chowder, the kind made with cream instead of tomatoes, Molly was skeptical. "People here wear the same brand of Top-Siders from the cradle to the grave, Cheeseboy. I can't really picture them suddenly going for a new soup. Especially since Manhattan chowder is their specialty. They're so proud of it."

"You're the one who told me they keep inventing new bagel flavors in New York. And what's more New York than a bagel?"

"Are you really going to compare North Hampton to New York?"

"I guess you're right. North Hampton has so many distinct advantages."

She laughed. "Like?"

"It has fewer roaches. Fewer rats. And it has outdoor opera on the Fourth of July, which is tomorrow night by the way. In case you don't have plans. How about some Wagner under the stars? I make the best picnic in town."

"Am I dreaming, Cheesefriend, or are you actually trying to ask me out again?" Her joking tone took the edge off. "Are you one of those people who doesn't learn from experience? Like the mice who keep reaching for the electric shock button even after the hundredth time? Because the button looks like a piece of cheese?"

He laughed. "Are you really calling your boss a lab animal?"

You had to hand it to Cheeseboy. Against all odds, he remained playfully persistent.

"Oh, my God, I forgot you're my boss!" She covered her face with her hands in mock drama, peeking through long manicured fingers at him as he dropped handfuls of parsley into his creamy chowder. "I depend on you, *Mr.* Cheeseboy, for such a huge part of my up-keep!" She gestured up and down the multicolored designer sundress that had surely cost more than a week's paycheck from the Cheesemonger. "I mean, this job almost covers my sock budget. Not stockings. I didn't say stockings. That would be asking too much. Besides, they don't sell Wolford in this town. But it pretty much covers my athletic socks. So, I guess I better not blow it and alienate you. I guess I have to say yes to your date. So, what time is that opera thing tomorrow? And what is it again? Wagner? Do I like Wagner? By the way, does this count as sexual harassment? Because you're my boss and all."

Partly, she wanted to make Tris a little jealous, since he hadn't mentioned any plans for the Fourth of July. Although in all fairness, they hadn't done much talking once they had started making out the other night. But partly, Molly couldn't help but find Cheeseboy cute, even if he was, you know, Cheeseboy.

She could see that he was so stunned and happy by her acceptance that he had to pretend to be absorbed in his cooking while he scrambled for a comeback worthy of her banter. After a few seconds, he said, "I think you'll like the Wagner a lot. The concert is a little, um, cheesy in that it's a 'greatest hits' of the Ring Cycle. So it's sort of high art meets Americana. But that's sort of how I think of you. You're an exquisite, yet all-American beauty."

"You think of me as 'high art meets Americana'?" She was trying to hold up her end of the conversation, but something about the words *Ring Cycle* was throwing her. Her body surged with the same otherworldly tingling she had felt during that creepy memory therapy session at Freya's house when that old Frenchman with the cool pocket square, Jean-Baptiste, had taken her and Mardi back to that weird night at Bret's. Scared that she was losing her balance, she gripped the counter.

Marshall didn't seem to notice. "Do you want to try my soup?" he asked.

"I guess," she managed. "Do I have a choice?"

He held out a spoon to her mouth. As she leaned toward it, she felt herself swoon. There was heavy music pounding in her head. Images of her and Mardi's ring snaked across her field of vision, and she lost her balance.

"Are you okay?" Marshall yelled as he saved her from face-planting into the chowder pot.

The next thing she knew, she was draped across the shop's gingham-upholstered window seat with a cool wet washcloth pressed to her forehead. Marshall was standing above her, slowly coming into focus as her nausea ebbed. From below, his ordinary features appeared reassuringly familiar, but also strikingly handsome.

"I don't know what happened," she said, slowly sitting up.

Just then, her phone rang. It was Daddy. His ringtone was "We Are Family" by Sister Sledge, which always brought an ironic smile to Molly's glossy lips, because she, Daddy, and Mardi were hardly a traditional family. They were no more than three strong-willed individuals bound up together, with no rhythms, no traditions, no center. Living with Ingrid, Matt, and the kids, with their aromas of home cooking and their chore lists taped to the fridge, was really bringing this fact home.

Marshall handed her the phone.

"Thanks, Ch—I mean, Marshall."

"You're welcome."

He was so kind. And not bad-looking either. Cute, really. Something was melting inside her.

"I really mean it. Thanks."

He winked and went back to his place behind the counter.

"Hi, Daddy," she sighed into her phone.

"Sweetheart, you sound upset. You must have heard the awful news. Did Ingrid tell you?"

"Daddy, I can't deal with your hysteria right now. I'm not feeling so great. Can we talk later?"

"Molly, this is serious. There's a formal accusation by the dead girl's parents. They have testimony from some of the kids and teachers at school about your outrageous pranks. The word *witchcraft* is actually being used. It was in the *Post* today."

"Daddy, this is the twenty-first century. No one is going to get tried for witchcraft in New York City." She tried to sound blithe, but she was starting to feel some of his anxiety. Her usual steely self-confidence was beginning to falter. So she did what she always did when she felt threatened. She said something mean.

"You live in an ancient fantasy world, Daddy. We're never going to be able to return to Asgard, and the mortals of this world think you wear a red cape and hold a hammer, okay? I gotta go."

Molly wasn't stupid. She knew that if there was a trial it would end up being about what mortals considered "facts," and not about witchcraft. But she also knew that the witchcraft thing could easily take hold in the public imagination, that people could start talking and asking questions, and that the White Council would not be remotely psyched about this, which was why Daddy was so stressed. Even if he was an absent single father, she had to admit that he did have some protective instincts. Maybe he was acting so crazy now in an attempt to make up for lost time.

To reassure herself, she felt for the ring on the chain around her neck.

But it wasn't there.

She panicked and began to look around frantically.

"Are you all right?" Marshall sounded concerned from behind the counter.

"I'm fine. It's nothing," she said, beginning to tremble. Was it possible that she had unhooked the chain and slipped it onto Mardi's neck, or that Mardi had taken it and slipped it on her finger? She didn't have the faintest memory. She would have to discreetly check Mardi's neck and hands later. Still, all of Molly's intuition told her Mardi didn't have it. No, Molly had misplaced it herself. But where? And when?

It came to her. It must have somehow fallen off in Tris's library while they were hooking up. Her memory of the evening was hardly sharp. The thick chain was long enough to fit over her head without unclasping it. It must have come off when other things were coming off.

Trembling, she felt the empty spot on her chest where the ring had lain. Although she did not know exactly why, she knew that losing her mother's ring could be disastrous. How could she have been so delirious?

She would double-check tonight that Mardi did not have it. And if it wasn't around Mardi's neck or on her hand, then she, Molly, would go back to Fair Haven and find it.

Soon.

TAKE ME TO THE WATER

*T*he smell of chocolate cake was growing stronger and more delicious by the minute, filling the house with a sense of promise. Mardi had never baked before, and she was amazed by the simple pleasure of mixing the sugar, butter, eggs, flour, chocolate, and buttermilk under the tutelage of Ingrid and Jo, while Henry licked utensils. She had always thought you bought cakes at bakery counters, usually at the last minute when you remembered it was someone's birthday. This experience of actually making one with her hands unveiled a whole new realm of magic to her.

"Smells good in here," Matt sang out as he came through the sliding glass doors that opened onto a deck on the beach. He was wrapped in a towel after a swim. "Looks good too," he said to Ingrid, giving her what Mardi couldn't help noticing was a deep kiss. *Maybe they weren't so uptight after all,* she thought. And then it occurred to her again that because he was mortal, he would die before their passion did. That sucked.

Jo and Henry came running up to their father. Henry leapt into his arms, and the family portrait they made was so charming that Ingrid's choice was beginning to make some sense.

"Daddy!" Jo squealed, "We're baking a Fourth of July cake for our picnic! It's going to have whipped cream frosting and red and blue sprinkles. That makes red, white, and blue! Get it? Mommy, can we decorate it soon?"

"It has to come out of the oven and then cool first, sweetie. *Then* we can frost it." Ingrid smiled as she went to answer her ringing phone, wiping her hands on her apron so as not to get flour on the phone. "Hello? Oh hi, Troy, how are you? . . . You're kidding." With a furtive and anxious glance at Mardi, she went out onto the deck, sliding the glass door behind her, and began to pace as she talked.

Matt went upstairs to take a shower, leaving Mardi to watch Henry and Jo, who were wild with excitement about the picnic tonight with the opera on the big town green overlooking the sea. Poor kids had no idea they were going to be subjected to a bunch of fat people screeching in German all night.

Mardi was relieved that she wasn't going to the concert. Trent had invited her out on the *Dragon* to see the fireworks up close—they were going to be launched from a barge off Gardiners Island.

Mardi felt sure that tonight was the night they would finally kiss. It would be just the two of them, with a bottle of wine and one of his delicious meals, watching the rockets fire and the colors rain through the night sky. She'd foraged a great outfit from Freya's attic closet: a dress from a '60s love-in, made out of an American flag with peace signs graffitied between the stripes. It was sewn into a toga, a very short toga, with fringe. To match it, she had star-spangled garters from Freya's vast lingerie collection. It was going to be a good night.

Henry broke her reverie by squealing one of his few words over and over: "Beach! Beach! Beach!" He tugged her out the door, past Ingrid, who was still on the phone, in an apparently stressful and all-consuming conversation. Impatiently, she waved Henry and Mardi past her on the deck, then ignored Jo asking her when the cake would be out of the oven.

After about fifteen minutes of halfheartedly helping Henry load and unload a plastic dump truck full of wet sand while Jo worked on a sand castle, Mardi saw a stone-faced Ingrid heading toward them.

"Jo!" Ingrid snapped. "How many times do I have to tell you, no magic sand castles!"

Jo was busily constructing a latticework palace with simple waves of her shovel.

"Use your hands like a normal kid," Ingrid went on relentlessly. "We don't do 'special' in our family."

"But that's so boring," Jo whined as she watched her beautiful construction crumble into a heap on the ground.

Ignoring her daughter's complaint, Ingrid gave Mardi a long and serious look. "I just spoke with your father," she said. "Things in New York are not looking good." She proceeded to explain that there was a formal accusation against the Overbrook sisters by the family of the dead girl, Samantha Hill. Mardi and Molly were accused of brainwashing with an intent to kill, but the subtext was witchcraft.

When Mardi tried to interrupt in her own defense, Ingrid told her that there was another development. Right before calling her, Troy had received a warning from the White Council. The Council was concerned that the twins were not only wantonly disrespectful, but that they were unleashing a rash of bad magic into Midgard.

"What exactly did the Council's message say?" Mardi asked as they headed back toward the house with the kids in tow.

"It said, 'Beware the storm of retribution.'"

"Well, that could be a metaphor for almost anything," Mardi laughed nervously.

"No," Ingrid corrected her, sliding open the screen to the deck. "It could be a metaphor for almost anything *negative*. We're going to have to do another session with Jean-Baptiste as soon as possible to figure out what happened that night and clear your names."

Coming into the house, they were assaulted by a burnt smell and a haze of smoke.

"The cake!"

Henry and Jo both burst into tears. Mardi tried hard to stifle a grin. These people were so earnest.

Ingrid and the kids ran to the oven. Dropping the pretense of oven mitts, Ingrid pulled out the blackened cake with her bare hands. It was a sad sight, a steaming lump of coal.

"Please, Mommy, please fix it," Jo begged, while Henry gazed at her with huge imploring eyes.

Mardi watched carefully as Ingrid caved, her face melting into a smile. "Okay," she said, "I'll do it for your grandmother Joanna. She would have loved you so much. And spoiled you so rotten." As she murmured an incantation over the pan, the smoke cleared, the delicious odor of chocolate returned, and the cake rose again. Jo and Henry squealed with delight. Promise was restored to the day.

Ingrid gave Mardi a sheepish smile as she put her finger to her lips. "I know, I know. All right. You got me. Why don't you go get ready for your date."

Mardi slipped into her vintage red, white, and blue. Then she gunned the Ferrari down to the docks, trying to banish negative thoughts brought on by her father's drama queen antics. What the Hell was a "storm of retribution," anyway? A lot of hot air was what it was. Dad might even have been making up the whole White Council thing to freak them out. Since he had no control over his daughters, he was always trying to get higher authorities to step in and parent for him. A summer at Ingrid's with the threat of divine punishment if she and Mardi didn't shape up might well be nothing more than his latest desperate stab at being a father. Pathetic. Not for the first time, she wondered what her mother had been like.

It took her a while to find Trent. When she finally did locate him, he was sanding a countertop in the kitchen of his friend's soon-to-open new restaurant. He was shirtless. His back was sculpted, every lean muscle defined, alive, and alert. His chest and stomach were toned by swimming in the ocean and working on the docks rather than lifting weights. His beauty was unconscious, carefree. It was all she could do not to run her fingers up and down the grooves of his muscles.

"You look incredible," Trent said when he saw her. He apologized for not being quite ready to set sail and promised that there was wine and a killer picnic on the boat if she wanted to go wait for him on the *Dragon*'s deck.

She went to hang out on the boat for a moment, thinking she would enjoy the calm of the sunset and the distant strains of the orchestra tuning as all of North Hampton gathered on the town green for the annual Fourth of July concert. But instead of feeling peaceful as she sat on the *Dragon*'s cushions, leaning on a pile of orange life jackets, she felt a tempest brewing inside her from the White Council's warning. It was so unfair! They hadn't done anything. Every gentle lap of the sea against the side of the boat set off a flurry of furious reverberations in her soul. She was like Jo or Henry on the verge of a tantrum. Only instead of pounding little fists on the floor, she had the urge to set fire to every boat in this harbor, to watch the sails go up in a vast conflagration of her own making, and to feel herself burn among them. She hated the White Council. They had nothing to do with her life, and yet they were threatening to wreck it.

She hadn't done anything to those kids back in the city. She and Molly were spoiled rotten, wild and selfish and heedless, but they weren't murderers. Except she was beginning to wonder now how well she actually knew herself and just how much evil she might be capable of. What had Jean-Baptiste called them? Twin goddesses of strength and rage? Of course since Thor was their father it made sense. But did that make them She-Hulks or something? Maybe she and Molly had bewitched and killed those kids. Maybe they *were* evil.

"Mardi, are you all right? You look upset," Trent said, with a worried look on his face.

"What are you talking about? I'm fine."

"All right, then, look what I stole from the cellar of Fair Haven." It was a 1999 bottle of Château Lafite Rothschild. "A very special year."

"I was born in 1999," she said, impressed.

He winked as he uncorked the bottle and poured two glasses. The ruby liquid sloshed a bit more than usual. Everything around her seemed to be surging with secret power, even though the night was beautifully calm.

You're projecting, she thought. Aloud she simply said "cheers," as he started the motor.

After a short ride, they anchored off Gardiners Island at a safe distance from the barge that would set off the firework display that the Gardiner family organized every year for the citizens of North Hampton.

Trent had put on a light blue linen shirt. As he set out their picnic of smoked bluefish, oysters, and lobster salad with tarragon from his greenhouse garden, the breeze began to pick up so that his shirt billowed in a pale blue cloud and her American Flag dress flew up to reveal Freya's funky garters.

Trent raised his eyebrows in amusement and wolf whistled.

Mardi tried to meet his smile head-on, but felt a momentary shyness. She looked down at her bare feet only to be surprised by a sudden wave washing across the deck over her toes. She scanned the water for a big vessel that might have caused the surge, but saw none. Then she noticed Trent doing the same, a tinge of anxiety in his eyes.

"Isn't the weather supposed to be perfect tonight?" she asked.

"Everything about tonight is supposed to be perfect," he said over the howling rising wind.

* 18 *

DAS RHEINGOLD

Cheeseboy had gone all-out on his picnic for Molly. He had brought a plaid cashmere blanket, the chic wicker basket, overflowing with delicacies, that had first attracted her to the Cheesemonger's window, and a cooler packed with oysters and champagne. He had shucked the oysters before her eyes, arranging them on a bed of ice as the orchestra tuned.

She commented on the rough sea and darkening sky. What was going on with the weather? Wasn't it supposed to be a beautiful evening?

Of course it was a beautiful evening, he said almost defensively, filling two champagne flutes, acting as though she were wildly exaggerating the effect of a gust of twilight breeze. He obviously didn't want some surprise storm to ruin the effect of his long-planned evening.

As the overture to the Ring Cycle began, an expectant hush came over the crowd on the green. A single note repeated, at first only on the strings. As the rest of the orchestra progressively joined in, and the note took on volume, there was a thunderclap from the east. The sound of pounding surf from the nearby beach competed with the percussion section to dominate the rhythm of the music. It was as though a battle were rumbling to life.

The tune was hauntingly familiar, although Molly couldn't think why. She wasn't exactly an opera buff. Once, she had gone to a benefit at the Metropolitan Opera House because the chance to wear her favorite floor-length Versace gown was too good to pass up. She couldn't even remember who the composer was. Mozart? Verdi? They all sounded the same. The only thing she clearly recalled was that she had fallen asleep during the first act and made her date take her home early.

For some reason, though, this music was echoing deep inside her, connecting with her unconscious. "What's this opera about, anyway?" she whispered.

"See those mermaid-like creatures 'swimming' on the stage?" he said, referring to three large, lusty singers in big iridescent dresses floundering around in billowing sheets of blue plastic that Molly assumed were supposed to represent water.

"Yeah?"

"Those are the Rhinemaidens, and they possess something called the Rhinegold, a magical gold. Whoever forges a ring from the Rhinegold will have immense power."

Shivering in her sheer wrap, Molly felt instinctively for her ring on the chain around her neck. Nothing. It was really lost. And this silly opera plot was randomly driving the point home.

"And see that guy who just rose up from the 'crack in the Earth'?" Marshall went on enthusiastically.

She nodded. There was a stocky bearded man pursuing the Rhinemaidens through gusts of steam coming out of the floor while everyone sang loudly in incomprehensible German.

"That's Alberich, the Nibelung. Since the Rhinemaidens won't love him, he's going to steal their gold to forge a powerful ring. It will make him lord of many lands, and, most importantly, it will allow him to subjugate the women who have hurt him, to take revenge on the female race, and—" Marshall was interrupted by more thunder and a wild streak of lightning as the sound system died with a fierce screech and the music was replaced by a crashing rain and screams from the crowd.

The lights on the boats, which had gathered around Gardiners Island for a close-up view of the fireworks, were darting up and down on the suddenly hectic sea. Several of them were sending out flares of alarm, which flickered, barely visible, in the rain-blackened sky. A coast guard siren blared as rescue boats sped out toward them. People everywhere were screaming, running from the green with their picnic blankets flapping behind them like ghosts.

No weather news source had predicted this. Nature was throwing a tantrum. Unannounced.

"Let's go!" Marshall yelled over the din, taking her hand and pulling her toward town. "We can be inside the store in five minutes."

But Molly could not take her eyes off the raging sea. She stood, drenched, fixated on the lights of the stranded boat. "My sister's out there!" she cried.

Mardi had been making obnoxious comments for the past couple of days about how she would be seeing the fireworks from the deck of a yacht off Gardiners Island. She wouldn't say whose yacht, but she implied that she was going to have way more fun than anyone else in Ingrid's house. No boring concert on the green for her.

Molly had been annoyed, dismissive, and secretly a bit jealous of Mardi's date, since Tris seemed to have disappeared for the holiday and she was stuck on a boring picnic with Cheeseboy. But as it hit her now that Mardi might be in real danger, her irritation vanished in a desperate surge of fear and love.

"Mardi!" she screamed, her voice carrying across the water with a force that put the local opera singers to shame. "Mardi, where are you?"

"Please, Molly," Marshall tried to reason with her, "if your sister is in any trouble, the coast guard will rescue her. They can do much more than we can."

Ignoring him, she rushed to join Ingrid and Freya, who were pushing through the crowd toward her. As the three witches fell into an embrace, they sang out Mardi's name in unison. It was an incantation. They had no doubt that Mardi would now know that they were coming for her.

Marshall looked on, soaked and bewildered but unwilling to abandon Molly.

"We need a coast guard boat!" Freya shrieked. With that, she turned and led the others to the docks, running as fast as her heels would allow. Molly assumed they would lose Marshall at this point, but, amazingly, he kept up, his eyes pulsing the brightest blue through the storm, as though he had somehow been touched by their magic.

Molly watched in admiration as a shivering Freya ordered a member of the coast guard to hand over the keys to his boat. Although he had been ready to spring into action, he simply stepped aside and allowed the three drenched women and their gangly sidekick to commandeer his motorboat.

"Look, I have to go," she said to Marshall. "Stay here. Please."

Marshall shook his head. "I won't leave you!" he said bravely.

But Molly couldn't risk his life as well, and she mouthed a spell to send him to safety.

He ran back to shore, and she joined Freya and Ingrid on the boat.

All three of them honed their perceptions on Mardi's aura. They sensed distress, but they also sensed a strong life force. Without bothering to turn the key, they revved their boat's engine. They didn't steer or even seem to get their bearings as they maneuvered at supernatural speed, unperturbed by the giant swells and echoing cries for help all around. In a flash, they were at the side of a large sailboat floundering between the bridge and the firework barge. Its name, *Dragon*, was written in red script across the hull.

Molly had a flash of recognition. Wasn't that the name of the Gardiner brother's boat? Had Tris mentioned it? Had she heard it somewhere else? Why would Mardi be on the Gardiners' boat? But this line of suspicious questioning was quickly subsumed by the urgency of finding Mardi.

A huge wave washed over their commandeered boat. The witches withstood it like pillars of stone. They scanned the black storm for Mardi's even blacker hair and dark eyes.

Freya stood, spread her arms, flew onto the *Dragon*, and disappeared belowdecks, only to resurface a moment later and cry out, "No one's left on the boat." She leapt back among them. "She's either on a lifeboat or she's swimming for shore."

The raging sea was dotted with orange lifeboats, tossing every which way. Coast guard boats were trying to tow them, while stopping constantly to pull people from the water. It would be a miracle if no one drowned on what had been, less than an hour ago, the most promising night of the summer to date.

Molly secretly began to bargain with fate to get her sister back. She swore under her breath to appreciate Mardi more, to share her best clothes after they had passed their prime instead of consigning them. She also promised to work closely with Mardi to solve the mystery that was plaguing them. If only she could have her sister stay in this world now, they could prove their innocence together. No power could deny them that. "Please!" she cried. "Please!"

In silent accord, like hunting dogs on a scent, Molly, Ingrid, and Freya began to sense Mardi's energy in the water nearby. They scanned the foam swirling around the *Dragon* as they slowly moved their little boat in the direction of her aura. Their impression grew progressively stronger as they headed toward the bridge. She had to be swimming, or drifting on a lifeboat, in the direction of Gardiners Island, where Fair Haven was now lit up from every window to provide a beacon of light in the tempest.

As they were searching the foaming water, Freya screamed, "A boy! Floating over there in a life jacket!" The boat veered in the direction of the bright yellow splash of color. Sure enough, there was a small boy, floating limp and lifeless, his hair splayed around him as if it were turning to weeds.

Molly burst into tears as Freya pulled the drowned child on board. The boy looked about six. Jo's age.

Ingrid raised her arms to the angry sky. "Mother! If you can hear us, you have to help us now. He's only been gone a few minutes. His soul is still lingering in this world. Mother, please! Send him back!"

From nowhere, Freya produced a lantern that she shone onto the boy's chalk-white face. They all held their breath. Nothing. No sign of life returning. If anything, his jaw appeared to clamp into an even tighter mask of death.

Molly knew enough about resurrection to know it was a dangerous proposition. You could only bring people back if they hadn't crossed to the other side yet.

Muttering spells in unison, Ingrid and Freya acted as one. Molly watched with astonishment. She and Mardi had never worked their magic together except to play tricks on people. She stared at the child's pale, lifeless face. So this was what death looked like. This was what had happened to Parker and Sam. It was horrible.

Ingrid and Freya's voices grew louder against the howling wind. But despite their spells, the boy remained limp in their arms. His face in the lantern light turned to marble. His childish lips went pure white.

"Please, Mother," Freya whispered.

Then, from out from the heart of the storm shot a bolt of lightning. It hit their boat, electrifying it in a bright and terrifying flash. Molly screamed, but Ingrid and Freya continued their chanting unbroken, staring at the boy, allowing themselves to smile as a dusky color returned to his cheeks and he began to cough up seawater, gasping his way back into the life he would never know he had lost.

Molly was awestruck. So this was what witchcraft was all about.

As Molly, Ingrid, and Freya all leaned in to comfort the confused and terrified little boy, they were stunned by the sound of Mardi's voice.

"Finally! I thought you'd never get here," she said as she hoisted herself onto the boat.

Molly wrapped her sister in a tight embrace. "Mardi! We've been so scared. *I've* been so scared. What happened to you?"

Mardi looked over at the *Dragon*. "I'm not totally sure," she said. The fact that they could hear her clearly, even though she was speaking in a normal voice, made them suddenly aware that the storm was dying down as quickly as it had appeared. Within moments, the sky was clear and the tempest was fading to a dream. The *Dragon* bobbed peacefully on a glossy sea.

"We thought we were going to capsize." Mardi seemed to be straining to remember. "Trent put me on a lifeboat. I thought he was going to jump into the lifeboat with me, but once he saw that I was safe, he disappeared."

Molly wanted to ask who Trent was, but she didn't want to interrupt the flow of Mardi's story. She told herself he must be the captain the Gardiners had hired for their boat. There really wasn't any other possibility, was there?

"I figured," Mardi continued, her eyes glittering with the intensity of what she had just lived, "that he had gone to rescue people in the water. There was no way I was going to sit there like some pathetic girl when I can swim as fast as he can. So I went after him, and I found him helping with the coast guard, dragging people to their boats. We worked side by side for a while. Then we were separated by an enormous wave. I've been treading water, looking for him, for a while now. I'm exhausted. If you all hadn't come . . ." Her voice cracked, and she lost her veneer of toughness. "Thank you," she said. The three women embraced her.

Everything was going to be fine. The stars were not only visible again but twinkling happily. The whole upheaval had lasted barely an hour.

"I hope Trent is okay," Mardi said to no one in particular. "He's so strong, though. I'm sure he made it home."

And where was home? Molly burned to ask, but for once she held back so as not to start a stupid fight. She might never be this happy to see her sister again. It was a moment to savor.

Molly took Mardi's hands in hers and said nothing. She could not help but notice that her sister's fingers and neck were bare. The ring they had shared since before they could remember, their only heirloom from their vanished mother, their magical ring, was truly gone. Worse, Molly knew she was the one who had lost it.

19

SHELTER FROM THE STORM

$\mathcal{M}$iraculously, no one had drowned in the freak storm
on the Fourth of July, and there had been no severe
damage to the docks or beaches, no flooding or erosion.
It was as though the sudden gale had been a threat, a
warning, or a test. But in the days that followed, as calm
was restored to the town of North Hampton, a charac-
teristic forgetfulness set in among its inhabitants. Since
it left no visible traces and had not touched any other
part of East End except for the little town, the storm
quickly faded from conversation and from conscious
memory.

Despite the general amnesia, there were a few in
North Hampton for whom the events of July Fourth remained starkly clear and menacing.

Freya and Ingrid had summoned Mardi and Molly to
another memory session with Jean-Baptiste in Freya's
living room to talk about the storm and its possible connection to what was happening back in New York, to
try to stimulate their memories again. The session was

to take place at eleven P.M., which was around the same time that Mardi and Molly became vague about the sequence of events at Bret's party. Jean-Baptiste felt that holding their session at the corresponding time of night might be a way to harness some power of suggestion. Only the twins were late.

Ingrid, Freya, and Jean-Baptiste had gone ahead to the lobster dinner Freya had cooked to raise everyone's spirits. But at the last minute, Mardi and Molly had to babysit the kids until Matt, who was working late on a case, could get back from the precinct.

It was close to midnight when they began their drive out to the isolated stretch of beach where Freya's unexpectedly sleek house nestled in the dunes. As Mardi sped along the empty roads, past dark farms and shadowy dwellings, she knew Molly was probably freaking out. Molly was clenching her teeth, but she wasn't screaming, as she usually did, about how she didn't want to be decapitated in her prime. Ever since the rescue at sea, the sisters had been holding back from lashing out at each other. In fact, they were being almost pleasant.

Whereas normally they would have spent the entire drive bickering and insulting each other, with Molly yelling that Mardi should have her license revoked and her ridiculous car impounded, while Mardi called Molly a lame princess, they were now chatting amiably, even giggling together about the makeshift dinner they had just pulled off for Henry and Jo.

They'd never made pasta before. They hardly even knew how to boil water. And yet somehow they had managed linguine with pesto sauce this evening.

Jo had explained to them that you salted the water and didn't put the pasta in until it was boiling. She showed them the big pot, the colander, and the pesto sauce in the freezer that her mom made every year with basil from their garden. Mardi had left a plastic lid on the first batch in an attempt to defrost it in the microwave. That hadn't gone so well, much to the kids' delight. But she'd nailed the second batch, and everyone had been cheerful. The linguine had even come out al dente.

After dinner, as instructed, they had put on an episode of *Little House on the Prairie* for the kids. Mardi was immediately sucked into some drama involving stolen candy at Mr. Oleson's General Store. She would have been embarrassed in front of Molly if she hadn't seen that Molly was also glued to the screen. It had taken them a while to notice that Henry had wandered off.

They found him sitting on the kitchen island. He had built a pyramid out of steak knives. Before they could stop him, he slammed a rolling pin into the heart of his creation and sent the blades flying all around his little body. Molly screamed, but he remained unscathed, and unperturbed, as the blades stuck into the wooden countertop, surrounding him in a jagged circle.

Mardi and Molly laughed about it now, as they drove through the warm night, top down, their long dark hair flying. "Either that kid is a budding warlock or he's a total klutz," Mardi said.

"What do you mean, he's a klutz? He never gets a scratch."

"I mean that maybe he's such a spaz that Ingrid has covered his little diapered ass with the most powerful protection spell out there. Hasn't that occurred to you?" Mardi asked.

"I guess that's the kind of thing mothers do?"

"I guess. . . . Not that *we* would know."

They drove on in companionable silence. Mardi even slowed down a little.

It had been several days now since the storm, and Mardi caught herself wondering how long this cease-fire with Molly could possibly hold out. She was stealing a glance at her gorgeous sister as she pulled into Freya's driveway when her phone beeped from beside the gearbox.

It must be Trent again. They had been texting one another, trying to set another date to go out in the boat and make up for their disastrous attempt to see the fireworks together. As Mardi had guessed, Trent, sensing that Mardi was safe, had made it to shore that awful night, after making several rescues.

Even though they had barely touched, the two of them had an understanding now. She slid her tongue stud back and forth over the roof of her mouth in anticipation.

But the text wasn't from Trent. It was from a blocked

number. She lifted her glowing phone to her face as she killed the motor.

I know what you and your sister did. You're not fooling anyone.

Mardi's first impulse was to share this freaky message with her sister. How bizarre that it was coming through at the very moment they had arrived to begin their memory session in order to recover more details of the night of the murders. She began, "Molly, you're never going to believe this—"

But as she was handing over the phone, she was stopped by a continuation of the message, scrolling before her in real time.

If you share this message with anyone, especially her, something terrible will happen to your twin. I'm warning you.

Mardi snatched the phone back and held it close. Molly, her curiosity piqued, lunged for it.

"Come on, show me! What is it?" Molly's tone was playful at first, but once she saw that Mardi wasn't joking and really wasn't going to show her the phone, Molly's whole face darkened.

Mardi recognized a tantrum brewing and tried to stave it off. "Look, I'm sorry, Moll," she said. "It was a mistake. It was nothing."

"If it's nothing, why won't you show me?"

"Look, I can't, okay? You have to trust me."

"Trust you?" Molly hissed. "How do you expect me to trust you if you're keeping secrets all the time?"

Mardi found herself in the absurd position of having

to protect her raging sister from an unknown enemy. She was sorely tempted to hurl the phone at her. But Mardi held strong, jumped out of the Ferrari, and made for Freya's front door, with Molly screaming up the walkway behind her.

"You know I saved your life in the storm! You are so ungrateful!"

"Look I can't show you what's on my phone 'cause I'm only trying to protect you!" Mardi screamed.

That gave Molly pause. "From what?"

"I can't say, okay?"

"No, not okay!"

"Be careful," Mardi taunted. "If you keep gritting your teeth like that you're going to have to start wearing a mouth guard. Not a good look."

"I should have let you drown!"

The door to the house swung open, releasing a delicious odor of lobster broth. Freya, Ingrid, and Jean-Baptiste looked out in alarm at the battling twins.

"Girls," said Jean-Baptiste, "I'm afraid you are not displaying the spirit of harmony required for our important task tonight."

Mardi and Molly glared at each other, then said in unison, "It's her fault."

"Let's leave notions of fault behind," he urged, ushering them inside. "It's time for you to come together, Mooi and Magdi. We all know the storm on July Fourth was no accident."

Mardi was startled into a feeling of gravity by the

sound of her given name, Magdi. She snuck a glance at Molly and saw that she too was suddenly struck by a sense of urgency at hearing herself called by her ancient appellation, Mooi. They were made from their father's spirit; when they were born, Thor had given up some of his powers and instilled them in his daughters.

Quietly now, the twins followed the god of memory into Freya's living room and took their places on the Le Corbusier sofa looking through the giant window out onto the moonlit sea, while he sat in the Eames chair facing them.

"Before we begin," said Mardi, "can you tell us, Jean-Baptiste, if you think the storm was a warning from the White Council?"

"I am convinced it was not," he answered.

All four women stared at him in surprise.

"The White Council does not need to act in such underhanded ways. They are a legitimate body, not a terrorist group. That storm was an act of rogue black magic. The same black magic, I fear, that the White Council fears you girls are releasing into the world."

"Wait!" Mardi jumped up from her seat. "You're saying that, according to the White Council, *we made the storm*? That's insanity. We had nothing to do with it."

"You did not intend for the storm to happen. Nor did you know of it beforehand. But"—he sighed—"I'm afraid that does not mean you had nothing to do with it."

"Girls." Freya spoke soothingly as Molly sank back into the sofa. "I think we can all agree that the only way to figure out what is really going on here is for you to clear up your amnesia. The answers lie on that night back in April."

Freya and Ingrid looked on as Jean-Baptiste quietly spoke. "Please, let's begin. Can you tell me anything you recall about the victims on the night of the party? How they looked? What they wore? What they did?"

The twins squinted inside, homing in on a visual of Sam and Parker.

Sam was überthin in that rich New York way, with bony wrists and a silken curtain of white-blond hair swinging breezily across her pointy, lightly freckled face. She had such a conservative, preppy style that pretty much anything she wore in warm weather could be mistaken for a tennis dress of some kind, and anything she sported in cold weather looked like Vermont après-ski. With some prompting from Jean-Baptiste, Mardi and Molly could recall that on the night of Bret's party, Sam had been wearing a navy-and-white sleeveless jersey dress with navy flats and a rather sweet cropped cream-colored Burberry jacket with a plaid lining and had been carrying a truly unfortunate floral Lilly Pulitzer tote.

Meanwhile, her boyfriend, Parker, had been experimenting with the Brooklyn hipster aesthetic. The results were mixed. He was tall and well built enough to carry off the plaid flannel shirt and suspenders that the look required. The work boots were borderline cool. But the facial hair was an unqualified disaster. Molly could picture him in Bret's living room, rolling his own cigarette, probably from tobacco grown on someone's roof in Red Hook. His beard, such as it was, fell dramatically short of the Brooklyn boy ideal. It grew in soft patchy wisps on his otherwise baby-smooth chin.

But besides noticing the details of their appearance, the twins couldn't say anything about them. They weren't sure how long they had been dating. They assumed they both lived on the Upper East Side, but it was possible that Parker hailed from downtown, or even perhaps from Brooklyn itself. The twins really had no idea.

"Honestly, we didn't know them enough to like them or not like them," Mardi said. "I don't mean to be insensitive, because it's terrible what happened to them. But they were totally random."

"Did Bret know them well?" asked Jean-Baptiste.

"I don't think so," Molly answered. "In fact, now that you mention it, something else is coming back to me. Bret did make noise at some point about how there were a bunch of crashers at his party. But he didn't seem that annoyed. It was more a way for him to show off, saying there were all kinds of kids who wanted to be at his pad, under his ridiculous giant spider sculpture, swimming naked in his indoor pool. I mean, Bret is a super-pretentious guy."

"Maybe that's why you liked him," Mardi chimed in.

"Why *I* liked him? *You're* the one who practically straddled him against one of those disgusting million-dollar tarantula legs."

"Girls, let us stay on track, so to speak." Jean-Baptiste was firm and calm. "You say that this young couple was not particularly meaningful to you or to your host. Would it be fair to say that they were expendable?"

"Harsh!" the twins exclaimed in unison.

After that they saw no more. Their minds were blocked.

The storm of retribution was blowing all right. But from where?

✳ 20 ✳

COME TOGETHER

$\mathcal{T}$he next night, after a busy day at the Cheesemonger, Molly was about to head home to Ingrid's for yet another stultifying family dinner when she got long-awaited word from Tris.

Sorry to be MIA. I was out of town surfing in Montauk for a few days. I missed you. Still do. Any chance you could come over for dinner tonight?

She was reminded of how much she loved the long-form, old-fashioned nature of his texts. Normally, she would have nothing to do with a guy who made her wait this long for a sign of life, especially after they'd hooked up. She was Molly Overbrook, after all, one of the very hottest tickets in New York City, if not the hottest. She needed no one. Yet somehow he was reeling her in. She told herself it was only a summer fling, that there was nothing else going on in North Hampton. So she might as well have her fun.

Besides, she absolutely had to go to Fair Haven to search for the ring in the library. Mardi still hadn't noticed that it had gone missing, and Molly had to find it before her sister realized and completely freaked out.

Molly waved good-bye to Marshall as she pedaled off in the direction of the bridge to Gardiners Island.

Luckily, she was wearing a silvery shift that moved perfectly from day into night. Her wedged espadrilles in black patent leather also segued beautifully. She smiled a self-satisfied smile. Somehow she must have known, as she was getting dressed earlier, that she had a reason to look good this evening. Despite her banishment, she hadn't lost her groove on the East End. She hadn't succumbed to rubber flip-flops, Top-Siders, or, God forbid, fleece.

As she started across the bridge, a crescent moon rose, filling her with a sense of possibility. She tingled with anticipation.

"Harsh," Molly whispered to herself, recalling the end of last night's session as she leaned her bike against a dune on the other side of the bridge. "Expendable? Sam and Parker weren't, like, the most gripping, beautiful people in school. But, expendable?" She shook her head.

The whole mystery was a drag. Molly decided that there was no point in driving herself crazy with it. She wanted to block it out of her mind and have a totally oblivious and irresponsible good time with Tris right now.

As if reading her mind, Tris appeared at the base of the garden path carrying two bottles of beer.

Tris's deep, sparkling eyes were as powerful as she recalled. Damn, that boy was sexy. As he leaned in for a kiss, she melted.

Slowly, he pulled away in order to hand her a bottle. "This is exactly what you need right now."

"And how would you happen to know exactly what I need?"

"We're in the same place, remember? I'm right here with you, doing time in the world's most boring town because I refuse to be who they want me to be. Doesn't that sound familiar?"

As they walked arm in arm toward the magnificent house, Molly decided on a whim to find out more about the story of this place that Freya had begun to tell her about the other day in the Cheesemonger.

"So, is it really true," she asked, "that Fair Haven is built on a seam between Midgard and the Underworld? Are we walking through the gloaming right now? Is that why it's so misty even though the sky is clear?" Although she kept her tone light, she realized as she spoke that she really did want to know the answers to her questions.

But Tris seemed completely nonchalant about the history of his ancestral home. "I don't know. I'm a prisoner here, remember? The only thing that I find engaging about Fair Haven at the moment is that you're here."

Inside the vast, low-lit house, Tris guided her gently

back to the library, which was one of the few rooms small enough to feel intimate when there were only the two of them.

"It feels especially empty inside Fair Haven tonight," she said.

"Most of the staff doesn't live in the house. I think the housekeeper might be down in the kitchen. But otherwise it's just us." He winked. "And, of course, the madwoman in the attic."

"You mean your stepmother?"

"Bingo." He laughed. "Ask Freya. Mother doesn't think anyone's good enough for a Gardiner boy."

She raised her eyebrows as they sank into the club chair that had become their particular haven of softness and comfort amid the grandeur of the mansion. The caress of the worn leather was as exciting and warm as his skin. "You really think she wouldn't approve of even me?"

"Do I look like I care, Molly?" he whispered, leaning down and pressing against her. As his tongue caressed hers, Molly felt that she had never existed so fully in a moment. She did not step outside herself to wonder what she looked like, nor did her mind wander, as it usually did, to the next conquest she planned to make.

She had no idea how long they had been entangled when he nibbled her earlobe and tickled her every sense with his voice. "You're making me hungry," he said, and pulled away.

She leaned back, expecting him to start unbuttoning her shirt.

Except he meant it literally.

Tris nodded toward the kitchen. "You want anything? I'll make us something. Stay here."

She had the fleeting sensation that he did not want her to leave the library. Was he hiding her from his stepmother? She supposed she didn't really mind. When in doubt, being served was always the best option. She stretched catlike as he released her from his embrace. Her entire body was flushed.

As soon as he left, though, a current of alarm ran through her. She remembered the missing ring. This room was the only place it could possibly be. It had to have fallen off the last time she was here. That was the only answer. Maybe Tris had unhooked the clasp of her gold chain, sometime around the moment that he had unhooked her bra. Or maybe the chain had slipped over her head. It was all a blur. She scoured her memory for some detail, the clink of metal hitting the floor, the feel of it sliding down her body. But there was nothing. Logic told her the ring had to be here, yet she had no sensual impression of losing it.

She felt several times in the cracks of the chair. To no avail. She moved every piece on the ivory backgammon board. Nothing. She checked along all the mahogany bookshelves in case a maid had found the ring and decided to put it up in a safe place where it could easily be spotted. No such luck. She ran her eyes and fingers over every surface, the side tables, the windowsills, the elaborate bar cart. Then one by one, she took the cushions off the antique sofa and checked underneath them.

Her heart was beginning to pound. Anxiously listening for Tris's footfall, since he had been gone a while now, she got down on her knees to check under each piece of furniture. She did not spot anything, not even a speck of dust. The once cozy little library was yawning with emptiness because it did not seem to contain the one thing she needed.

The only place left to try was the oriental rug. Its rich silken fibers gleamed in the room's low lamplight. Suddenly her searching gaze caught on a shiny gold band. She lunged for it, practically splaying herself on the floor. But the sparkle proved to be a mirage, the mere illusion of a ring in the rug's intricate Persian pattern. Molly sighed and kept looking, more determined than ever, her eyes inches from the ground.

"What the— What are you doing on the floor?"

Tris loomed above Molly in his crisp whites, carrying a silver tray. His expression as he stared down at her was inscrutable. Was he suspicious? Amused? Angry? As he put the tray down on a low table, she saw that it bore two cold lobsters, an heirloom tomato salad, a baguette, two crystal wineglasses, and a bottle of white Burgundy in a slender ice bucket. This was a far cry from the usual late-night fare of fast food and beers that most guys under twenty-five, even the sophisticated, jet-setting ones, would proudly produce. Tris was something else.

And she may have just totally blown it with him.

She started to get up.

"Don't," he commanded softly.

"Don't?"

"Don't move. Whatever you are doing down there on the floor, I like it. You look so hot right now lying on the rug. You have no idea."

Oh, but she did. She had a very good idea.

As he lay down beside her, she met his wicked smile with her own.

✳ *21* ✳

THE TEXTING SONG

The texts were freaking Mardi out. Since receiving the creepy note right before the memory session with Jean-Baptiste, she had gotten three more. Each one implied that the texter knew something incriminating about "that night." Then whoever it was threatened to hurt, or even kill, Molly if Mardi said anything to anyone.

I saw the evil you allowed to take place that night. . . . It was your power that killed them. . . . It will soon become clear that you are the guilty ones.

If you tell anyone about me, especially her, she will be . . . destroyed . . . cast down . . . forever lost to you.

Could this be some kind of warning from the White Council?

No, of course not. The Council did not traffic in blackmail. It was someone who knew their secret—the only problem was that Mardi herself had no idea what their secret was.

She was tempted to turn her phone off, but she was also secretly hoping to glean some information from whoever was torturing her. She tried answering the texts with Who are you? How can I help you? But there was no reply.

For once in her life, Mardi craved advice from an adult. But who to turn to? And how to get help without giving too much away and putting her sister in potential danger? Of course, this so-called stalker could just be some lame-o. But there was no way to be sure. And as much as Molly could drive her crazy, Mardi didn't want to live out eternity knowing she had sent her own twin sister to the Underworld.

Dad was *so* not a good candidate for someone to talk to. He would panic, and he would press her for specifics. If she mentioned her dilemma to Jean-Baptiste, he might put her into one of his involuntary memory trances and get too much information out of her. This pretty much left Ingrid and Freya.

It was about nine in the morning. Mardi rolled out of bed and went to splash some cold water on her face. She remarked to herself that it had been a while since she had had the ring. The rose gold band should pass any moment now from Molly to her. It was time.

Should she turn to Ingrid or Freya for her problems?

As she weighed the two options, she craned her neck in order to see her snaking rainbow tattoo from various angles. The colorful reflection glistened as it undulated. It seemed to have a life, and will, of its own.

As she stared into the mirror, it dawned on her that

the bridge tattooed on her shoulder no longer existed. This was the bridge that had collapsed centuries ago, stranding several hundred gods and goddesses in Midgard, including their father. The rainbow bridge etched into her skin was a powerful symbol of a lost time.

Mardi looked deep into the reflection of her own dark eyes. She saw a sixteen-year-old witch with symbols of ancient history engraved on her body. She wasn't just some stupid club kid with a random tattoo and a tongue stud. Mardi Overbrook was the real deal. And it was time for her to step up.

In that instant, she realized that she didn't have to decide between Ingrid and Freya. This wasn't a competitive twin thing where one sister got to win out over the other. Mardi had to stop thinking like a kid. She decided that she would speak to them both, to gather as much wisdom as she could. She would start with Ingrid, because Ingrid was downstairs.

Mardi came upon Ingrid in a rare moment of stillness. She was sitting barefoot at the kitchen island, still wearing her simple white cotton bathrobe, her blond hair pulled back into a ponytail, exposing her delicate features and translucent skin. In front of her was a steaming cup of coffee, a china plate with a blueberry muffin from a batch she had baked yesterday with Jo and Henry, and a dog-eared paperback of her favorite novel, *To Kill a Mockingbird*.

No one else was visible in the big, bright, open family living space. Molly was probably still asleep. And

Matt must have taken the kids outside to give Ingrid some peace. But Ingrid did not look peaceful. She looked drawn and worried. In this unguarded instant, she had let down her perfect posture and had allowed her expression of motherly kindness to fade away. She was frowning. There was a sad droop to her shoulders. She hadn't touched her muffin. The book on the counter was closed.

"Good morning, Ingrid," Mardi said softly, so as not to startle her.

"Mardi, dear, good morning. I didn't see you." Ingrid turned and forced a smile. "Let me pour you some coffee. You take it black, right? And here, have a blueberry muffin before the rest of the gang gets here and they vanish. You know, we picked these blueberries ourselves on the farm down the road."

Ingrid, Mardi understood as she watched her fussing over the coffee and then carefully placing the muffin on a pretty floral plate, was a compulsive nurturer. She put a perfect pat of salted butter next to the muffin, because she knew that Mardi only liked her butter salted. That was how attentive she was.

But even though Ingrid was doing her usual bustling in order to take care of someone other than herself, her movements were distracted. It was as though she were on autopilot. Something was wrong.

Mardi sat down beside her at the island counter, trying to figure out how to approach the subject of her mysterious texts without directly mentioning them. She had no idea where to begin.

"Ingrid, is something wrong? You look upset."

"I'm worried. You know, part of my work at the library is counseling women with health issues or psychological stress. And there has been a rash of domestic violence in town. I don't like it all."

"You think it might connect to the other weird stuff that has been going on here?"

"I'm certainly starting to think that whoever, or whatever, is causing these disturbances has it in for women in particular."

"You don't think it's random at all, do you?"

"I'm afraid I don't."

At a loss for what to say next, Mardi took a bite of blueberry muffin with a dab of butter.

"Wow, Ingrid," she said. "This is delicious. Thanks."

"Can you taste the lemon?" Ingrid asked, suddenly very intense, like her mind had shifted to a distant place where lemons were somehow really important.

Mardi took another bite. "I think so. Did you squeeze in some lemon juice or something?"

"It's lemon rind," Ingrid said sadly. "It's was my mother's recipe. She always took such care grating the lemon rind because she said it brought out the flavor of the blueberries like nothing else . . . You'll see, Mardi, if you ever lose someone, it's the details that will haunt you, all the tiny ways they expressed their love," she said, her voice hoarse. "Joanna has been gone ten years, but the grief never ends. You just get used to it."

Tentatively, Mardi put a hand on Ingrid's thin shoulder. She wasn't in the habit of comforting other people, but this gesture felt right.

"How did your parents get stuck in the Underworld?" Mardi asked.

"They sacrificed themselves in order to save Freya. It's a long story." Ingrid sighed. "They had watched both of us hang once, during the Salem witch trials, and they couldn't face the sight again . . . "

Ingrid seemed to lose her train of thought. Mardi did not prompt her, but stayed very still, waiting while Ingrid stared at the pattern on her plate without really seeing it.

Mardi shuddered. The White Council's threats to damn the sisters forever if they were found guilty of murder were starting to seem a lot less abstract.

"My mother's gift as a witch was bringing souls back from the dead. That's why I called on her to help me save the little drowned boy during the storm on the Fourth of July."

"You mean, the kid on the boat with you?"

"Yes, he was technically dead when we pulled him out of the water. But we were able to intervene. It's very, very rare to be able to pull off a resurrection. Even for us with our direct connection. We were incredibly fortunate that our spells were heard." Ingrid paused to gather her thoughts. "I don't mean to be preachy,

Mardi, but the situation you and Molly have gotten us in with the Council puts all this in danger. If we couldn't practice magic anymore, we would have had absolutely no chance of saving that boy."

"I get it, okay!" Mardi recoiled defensively.

"I think maybe you finally do get it," Ingrid said softly. "Anyway, my mother's sister, Helda, lords over the Underworld. And my mother knows every twist and turn of the path a soul takes to get there. She knows all the rules. And one of those rules, Mardi, is 'a soul for a soul.' The little boy we rescued the other day from drowning, his soul was still in the mortal world, his name was not yet written in the Book of the Dead, so we were able to snatch him back without sacrificing anyone . . . But, when Freya was hung in Salem, she was lost. My mother and father decided to drown themselves in the deep water you see through these very windows, to exchange themselves for their daughter so that she could come home."

"But wait, why did your dad have to go too?"

"He didn't. He chose to."

"Why?"

"Because my mother is his eternal mate. They had just reconciled after a centuries-long separation. They were madly in love again. He was going to die with her. No one ever found their bodies, of course. But they share a headstone in the town cemetery."

Gently, Mardi patted her shoulder. "Is it hard for you with Matt? Because he's, like, your soul mate, only he's not going to be around forever? He's a really great guy. And a great dad. I can see why you chose him. But, well, it must be really sad sometimes to think about all the time you're going to have to spend apart."

Ingrid nodded. "I think about it constantly but I try not to ruin the time we have together by mourning his death. Live in the present, Mardi."

Speaking of, the door to the deck clamored open and Matt and the kids spilled into the room laughing and shedding sand everywhere as they dove into the muffins.

Mardi's window of opportunity to tell Ingrid about the weird texts had closed. But she had learned something. She'd learned just how important it was, for the whole ecosystem of her people, that she and Molly get out of the mess they were in. If only they knew what exactly they had done so that they could actually defend themselves.

Seeing as she hadn't had a chance to talk to Ingrid about those weird texts, Mardi decided to go and lose herself in heavy lifting on the docks, to tackle a big shipment of equipment coming in for the new restaurant. Then, after work she would go to the North Inn to talk to Freya and see if she could get somewhere.

"I'm heading out! I'll see you guys later!"

The little family managed to return her good-bye through mouthfuls of breakfast. Ingrid gave her a wink.

She hopped into her convertible and put the key

in the ignition. Before she could turn it, though, her phone vibrated inside her favorite vintage bag. The bag's brown suede fringe trembled against her bare arm. She instantly knew what this was. She wished she didn't feel compelled to pull out her phone and look at the screen, but she had no choice.

Meet me tonight at ten in the dunes by the bridge on Gardiners Island. Or else.

* 22 *

A SKY FULL OF STARS

*A*lthough she was infatuated with Tris, Molly felt a little tug at her heart as she left Marshall behind after a charm-filled afternoon with him at the Cheesemonger. Cheeseboy was growing on her like a fine mold.

Today she had been complaining that she was addicted to the New England clam chowder he wouldn't stop making. (Her doubts about the people of North Hampton being ready to embrace a chowder other than their signature Manhattan had been way off—they were lining up for the stuff.) She told him how fattening it was and teased him about being a soup dealer who ought to be arrested for peddling the stuff to poor teenage girls with no willpower.

"You have more willpower than I've ever seen!" he'd said, interrupting her.

"What do you mean? I just told you I can't stop eating your creamy, starchy, potato-filled soup. Not to mention your brownies."

"I mean that you have willpower because you take

what you need. You don't look like a girl who starves herself to be beautiful. You look like a girl who gets what she wants, which makes you beautiful."

"If you say so." She shrugged. But she was secretly pleased. Marshall might not have a chance against Tris, but he sure knew how to appreciate her like she deserved to be appreciated.

So it was with a twinge of something like regret that she said, "Later, Cheesepal," as she rode off to do a quick change for her evening among the dunes with Tris. He had told her to meet him that evening on the other side of the bridge, and to dress for a night under the stars.

All day, she had been thinking through her outfit. She had settled on a light gray cashmere hoodie over a whisper-soft black tank top, cropped white jeans, and flat snakeskin sandals. Underneath it all, a creamy lace ensemble.

Once she was ready, she went downstairs to ask Ingrid and Matt if she could borrow their car. She didn't feel like biking all the way to Fair Haven in the dark and then pedaling home at sunrise. She was starting to get circles under her eyes from her late nights with Tris, and it was impossible to find decent concealer in this lame excuse for a town.

"You look nice," Ingrid said as Molly appeared. "I'm sure you're on your way out, but would you like a glass of wine with us first? We're celebrating getting the kids down."

She and Matt smiled at one another over the wide rims of their Burgundy glasses.

"Hey, guys, can I borrow the car tonight?" she asked.

"I'm not so sure that's a good idea," Matt said, furrowing his brow.

What? Was he actually getting precious about the family Subaru wagon all of a sudden?

Molly was tempted to hex him so that he would pour his wine into his ear and get over himself, but she felt Ingrid's eyes on her and reined herself in.

"May I ask why it might not be a good idea, Matt?"

"You haven't heard?"

Molly shook her pretty head.

"There's been a rash of traffic light outages today all over town. It looks like vandalism, but it's pretty strange because the power goes in and out randomly in isolated sets of lights, without warning, for only a few minutes at a time. It's like someone who has no real plan of action is playing with the power grid. There've been four car accidents so far, and strangely, all of them involve girls your age. No one has been seriously hurt, although one teenage girl is in the hospital for some broken ribs . . . I'm not so sure it's safe to drive until we know what's going on."

"Don't you think it's just a coincidence? I mean, there's no way whoever is doing this can see who is driving the cars, is there?" Although Ingrid directed her questions at Matt, she gave Molly a significant look.

"Well, the outages certainly aren't systematic, if

that's what you mean. Something is short-circuiting in the grid. Or else someone is messing around with our power—and putting innocent people in danger. But you're right that they couldn't target specific cars, though."

Molly's head started to spin as she sank into a chair with her wine. Innocent people . . . random accidents . . . The parallel hit her hard.

Or was she reading too much into things? Seeing symbolism where there was none? Was she falling victim to Daddy's and Ingrid's paranoia?

Through the static of her thoughts, she heard Matt and Ingrid tell her to go ahead and take the car, but to be really careful. They even made a lame joke about her being in the "unlucky demographic."

"Thanks," she said, jumping up before they could change their minds. "Don't wait up for me!"

She grabbed the keys from a hook by the front door and raced off, trying not to freak out about the connections between random traffic accidents and random subway deaths. Or about her growing suspicion that her missing ring might have something to do with both of them. Whatever. She had a date.

As she neared the end of the bridge, she saw Tris outlined in her high beams, glowing like a bronze Adonis. He was wearing jeans and a soft brown sweatshirt. But nothing could take away from the overall impression of elegance that he radiated, an elegance which Molly felt was uniquely worthy of her own.

He raised his hand, and she slowed down to kiss him through her open window. She slid into the passenger seat and let him take the wheel. For the short ride to Fair Haven's sandy parking areas, his strong, graceful movements transformed the lowly maroon station wagon into a timelessly cool vehicle.

Once they had parked in the garage of one of the estate's outbuildings, he told her to close her eyes. He then blindfolded her with a silk scarf and led her through the dunes for what felt like ten minutes. As he brought her to a stop, the insides of her eyelids were suffused with orange light and her body was filled with warmth. She had to be standing in front of a fire.

Gently, he untied her blindfold to reveal a bonfire encircled in beautiful carpets like a Bedouin encampment. There were cashmere blankets and piles of Moroccan pillows in all sizes. High wooden posts bearing large osprey nests gave the scene the aura of a sacred temple guarded by rare and magical birds. The stars twinkled above.

A golden bowl heaped with caviar caught the firelight. Two bottles of champagne were nestled in an antique silver ice bucket, radiant in the starlight and the glow of the flames.

"Wow," she said. "And I'm not easily impressed."

"I knew you wouldn't be," he whispered, threading his strong arms around her and pulling her toward him, his blue eyes glinting orange, gold, and hypnotic. "That's why I tried so hard."

They fell into each other, rolling among the blankets and pillows in the gorgeous shadows created by the flames. Every once in a while, they would come up for air. He would feed her some Beluga from a pearl spoon and they would swig champagne straight from the bottle. She could feel herself giving in to him. There was something deep and eternal about their connection. But he also gave her the thrill of the unknown.

As she was unbuckling his belt, slowly, savoring the moment, he suddenly leapt to his feet in a single athletic bound, with all the speed and grace of a startled deer.

"Molly, I'm so sorry. I'll be right back."

She couldn't help but be a little taken aback by his sudden exit. What was that all about? Things were just getting fun. She tucked her knees into her chest, stared into the bonfire, sipped some champagne, and listened to the sound of the sea lapping the beach, feeling a little frustrated.

She began to wonder where he was. How long could it possibly take a guy to pee? Molly looked at her watch. It was close to ten o'clock. She took another drink, spaced out into the starry sky, and tried not to check the time again. When she finally gave in and looked at the face of her Rolex again, she saw that almost ten more minutes had elapsed.

Where was he? Had he ditched her? She felt her eyes begin to shoot angry sparks. Her ancestral rage rose up with the swiftness and fury of a tidal wave. She toyed with the idea of collapsing the osprey nest platforms into the bonfire. But it didn't seem right to make a bunch of endangered birds suffer for his rudeness.

He was always doing this—disappearing for no reason. What was up with that?

She felt around in the soft, luxurious mass of fabrics for her sandals. Once she had slipped them on, she stood and brushed off the sand, making sure to get some in the caviar.

Then she heard footsteps approaching.

So he *was* coming back, after all. He'd better have a great excuse. It was going to take a lot for him to explain himself.

As she was composing her face into her signature unreadable and hard-to-get expression, she heard the footsteps grow fainter. Was he walking away from her now? Was he toying with her?

And then he started walking toward her again, running even. It was as if he had forgotten exactly where he had made their love nest and had circled around before finally spotting the smoke from the fire and orienting himself in the right direction. But this made no sense because he knew these dunes inside and out.

What was going on?

As Tris came around the side of the dune toward the bonfire, she thought she heard him humming a familiar tune. What was this song again?

She turned to confront him. She was going to let him

have it. By the time she was through, he would be a puddle of tidewater, because nobody, no matter how rich or how beautiful he was, kept Molly Overbrook waiting this long.

Only it wasn't him. The person who stepped into the firelight was not Tris Gardiner at all.

23

GIRLS JUST WANNA HAVE FUN

$\mathcal{M}$ardi and Trent had been working side by side all day, unloading kitchen hardware and cases of wine, stocking the cellar of the restaurant, which the owner, Joshua Goose, had decided to call Goose's Landing. Her body was electric with Trent's presence. The space between them was charged with everything they dreamed of doing together.

When they finally kicked back for a beer after a job well done, with Luis and Mario, the brothers who were helping out with the construction, Molly sat next to Trent on the dock so that their knees touched and their bare shoulders rubbed. He was shirtless, and she was wearing a lime green halter-top that Molly liked to tease her was straight out of a '90s Spice Girls video. Their dad had had a fling with Posh—or was it Scary?—in the '90s, and they were never going to let him live it down.

The brush of Trent's skin made Mardi tremble. She wanted him. And yet she was the one who kept making excuses to avoid intimacy. She could not overcome her defensive and off-putting nature. Precisely because she was so attracted to Trent, she always had a reason why they couldn't be together. On July Fourth, she had finally been ready to let go, but the crazy storm had spectacularly ruined their moment. Since then, the time had never been right again for her to lose control.

She took a long, deep sip of beer and decided that she would finally make something happen this evening before she took off to her rendezvous in the dunes with her stalker. Maybe she would ask Trent to come to Freya's bar with her. She pictured him pressing her into one of those wooden booths to the sound of blaring '70s rock, and she glowed inside.

As though he could read her thoughts, he flashed her a big open grin. If they had been alone, she would have kissed him. But they never seemed to be alone at the right time.

"Another round of Brooklyn Lagers?" Trent asked.

But before anyone could answer, there was a violent crashing sound from inside the restaurant, the clang of smashing glass.

Trent, Mardi, Luis, and Mario leapt up and ran inside to find that several beams had collapsed in the cellar, breaking hundreds of bottles and flooding the basement in a bloodred river of wine.

"How the Hell did this happen?" Trent's face went dark.

"Those beams were very secure," said Luis, utterly baffled.

"The engineer signed off on them yesterday," Mario backed his brother up. "We do good work! Someone else has been down here."

"Is there someone who doesn't want this place to open?" asked Mardi.

"Not that we know of," said Trent. "Right, guys?" He focused his piercing blue eyes straight on the brothers.

Mario and Luis shook their heads. Then they looked at each other questioningly, their eyes full of discomfort.

Trent practically leapt at them. "What's going on here? What are you not telling us? This is serious."

"Whoa," said Mardi, touching his hard, tensed arm. "Relax. Don't be such a bully." She had never seen him so revved up.

"Relax? Mardi, it's dumb luck that one of us wasn't down there just now when the ceiling caved. We could have been killed." Then he turned again to Luis and Mario. "Sorry, guys. I'm not accusing you of anything. You do good work. But if you know of anything that could help us figure this out, you should say something.

"It's weird, this collapse," Mario said. "Like that accident yesterday in the farmhouse where we have been working out on Anemone Road."

"What accident?" Trent couldn't control the alarm in his voice.

"It makes us look bad, but really we're very careful," Luis jumped in. "It's like someone is trying to make it look like we don't do our job. But this accident at the farmhouse, it couldn't have been our fault."

"I can explain what happened," Mario interjected, seeing that Trent was about to explode with impatience. "We redid the baby's room in the attic. But we didn't touch the structure. We built some shelves and painted and fixed some wiring. So it couldn't have been our work that made the roof fall in yesterday."

"Was the baby okay?" asked Mardi as Trent squeezed her hand.

"Yes, thank God, the baby wasn't in there sleeping. The beam that fell from the ceiling split and drove a stake through her crib." Mario gave Trent and Mardi a searching look as if to ask whether they really believed him. "We are very sorry, but it wasn't our fault."

"We trust you. But we need to find out what the Hell is going on," said Trent with a quiet yet strong anger that sent a thrill through Mardi's body. She was furious on these guys' behalf too. As she squeezed his palm, she felt a searing heat pass between them.

"Mario, Luis. Don't worry," Trent continued. "We'll get to the bottom of this. My guess is that it has nothing to do with you at all."

"You think it's random? Like the messed-up traffic lights?" asked Mardi.

Trent released her hand and squinted into the horizon, as though the sunset might hold some explanation. "It's random . . . and it's also not at all random," he said. He was silent for a while.

Mardi sensed his profound confusion—and she also saw the fierce intelligence with which he was fighting that confusion. In that moment, she felt she embodied the very same struggle that he was caught in.

"There is something evil in the air," he said, looking her straight in the eye.

She met his blue gaze. "You mean like black magic?"

"I think you know what I mean."

"You're just like me, aren't you, Trent?" Made of myth and magic.

Slowly, he nodded.

"Trent," she turned his face gently toward hers, "let's go get a drink at Freya's bar and talk this over." Now that they had told each other who they really were, she wanted to talk to him about what had happened back in the city and explain how she was trapped in it. Maybe he would be able to help her figure out how it was all connected? Maybe the same evil force that had murdered those kids in New York was now tracking Molly and Mardi down here on the East End? There were so many questions.

And Trent was the only soul she wanted to open up to right now.

But before she could speak any of these thoughts, he was turning away from her. "Guys," he said to Mario and Luis, "don't worry about cleaning up the restaurant yet. It might be dangerous down there. Just leave it for now, okay?"

The brothers nodded.

"Mardi, I've gotta go." He took her hands in his and scrutinized them for a few seconds, then looked up and met her dark eyes. "There's something I have to do."

"What is it?" She was stunned. Hadn't they just made a deep connection? Where the Hell was he going?

But he wouldn't say.

Instead of going to the North Inn to talk to Freya, Mardi sped aimlessly in and around town, killing time until her rendezvous with her stalker. She was trying to temper her anger at Trent's bizarre brush-off. She wasn't the only one who pulled back every time something was about to happen. They were acting like repellent magnets. The closer they almost got, the harder they pushed each other away.

The streets were empty, probably because of the traffic light scare. North Hampton felt even more dead than usual. She wanted out of here so badly, she could scream. She knew Freya and Ingrid kept brooms hidden in the house. Maybe it was time to fly this coop.

But she couldn't fly now. She was trapped by this stupid feeling of responsibility creeping in on her from all sides. It was so unfair. How did a teenage prankster like her end up at the heart of some big, life-threatening power struggle that she wanted nothing to do with? Why couldn't she have the fun of being a witch without the heaviness of being a goddess? Why was she wasting a gorgeous hot summer night going to meet some psycho in the deserted sand dunes?

She supposed it would be worth it if the psycho could at least tell her what she and Molly had done to deserve all this. But still it was a good thing she was alone in the Ferrari, because the angry magic sparking from her every pore would have hexed any mortal within spitting distance.

At a few minutes before ten, Mardi set off across the Gardiners Island Bridge. She hadn't been there since the party on the night of her arrival. Unlike that evening in late June, Fair Haven was not ablaze now with festive torchlight and gleaming chandeliers. The house glimmered so faintly that it might be an illusion. The wind in her hair became icy, and she had to suppress the urge to turn back. What if the stalker was violent? After all, he or she had threatened to hurt Molly. Not that Mardi couldn't handle anything that came her way. But still . . . She steeled herself and pressed harder on the gas. The urge to know what was going on was a lot more powerful than any fear.

Just off the bridge, she pulled over on the side of the road, got out of the car, and waited at the edge of the dunes. She noticed that there was another car parked in the distance and wondered who else might be there.

After a few minutes, she called out a soft "hello."

No response.

She decided to start looking around, to show who-ever was messing with her that she was not afraid.

As she began to wander into the dunes, she smelled smoke. Her animal instincts came alive. She looked up to see gray wisps floating skyward about a hundred yards away. She went straight toward the smoke only to find herself blocked by a large mass of sand. She could hear rustling and the popping of dry wood in flames. Whoever had summoned her had built a fire under the stars.

Mardi did not try to tread lightly. In fact, she stomped, making sure to show that she wasn't the one sneaking around here. She had nothing to hide.

She followed the smoky odor and the faint sounds until she found herself up against a large dune. The fire had to be on the other side, along with her stalker. Humming to keep her spirits up, she went around the mass of sand. At first, she was hardly aware of the tune she was channeling. But after a few bars, she realized it was "Wannabe," the Spice Girls song she and Molly used to play at full volume in order to torture Dad and tease him about his series of one-night stands with the '90s ingénues. It was one of the few truly joyful memo-ries that she and Molly shared. She wondered why it had popped into her head at this bizarre moment.

As she came around the dune, she caught her breath. There was a fire here, all right. A bonfire surrounded by fancy oriental rugs and huge silk pillows, blankets, champagne bottles, the remains of a caviar feast now covered in sand. It looked like the aftermath of some exotic orgy. And right in the heart of it sat her sister, looking a little disheveled and totally shocked.

"What are *you* doing here?" Molly jumped up and tried to smooth out her clothes.

"I could ask you the same question." Mardi tried to keep her voice steady. "Did you ask me to come? Is this your idea of a sick joke?"

"Of course not. Why would I invite *you* to Fair Haven? This is my territory."

Instinctively, Mardi believed her. Molly had not summoned her here. She could always tell when her twin was lying. But what did she mean that Fair Haven was hers?

Molly looked into the night, beyond Mardi, as though she was waiting for someone else to appear.

"So, who were you here with?" asked Mardi. "Who built you this fire?"

"How do you know I didn't build it?"

"Come on, Molly. Campfires are so *not* in your skill set. Just tell me, who's the lucky guy?" Mardi gestured to the dregs of the Dom Pérignon.

"Flattery will get you nowhere. And it is totally none of your business who I happen to be seeing."

Mardi couldn't take the suspense any longer. It couldn't be Trent, it just couldn't . . . He wouldn't do this to her. But she had to clear this up. "His last name doesn't happen to be Gardiner, does it?"

"I told you, it's none of your business."

If only Molly would come out and say yes or no, Mardi would be able to tell where the truth lay. And Molly knew this, which was why she was torturing her with evasion.

"Fair enough," said Mardi. After all, she hadn't told Molly much about Trent. Not that there was anything to tell.

"But I *will* say that the lucky guy, as you call him, might actually be something of a disappointment." Molly dug her perfectly pedicured toes into the sand.

"I can relate to that." Mardi sighed, thinking back to Trent's abrupt and chilly departure from the docks earlier this evening. "Guys aren't necessarily worth it."

Nodding her head in agreement, Molly asked, "So how did you end up here tonight, anyway?"

"I was exploring, okay?"

"No, that's not true. A minute ago, you said that someone asked you to come."

"Okay, you've got me. Believe me, I want to tell you who it is. But I can't."

"Wait, but if you know who told you to come here, then why did you just ask if it was me? You're not making any sense, Mardi."

Molly sounded more worried than angry. Perhaps she too was beginning to sense that something was really amiss tonight.

"Can we call it a premonition and leave it at that, for now?"

As Molly squinted at her, Mardi wondered nervously if her sister was going to buy this incoherent explanation. She was also trying to figure out how to convince her to get the Hell out of here, because she was beginning to suspect that this whole setup was some kind of trap.

"Whatever you want to call it." Molly shrugged, obviously not up for a fight. "By the way, were you really humming the Spice Girls just now when you found me? Or did I imagine that?"

"I think I was. Maybe it was my way of reaching out to you. I mean, it's kind of our song."

"Wait a second." Molly laughed. "You're even wearing the Scary Spice green tube top. This is cosmic." She started to hum the tune herself.

"Molly," Mardi interrupted her, "let's get out of here."

As Mardi spoke, the massive bonfire doubled in size, its flames appearing to lick the stars. Both girls jumped away from the scorching heat and ran as the carpets and blankets all caught fire and the air filled with smoke.

Together, the twins raced through the dunes toward the entrance to the bridge where Mardi had left the Ferrari. They arrived panting at the car to find a message scrawled bright red across the windshield: *Bitches burn in Hell.*

"Do you think this means us?" asked Molly.

They could hear the fire crackling and raging. The

moon and stars were hidden by a thick curtain of black smoke.

"Wait a second. Do you remember? 'You bitches are gonna burn in Hell'?"

"You know about that night . . . " Molly's voice trailed off into the fiery night.

Mardi looked at her twin. "Molly," she said, "where is our ring?"

24

WAKE ME UP WHEN IT'S ALL OVER

The next morning, Molly awoke in a funk. Her eyes were puffier than ever from too much alcohol and not enough sleep. She was down to her last stick of concealer with the awesome brush applicator, and it was only the first day of August. She was going to have to stretch the concealer through Labor Day, when she would finally return to civilization, a prospect she would have greeted with pure joy and utter relief if it weren't for the fact that she was a suspect in an ongoing police investigation.

Although it was hard to believe that anything terrible would actually happen to her and Mardi, it was no longer an impossible scenario. Especially not after last night's conflagration and freaky misogynist message. The thought that Daddy might be right about the trouble they were in was now gnawing at her insides. Why had Tris deserted her last night, leaving her to the mercy of some psycho spirit? Where had the ring gone, and why did it seem to matter so much? She hated the feeling, which she had all the time lately, that there was a lot going on that she didn't understand. Molly was so not used to being in the dark.

Downstairs, Ingrid's happy little family was cooing over their homemade granola. It was more cheer than Molly could take right now. She felt like making a twister out of the stuff and causing it to spiral out to sea while the children cried inconsolably. Seeing Mardi slumped over her coffee cup desperately trying to ignore the self-congratulatory granola fest, Molly understood that at least her sister felt the same way she did.

Get us out of here. Now. We don't want your life. We like takeout! And we miss our dad.

"Who would like to try some of our granola?" Ingrid practically sang. "We made it with organic oats and locally foraged honey."

"Tell them about the raisins, Mommy!" cried Jo.

"Raisins!" Henry echoed from his grubby high chair. Molly shuddered, remembering what had happened to her shirt earlier in the summer.

"Oh, the raisins! We dried them ourselves in the sun, from grapes grown at Duck Walk Vineyards down the road. Can I give you girls some? With yogurt or with milk?"

"Midnight likes hers with milk!" Jo squealed, pointing to the cat who was lapping at a bowl on the floor.

"I'm not hungry," the twins groaned in unison.

"I'm sorry, but I can't let you two leave the house

without breakfast. It's the most important meal of the day."

"You're not our mother, Ingrid!" Molly snapped, immediately regretting her words when she saw Ingrid's face fall. She attempted some damage control. "It's just that we aren't used to having a mother. Daddy somehow gets cereal and milk into the house, and we manage just fine on our own. We're not really used to this whole domestic thing."

"What you call 'this whole domestic thing' is what we call life," said Matt, putting his arm around his wife.

"That's great for you," said Molly. "But I'm really not hungry."

"Just a tiny bit, please?" begged little Jo. "We made it for you guys."

Wow. Who knew cooking and guilt were so intricately bound together? Molly supposed this was one of the things a mother would have taught her.

Jo leaned into her and whispered, "I did a doubling spell on the brown sugar while Mommy wasn't looking. It's so much sweeter than she thinks it is. Shhh."

"Okay." Molly gave up. "I'll try some. With milk."

"Me too," said Mardi. "With yogurt, please."

Begrudgingly, Molly admitted to herself that this granola was even better than the stuff she always ordered at Balthazar back in the city. Much to the general delight of the family, she and Mardi each had two helpings, heaping with fresh-picked berries, before getting ready to face the day.

As Molly left the house to head to work, Mardi followed her outside toward her bike.

"Um, Molly," she said tentatively.

Before her sister spoke, Molly knew what it was about. "Look, Mardi, I should have told you the ring was gone, okay? I thought I could find it myself before you noticed."

"What the Hell? Why didn't you tell me right away? Where did you have it last?"

"I'm not exactly sure." Technically, this was true. "Look, I've had enough drama for now after last night. Can I just please go have a normal day at work, and we'll talk about this later?"

"Molly, it's our mother's ring. It's all we have of her. *And* it turns out it may have some kind of power that we don't even understand. I think that guy in the pool wanted our ring. Remember?"

Molly's mind started to reel. The creepy dude. The ring. The story from that opera Marshall was telling her. Somehow it all clicked. She had to go talk to Marshall. Even if he had no clue what was going on in her life, he might unwittingly hold a key.

"We'll get it back, okay? I have to go."

"We really need to talk about this, Molly!" Mardi's voice carried after her as she pedaled off toward town.

At the Cheesemonger, everything about Marshall seemed particularly sweet today. In contrast to Tris, he was open and funny. He had no idea about the White Council and the murders and threats of the Underworld. He was simply happy to run his mother's little store in this mellow town, where the biggest thing going was outdoor opera, and the biggest risk you could take was making New England clam chowder instead of Manhattan. He was so cute and didn't seem to notice a lot of girls patronized the shop just so they could flirt with him.

In the lull after the lunch rush, she sat down on a stool quite close to where he was chopping celery and decided to open up a little about some of what was weighing on her, without, of course, venturing into forbidden territory. She was craving sympathy, and Cheeseboy was pretty much a font of the stuff. And she also wanted to know more about the legend of the ring.

"Cheeseboy," she began, "I've had this weird thing happen. Remember the gold ring I had, the one that I started wearing on the chain around my neck?"

"Sort of," he said. He sounded attentive, but he couldn't look at her because he had to keep his eyes on his chopping knife.

"I lost it."

"Do you ever take it off to do prep work? I don't think I've seen it lying around, and I'm pretty observant about that kind of thing in the shop. I'll keep an eye out, though. I'm sure you'll find it. Stuff like that is usually under your nose. You're so used to seeing it all the time that sometimes it's hard to actually notice." He sounded considerate and concerned, not belittling her anxiety, but also not stressed out, because his general vibe was one of mellow optimism. She appreciated him so much right now.

Suddenly, he started to sing a rousing tune that sounded like an air from the Wagner opera she wanted to ask him about. It was as though he anticipated her every need. Cheerfully, he was hitting his cleaver into the chopping block in time to the music so that the pieces of diced celery hopped and skipped onto the counter.

"That's from the Ring opera, right?" She smiled.

"Yes, it's 'The March of the Valkyries.' Your ring dilemma has inspired me. As you've probably noticed by now, I take all my musical cues from life."

"So, I've been wondering something." She grabbed a celery stalk and pensively bit into it. "On July Fourth, before the thunder and lightning started, you were telling me the plot of the opera. About the ring. It started out with these three enormous mermaids swimming around in a plastic pool."

"Rhinemaidens," he corrected her with an impish wink. "They are Rhinemaidens. And they were being chased by Alberich. He wants their love, but since they won't give it to him, he steals their magical gold. Whoever makes a ring from their gold has ultimate power. So, the ring is pretty much the most desirable object in the world."

"So, Alberich wants to take over the world?"

"What he really wants is to use the ring to subjugate and punish the maidens who have humiliated him. And if the world gets in the way, then, sure, he'll take it over and destroy as much as he has to. That's the way he rolls."

Molly grew quiet, thoughtful. In his geeky enthusiasm for an opera based on what he assumed was myth, Marshall night have unwittingly guided her to a clue about that fateful night in April. Someone had been wielding unnatural power over events. Someone who hated women had been threatening Molly and Mardi. She sensed that the threat had something to do with the ring. It was clear now that the ring had powers she and her twin had not fathomed. Had it fallen into the wrong hands?

She couldn't, of course, mention any of this to Marshall, but she could express her gratitude to him for giving her some insight into her nightmare. He may have just gotten her closer to the moment when she could finally wake up and live her life again. Gratitude was not a familiar emotion for Molly. She tried to imagine what would make him happy.

It wasn't very hard. She took his chin in the palm of her hand and lifted his sweet face to hers. Then she kissed him.

He reeled backward, so amazed at his luck that he had no idea how to react.

"Marshall, you're the best. If you were a cheese, you'd be the Brillat-Savarin!"

"The cheese of the gods?" He laughed, blushing to the roots of his sandy hair.

"Exactly."

25

I KNEW YOU WERE TROUBLE, PART TWO

*A*fter the feel-good granolafest, Mardi put on her black racing suit and silver goggles. Then she took off for a long swim in the bay. She needed it. She had a lot to process. As she pulled her body fluidly through the water, stretching her arms, rotating her core, kicking, awakening her every muscle, she was able to align her thoughts and questions.

How had Molly lost the ring? Why did she race off just now instead of talking about it? It was almost like she had an idea and had to act on it right away.

Mardi now knew from the memory sessions with Jean-Baptiste that the ring was way more than a keepsake from their mother, whoever she was. They had always assumed it was a benevolent, private symbol between them. But Mardi was sure now that it harbored powers, and that those powers could be terrifying.

With Mardi and Molly, the ring was safe. In the

wrong hands, it was a mortal threat. Someone else had it now, and that someone was testing out its powers on this poor unsuspecting town, targeting its women most of all.

The weirdo in the pool had wanted their ring, seemingly to punish the twins. He hated them. But why? Granted, she and Molly were obnoxious, but they didn't deserve the flames of Hell. Did he despise all women, or "bitches," as he called them? Or was it personal?

Was he the stalker?

Although she swam and swam, Mardi came no closer to any answers.

She moved on to her next dilemma: Trent. Why had he ripped himself away from her yesterday, acting like he had important business that she couldn't come along on, right after they had officially recognized each other? She hated being pushed aside. She had offered to have a drink with him, and instead of letting her in, he had pulled a typical lone-male-wolf act. If he hadn't been a warlock himself, she would have turned him into a wolf cub for a few hours just to show him what an idiot he was being.

Could he have been racing off to meet her sister on Gardiners Island? That would qualify him as a psychopath, and she so didn't want to go there. But every time she tried to figure out who else Molly could have been seeing in her Bedouin love den in the dunes, she came up blank. It was infuriating.

All this anger was causing her to swim so fast that

she was out of breath. She forced herself to stop and float on her back for a couple of minutes to reassess. She felt a wave of appreciation for this beautiful sea and this quiet, leafy town, a town that seemed so sleepy and peaceful and yet was full of magic and mystery. She certainly couldn't complain that her life was boring here. Even if it was stressful.

She tried to slow down and think more rationally about Trent. Assuming he wasn't messing around with her sister, she should write Trent off for acting like such a jerk on the docks last night. But she didn't want to, and not just because she was so attracted to him. There was more to it than that. There was something deep going on with him, but he wouldn't share it with her. Did he think she was stupid? Immature? Selfish?

Mardi sighed across the glassy sea. Slowly, methodically, the bulk of her anger spent for the time being, she made her way back to shore and a shower before going down to Goose's Landing to help with the cleanup.

She put on an old Black Flag cutoff T-shirt for the occasion, with frayed denim shorts and black Doc Martens. And she wore a spiky dog collar and black lipstick.

"Wow, Mardi," said Freya, who had stopped by for a cup of coffee with Ingrid on her way to set up the bar. "Are you trying to look scary for anyone in particular? Who's the lucky guy?"

"Not scary," Mardi snapped. "Just totally unavailable." And before either Freya or Ingrid could respond from behind the steam of her fresh-brewed latte, she was out the door.

She found Trent alone on the dock outside the restaurant, picking up their beer cans from the evening before. He was frowning, and there were dark shadows under his eyes.

"Hey," she said.

At the sound of her voice, he smiled instantly, but when he looked up and saw how severe she had made herself look, he seemed to remember how things stood, and his happy expression disappeared.

"Hey," he finally managed. "I'm glad you showed up today. It's gonna be a tough one. It's a nightmare down in that cellar."

"Yep." She wasn't going to give him an inch. "Should we get started?"

"We can't go down there quite yet. We have to wait for the fire department to give us the go-ahead. They should be here in a few minutes. Want to go hang out on the *Dragon* until they come? I got this new sandwich press I want to try out. Do you like panini?"

"What is with you, man? Last night, you're all doom and gloom, and you won't even tell me what's going through your head. And when I show up today, you want to talk about panini? I'm not going to pretend like nothing's happening just because you don't feel like dealing with it. Either tell me what went down last night or tell me you're not going to tell me. But quit messing around."

"I'm just trying to be friendly. I could tell I pissed you off last night, and I thought I'd see if I could lighten the mood."

"Bad idea."

"So I see."

"I'll come hang out on the *Dragon*, but I don't want some stupid sandwich. I want answers."

"Okay." He looked straight at her. "I promise. Answers. No sandwich. Let's go."

They walked silently through the noonday sun to the boat and climbed aboard. She could see salt crystals dazzling in the soft hair on his arms. He must have taken a swim this morning too, but he hadn't showered yet. He often worked through the day with the sheen of the ocean on his skin. This was one of the things she used to think she liked about him.

As soon as they climbed onto the deck of the boat, he went into the cabin and returned with his panini press on the end of an extension cord, along with a cutting board, a knife, some focaccia and ham, cheese, and basil.

"I don't want there to be any more misunderstandings. I'm not offering you a panini," he said matter-of-factly. "I'm making one for myself. I'm starving."

Looking at the food, smelling the basil and fresh bread, Molly realized that she was starving too. But there was no way she was going to admit it.

"I owe you an apology," he continued.

"I don't care about apologies. I want an explanation. I want to understand what's happening."

"I wish I knew. But what I can say for sure is that someone with unnatural powers is messing with this town. I don't think it's the White Council trying to show disapproval. I think it's someone else, someone playing with a great power they can't necessarily control. It's an ancient power of some kind. I needed to talk to Jean-Baptiste last night, to see if he had any notion of what I should do."

"You sure you weren't at Fair Haven last night?" she hissed.

"What?" He looked genuinely confused.

"With a girl who looks identical to me, only more Fifth Avenue and less Williamsburg."

"Are you talking about your sister, Molly?"

"That's the only sister I have."

"Mardi, I have no idea what you are talking about. Why would you think that? I was with Jean-Baptiste last night. And I swear he looks nothing like you. Although he is very Fifth Avenue. You gotta give him that."

In spite of herself, she cracked a smile.

"Okay, so you were with Jean-Baptiste. And?"

"And there is something else, but the problem is that I can't tell you any more or someone may get hurt. It's not that I want to be secretive. I'm in a bind, Mardi. Please believe me. Haven't you ever been in a bind before?"

"I guess so." She found herself wanting to tell him about the blocked texts from someone claiming to have incriminating information about Molly and her, threatening her sister if she told . . . *anyone*. She realized she couldn't even explain the cause of her suspicions without risking her twin's life. She too was in a bind. "Yeah, I have a potential source of information too. Maybe. It's either a real source or a totally sick joke. But there's a threat if I reveal too much that someone might get hurt."

"So, it seems like, for now, we can only tell each other without telling each other."

"I guess that's right," she admitted, deeply grateful for the fact that he wasn't pushing her to talk.

"Is that going to be okay with you, at least for now?" he asked, constructing a sandwich on two thin slices of golden bread.

"I guess it has to be." She shrugged.

He nodded, closing the hot press so that the cheese began to sizzle. "You sure you don't want one?"

"I might have changed my mind," she admitted.

He lifted the perfectly grilled sandwich and handed it to her in a blue cloth napkin. "Here." He smiled. "All yours. No strings attached and no questions asked."

26

LOVE ME TWO TIMES

*T*he North Inn, like the neighborhood dive it was, often smelled like spilled beer, but because it had a witch for a bartender, it also smelled like the fresh herbs and fruit juices that went into Freya's potent cocktails. The wooden booths were beaten up and carved with countless sets of initials and messages that had completely lost their meaning over the years. It shook to the rhythm of rock and roll, beating time with the slap of glasses and dollar bills on the counter. Even Molly, through her crinkled little snub nose, was able, on some level, to appreciate its undying energy.

Freya was known for her ability to cure heartbreak, for dispensing magic that kept many relationships alive. Somehow, the people of North Hampton never noticed that she did not grow old alongside them, but stayed timelessly gorgeous with her lush mane of hair, tiny waist, and breathtaking cleavage.

When Molly came in on a hot Friday evening, having just kissed poor Marshall and left him beaming and wordless, the North Inn was heaving. It was karaoke night, and even though it wasn't even nine o'clock yet, the microphone was starting to get some play. A mousy young woman, whom Molly recognized as one of Ingrid's fellow librarians, was crooning Beyoncé's "Halo" to her boyish, smooth-chinned fisherman boyfriend, who, Molly noticed, was still wearing his waders. Beaming up at his librarian, Fishboy sipped a pink cocktail from a wide-rimmed glass. Whenever there was a musical interlude that gave her a break from singing, he passed the glass to her.

"Want an Infatuation like that happy couple?" asked Freya, leaning over the bar toward Molly.

"What is it?"

"Hibiscus, rosewater, and English gin. Or maybe you'd care for a Forever, like the mayor and his husband?"

Molly looked over at two trim men in their early forties, dressed in striped button-downs. While they waited for their turn, they looked intently through the karaoke songbook, discussing the possibilities with much animation.

"Is it good?"

"Champagne fortified with fresh daisy petals is always good."

Molly smiled at Freya's ingenuity. Having taken the only available stool at the bar, she was surrounded on all sides by locals. From working in the shop, she recognized many faces. But she realized now that she knew no one beyond smiling distance. For a second, she felt sad that she had made almost no inroads in North Hampton. In just over a month, apart from having won over and then broken two hearts, she would leave the East End without a trace . . . Although maybe she would come back next summer? She was taken aback by the thought. Was this tacky, disorienting place actually growing on her?

"So what'll it be?" asked Freya.

"Do you have a drink called Clarity? I'm so confused right now."

"Let me guess." Freya smiled, reaching for an unlabeled bottle of honey-colored liquor. "Too many men in your orbit?"

"Not exactly," Molly began to fidget with her beaded clutch. "I'm used to having a lot of boys circling around. But this time, I sort of like two guys at the same time. Like, I'm being pulled in two directions. I don't know how to choose."

"Who says you have to choose?" Winking, Freya poured a shot of the golden liquid from her mystery bottle into a shaker and added some sort of green cordial.

"I don't know why I have to choose, but it feels like I do."

"It sounds to me like you don't need to ask that question because the answer is already blazing inside you." Freya laughed kindly. "Molly, you seem like you could handle it all."

"How do you know?"

"Because I've been there. I thought I had to choose between two guys, and it almost destroyed me." Freya paused to muddle some blackberries with several kinds of herbs that she snipped from bunches in tall glasses on their own dedicated shelf behind the bar. When she was satisfied with her mixture, she added it to the shaker.

"So what did you do?"

Freya smiled mysteriously as she gave her cocktail a couple of hard shakes, then poured the glistening concoction into a rocks glass over ice and handed it to Molly. "I'm still working it out. Things are always evolving between the three of us. We'll see what happens." She winked. "I like to live in the moment. So should you."

Molly raised her glass in Freya's direction and took a sip of her cocktail. She had no idea what it was. There were traces of fruit along with vaguely medicinal notes and a deep, rolling, satisfying flavor whose name was just outside her grasp.

"This is awesome," she said, "better than anything I've tasted in any pretentious mixology place in the city. What is it?"

"It's called Embrace. But it's not a regular menu item. I just invented it for you. And you, Molly, are the only person I will ever mix it for."

"I'm flattered. What's in it?"

"If I tell you, it will lose its potency. I have to watch my secrets around fellow witches," Freya teased.

"What do you mean, potency? What's it going to do to me?" Molly was intrigued. After one swallow, she was already starting to picture kissing Tris and Marshall at the same time. She felt her face flush, just thinking about it.

Molly drained her glass and pulled Freya out from behind the bar toward the karaoke machine. Too impatient to bother with flipping through the index of the songbook, she muttered a little incantation causing it to open to the page she wanted.

Freya threw an arm around Molly. "Now, this is my kind of music! I love the Doors!"

"So does Daddy," Molly yelled over the intro, grooving to the fact that she and Freya were both wearing short, fitted white dresses. Freya's was flared and retro, while Molly's was a slinky number from the latest designer collection. Yet despite the differences, they both wore their dresses so well that it looked like they could have planned their outfits specifically for their star turn at the North Inn.

As they launched into the song, the entire bar fell under their spell. Conversations came to abrupt ends. Drinks sat untouched. At first, everyone appeared to be in a trance. Then Freya moved her hands in a come-hither gesture that got people singing along, one by one, until the whole Friday-night crowd was belting out Jim Morrison's lyrics.

Molly had never done anything this fun and silly.

North Hampton was beginning to grow on her, lyric by lyric.

But just as effortlessly as she had drawn them into the song, Molly silenced everyone with a simple finger to her lips. Not a soul could disobey her. The room went silent except for the two gorgeous white-clad witches finishing out their anthem.

There was rapturous applause, whistling, and many rounds of drinks were offered and bought. But Molly couldn't manage to take another sip. She felt the effects of Freya's cocktail growing stronger and stronger, and was soon barely able to fend off the random guys who wanted to do shots with her. The room was starting to spin.

"Are you okay?" Freya asked as she busily attended to the rush their song had created behind the bar.

"Not really," Molly admitted. "I'm not usually such a lightweight. But I think I might get sick."

"I'm so sorry, sweetie. My potions can be pretty strong. Why don't you go outside and get some fresh air? I'll be out in a few. And don't you dare get on your bike. I'll call you a cab."

Stumbling out into the parking lot, Molly kicked off her heels and stood barefoot, head in hands, trying not to puke. So, this was the underside of the Embrace. The effects of the drink were showing no signs of wearing off. But instead of keeping her on top of the world, with heady visions of boys submitting to her will, her buzz was going sour.

Her head was filling with the recollection of the one boy back home she had never been able to control. Bret. She hated to pronounce his name, even if it was only in her head. And she hated the memory of his chiseled face from the night of the party in his Upper East Side penthouse. For as long into the evening as she could remember, he had toyed with her and Mardi alternately, never committing to one, driving them both crazy with jealous rage. They had never liked the same boy before, and it was awful.

What a bullshit artist that boy was. A rich bullshit artist with bleached blond hair. Why was she thinking about him now? Was it the potion? Was Freya's handiwork causing her to see all the boys she wanted to be with? Did she want to be with Bret?

No, no, she told herself. Absolutely not. But even as she insisted inside that she had never wanted him, a new recollection surfaced to contradict her.

It started out like that vision she and Mardi had had during Jean-Baptiste's first memory session, the one where they were naked in a black swimming pool and being chased by some weirdo. As they slithered and swam away, the three of them were trapped in a dreamlike loop.

The vision rose up again inside her, vivid and terrifying. Had Freya meant to do this with her cocktail? Molly heard powerful strains of opera blaring in surround sound from the black marble walls. She saw the guy with her and Mardi in Bret's penthouse swimming pool. He was saying something, something hostile. It sounded like "bitches burn in Hell . . ." Feeling sicker and sicker, Molly strained her senses through time and space to catch his words. *Bitches burn . . .*

Deep in a trance, she could finally hear him hissing through the steam of his overheated pool. The weirdo didn't just look like Bret. He *was* Bret. She was sure of it now, as sure as she had ever been of anything. They were the same person—or the same creature.

"Don't touch us!" Mardi screamed.

"You stupid witch. I have no interest in you or your sister. I hate you both. I hate all you bitches! It's your gold I want! Give me the gold!"

"Not our ring! Never!" Molly found herself yelling hysterically out into the emptiness of the North Inn parking lot. The sound of her own voice roused her from her nightmare.

Now Freya was holding her, pressing a cool, wet washcloth to her forehead.

"Whoa, relax, relax. Molly? Earth to Molly. Are you with me?"

"I think so." Molly thought she was speaking out loud, but she was so disoriented that she couldn't be certain.

"This is all my fault. I'm afraid I went a little too heavy on the absinthe. What were you screaming just now about a ring?"

"I—I don't really know," Molly stammered. She was shaking, scanning the road for her cab. Ingrid's house was only a ten-minute ride from here. She had never wanted so desperately to be in her bed. "Can—can I sit down?"

"Sure," Freya said, leading Molly toward the three stairs to the North Inn's door.

But just as Molly let herself collapse onto the bottom step, a pair of headlights pulled into the lot, followed by a Subaru wagon with Matt behind the wheel.

"Your chariot has arrived." Freya couldn't completely repress a smile.

"Evening, ladies," Matt said pleasantly through his open window. He was wearing his detective uniform— a nondescript sport coat and tie. "Ingrid sent me to pick her up; she had a premonition she'd need a ride home," he said.

Molly frowned and glared at Freya. "If I throw up in his car, I'm never speaking to you again."

✳ 27 ✳

RED, RED WINE

$\mathcal{S}$o, my sister was so drunk when she got home last night that she told me Freya is basically seeing both of your brothers, and that supposedly Freya and Killian used to shack up right here in this cabin. Is it true?"

"Which part?" asked Trent with a smile.

"Any of it?"

"I don't know what's going on between the three of them, and it's none of my business. But this is Killian's boat . . . my brother, the lady-killer," He gestured with mock grandeur to the cherrywood and leather interior that was his home here on the East End. Then he put on a silly Dracula accent. "So prepare to be seduced."

They had repaired to the *Dragon* after mopping out the flooded wine cellar of Goose's Landing. When no one was looking, they had resorted to a little magic to undo some of the more alarming red stains. Mario and Luis were going to start repairing the structural damage tomorrow morning.

Trent told her he'd swiped a really good bottle of

Bordeaux from the cellar at Fair Haven. As he uncorked it, he hummed the old reggae tune "Red, Red Wine."

"What else did your sister say about my family?" Trent asked.

"Not much. She was pretty incoherent. Freya gave her one of her cocktails. But it was one she'd never mixed before, and it got a little out of hand. Poor Molly. I usually think she deserves what she gets, but no one deserves to be that sick. She spent half the night curled up on the bathroom floor throwing up. It was really a bummer."

"Is she okay this morning?"

"She's fine. Ingrid gave her a pretty radical hangover potion. I'm going to have to steal the formula from her. I've been thinking that if Molly and I ever have to go underground we could always support ourselves by selling the stuff on the black market. Seriously, it works wonders. Molly looks like she slept ten hours last night. She's so happy that she's not even a tiny bit bloated. It's like Christmas!"

"How come I haven't met her yet? I guess I've been hanging at the docks too much. I hear she's quite a stunner," he said, his eyes twinkling.

Mardi curled her lip. "Don't worry. She's not your type."

"Aren't you guys really identical?" he teased as he handed her a full glass of dark wine, his eyes twinkling blue as a sun-kissed sea.

She ignored him. "Yeah, but you wouldn't be able to stand her for five minutes."

"And I can stand you for at least five minutes?" His eyes were definitely shining.

"Besides, she has a boyfriend." Mardi couldn't help but feel jealous at Trent's interest in Molly.

"Oh, yeah?"

"She's been hanging out at Fair Haven. That's why I thought—"

"I think we've established it's not me. So, then, who?" Although he was trying to keep his tone light, she could tell this was an important question.

"No idea." Mardi was suddenly concerned. Who *could* Molly be seeing? She'd never stoop to dating an employee of the house. Was there yet another brother lurking at Fair Haven? A stepchild? Some relative Trent didn't want to acknowledge? Could she really trust Trent? She wanted to. More than anything.

"So, cheers to cleaning up gallons of this stuff!" Mardi touched her wineglass to his and took a big sip. As if it fortified her courage, she put the glass down and stood up next to him. "This is great, but you know what could be better?" she asked huskily.

He raised his eyebrows and put down his glass. "I think I do."

She leaned toward him but he was faster, and he pulled her into his arms. She closed her eyes and their lips met, slowly at first, then harder, and faster, more urgent, until they had knocked the wine off the table in a hurry to fall into bed, so that the red wine bloomed like a cut on the carpet.

PERFECT DAY

$\mathcal{M}$olly needed to appear innocent while delivering a message that could, potentially, make her seem pretty guilty. She had to look her best. She thumbed through the possibilities on the rolling clothes rack she had swiped from Freya's enormous attic wardrobe. She hadn't wanted her beautiful stuff to get all mussed in Ingrid and Matt's small minimalist guest room closet.

She looked over the hangers out onto the beach and the sparkling bay. It was gorgeous outside. She had texted Marshall that she needed to take the day off for "personal reasons." Velvet Underground was playing in the background, Lou Reed crooning about a perfect day, just like the one she was about to have.

She toyed with the idea of a cap-sleeved orange sundress, but decided it would be a mistake. Yet the baby blue romper was too babyish. On the other end of the spectrum was a fitted navy button-down dress she had bought for a funeral. She tried it on with a pair of beige pumps and checked herself out in the full-length mirror that she had also borrowed from Freya's stash. It was all right for a funeral, she thought, laughing to herself.

There had to be a happy medium. She went back to her rack. Her solution jumped out at her in the form of a lightweight Chanel suit. Freya had had the hemline taken up, but not too much. The jacket was cropped, but she had a great silk tank that would cover her belly button. And she could finish it with some cork wedges that were fun yet discreet.

As she put the final touches on her hair and makeup, she smiled at herself in the bathroom mirror. "Perfect for a perfect day," she whispered.

Molly's mission was a delicate one. She had decided to seek out Jean-Baptiste and tell him about the vision she'd had of Bret chasing her and Mardi around because he wanted their ring. She was starting to think that the scene she had relived in her absinthe delirium in the parking lot of the North Inn wasn't a simply a paranoid vision, but a memory. Hazy as it was, it had a feel of truth to it.

Slowly, painfully, the night of the accident was coming into focus. And she had a feeling that the ring, missing now, had also briefly gone missing that night.

Molly realized that she could potentially incriminate herself—and her twin—by telling Jean-Baptiste that she had recalled events leading her to believe that her and Mardi's ring was a factor in the killings. Maybe this would make her look guilty. But maybe she was?

No way. They were being framed—she was sure of it. Someone knew that they were considered trouble-makers at Headingley and in bars and clubs all around the city, that they were constantly on the verge of being expelled but always managed to charm their way out of trouble at the eleventh hour. And this same someone was well aware that the White Council wouldn't mind having an excuse to put the Overbrook sisters out of harm's way for a few thousand years.

Could it actually be Bret who was trying to banish them to the Underworld? That phrase, "bitches burn in Hell," pursued her and Mardi like an echo through time. First the night of the party. Then on the wind-shield of the Ferrari while a freak fire raged in the night. Could it all be Bret? Who was Bret, anyway? The sisters had always guessed he was paranormal. But how? And why would he have it in for Mardi and her? What had they ever done to him?

If she could get Jean-Baptiste to see through her eyes, perhaps he could shed some light on this thicket of images and impressions. Perhaps he could help her to remember a little bit more, and more clearly, so that together they could unravel the facts, clear the Overbrook name—find out what really happened that night and what was going on right now in North Hampton.

. . .

Briskly and purposefully, Molly knocked on the pale pink door of Rose Cottage, the bed and breakfast where Jean-Baptiste was spending his East End summer.

In seconds, as though she had been lying in wait for a visitor, Mrs. Ashley Green, a pleasantly plump woman in her late fifties, wearing a flowing lavender-and-white batik dress, opened the door with a gracious smile.

"Well, don't you look lovely," she said. "I believe I recognize you from the Cheesemonger. I buy all of my scones from you for my guests. I used to bake them myself, but yours are so much more divine than anything I could produce. My favorites are the apricot currant. Do you have a favorite?"

"Um, I really like—"

"You also do wonderful soups. At first I was skeptical, like everyone else in town, of the New England chowder, but I have to say that I'm now a convert. An absolute convert!"

"Yes, it was a big risk, but it paid—"

"It paid off. Why, yes it did! Come in dear. What can I get you?"

"Actually—"

"No, don't say it. I can read it in your eyes. Such pretty dark eyes. And what lovely dark hair you have. I can see exactly what you want. I have a gift for reading people you know. I can say beyond a shadow of a doubt that you would absolutely kill for some lemonade and shortbread right now."

"Excuse me, but—"

"This way. Come this way."

Before she could object, Molly was led through a fever dream of chintz and Victorian antiques into a kitchen whose walls were covered in mounted floral china plates. She was seated at a table and presented with a tall glass of lemonade and a plate of shortbread.

"This is really lovely of you, Mrs. Green, but I'm not—"

"Now, don't you try to be polite. I'm sure your mother taught you never to act hungry in a stranger's home, but I'm no stranger to anyone in this town."

At the mention of a mother, Molly's heart sank a little. No one, except a couple of unfortunate and short-lived nannies, had ever attempted to teach either of the twins manners of any kind.

She suddenly grew impatient with the aggressively friendly Mrs. Green and whispered a spell that stuck the dowdy woman's lips together long enough that she could get a word in edgewise.

"Listen, I'm not hungry, and I don't eat cookies that are pure butter anyway, and I need to see one of your guests. A Mr. Mésomier."

Frightened and confused, Mrs. Green stared bug-eyed at Molly, as if from underwater, making the faint guttural sounds of the gagged and the drowning.

Molly released the poor woman, who immediately went off on a tangent about how the strangest thing had just happened, and had Molly noticed that her mouth wouldn't move for a few minutes there?

Just as Molly was ready to turn Mrs. Green into a gingerbread woman, take a bite out of her, and put her remains on the hideous china plate next to her vile shortbread, Jean-Baptiste stuck his elegant head into the kitchen.

"Why, Molly, how wonderful to see you," he purred, not appearing remotely surprised. Within moments, he had dispatched his annoying hostess and was seated across from Molly, shrink-style, on a brown velvet settee, while she was perched nervously in a toile-upholstered window seat.

"You look smashing," he opened.

"So do you," she replied. She meant it. He was wearing an impeccable canary yellow linen suit. And his pocket square today was kelly green. "Do you always do solid-color pocket squares?" she asked, genuinely curious.

"I do," he answered. "If you ever see a man who looks like me but is wearing a patterned pocket square, you can be sure he's an imposter."

"Good to know." She smiled.

"But I don't think you came here to ask about my sartorial preferences. To what do I owe this pleasure?"

With that, it all came pouring out of her. The images of the pool, the ominous sounds of the opera overhead, the bitches burning in Hell. The shared ring that Bret had been after, which she thought went missing briefly that night; the fact that it was now missing again; all the intertwining themes and variations.

She tried to describe the wall of secrecy that was coming up between her and her twin. The two of them had always butted heads, but they had never been such bitter rivals as on the night of the party. And every time they tried to get close here in North Hampton, they inevitably started to argue.

"It's weird. I don't know what's going on with us. I mean, we've always fought, but we've also always known what's up with each other. I feel like someone's using our competitiveness to keep us apart. Is that weird?"

Jean-Baptiste nodded. "Yes, you and your sister must make every effort to unite your powers. The two of you must tell each another everything that you recall, even if it feels like nothing more than a dream. I believe that the ring may hold the answers we are seeking, although truly it is the power of your memories that will ultimately uncover the fates of those poor murdered children and prove your innocence.

"Whoever is behind these crimes is trying to divide the two of you—and I have to say you are easy targets for discord—so that you will not combine your recollections and come to the solution. You are being kept in the dark by your own inability to work together. If you and Mardi can find the strength to work together, you will be able to remember exactly what happened that night."

"And do you think that remembering what happened will help us understand what is going on here, now? All the random acts of evil and hate?"

"I'm afraid they aren't so random, Molly."

"There *is* a pattern. Whoever is behind this craves power. And hates women."

"Yes, Molly." He closed his eyes to concentrate. "You are beginning to see clearly now. I believe that, united, you and Mardi have enough clarity to combat this evil."

With Jean-Baptiste's wise words ringing in her ears and heart, Molly rushed from Rose Cottage, leapt onto her shiny red bicycle, and began to ride toward the docks, where she hoped to find Mardi and come clean. But she had only pedaled for a block when she heard her phone beep.

A text. Could it be Tris? Was he finally going to tell her why he had vanished from the dunes the other night? Although she knew she should be furious, she wanted more than anything to give him the benefit of the doubt, to join him again among the cashmere blankets. And maybe even to confide in him about all the crazy stuff that was going on in her life. He was, after all, her kind.

She pulled out her phone. OMG! It *was* him. And he was saying all the right things.

I'm so sorry. I can explain everything. Meet me as soon as you possibly can inside the greenhouse on the west side of Fair Haven.

Without hesitating, Molly changed direction and began to speed toward the Gardiners Island Bridge. It wasn't that she had changed her mind about bonding with Mardi. She had every intention of doing so. She knew it was important.

But first, she had an urgent booty call to answer.

✳ 29 ✳

BAD BOYFRIEND

$\mathcal{P}$lease, Mardi, don't go. Spend the night with me on the *Dragon*." Trent's voice was at once silky and rugged.

"Believe me, I don't want to go." It was true. She felt amazing. As the sun began to dip, bathing the boat's deck in soft pink light, every nerve in her body tingled with pleasure. She stretched, long and feline, within the comfort of his muscular embrace. "But I promised Ingrid and Matt I would be home by seven to babysit."

This was true. But it wasn't the only reason she gave herself for wrenching her body from his. You always wanted to leave a fresh situation with a boy on a high note, with a lingering sense of possibility. There was no point in exhausting your options right after the first kisses. Mardi was a sucker for the exquisite torture of the long, drawn-out conquest. August was going to be an eventful month.

He waved sweetly as she climbed off the boat. And

she was sure she could feel his melancholy gaze caressing her sinewy back as she walked along the dock toward shore. But when she turned for a last look from the harbor, he was gone.

Sinking dreamily into the driver's seat of the Ferrari, she felt the vibration of her phone in her back pocket. It was probably Ingrid reminding her that she and Matt were going on a date tonight and that Mardi needed to be home soon or else telling Mardi what she had prepared for her and the kids for dinner (Ingrid loved to discuss dinner).

But of course it wasn't Ingrid.

Meet me at greenhouse at Fair Haven ASAP. You know where it is.

Buzzkill.

Psycho stalker.

Mardi kicked one of her tires, then texted Ingrid that she was sorry she was going to be late. Something had come up at work.

Ingrid immediately messaged back that this was *disappointing*. She and Matt were now probably going to lose their table at the coveted Bistro Margaux and possibly even miss their movie.

I have come to expect more from you, Mardi.

Mardi wished she could tell Ingrid what was going on.

Her wonderful mood shattered now, Mardi gunned it across the bridge to Fair Haven. *You know where it is,* the stalker had written, which meant whoever was texting her knew Mardi was familiar with the greenhouse. They had been spying on her while she ate dinner there, among the potted palms and ferns, with Trent on the night of the party. She had a mental flash of the Venus flytrap snapping its green lips around a live worm.

As she was parking the Ferrari, her eye caught on a flash of red against one of the dunes. It was a bicycle. *Ingrid's* bicycle. The one that Molly rode everywhere. Why was her sister here now? Shouldn't she be at the Cheesemonger finishing up her shift?

Molly was here again? Like the last time Mardi was summoned? It had to be more than coincidence.

Mardi glanced at the massive house, which looked deserted at first, all of its windows shuttered and draped—although on closer examination, there was one parted curtain on the top floor. She felt as if she was being watched as she crossed the vast green lawn of the estate toward the western side of the house to the beautiful wrought-iron and glass structure where she had first gotten to know Trent. So much had happened already this summer that the June evening of the party seemed distant and rosy, from a different time.

In order to show whoever was observing her that she was not afraid, she took strong purposeful strides.

As she approached the greenhouse, she saw that there was a figure pressed against the glass. It appeared to waver slightly among the fronds and branches, as though it were flickering, only half real. Maybe it was a trick of the light, a tree with a vaguely humanoid shape that struck her nervous imagination. But, from a closer vantage point, Mardi saw clearly that this was no tree. And it was not one, but two people, two people writhing as one.

What she finally witnessed was so bizarre that at first she could not process it. The guy and the girl pawing one another in the greenhouse were none other than Molly and . . .

Trent?

Trent? Her Trent?

He had the same dark hair, the same expression on his face . . . the same one he'd made when he'd kissed *her* earlier that day.

Mardi watched, her heart falling into her stomach, and felt as if she might vomit. Her most far-fetched suspicions were actually true. This was a nightmare.

Molly had her back pressed into the glass wall, her skirt hiked to her waist, and her legs wrapped around Trent's hips.

Trent was holding her up against the glass, his face buried in her neck.

So this was what her stalker wanted her to know.

Mardi had never felt so betrayed—or so stupid. Only a few hours ago, she had finally let herself trust Trent, and he had been playing her all along. *How come I've never met your sister . . . I hear she's quite a stunner . . . Aren't you guys really identical?*

Mardi couldn't move. Not even when he began to unbutton the front of Molly's dress, not even when Molly pulled off his polo shirt.

Mardi felt sick. How could she have ever touched him? How could she have been so completely wrong about him? If the world was confusing before, now it had stopped making any sense at all.

She and Molly never liked the same guy. They had sort of fought over Bret, but they were sort of repulsed by him too. It wasn't the same. This was different. There was a *code*. No matter what happened—no matter how much she and Molly bickered and fought, they were *sisters*. Twin sisters.

If Trent liked Molly better, then there was nothing Mardi could do about it. She would step aside.

She was about to leave when Trent looked up and caught her eye.

She froze.

But he only smiled.

A malicious, terrifying grin.

A shit-eating grin.

One that confirmed all her fears. He'd *wanted* her to

see this. He had sent her all those texts! He'd wanted her to know he was toying with her all along. Toying with them. Two-for-one special. Maybe it ran in the family, what with the weird triangle of his older brothers and Freya Beauchamp.

For the first time in her life, Mardi Overbrook was too hurt to fight. She had no rage left in her. She turned away and ran.

30

FOUND OUT ABOUT YOU

$\mathscr{I}$t was four A.M. Molly opened the front door quietly. Her head was still swirling with African violets, pink and white water lilies in a trickling fountain, lacy ferns, exotic herbs, and that awesomely weird Venus flytrap that Tris had fed from a stash of writhing worms. He had told her that he was taking care of the plant for his brother Killian.

She had never felt so jazzed by a boy in this life—maybe ever. Of course, Cheeseboy was a wonderful side dish, and there was no reason not to keep him warm, but for now, she was going to focus on the young heir to Fair Haven.

Tris had explained his disappearance from the dunes. His stepmother, Mrs. Gardiner, was not only chilly, judgmental, and overly fond of gin. She was also mentally unstable and sometimes self-destructive in her cries for help. She had been acting strange all that day, saying dramatic good-byes to Tris and the staff for no particular reason, since she wasn't going anywhere they knew of. And she would not take off her fur-collared "traveling coat," even though it was the first week of August.

While Tris had been with Molly in front of the fire that night, he'd had a sudden, strong premonition that Mrs. G had done something awful. He'd rushed off to go check. Sure enough, there was an empty bottle of sleeping pills by her bed and she was turning blue. He'd had to call 911 immediately.

"That's weird," Molly said. "I didn't hear an ambulance."

"They always come by boat. It's faster. And more discreet."

"Got it." She nodded. "I'm really sorry. Do you think she'll be okay?"

"Depends on your definition of okay. But I don't want to think about it anymore now."

He kissed her.

The kisses had led to so much more, she thought dreamily, remembering their hot make-out session. Tris had wanted to go all the way, but Molly had stopped him. He had taken off his shirt and she was half undressed, but that was as far as she had allowed him to go.

She wanted to tease it out.

"No," she'd said. "Not yet."

"But I want to," he'd begged. "I want you so much. I've wanted you for so long."

"I do too," she'd told him. "But good things come to those who wait."

She smiled, recalling the musky scent of his cologne and the intensity of his touch, as she closed the front door softly behind her, took off her shoes so as not to make noise on the wooden floors, and tiptoed into the dark living room.

"Where have you been?" Mardi's angry whisper hit her out of nowhere.

Molly steeled herself. She wasn't going to let a fight with her sister wreck a perfect night. She was going to keep things under control.

"I saw you."

As her eyes adjusted to the darkness, Molly saw Mardi as a long shape coiled on the sofa like a snake preparing to strike. Midnight was nestled in the crook of her knees.

"And what exactly did you see me doing, perv?" Molly knew she shouldn't engage, but the urge was stronger than ever. She couldn't let Mardi have the last word.

"You were in the greenhouse at Fair Haven, making out with Trent."

"Trent? Who's Trent?"

"Trystan Gardiner. My boyfriend. Everyone calls him Trent."

"Mardi, you're delirious." Molly moved toward the couch. "Trystan Gardiner is *my* boyfriend. And he doesn't go by Trent, everyone calls him Tris, including me."

"He's Trent, you idiot."

"Nuh-uh. His name is Tris! Trystan, get it? Tris!"

"Trent!"

"Tris!"

They were still whispering viciously, their faces now just inches apart so that to each one the other's features looked distorted and gray in the darkness. Midnight was looking from one to the other. The kitten's wide copper eyes flashed between them.

"Wait—there's only one Gardiner brother in town this summer, isn't there?" Molly asked suddenly.

"Duh! Haven't you heard a word I said?"

"Then that means your Trent and my Tris are the same guy?"

Mardi rolled her eyes. "What do you think?"

"So you didn't know you were with my guy?"

"Of course I didn't know," Molly snapped, deeply offended. "Did *you* know?"

"Of course not."

"So why did you ask if I knew? Tris or Trent, or whoever he is, the guy has been playing both of us."

Molly was devastated. "But Tris is so not your type."

"Trent is so not yours. I met him first at the party at Fair Haven."

"No, *I* met him first at the party at Fair Haven!"

As they glared at each other, the kitten arched her back and hissed. But they paid no attention.

Molly decided she had to leave. She had never been this humiliated before. In fact, she had *never* been humiliated. She couldn't stand it. And her sister, whom she was supposed to be bonding with, was driving her even more insane. As much as she hated Tris now, she hated the idea of Mardi having him even more.

She had almost . . . and her sister . . . what had she done?

"Ew! Did you sleep with him?" Molly demanded.

"No! Did you?" Mardi asked.

"No!"

But even if Mardi hadn't slept with him, it still didn't make it okay. They had kissed, that was for sure, and that was enough for Molly.

She hated this house. She hated this town. She hated everything. She didn't know where she wanted to go. But she knew she wanted out of this hellhole. Now.

She ran upstairs, threw a few clothes and a tooth-brush and makeup bag into her Hermès tote, and, without so much as a good-bye to Mardi, who might still be stewing on the couch for all she cared, Molly stormed off into the breaking day, with Midnight's eyes shining after her in the dawning light.

*

PART THREE

SUMMER LOVING! HAD ME A BLAST SUMMER LOVING! HAPPENED SO FAST

*

31

I WILL SURVIVE

𝓜ardi was still lying on the sofa, staring at the living room ceiling, when Ingrid came down in her simple white cotton bathrobe, looking fresh and wholesome, to grind the coffee.

"Good morning," said Ingrid. "Did you sleep well?"

Mardi hadn't slept at all. What had just happened? She and her sister had been seeing the same Gardiner brother. It was unbelievable. And to think she had actually liked him—Trent or Tris or Trystan, whatever his name was. And he had liked her too—just as much as he'd liked her sister, that was clear.

It was so gross and so awful.

"Coffee?" Ingrid chirped as she poured fresh grounds into her elaborate coffee machine.

Mardi grunted.

"Hang in there. The java is percolating. Help is on the way." Ingrid appeared to have forgiven her for never showing up to babysit last night.

But apparently Jo and Henry, who came bounding

downstairs at the sound of her voice, were not so understanding. They both jumped on her and started hitting
her with their stuffed animals. "Where were you? We
were supposed to have a dance party with Mini and
George. You promised!"

"Party!" Henry echoed.

Mini and George were a toy mouse and a monkey
puppet. Whenever Ingrid and Matt were safely out of
the picture, Mardi and Jo animated them, making them
sing, dance, and fly all over the house, much to Henry's
delight.

"I'm sorry guys." Mardi rolled over to escape their
soft blows. "Something came up."

She put her face in her hands and pressed her fingers
into her forehead, trying to fight the grogginess invad-
ing her body. And then she felt it. The ring. That tiny,
deeply familiar weight on her right hand. Her eyes
widened as she pulled her hands from her face to ex-
amine it. She completely forgot that she was supposed
to be upset. Lovingly, she twisted the ring around and
around, marveling at its simple carved diamond design.
How long had it been here?

Her first instinct was to find Molly and tell her. Then
she remembered she was in a huge fight with Molly.
Then she remembered why, and she was overcome by
a wave of sadness and anger so strong she grabbed the
suede fringe bag she had dumped on the floor next to
her and bolted from the couch for the front door. She
didn't need Ingrid's organic fair trade coffee. She didn't

even need to brush her teeth or wash her face. What she needed was to make Trystan Gardiner pay. Now.

"Mardi!" Ingrid ran to stop her. "What's this all about? Is there something you need to tell me?"

"No."

"Where's Molly?"

"I don't know."

"You don't have any idea where she is?"

Mardi shrugged and made for the door again.

Ingrid frowned. "Listen," she said, "I'm responsible for you two here this summer. Your dad is an age-old friend of mine. I promised him to keep an eye on you. And I promised to help you get to the bottom of that accident in New York so that we wouldn't all suffer for your carelessness. Now, if something serious is going on, you owe it to me and to Freya and Jean-Baptiste to let us in."

"Oh, my God, Ingrid, this has nothing to do with the White Council or the investigation. If you must know, it's about a guy. It's kind of a rude awakening, but it's not life threatening, except maybe to him when I get a hold of him."

"What did he do?"

"He was playing both of us."

"Playing both of you? You don't mean . . . ?" Ingrid softened her tone.

Mardi nodded, her eyes filling with tears.

"Oh! How awful! Who is he?"

"Trystan Gardiner."

"Trystan Gardiner?" Ingrid said, taken aback. "Are you sure?"

"I think I know who we were both dating, Ingrid."

"But it doesn't sound like him. I *know* Trystan . . . He's a bit rough around the edges, but he's got a good heart."

"A heart that's big enough for two, clearly." Mardi cracked a bitter smile. "Can I go now?"

"Are you sure you don't want any coffee?"

"No thanks, Ingrid. I'm pumped up enough as it is."

"Okay, I know I'm not your mother. I'm sorry about Trystan, but it's hard to believe he would do such a thing." She gave a sad little smile. "Do you mind keeping an eye on the kids for me for a minute before you go? I need to get some zucchini from the garden."

"Yeah, whatever."

Once Ingrid was out the door, Jo came up to Mardi with her hands behind her back and a wildly happy expression on her little face. Henry was trailing her, meowing like a cat.

"We have a surprise for you!" Jo was trembling with excitement.

Mardi tried to pretend she cared. After all, these kids weren't to blame for the fact that she was miserable. She mustered as much sham enthusiasm as she could. "No way! You guys are the best! What could it be?"

"Look!" From behind her back, Jo produced a small, purring Siamese cat.

"Killer?" Mardi experienced a wave of the purest

delight. "Killer, it's you!" The cat leapt into Mardi's arms, nestled in the crook of her neck, and gazed up adoringly into her face. Midnight looked on with a gentle curiosity.

"I thought you might miss your familiars. It seemed so unfair that your daddy made you leave them behind. So I transported them for you. It was the hardest spell I've ever done."

"This is amazing, Jo. You are one talented little witch." She scratched Killer gently under the chin, loving the familiar feeling of her short fur. Never had she been so happy to see her constant companion. "But what do you mean by 'familiars'? I only have one familiar. It's just me and Killer. Killer and me."

"Oh, but I rescued Molly's familiar too!"

"You mean Fury is here?"

"Yes. She's in Molly's bed right now. She's a really funny-looking doggy, right?"

Mardi had to laugh. "Miracles never cease."

Jo and Henry stood beaming at her.

After a few minutes of bonding and reconnecting with the beautiful creature, she handed Killer back to Jo. "I need you to take care of her for me for a few hours, okay? I'll be home soon. And try to make sure she and Fury don't see each other. They tend to fight a lot."

"Sort of like you and Molly?"

"Something like that."

32

THE BEST DAY OF MY LIFE

𝓜olly knew that there was one person in this town whom she could count on to help her no matter what, without judgment and without asking anything in return. And he would do it with a smile and a sense of humor.

Marshall would be at the store by now, baking muffins and scones, prepping for the day, singing some goofy song. She would ask him to help her get out of here for a few days, to lend her his car and hook her up with a hotel recommendation somewhere on East End, anywhere that wasn't here. Better yet, she would have him drive her out of town so that she wouldn't have to deal with crossing that weird misty force field that surrounded North Hampton all by herself. Maybe she should have been with Marshall all along.

She still couldn't believe what had happened.

Tris had ingratiated himself so smoothly, pretending to be banished to North Hampton just like her, giving her the sense that he was uniquely qualified to understand her. But what infuriated her even more than the emotional betrayal was the physical one. She had practically begged him to touch her. She had craved his kisses, the feel of his tongue and hands all over her body. Even now that she despised him, she could not help but feel turned on when she pictured herself with him. Physical attraction, she was learning, was a cruel, cruel thing.

She got it now—"Tris" and "Trent"—he thought he was so clever! Why not just call himself "Tryst"? That was probably the most appropriate name for him. She realized that in order to exact the true punishment he so richly deserved, she was going to have to ally herself with Mardi. United in fury, they were a terrifying force. And she knew she also had to ally herself with Mardi in order to solve the mystery of the disappearing ring and get to the bottom of the murders. The summer would be over soon, and if they didn't clear things up before then, the White Council would lay down the law and Daddy would freak. But for right now, she simply couldn't deal. All this anger and responsibility was giving her a migraine. Her skin was a mess. She needed a break.

Having applied her lip gloss and checked her hair in her compact mirror, she tapped on the glass door of the Cheesemonger. As she expected, Marshall lit up like a puppy the moment he saw her. He came running to open the door for her.

"Molly! What's up? Why are you here? You're not

supposed to be working today." He moved to hug her, but then stopped himself, obviously not sure where he stood, despite the kiss she had bestowed on him the other day.

She got straight to the point. "Marshall, I need your help. I can't really get into it, but things are incredibly rough at Ingrid's, and with my dad and our New York legal problems, and with other stuff here in town. I have to get out of here for a few days, or I'm going to explode."

"Gee, I'm sorry to hear that."

"Do you think you can get me out of here? To Shelter Island or Montauk or anywhere reasonably close by that isn't *here*? I've never been to either Shelter or Montauk. I hear they both have some cool new boutique hotels. Sunset Beach sounds like heaven right now."

"I'd love to go away with you, Molly," he said. "But I don't know if I can leave the shop. No one else can run it."

"What about your mom? Won't she cut you a break? Where *is* your mother anyway? Why is she leaving all the work to you? When is she coming back?"

"I'm not exactly sure where she is." He winced down at his shoes as though the subject was painful for him. "Somewhere in South America, I think. And she may never actually come back."

"If it makes you feel any better, my mother is totally MIA too. I don't even know her name. The only thing Daddy has ever said about her is that she was a . . . "

Molly almost said *giantess*, which was in fact what Daddy had let slip once when he was very drunk, but she caught herself in time and improvised: "A lot to handle."

He nodded.

"Maternal love is overrated. Case in point: we've both turned out just fine without it. Let's stop feeling sorry for ourselves and blow this Popsicle stand. I can't take another minute of it. If we hurry, we can be gone before you're supposed to open the shop. Then no one will be able to stop us."

He began to waver. "Yeah, who needs mothers anyway?" he whispered. She could see that he was unable to resist her charms. Who could?

"I guess we could check out Montauk for a few days." He gave a shy smile. "I've been wanting to eat at this new place for ages. It's called the Crow's Nest. Apparently, they do a beautiful mezze plate. And we can stay there. It's one of those trendy repurposed motels."

"Don't say 'trendy.' It sounds terrible. Like the exact opposite of what you want it to mean." Molly was relieved to find that, even in the throes of fury and exhaustion, she had not lost her critical faculties.

"Sorry," he said. "I get really goofy when I'm excited. And this idea is growing on me fast. You're so right that we should take a vacation. We deserve it! It'll make our customers miss us. They'll end up appreciating us more because we're not always at their beck and call.

Right? I hate being taken for granted. More than anything."

"That's the spirit! Let's go!"

"Okay. I guess I just need to pack and take care of a couple of things at home first. Do you want to wait for me here? There are plenty of breakfast treats! I made the blueberry scones you like." He laughed, half nervous and half triumphant. This was probably the best day of his life.

He was such a spaz. But Molly had to love him.

"So we're good?" she confirmed. "You'll be back soon?"

"Golden."

* 33 *

RING OF FIRE

*M*ardi found Trent or Tris or Trystan, or whoever the Hell he was, climbing off the *Dragon*. He gave her a big open smile that implied he was ready to pick up where they had left off yesterday. What kind of idiot did he take her for?

"Hey, beautiful, I missed you last night. You should have stayed," he said with a slow, sexy grin.

She put her hands on her narrow hips and glared at him with the full force of her dark, dark eyes.

He returned her cruel stare with a confused look. How had she ever been drawn to those blue eyes? She saw them now for what they really were: watery, shifty, weak.

"Mardi, is there something wrong?"

"You are scum, and the only reason I'm stooping to talk to you right now is to tell you that I'm never going to speak to you again. Oh, and also that I'm quitting my job. In case that isn't obvious."

"What are you talking about?" He looked and

sounded genuinely baffled. But she knew now what a skilled player he was. To assume such divergent parts as to be able to seduce both Overbrook sisters at once, in alternating moments, you had to be more than a brilliant actor; you had to have a split personality.

"Give it up will you?" She seethed. "Dude, I think you're a psychopath. If I cared about you even one little bit, I'd consider having you committed. But I wouldn't lift a finger to help you now. I saw you with her yesterday. In the greenhouse at Fair Haven."

"With who? I wasn't at Fair Haven yesterday, Mardi. I was here, with you."

"Are you really going to make me spell it out?"

He looked at her expectantly.

"Fine, Trystan Gardiner. Here is how it went down. After we hung out on your boat yesterday afternoon, I got a text telling me to go to the greenhouse in Fair Haven. I assume it was from you, since you obviously enjoy messing with people's heads. I went because you've been threatening to hurt my sister if I don't do everything you say. But you know that, of course."

The color drained from his face.

Mercilessly, she continued. "And when I got to the greenhouse, what do you think I saw? I saw you sucking face with my twin sister, yeah . . . we're identical . . . whom apparently you've been leading on whenever you aren't busy trying to get in *my* pants."

"Mardi, wait. I think I might know what's going—"

"I know what's going on—you're sick!"

"Mardi," he thundered, taking a step toward her, his face red with frustration, "listen, will you? Whoever that guy was, it wasn't me."

"Oh, right. As if there are two of you—"

"I was here with you. I was here all night. I wish you'd stayed with me. I've never met your sister before. Listen to me."

"I saw you!" Hadn't she? Hadn't she gotten a good look at him as Molly pulled his pastel polo off over his head.

Pastel polo?

When did Trent ever wear polo shirts?

Not to mention Bermuda shorts.

But it was definitely Trent, wasn't it?

The doubt must have showed on her face, because Trent began to talk again. "Look, I think I know what's happening here. I think I know who's been sending you those messages and who was with your sister. And if I'm right, he's very dangerous. We have to make sure your sister isn't with him. Do you know where Molly is right now?"

"Nice try," she sneered, turning to go.

He tried to hold her back by the shoulder. As she turned around to punch him, he blocked her, grabbing her wrist.

"Get your hands off me!"

"Mardi, please listen." He let go of her wrist.

"To what? More lies?"

"Look down at your right hand," he said.

"Why?" she asked. Yet even as the question escaped her lips, she knew the answer. It was on her middle finger.

Her ring.

"I slipped that ring back on you yesterday. I needed to get it on your body without you knowing in order for you to assume its power again. That's the way the curse works. If you demand the ring, it assumes its destructive power. If you receive it, it becomes pacified. And that's why I haven't been able to be open with you until now. I had to wait until the ring was restored. And for that to happen, I had to find it."

"Where? What?"

"I stole it back for you, Mardi. It was taken from your sister in an unconscious moment, and I retrieved it. Whoever possesses that ring has massive power. All those accidents, those near deaths in town over the past week, those beaten women, were the ring bearer's experiments with his newfound domination. If I hadn't gotten it back to you, anything could have happened. Hold on to it, please. Don't let anyone take it from you until we figure out what to do."

Although she was beginning to believe him, Mardi was still on guard. "So if that wasn't you in the greenhouse with Molly, who is the guy who looks *exactly* like you except for the clean-cut clothes?"

"I think his name is Alberich. He's a shape-shifter

who's long been in disfavor with our kind. He's been after your ring for centuries, while your mother and her sisters shared it."

My mother and her sisters?

The maidens in the pool.

Rhinemaidens.

Thor had said their mother was a hottie, and more importantly, that the twins carried part of their parents' spirits and memories with them.

"Okay, so let me get this straight. You stole our ring back from a creep who passes himself off as you."

"Well, not exactly. When the wine cellar caved in, and I realized I hadn't seen the ring on your finger in a while, I went to talk to Jean-Baptiste. He had noticed that neither you or Molly had it in your last session with him, and he was very concerned. I couldn't tell you directly, and neither could he, because if you yourself had gone after the ring, knowing what it could do, its power could have turned on you. It's cursed, Mardi. You dominate it while it is on your person, but as soon as it leaves the warmth of your—or Molly's—flesh, it becomes incredibly, irrationally dangerous. Alberich thinks he can harness its power for himself, but he has no real control over it, not the way you guys do. He wants to use it to take revenge on the women of the world, to subjugate them and make them suffer, because he has felt humiliated for centuries by their rejection. He wants to enslave them. To see them burned by the state as witches. He wants to unleash the kind of wave of lawless paranoia that the world hasn't seen since the Salem witch trials."

"So you're saying he made himself look like you in order to convince Molly that he was Trystan Gardiner and seduce her to get ahold of our ring? So he could punish us for being powerful female witches?"

"Something like that. As I said, he's a shape-shifter. So he could take my form, but he could also take others. He could have looked like almost anyone in town when he got the ring off her body. The only feature he can't change is the color of his eyes, which, if you look closely, are a much lighter, colder blue than mine. That's how you could have told us apart if you'd gotten closer."

She stared at him, at his warm blue eyes that shone with affection.

"I'm telling you the truth," he said. "Please believe me."

She looked into his eyes, and somehow she knew he wasn't lying. Ingrid herself had said she couldn't believe Trystan would do something so awful.

"The eyes aren't the only difference," she finally said.

"Thanks. That means a lot." He took her hand. "The reason Alberich became Tris was to keep a constant eye on Molly once he had taken the ring. He's a maniac. He's experimenting right now in order to harness the ring's power for his master plan. In the meantime, he doesn't care who gets in the way."

She gasped.

"What?"

"Those kids who died in the subway accident in New York. The ones we're accused of killing or brainwashing or whatever. We've been trying to figure out why they were targeted. But now I see they *weren't* targeted! They were anonymous victims, collateral damage. Alberich stole our ring and was going after us, trying to get us accused and punished." Mardi was shaking. "They just happened to be in the wrong place at the wrong time."

"I'm sorry," said Trent.

"Bret! He's Alberich!"

"Who's Bret?"

"The host of the party. It was his penthouse. He must have drugged us, stolen our ring, and entertained himself by sacrificing two of his party crashers on the tracks of the 6 train, then he framed us for the murders. And now he's morphed into Trystan Gardiner . . . Wait, I can't believe I haven't asked you—how'd you find the ring?"

"He's a Nibelung from the shadow world. He likes to burrow. I knew he would bury it. And his arrogance would push him to bury it somewhere symbolic."

"But how did you know it was the greenhouse?"

"I didn't. I got really lucky. I was feeding Killian's flytrap, and I noticed the dirt under the box of worms was loose. I had a premonition, and I started to dig."

She looked at him admiringly. "I think someone

guided you to the ring. Someone powerful and benevolent. I think someone is watching over us."

"Listen, we have to find your sister before she tries to get to Tris and give him Hell like you gave me. That wouldn't end well. Alberich does not respond positively to criticism."

"I can try texting her, but she'll probably blow me off."

"Tell her it's an emergency."

"I have a better idea."

✳ 34 ✳

LEAVING HERE

$\mathcal{M}$arshall should have been back by now. Molly had made herself two cappuccinos, eaten a morning glory muffin and a blueberry scone, bemoaned eating so much, and rearranged the cracker shelf in the store so that it moved from lightest to darkest packaging. If he didn't get there soon, she was going to start messing with the geography of his cheese case, switching the French chèvre with the Italian capra. She had never been so anxious to get moving in her life.

Her phone vibrated, and she pulled it from her tote, hoping it was him. No such luck. Just a message from Mardi. Great. She didn't even want to read it.

Technically, what had happened with Trystan wasn't Mardi's fault. It was Trystan who was the total sociopath, just like the rest of those Gardiner brothers. Rationally, Molly knew this, and deep down she knew that her sister was as hurt and humiliated as she was.

The only reason they'd had a fight was that they were both mortified, and neither one could handle seeing her mirror image reflected in the other. They liked to think they were so different. And yet they had been fooled by the same guy.

She didn't read Mardi's text, because she didn't feel like answering it just yet.

Still, Molly figured that once she'd had a bit of time to simmer down, she would return to town and ally herself with Mardi, and together they would take the sleazebag down. *Hard.* Even if he was a warlock like he claimed, he would be no match for the two of them in full fury mode. He'd better be taking his vitamins right now. In a few days, his sick joke was going to turn on him.

But right now, she wasn't ready to do anything except run away and forget. Marshall, she realized, was what she had wanted all along. He was kind and funny and creative, and he made her feel like she was all these things too. He believed there was sweetness in her. And the force of his belief made her feel as good as she ever had.

She knew now that Marshall was a great guy. But what was taking him so long? If he didn't drive up soon, customers were going to show up and ruin everything.

She fiddled with the window display. Maybe she should read her sister's text. It might be important. Okay, she would read it, but she certainly wouldn't let Mardi know her whereabouts or her plans. She had to retain at least some dignity in this disaster.

Molly flicked on her screen and gasped. Mardi had sent a photo of their ring, on the middle finger of her right hand.

Look familiar? It's back. Where r u? Need to talk.

She typed back: I'll tell u, but only if u promise to give it to me.

Even as she finished typing, she was surprised by her reaction. She'd never been covetous of the ring before. It had always been the one thing that escaped the realm of their competition, like a free radical hopping between them. But something had changed since she discovered they were kissing the same guy.

Seeing the ring on her screen had made her sick to her stomach. She wanted it back, and she didn't want Mardi to have it. Couldn't she have one thing that was hers alone? She and Mardi shared everything—the same lustrous dark hair, the same blue-black eyes, the same nose, the same dimple on the right cheek!

She was tired of sharing everything.

A thought occurred to her that made her suddenly furious. What if Mardi had actually been hiding the ring from her this whole time? She knew it was irrational, but stranger things were happening these days.

Molly got so mad at her hypothesis that she burst all the jars on the pickle shelf. When that didn't quite satisfy her rage, she glared at the bottles of homemade organic ketchup until, one by one, they smashed, dribbling a reddish brown glop down the glass of the counter. It looked like a crime scene.

There. She felt better.

Marshall finally pulled up at the curb in the old yellow pickup truck he used to gather local produce. Only now she wasn't quite ready to go with him.

Mardi had texted back: OK. You can have it. Just come back will you?

Molly smiled triumphantly. At shop. Meet me here.

"Ready to go?" Marshall called through his open window with a touch of nervous impatience.

"Actually, not quite."

"Do you need me to come in and help you carry anything?"

"No, I'm fine." The last thing she needed was for him to see the havoc she had caused with her little tantrum just now. He'd never be able to leave his controlling mom's precious shop in that state. They'd be stuck here cleaning for days. If they left now, it would be easy to blame on vandals when they got back. After all, there had been such a rash of seemingly random destruction in town. Her mess would fit right into the pattern. And someone else, as always, would clean it up.

She just had to stall him long enough for Mardi to arrive. She might have to resort to magic if her sister didn't show soon. There was no way she was leaving that ring behind.

"Molly, we really should get a move on. It's getting late."

"Hold your horses. I'm waiting to say good-bye to my sister, okay? She's on her way."

"What? Why?" he asked, sounding uncharacteristically annoyed.

Before Marshall could protest further, the Ferrari came screeching around the corner of Main Street. It stopped right in front of Molly. Mardi rolled down the window, and Molly was instantly mesmerized by the ring glowing on her hand.

"Mine," she said.

"Fine, Molly. But we need to be careful." Mardi slipped the ring off and handed it to Molly. "Please get in the car."

"Give me a minute to close up the shop," Molly hedged. She looked back at Marshall in the cab of his truck, but couldn't see him.

She ran into the quaint little wallpapered bathroom at the back of the shop, unhooked a thin gold chain around her neck, slipped the ring around it, fastened it carefully, and checked her reflection in the mirror over the washbasin. The ring was much shinier than she recalled. The diamond etchings in the band seemed more pronounced now, and the metal was radiant. It was as though she had never really looked at the ring before and was finally seeing it for the treasure it had always been.

Feeling stronger and steadier now that she had it back, she rushed outside and was startled to see her sister standing right at the door with a serious look on her face.

"I get it," Molly said, preempting the lecture Mardi

was sure to deliver. "We have a lot to talk about. But right now—" She froze midsentence. There was Tris himself, running up behind Mardi. And Mardi was turning to him as if he was a close friend.

"Mardi, have you completely lost your mind? What is going on? Do you remember what this guy did to us?"

"We can explain," Mardi said, her face hopeful and pleading.

"Uh-huh!" Molly said. "It's all falling into place now. You've been in on this all along, haven't you? That whole act back at Ingrid's about how shocked you were to see me kissing Trystan in the greenhouse was a total scam. The two of you have been playing a joke on me!"

"Molly, come on. Please don't be so paranoid! I would *never* do that to you. And I wouldn't be able to stand you kissing a boyfriend of mine even if it was the best joke in the world. You're not being logical."

But now that she understood the magnitude of the deceit all around her, Molly couldn't bear to listen to her sister pretending to reason with her. Not for another second. It was simply too offensive. She turned to Tris. "I don't know who or what you are, but get out of my way."

But Tris didn't move. Instead, he attempted yet another one of his tricks. "Molly, I'm not Tris, and I never have been. I've never met you till today. I go by Trent. Everyone in town knows me by that name. There's never been anyone named Tris Gardiner."

"What are you talking about?"

"Please let me try to explain," he said, actually sounding sincere.

"Come on, Molly," Mardi pleaded. She was truly an excellent actress. "Hear us out."

Did they take her for an utter moron? "No way. You guys are the people I least want to hear from right now."

With that, she ran to the truck, opened the door, and said, "Okay. I'm ready."

"Great," Marshall said with a broad smile, gunning it out onto the road.

"If my sister thinks I'll listen to anything they have to say, she has another thing coming. I'm never setting foot in North Hampton again."

They drove in silence for a while. Not until they were on the outskirts of town among the fields of potatoes and corn, where the old farmhouses were acres apart, did Molly begin to exhale. She fingered the ring she wore around her neck. "We never really learned the Cookie Monster lesson," she said, touching it gently.

"It's all right," he said. Then, still driving fast, he reached over with his right hand to carefully take the ring between his thumb and forefinger. "Pretty." His fingers were sort of grimy, she noticed.

"Thanks," she said, then pulled it away, uncomfortable at the thought of anyone else touching it right then. It was hers.

The ring was finally hers alone.

* 35 *

YOUR LYIN' EYES

Mardi watched with a sinking feeling as Marshall's yellow pickup disappeared down the lane. Did Molly really believe Mardi was capable of playing such a horrid prank deliberately? It was an awful blow to realize how estranged they were. Sure, they bickered and scratched at each other, but in the end, they were sisters . . . twin sisters. They only had each other, really.

"I can see why she doesn't believe us," Mardi sighed. "You and me showing up together when she still thinks you're the one who totally screwed her over and made her look foolish. Looking foolish might be Molly's worst nightmare. And as far as she's concerned, that nightmare has come true. I know, because I felt the same way she does until only an hour ago. I just wish I could have convinced her to let me explain."

Trent put his arm around her. "It's not your fault. Give her a day or two to calm down, and then you'll be able to reach her. As long as she doesn't have the ring, she's safe. But for now, you and I need to figure out what to do with that toxic thing."

"What do you mean?" Panic rising, Mardi looked at her bare hand.

"You gave her the ring?"

"She's my sister—we share it! She asked for it back."

"And you gave it to her?"

"Yes! That's the way we operate. It's both of ours! It's our only bond. I had to give it to her, especially now. I thought it would make her trust me. Also I sort of felt like the ring wanted to go to her. I don't know, maybe I'm imagining it. It's hard to tell anything for sure right now, when we're all in such high gear. But I wanted it off my finger. The urge was stronger than I am."

"Nothing is stronger than you, Mardi," he said.

His words flooded her with a new sense of purpose. He was so beautiful, his skin golden in the morning sun, his muscles taut in anticipation of the challenge ahead. She wanted to pull him back into the Ferrari and have her way with him in the passenger seat, but this was no time to let herself be distracted.

"We have to think . . . Molly is in danger from Alberich as long as she's got the ring. And she has no idea that Tris is really Alberich. So if he finds her . . ."

Trent scratched his nose. "You saw the way she reacted to me just now, when she thought I was Tris. She's not going to let Tris anywhere near her, except maybe to try to blow his head off. And I'm sure Alberich knows that. He's going to try to get to her as someone else."

"Yeah, thankfully, I don't think she'd be all that delighted to let Bret into her personal space right now either."

"No one she trusts?"

"Well, there's Cheeseboy, but he doesn't cou—" Her heart leapt into her mouth. She had a sudden vision of Marshall's blue eyes twinkling. The image superimposed in her mind with that of Bret's baby blues lit up under the body of his giant bronze spider.

Her memory was kicking back in. The haze of forgetfulness was clearing. She knew with absolute certainty that Marshall's eyes were Bret's eyes. They both had the same long tapering fingers, so appealing at first and ultimately so menacing. "Trent, that guy who just drove her away in his pickup—that's him! Bret! I mean Alberich!"

"Wait—what—who?"

"The guy—in the pickup truck—he owns the cheese store?"

"What guy?"

"Marshall Brighton—he grew up here with his mom. He runs the store for her while she globe-trots or something. He said it's been here for ages."

"His mom?" Trent frowned and his eyes were cloudy and confused. "No. That's wrong. That place popped up a few weeks before you two arrived."

"He seemed like such a great guy. He was always trying to show Molly and me how to forget our differences and bond."

"Sound familiar?"

"What are you saying?"

"Think about the nature of the ring itself. For as long as you can remember, it's masqueraded as a sisterly bond between you. For years, it's been hiding its destructive power. Evil can lurk for a long time in the sweetest of guises."

"Well, we have to get it back! And we have to get my sister back!" They ran back to the car and slammed the doors. Mardi hit the gas and floored the pedal, but even as they drove quickly through town, she knew they could be anywhere by now. Even the Ferrari wasn't fast enough to cover every possible hideaway on the East End before it would be too late.

"I can't believe I let her leave with him!" she cried.

"It's not you. It's the ring. It's Alberich. It's fate. But we can turn it around. There has to be a way."

"Jean-Baptiste! He can help! Maybe he'll have some guidance or know some way to visualize their whereabouts."

"Good idea."

They drove to Rose Cottage, where Mrs. Green told them that Mr. Mésomier had gone out earlier.

"Did he say when he would be back?"

"No, I'm sorry, he didn't. Would you like to come in and wait? I have delicious coffee and fresh-squeezed orange juice and a basket of scones from that lovely Cheesemonger shop. I'd be so delighted to entertain you until Mr. Mésomier returns. I'm so very fond of you young people."

As fast as they could, Mardi and Trent begged off and jumped back into the car.

"Where to now?" she asked, agitated.

"If only we could find a way of scanning the landscape for that yellow truck. We need a bird's-eye view . . . I've got it! There's an airport in East Hampton! We can charter a plane! How fast can this old girl get us to East Hampton?"

"The Ferrari isn't old—she's experienced! There's a big difference." She couldn't believe she was arguing this point right now. Like anything mattered except finding her sister. But somehow it seemed important to keep perspective.

Perspective. A bird's-eye view. When in her life had she ever really had perspective?

Then it hit her. The answer.

"We're not going to East Hampton. We don't need a plane." Without another word, she turned on her ignition, shifted into gear, and drove like lightning, tearing through the sleepy streets of North Hampton, heading to the only recourse she knew.

✳ 36 ✳

MONTAUK

𝓜olly sat across from Marshall at the breezy outdoor restaurant of the Crow's Nest, atop a gentle hill sloping down to the shore of Lake Montauk, about a mile outside the groovy surfer town. She was trying to relax, but she was still angry at Trystan as well as the whole confusing mess in New York, angry at Daddy for sending her to East End in the first place. Worst idea ever. But her fiercest fury was reserved for her sister. Mardi was dead to her. And yet Molly couldn't get Mardi out of her mind.

"This will help," said Marshall as their waiter uncorked and poured a French Provençal rosé.

"Yeah," she said, trying to muster some enthusiasm. "Daddy always says there's nothing like a little wine at lunch to make you feel like you're on vacation. Which basically means that he's been on vacation every day of his life."

The waiter placed a dish of grilled octopus on a bed of spiced yogurt in between them along with two small share plates. Delicately, Marshall cut the octopus in half. She admired the precise motions of his long graceful hands, which were almost clean now. He'd obviously scrubbed them since they arrived at the hotel, although there was still a trace of dirt beneath his fingernails. She noticed for the first time that his spidery fingers were not unlike Tris's, a weird coincidence that made her stomach twist. She had to get ahold of herself.

"Look, whatever happened between you guys, it's over. And whoever he is, he never deserved you. We're out of North Hampton now. If you don't want to go back, we never have to."

"What do you mean, never go back? What about your mom's shop?"

He shrugged.

Was he proposing or something? All the other tables around them were laughing and lighthearted. She wasn't up for some big declaration of undying love right now. She was here to forget, not to fend off crazy propositions.

"Or if you'd like, we could talk about the weather, or the flight path of those ducks down there on the lake, or something really pleasant and meaningless."

Sarcasm? From sweet Cheeseboy? The last thing she felt like dealing with was his adolescent petulance right now. She decided to ignore it. "Anyway, cheers, and thanks for bringing me here." She lifted her rosé glass to his.

He looked down at his plate and batted around a

piece of octopus. He seemed to be groping for the right words to say. Finally, he said, his blue eyes blazing, "Everything I've done is for you."

His intensity was making her uncomfortable. She put down the fork she had been about to raise to her mouth and began to fidget with the neckline of her dress. There was something odd here that she couldn't place, something deeply amiss. Maybe it hadn't been such a good idea to bolt from reality after all. Maybe she should have stayed in North Hampton and faced the music. Maybe she was missing her last chance to solve the enigma of what happened in New York. What if her leaving with the ring meant that Jean-Baptiste could no longer help the others? He had been quite clear when she had gone to consult him: the ring was key.

As she reached to touch it where it dangled in her cleavage, Marshall grabbed her hand and caressed it with surprising skill. A totally unexpected jolt of excitement passed through her body. She felt herself give him an electric smile almost against her will.

"Is everything to your liking?" the waiter asked, interrupting.

Molly nodded, even if she couldn't keep her eyes off Marshall's blue ones as the waiter refilled their glasses and cleared their appetizer plates. "Your main courses will be out in just a minute."

She barely heard the waiter. "What were you saying before? About how everything was for me?"

"Everything I did this summer was for you," he whispered.

She knew he was cute, but had she ever noticed just how cute?

He strengthened his hold on her. "What do you say we skip dessert—"

Just then, the waiter chimed in. "I would wait to make that decision until the time comes if I were you. We have a pretty tempting dessert menu. I would personally recommend the peach and basil crumble and the wild blueberry crème brûlée, but if you are chocolate lovers, the mousse is incredible."

Molly had no idea what this guy was talking about. And, judging from Marshall's rapt expression, he wasn't paying any attention to the dessert options either.

She took a long cool drink. "I'm not hungry all of a sudden. Do you think we should just skip lunch entirely?" She was churning with desire. How had this happened so fast? One minute she was annoyed with him, and the next, she wanted nothing more than to hook up. How had it never happened before during all those hours working side by side at the shop? Had her infatuation with Tris blinded her to this awesome guy who was right under her nose?

"What are you suggesting?" he asked, a sexy resonance to his sweetness that she had never noticed before.

"It's like what you said that time I was looking for my ring in the shop. Sometimes you're so used to seeing something—or someone—all the time that it's hard to actually notice what's awesome about him."

At her mention of the ring, she reached for it instinctively, and again he seized the moment to take her hand.

"I never thought I'd hear you say anything like that." He was practically trembling. "I've—I've been infatuated with you, Molly. And not just because you are the most bewitchingly beautiful girl I've ever seen. Your potential is enormous. Together, we could be fantastic."

Although she wasn't sure what he meant, she was swept away by the grandeur of his language and the racing of her own pulse. Nothing mattered in this magical moment except for the here and now, in Montauk, with him. Not the looming trial in New York. Not the White Council. Not Daddy freaking out. Not her treacherous sister. And certainly not Trystan Gardiner.

Somehow they managed to finish their lunch and stave off the waiter's enthusiasm for dessert and coffee. Marshall signed the bill to his room number, and they set out arm in arm, hip to hip.

The minute they were outside the restaurant, he pulled her in for a deep kiss.

"What do you say we share a room tonight?" she sighed, whispering in his ear.

"I want that more than anything, believe me. I've waited so long."

* 37 *

LEARNING TO FLY

$\mathcal{M}$ardi and Trent burst into Ingrid's house to find Ingrid, Freya, and Jean-Baptiste in a cluster around the coffee table. For once, there was no food or drink in sight. All three looked tired and defeated. The kids' toys lay scattered on the floor, but the kids themselves were nowhere to be seen. Midnight meowed aimlessly through a picture window onto the empty front yard, a living barometer of the family stress.

Briefly, Mardi wondered where Killer was and how Killer and Midnight were getting along. But this was no time to ask about cats.

Barely registering the presence of Trent, Ingrid looked up at Mardi. She didn't even say hello. "Your father called about an hour ago. It seems there's fresh evidence against you. Apparently there are several witnesses willing to testify to the fact that you and Molly threatened that young couple who died. You told them you were going to mess with their minds. You actually came out and bragged to them that you were witches!"

"No, we didn't! Even if we did, we weren't ourselves. Listen, we know what happened now. But we need your help to make it right."

Jean-Baptiste let out a tired sigh. "I'm afraid it's too late, Mardi. We did our best. But evil has been unleashed and you are blamed. Now your fate—our fate—is at the mercy of the mortal realm."

"Yeah," said Freya bitterly. "And we know how well that turned out for us last time." She drew a deadly finger across her throat.

"Well, I don't know about you guys," Mardi persisted, "but I'm not giving up."

"And I'm right behind her," said Trent.

"Trystan!" Ingrid said. "What a surprise. Mardi, what's going on?"

"Look, there's no time to go into details right now. You were right about Trystan—I mean Trent. But um, we need your brooms. Immediately."

Ingrid went crimson. "If you think, young lady, that after all the trouble you've caused, I'm going to open up my broom closet just because you've asked—"

"Ingrid, please!" Jean-Baptiste interjected as Freya took Ingrid's arm.

Ingrid shook Freya off. "You and your sister have put our whole community at risk! Everything we've worked for! We are refugees here! We should be sticking together, taking care of each other. And you've broken that covenant!"

"I know." Mardi wasn't backing down, but she was

crying tears of regret—and tears of determination. "And I'm going to do something about it. If you really care, Ingrid, then listen."

"You should hear her out," said Jean-Baptiste.

"Come on, Ingrid," Freya pleaded. "Give them a chance."

Ingrid raised an eyebrow. "Fine. I'm listening."

Mardi stumbled over herself to get her story out, with Trent interjecting here and there to clarify where he could.

They explained that the ring that Molly and Mardi had been wearing on their right hands was a legendary ring. A cursed object of intense desire that possessed such power that, in the wrong hands, it could unleash terrible violence and cause great suffering.

Everyone wanted it.

And no one should have it.

They told them about Alberich transforming himself. In his New York incarnation as Bret Farley, he had murdered Parker Fales and Samantha Hill to test the power of the ring he had borrowed from the unsuspecting twins and to frame them so that they would literally be sent to Hell. He had used his newfound strength to cloud their memories, but had not been able to resist the temptation of torturing them by leaving them with certain vivid mental scraps from his triumphant night. That was why they had retained such striking images and impressions of the bronze spider, the black pool, the blaring Wagner.

He wanted to lord his power over the beautiful twins who were the talk of all New York. To take his revenge on the daughters of the Rhinemaidens who had taunted him centuries ago, and on all their kind, mortal and immortal.

Here in North Hampton, Alberich had taken on two alternating shapes. He was Tris Gardiner, and he was Marshall Brighton. The seducer and the sweetheart. He had managed to steal the ring from Molly yet again, which explained the series of accidents and near accidents plaguing the town. Alberich was playing puppeteer. And women were his primary victims. He hated women. Ever since his rejection by the Rhinemaidens, he had dreamed of growing powerful enough to subjugate and humiliate them for all time. That was why, now that he had the ring again, so many women were being threatened and hurt.

The ring had the power to unleash vast evil. For years Molly and Mardi had unconsciously kept this evil at bay. But in Alberich's hands, its gold was beginning to burn with a bright malice. While he was experimenting with it and learning to control it, Alberich had kept the ring buried in the greenhouse at Fair Haven, where Trent, who knew the ancient legend, had found it.

That morning, Trent had given Mardi the ring, but Mardi, desperate to earn her sister's trust, had passed the ring back to Molly. And Molly had immediately run off with it. By now, she could be anywhere on the East

End. She was with Marshall, but she had no idea he was really Alberich. If Marshall got ahold of the ring again, there was no telling what he would do to Molly this time. They had to save Molly. And they had to get the ring away from Alberich before he not only ruined the twins' lives but found all sorts of hideous outlets for his raging misogyny. If he realized his dream, powerful women were going to burn as witches again.

"And the only way to find them fast enough," said Mardi breathlessly, "is on your and Freya's brooms. We know you have them, Ingrid. Hiding in the attic. Jo showed them to us the other day."

Ingrid couldn't suppress a slight smile.

"Freya, Ingrid," Jean-Baptiste began with gentle authority, "I think you should give these two a chance. They've shown great ingenuity and a true desire to plumb their memories for the truth. If we don't empower them now, we give in to the forces that are out to destroy our way of life."

Freya didn't hesitate. "You're welcome to my broom!"

Mardi flew to embrace her and was consumed for a moment in Freya's sweet musky scent. "Thank you, Freya."

"All right." Ingrid was starting to give. "But we have to cast a very powerful concealment spell. The last thing we need is for the White Council to get wind of UFO sightings on the East End that look suspiciously like witches on broomsticks. We won't be able to give you full visibility, you know. It's going to be tricky." She was suddenly struck by a fresh doubt. "You *have* flown before?"

Neither Mardi nor Trent answered.

"Mardi?" Ingrid wasn't going to let this slide.

Mardi looked pleadingly at Jean-Baptiste.

He nodded with encouragement.

"Only a few times in the Caribbean with Dad," she admitted. "He taught Molly and me during our spring breaks, in empty skies. Kind of like driving in a parking lot, I guess. He told us that if he ever caught us flying in a populated area, we'd be grounded until the end of time . . . But I do know how to steer and stuff. And I'm super coordinated." Mardi realized she wasn't painting the ultimate picture of responsibility, all raccoon-eyed in yesterday's rumpled clothes. But she'd come too far to give up now.

"What about you, Trystan?" Ingrid asked.

Trent squirmed. "Ingrid, please call me Trent."

"Maybe I should call you by your real name, Tyr, the god of war? I can't help but think you are a little bit to blame for what has happened to these girls this summer."

He nodded. "But this time I'm on your side, Ingrid. It's why I came back to North Hampton. To help stop the spread of violence that Alberich and his ring have started. I've been practicing my tolerance for adversity and uncertainty. This is my calling. At the same time"—here he looked straight at Mardi—"I'm falling in love for the first time."

Mardi could only blush deeply to the roots of her dark hair.

"All right, I'll get the brooms," Ingrid said. "On one condition. Freya flies with Mardi. There's no way I'm calling Troy to tell him one daughter has been kidnapped and the other has wiped out against a telephone pole. Let's go, Freya."

Freya and Ingrid ran upstairs, with Midnight at their heels, to get their brooms from the hidden closet behind Freya's amazing array of clothes and shoes.

Jean-Baptiste closed his eyes and began to murmur a series of ancient protective spells. Mardi reached over to take Trent's hands.

"Hey, Tyr," she whispered.

"Hey, Magdi."

God of war. Goddess of rage. They belonged together.

When Jean-Baptiste opened an enquiring eye on them, they both giggled. "It always stuns me," he said, straightening the silver gray pocket square in his plaid jacket, "how quickly you young people can lose your gravitas even in the most dire situations."

"Sorry!" they said sheepishly.

"Oh, my goodness, don't be sorry. It's a gift you have, a wonderful gift. If we all felt the weight of the world in every single moment, we would be in a very sorry state. Please, keep laughing."

Ingrid and Freya, still shadowed by Midnight, appeared at the bottom of the stairs, broomsticks in hand. Mardi was struck by how ordinary looking the broomsticks were. Simple wood and straw. And yet they were the means by which she was about to save her sister, and hopefully save her family, such as it was, while at the same time squelching a force of evil that threatened the women of both the human and the witching worlds. These brooms looked like such a low-tech solution to a massive problem that for a moment she doubted everything.

Soon she was outside, high in the afternoon sky, the land and water rolling out below in a glorious patch-work. For a few moments, she could still make out Ingrid's watchful figure, the little black cat perched on her shoulder, taking it all in.

The Earth was beautiful from above. She was sitting behind Freya. Beside her, Trent looped and circled. She had never felt closer to people she loved. Except one of them was missing and in grave danger. *Molly Moll, where are you?*

As the magical rescue team broke through the misty barrier enshrouding North Haven, a protective layer created centuries ago by Joanna Beauchamp and main-tained now by her dutiful daughters, the East End opened up before them, a narrow strip of bright green-ery and golden sand jutting out into the bright sea.

Mardi felt something move in the suede bag she wore over her shoulder. She reached to adjust it and touched the top of a soft, familiar head poking playfully out from under the flap. But it wasn't her cat. She looked down to meet Fury's sorrowful gaze. Molly's familiar wanted his mistress back. "I know how you feel. We'll get her back, buddy—don't worry. I'm glad you came along for the ride."

38

I SHALL BE RELEASED

*M*olly's room at the Crow's Nest was the ultimate in beach chic, with white clapboard walls, blond floors, driftwood mirrors, a blue-and-white batik bedspread, and soft sheer curtains billowing with a late-afternoon breeze. It was like making out inside the pages of the Calypso Home catalog.

Marshall was an amazing kisser, and his wiry arms were proving strong and almost comforting. She felt lulled by his touch and was drifting softly into a beautiful oblivion.

So when she finally realized that Marshall was whispering the word *mine*, over and over again between kisses, she had no idea how long this had been going on and no grasp at all on what it might mean, although she felt a wave of nausea from hearing the word.

"What's mine?" she asked, trying to sound flirtatious.

"Why, Molly," he said, his tone suddenly cold and imperious as he looked down at her, and she realized she was almost naked and felt vulnerable beneath his steady gaze. "You're mine."

"Oh . . . right," she said, wondering why she suddenly felt scared instead of excited.

"But believe it or not, it's not you or your delectable body I really want, although I will take them as my due, but the Rhinegold you wear around your neck. Because the Rhinegold will let me keep you forever. All of you."

Molly pushed him off of her. "Rhinegold." She groped after the memory of that word, mustering all her remaining strength to pierce the fog clouding her mind, and she forced herself to look at him, really look at him.

"Who are you?"

He smiled and for a moment she thought she saw Tris Gardiner's handsome face. Then it changed again, and he was someone else entirely.

"No!" she screamed through a sharp pain in her throat. "Bret! You're Bret!"

Marshall was no longer Marshall. He had grown smaller, and his arm muscles had thickened. His face had morphed into that of the boy from the black pool in Bret's penthouse. Only the ice-blue eyes were unchanged. From his right hand he dangled the rose gold ring from her broken chain.

"I may not be a witch like you, but my sleight of hand is excellent." He cackled. "I ripped it from your neck without you even noticing."

She clawed at the empty space around her throat.

"Cheeseboy is in charge now. As I said, Molly, you're mine now. Along with this ring. And everything it can bring to me."

She tried to protest but discovered she couldn't, and Marshall was the reason why. For the first time in her life, she was on the wrong side of a serious hex. It was a profound lesson in how the other half lived.

But her fighting instincts had not abandoned her. She would bide her time like a reptile in the shade and wait for her moment to strike. She lay back on the bed, pretending to give up, and raised her arms above her head in a seductive pose.

"That's my girl. You looked just like this that night," he said. "Want to see?"

She nodded, thinking it was what he wanted to hear. He pulled her up to the head of the bed and propped her up against a mass of large decorative pillows. She found that her limbs had stiffened and her hands no longer moved at all. Her entire body, except for her eyes and ears, was in the process of shutting down.

"Now you know how it feels to be powerless." He laughed. "Get used to it, Goddess No More."

Instantly, the room darkened as the television screen on the dresser lit up to show a close-up image of Molly's own face. She appeared dazed, drugged even, her pupils dilated and her stare fixed. She looked almost exactly like she felt right now: terrified, yet somehow determined to pierce the veil of her enchantment. Next on the screen, there was an image of Mardi, similarly out of it, but biting her lip in an effort to remain connected to her inner strength. Seeing her sister so vulnerable yet so resolute, Molly wanted to reach out to her through time and space and tell her how sorry she was and how much she loved her.

But it was too late.

Mardi and Trent, she knew with sudden certainty, had been telling the truth that afternoon. She had been too angry to hear it. The curse of discord had been too strong.

Was there time left to fight it?

The screen went blurry, and when it focused again, it showed a shot of the two sisters side by side. They were sitting on a bench in the neon light of a subway platform, wearing their outfits from the night of Bret's party. Molly instantly recognized the red dress and the nude snakeskin pumps she'd bought that same afternoon. Mardi was wearing a skintight silver jumpsuit that she had found at a consignment shop called A Star Is Worn, where stars sold their old clothing and the proceeds were donated to charity. The jumpsuit had belonged to Cher, God knew how many years ago. Molly had made cruel fun of it that night, but seeing it pop out now in this grainy screen image, in all its shiny boldness, she was flooded with a new appreciation for

Mardi's quirks. What if she never saw all those wacky vintage clothes again?

The focus left the twins and started to dart and swerve around the station, finally settling on another pair of figures, whom Molly instantly recognized as Parker and Samantha.

Samantha was clutching her big floral bag. Parker was swaying from foot to foot in his Brooklyn-inspired faux work boots. They were biding their time, waiting for a late-night 6 train, craning their necks to look down the dark tunnel in search of the first glimmer of oncoming headlights. Molly hadn't taken many subways in her life, but from her few experiences, she recognized their gestures of vague impatience.

The camera image started to weave back and forth between the human couple on the edge of the tracks and the pair of dazed witches on the bench.

"You'll have to excuse the handheld look." Bret laughed. "I shot this on my phone."

Slowly, a deep rumble became audible beneath the images. Molly's heart started going wild. Then Bret's voice sounded, crackling through time. "Girls, this is your cue. Get to it!"

What was he talking about? What was he commanding them to do? Molly had a suspicion, but it was too awful to contemplate.

The phone camera zoomed shakily onto Molly and Mardi, who were slowly standing and starting to walk, zombie-like—in the direction of the doomed couple.

Molly's eyes widened in horror as she watched her former self, shot from the back. She was advancing in her high heels toward the unsuspecting mortal pair. Beside her, Mardi strutted, but not with her natural sultry gait. It was a stylized walk, like that of a robotic chorus girl.

Were they really about to push Parker and Samantha to their deaths? What had the poor kids done to deserve such a brutal end to their short lives? Crashed the wrong party? Been in the wrong place at the wrong time? How could she and her sister have forgotten everything about this night?

The answer to these questions flashed suddenly before Molly in the form of the ring, which Bret now held up right in front of the phone camera. It was in such close-up that the diamond pattern looked enormous. For the first time, this pattern struck Molly for what it really was: the motif on the back of a rattlesnake. She couldn't believe that she and her sister had been sharing it for so long. What did that mean, then—that they were evil in nature? Molly was ashamed of herself, ashamed of the two of them.

"The power is mine now!" the on-screen Bret howled with delight.

Even if they had been hypnotized, she and Mardi *were* guilty. And she was about to witness their crime.

As the sound of the oncoming subway train grew louder, Molly wished she could close her eyes to spare herself the sight of what she was about to do. However, not only was she now fully paralyzed on the bed, but her eyes were stuck wide open. With no control or dignity left, she was forced to be a spectator to her own horrific actions.

On-screen, Molly and Mardi approached the unsuspecting couple while Bret whispered triumphantly into his phone. "That's it, girls. A little bit closer, and then you can shove. Make sure you time it right. I think we have about thirty seconds to go." Then he started counting down. "Thirty, twenty-nine, twenty-eight . . ."

When he reached twenty-seven, an incredible thing happened. Molly and Mardi stopped in their tracks. Trembling with an otherworldly resolve, they turned toward Bret, grasped each other's hands, and cried out in unison, "No!"

"No? You cannot defy me! Obey the ring!" Bret's triumphant tone devolved into one of desperate fury.

But the twins were somehow standing firm.

Their eyes blazed as they held hands.

They were the twin goddesses of rage and strength. Thor's daughters, Magdi and Mooi, daughters of thunder, children of lightning, and together they embodied the spirit of their father's powerful hammer.

A hammer that was falling on the pathetic creature.

The image on the screen began to shake. Bret was getting angry and desperate. As the train lights came into view on the tracks, he suddenly screeched. "You! You, over there! Do it!" And seemingly out of nowhere, an older man with a briefcase appeared, sailing across the platform, barely touching the ground with his wing-tip shoes. He must have been a banker or a lawyer waiting for a late-night train home from some lonely weekend work at the office, but he had been of no interest to Bret and so had not appeared in his video until now.

It was only in the last seconds, since Mardi and Molly had somehow found it within themselves to resist, that this unwitting bystander was pulled in to commit murder so that the twins could be framed. With supernatural speed, he rushed at the doomed couple. Before they even had time to yell, they were shoved onto the tracks. The man turned to leave the station, oblivious to what he had just done.

Then the most extraordinary thing happened.

Molly's memory kicked back in full force. With every fiber of her being, she felt what happened next as it unfolded before her on the television screen.

Still holding hands, she and Mardi had flown into the air and onto the tracks after Parker and Sam.

Witches to the rescue!

Molly saw Mardi grab an astonished and uncomprehending Parker. She herself held Sam in her arms. The girl's face was frozen in a silent scream. And just before anyone hit the rails, the four of them began to soar upward out of harm's way.

Only they were a fraction of a second too late.

Before they were high enough to clear it, the train, its horn blaring wildly, barreled into them.

The last thing Molly saw was the golden ring sailing down after them, flashing into the void. Bret had hurled it at them.

The four of them were killed instantly.

As the screen went dark, Molly's memory went blank again along with it.

"Such useless valiance, such senseless courage," Bret lectured, caressing her motionless thigh. "You and your sister made a pathetic, ridiculous attempt to save those expendable mortals. You had the brazen stupidity to try to combat the power of my ring, but you were obviously no match for it. You will soon learn to obey."

No match for it? But how had they gotten from the horrifying moment under the 6 train to the following day, when she and Mardi had awoken a few minutes past noon, both of them in their beds, feeling a little hungover but not especially worse for wear?

"As you can imagine," Bret droned on, "you goddesses have a connection or two in the Underworld. That's how it always is with you people. You take care of your own. The rest of us, of course, aren't so blessed. Someone called in a favor for you, and you two beauties were returned to the present in the blink of an eye. You never even knew what hit you. Those mortals, not so much. They're not summering on the East End right now, are they? More like being devoured by worms."

Molly's first thought was that Daddy must have gone into overdrive to fix everything, and fast, that very night, to rescue his girls from the jaws of Hell. Then she realized it couldn't have been him, because he didn't know what had happened. If he had had this kind of proof, he would have taken it to the White Council long ago.

So, if not Daddy, then who?

And there was another unanswered question. Why, Molly burned to know, had Bret cast off the ring he was so obsessed with, so that it reappeared the next day on Mardi's right middle finger, as though nothing had happened?

With frightening insight, Bret answered her silent query. "The reason I threw the ring back to you bitches is this: I didn't want you—or anyone else—to link the ring to what had just happened. Now that I had learned how to use it, I wanted to bide my time until I was ready to harness its power to establish a pure world order, with women in their place. I knew I could get it back from you again quite easily when the time was right. Thanks to your vanity, you've been an easy target all along. Like all women, you live to manipulate and are blinded by your childish pride. You've proven quite susceptible to my charms, Molly Overbrook. You've fallen for me behind three different masks now. I've gotta hand it to myself, and you have to admit, you find me irresistible."

She realized now just when he had stolen the ring from her. He hadn't taken it when they'd hooked up at the Fair Haven library, when she assumed it had fallen off in the heat of passion. Instead, he'd taken it at the Cheesemonger, after she had fainted. He had probably caused her to her faint so that he could come to her rescue, so that he could charm her and rob her blind in one fell swoop. Even though she despised him, she couldn't help but recall how tenderly she had felt toward him in that moment. She glared at him now from among the pillows. If she could have moved, she would have scratched his eyes out.

"So, Molly, what you've just seen in my little homespun video was my test run, so to speak." He dangled the ring in her face. "Now we are on to bigger and better things. Too bad you won't be joining me in my glory. You would have made a stunning, if spoiled, queen. But the paralysis you are feeling right now is only going to get worse. By nightfall, your heart will stop. It's a potent spider venom. I distilled it myself and sprinkled it into your rosé. I've always been able to count on your appreciation of the finer things, haven't I? And, besides, I have a great fondness for spiders, in case you haven't noticed. In fact, I adore them. *Maman*, my glorious bronze tarantula, whom I believe your sister admired greatly in my penthouse, is my favorite object on Earth."

Although her nerves were filled with poison, Molly had not entirely lost hope of escape and victory. She might be stuck here on this bed right now, but her twin wasn't.

Although it was irrational for her to expect Mardi to burst into her hotel room at the Crow's Nest Hotel in the wilds of Montauk, when it happened, Molly was not at all surprised.

What took you so long?

39

SISTERS ARE DOING IT FOR THEMSELVES

$\mathcal{M}$ardi was standing in the open doorway, her mouth agape.

She, Trent, and Freya had found the yellow pickup truck parked outside the Crow's Nest and had asked about the young couple, casting a spell on the receptionist to learn where Molly and Marshall were staying. Marshall's room had been empty, so when they found Molly's door, Mardi kicked it down even though it wasn't locked.

The three of them found Molly lying on the bed while that vile boy lay next to her. His features morphed back into Trent's handsome ones, and she recoiled.

"Molly!" Mardi yelled. "You beast, get off her!"

What was wrong with Molly? She was just staring at them speechless. No matter—she, Trent, and Freya tackled Alberich and wrestled him to the ground. She grabbed the ring from his fingers.

Fury jumped out of Freya's bag and started to bark angrily and nip at Alberich's ankles.

Alberich was no match for the four of them. Without the ring in hand, his shrieking threats were empty. Freya and Trent tied him up with the curtain sashes.

"Give it your best shot," he sneered. "You're just as weak as your sister."

"Freya, may I?" Mardi asked.

"Do it," Freya urged.

Mardi punched him unconscious with her bare fists, and then, for good measure, hit him with a catatonic spell. Then she turned to her sister, whom Trent had covered with a blanket.

Her stomach twisted in jealousy a little at that, but she tried to push it aside. "Molly, what's wrong?"

Her sister was utterly still and stone-faced. Fury was nuzzling her neck to no avail.

"There's something wrong with her!" Mardi yelled, taking her sister's hand in hers and noting her dwindling pulse. "I think she's paralyzed!"

"Poisoned, more like it," said Freya, who was an expert. She found a sewing kit in the hotel bathroom, took out a needle, pricked Molly's left index finger, squeezed out three drops of blood onto her own thumb, licked them thoughtfully, and pronounced, "It's a neurotoxic spider venom. He must have transformed it so that it could be given orally. I know the antidote by heart. But I don't have the herbs here that I need to prepare it. We're going to have to get her home, and I'm going to have to rush to the greenhouse for my ingredients. We have to act fast. Mardi, gather her stuff."

"What about Alberich?" Mardi asked, looking at him bound and unconscious on the floor. "Even if we kill him, there's no guarantee he won't claw his way back somehow."

"You all go ahead and take care of Molly," said Trent. "I'll stay here. I've got him covered."

"But what are you going to do with him? I don't understand. How are we going to contain him?" Mardi asked, throwing Molly's clothes haphazardly into her Hermès tote, not even bothering to fold them. She knew Molly would be screaming at her now about being such a slob— if she could. She'd never thought she would want Molly to be able to scream. But she did. More than anything.

"I was thinking about calling the North Hampton police to take him back to town and arrest him," said Trent. "But I've changed my mind. Matt's strong, but I don't imagine he's any match for Alberich's evil charms. And I'm afraid that Matt doesn't know the way to Limbo, which is where he belongs. So I've called upon the Valkyries. They know the way. And they owe me many a favor. The Valkyries and I, we go way back. They'll be here soon, and we'll be rid of Alberich for the foreseeable future. Sound like a plan?"

"Valkyries, huh?" Mardi said, raising an eyebrow. "Those sorority girls?"

"Our brother Freddie knew a few of them quite well," Freya said, her lips curling into a smile.

But as they were lifting Molly to go, she seemed to be trying to tell them something. Her eyes were darting frantically around the room.

"What is it? What do you want to tell us?" Mardi asked, a little crazed. "We don't have time! If we don't get you back to Fair Haven, you're going to die!"

She wished she could understand what Molly was trying to tell them, but she had no idea. What did Molly want? Her tote? She had it packed.

"It's under control, I've packed all your stuff," Mardi said.

Molly emitted a low moan.

"Poor thing," said Freya. "She must be in pain. Don't worry. We'll have you back to yourself in a couple of hours. Stop trying to talk now. You'll only strain yourself."

They picked her up and walked out the door.

But at the very last second, Fury jumped onto the dresser, knocking what looked like a phone to the floor. Fury batted it with her paws so that it skidded across the wooden floor planks straight to Mardi's feet.

She looked down. Of course. This is what Molly had been trying to tell her. "Alberich's phone! Of course! It probably holds all kinds of clues." Mardi leaned down to grab the phone and give the dog a stroke. "Fury, you're a genius." She winked up at her immobile sister. "Who knew you're as smart as my cat?"

40

BLURRED LINES

$\mathcal{I}$t might have been the calming ocean breezes or the general air of forgetfulness that infused North Hampton. Some force, either natural or supernatural, was causing Killer and Fury to forget their differences as August drew to a close. In fact, along with Jo's cat, Midnight, they formed a rather merry band around Ingrid and Matt's house, frolicking on the beach, chasing squirrels, and generally making the resident kids, big and small, feel that all was going to be right with the world.

Mardi was relieved to see that Molly recovered quickly from the spider venom, although she secretly thought that it would have been nice to keep her sister quiet for a day or two longer.

Mardi had helped Freya gather the herbs she needed for the antidote: feverfew, catnip, and angelica root. Then they had gone into the woods, scavenging for very specific toadstools and for the skeletons of snakes and the skulls of small birds. Observing Freya at her craft, Mardi was mesmerized. Maybe she could learn to do the same thing one day.

But she was with Trent now. He had asked her to meet him on the *Dragon*.

"Took you long enough," he said when she arrived.

"I drove here as fast as I could."

Then he was kissing her, and it felt so perfect and sweet and right, and Mardi wondered why she had fought it for so long.

Mardi soon lost her desire to get back to her old life in New York. Her endless nights of underground clubbing were fading to a blurry smudge in her memory. They seemed empty, weightless. She had succumbed to the charms of life on the East End. Could it be, she teased Trent one evening, she actually might want to return to North Hampton next summer?

"Of your own free will?" he asked, gently kissing her eyelids.

"Of my own free will."

Mardi felt almost sorry for Molly, who was not nearly so fulfilled right now as she was.

But Molly was adjusting to her new circumstances without too much drama. She was spending a lot of time helping Ingrid and Matt with the kids and tending to the menagerie of familiar animals now inhabiting the house. Fury, the pricy Löwchen, was, of course, by far the highest maintenance of the family pets. And since there were no options in town for outsourcing the dog's walking, feeding, or ridiculously elaborate grooming, Molly was doing it all herself—with Jo and Henry's enthusiastic help. It was a brave new world of responsibility for Molly. And Mardi couldn't help but hint that it was good for her twin to get down and dirty. Well, relatively down and dirty at least. When she shaved Fury's hindquarters, leaving the hair long at the front and around the ankles, Molly donned a navy-blue Gucci coverall to protect her clothes. And she never failed to wear Ingrid's gardening gloves for any kind of manual labor. Before putting the gloves on, she would slather her hands in lotion, "just like at the salon." She didn't care if her sister teased her. These days, Mardi's teasing only made her smile.

With very little ceremony, the Cheesemonger had closed down. Ocean Vines, the tony wine shop next door that Molly had been briefly attracted to on her job search at the beginning of the summer, was quietly expanding to take over the gourmet store's narrow space. Ashley Green, for one, could already no longer remember when she hadn't risen early to bake for her guests in her own kitchen at Rose Cottage, since there was absolutely nowhere in town to buy a decent muffin or scone. Only Jean-Baptiste, as he prepared to return to New Orleans for the fall, recalled, wistfully, that the raspberry and ginger scones from the Cheesemonger had been nothing short of exquisite.

It would have been a happy and relatively carefree time for the twins were it not for two things. The case back in New York was still looming. Dad had called to somberly announce that a September trial date had now been set. And, even more urgently, no one quite knew what to do at this point with the ring. For now, it was "safe" on Mardi's hand. She seemed to be the only person who could keep its evil in check. Something about her skin nullified the curse. But still, she wanted it off her body. Even if it stayed inactive, it put her in grave danger.

Molly had made it very clear that she would never wear the ring again. It was too bound up for her with the nightmare of her escapade in Montauk. Whenever she looked at it, its pattern seeming to move like a slithering diamondback rattlesnake, she felt a wave of horror.

"Promise me," she said to Mardi, "that when we have our accounts back, we'll come up with a different symbol to float to each other. I never want to see that thing again."

"Of course," Mardi agreed. But that was the least of their problems.

Mardi suggested to Ingrid and Freya that they bury the ring. But Ingrid pointed out that it might poison the soil, ruining crops and causing strange cancers and birth defects.

"Okay, then. Scratch that," Mardi sighed.

"What if we melted it?" Molly asked.

"It wouldn't do any good," Freya said, glancing at the

light on Mardi's finger. "It's not the ring itself but the Rhinegold that's cursed. The Rhinegold can assume any shape at all and still wreak havoc in the world."

The four witches were gathered in Freya's airy living room, sipping fresh-squeezed lemonade from tall glasses on the coffee table, which was nothing more than a simple glass cube. Because this room was so uncluttered, they felt they could think clearly here. Even the piles of Freya's excess clothes were neat and streamlined, like colored pillars in a work of minimalist art. This was neutral territory, slightly outside of space and time, removed from the living chaos of everyday life. It was a place for introspection, and perhaps even for reason.

Mardi, Molly, Freya, and Ingrid were waiting for Jean-Baptiste in order to have a final session. This would not be a memory session per se, since, thanks to Alberich's overpowering need to brag about his crimes and his hatred to Molly, the facts about the fateful New York night had finally been fully recovered. Instead, the witches had asked Jean-Baptiste to help with their remaining dilemmas: how to deal with the ring, how to use the evidence on Alberich's cell phone to prove Mardi and Molly's innocence so that the White Council would be appeased, and how to find out who had saved them from the jaws of death that night, sending them back, oblivious, into the comfort of their beds. Even if the god of memory did not directly provide them with the answers they sought, they hoped that his guiding questions and eminent wisdom would help them come to these answers in his presence.

There was a polite knock on the front door.

Mardi jumped up to answer.

"Hello, Jean-Baptiste. It's really great to see you."

"The pleasure is all mine."

He seemed to arrive everywhere on foot, no matter the distance, without ever having broken a sweat, jacket on, pocket square freshly pressed. He was the incarnation of elegance.

Mardi took a moment to appreciate him. "You're pretty cool for an old guy."

"I'll take that as a compliment." He smiled.

"Come in," Freya said. "We saved your spot for you." She gestured to the tan leather Eames chair.

"I believe," he said, taking his accustomed seat, "that the painful part of our work is now behind us. We are now faced, at present, with practical concerns. These are urgent, yes. But the urgency is of a different nature from before. I hope I can be of some assistance."

They told him that their first order of business was to find a safe place to keep the Rhinegold. They weren't sure how much longer Mardi's magic would be able to neutralize it. The pressure was too great. She wanted it off her finger.

Having listened carefully, Jean-Baptiste began by putting an open-ended query to the witches: "Is there anywhere on this Earth that you could conceive of hiding it?"

Ingrid answered him. "On this Earth, no. Midgard is too fragile an ecology to absorb so much negative energy. With all the global warming and pollution and strife already affecting this planet, a curse this strong would push it into chaos. We can't let that happen. Midgard won't support it."

"Wait a second!" Molly stood and started jumping up and down in her steep wedges.

Mardi winced. She wished her sister could be a tad more dignified. But once she had she heard Molly's idea, she stopped caring. Between exclamations of "OMG!" and "I've got it!" Molly was able to articulate a plan to have Trent ask the Valkyries to come back for the ring and take it for safekeeping into Limbo. "Let it curse people down there for all we care!"

"I never thought I'd say this, Molly, but you're brilliant." Mardi beamed.

Jean-Baptiste was more measured in his response. "Freya? Ingrid? What do you say to this plan?"

Freya answered him first. "I say close, but no cigar."

"Yes," Ingrid echoed. "You're on the right track, girls, but it's not so simple."

The twins cried out in protest together. For once they were able to agree on something, and instead of celebrating with them, Freya and Ingrid were going to poke holes?

"We don't exactly want the Rhinegold in Limbo. There are too many unsavory characters languishing there. And if the Valkyries make a big deal of bringing it down, Alberich might somehow get his hands on it again."

"But," Freya took up Ingrid's thread, "Molly's idea of hiding the ring in another world is an excellent one. And, since North Hampton happens to be located on a seam, we're uniquely placed to get it into the gloaming space that borders the Underworld. If we could find the entrance to the gloaming within the renovated Fair Haven, we could bury the ring there and know that it would be safely out of the way for centuries, or until we find a way to undo the curse."

"The passageway used to be in the ballroom," Ingrid continued. "They changed the paneling in the renovation, but I imagine that beneath it the connection is still intact. I'm sure that Tyr will help us find our way."

"Of course he will," Freya agreed.

"It seems," said Jean-Baptiste in conclusion, "that you have found your solution. And that the four of you have found it together. Bravo."

Mardi tingled with restlessness. Now that there was an end in sight, she wanted to be rid of the ring immediately. "Great! What are we waiting for? I'll text Trent right away. Let's go."

Molly grabbed her bag. "What she said!"

"Just a moment, girls." Ingrid stayed resolutely seated. Why did she always have to be so slow and deliberate about everything? "I know you are eager to rid yourselves of the ring. We all are dying to get it out of our lives, believe me. But, as long as we are fortunate

319

enough to have Jean-Baptiste among us, don't you think we should let him help us come up with a way to prove your innocence in New York? After all, he guided you toward discovering what really happened that night. His instincts are invaluable."

Mardi had to admit that Ingrid had a point. She looked at Molly, who was gently placing her purse back on the floor, ready to stick things out a little longer. They both had realized by now that if they blew the police investigation, the consequences would be dire. The White Council had been quiet of late. No more warning notes to Dad. But this was not to say that the Council did not hold major punishments in store for anyone who threatened to reveal the covenant of its witches.

The twin goddesses of strength and rage looked to the god of memory for guidance.

"We have the phone that shows everything that really happened and proves beyond any doubt that we didn't kill them—in fact, we tried to save them—but we don't know how we can use it." Mardi spoke with a rare tentative quality to her voice. She pressed her tongue stud against her teeth in thought. It was so frustrating to have the perfect proof, and to have no way to use it. "It—it reveals way too much about magic to the mortals. The White Council would roast us alive if we introduced it as evidence. There's no way to prove what happened without doing exactly what we're supposed to never do."

"Yep," Molly summed it up. "We're pretty screwed."

"It seems to me," Jean-Baptiste mused, "that in this particular instance, Magdi and Mooi, you two have absolutely nothing to be ashamed of. In fact, if I were your father, I would be very proud of you. My advice to you is this: no matter what the ultimate outcome in the mortal realm, you have behaved overall with great honor and bravery. You risked everything. When the choice was before you, your true characters shone through. And since your arrival here in North Hampton, you have defeated both Alberich and the curse of the Rhinegold, two of the greatest scourges of our times. Your story is one of supernatural courage. And if I were your father, I would want to know it. And, as I say, I would be proud. Very proud."

"Well, when you put it like that . . ." the twins thought aloud, as one.

Immediately, they emailed their dad the video from Alberich's phone, along with a blow-by-blow of their exploits.

Within twenty minutes, Mardi's cell rang.

"S'up?"

"How about 'hello, Dad'?"

"S'up?"

"I see that some things are never going to change." There was a lightness to his tone that Mardi hadn't heard for a long time.

"Dad, I can tell you have good news. What have you done?"

"Well, first of all, I've convinced Headingley not to suspend you and Molly next year, provided there are no more bizarre incidents with flying lunch items and radical changes of hair color among the staff. I'm afraid this called for a very large donation on the part of our family foundation. We're endowing a scholarship."

"How nice of us. But did you look at the video we sent? Is there anything we can do?"

"You've already done it, Mardi."

"What do you mean?"

"Sometimes, believe it or not, honesty is the best policy. I've shared the tape with the White Council."

"Dad. You didn't! And, Dad, it's not called a tape. It's a video. You're, like, twenty-five years behind the times." She rolled her eyes. Dad was such a loser, but he was their loser. Molly, Freya, Ingrid, and Jean-Baptiste were all staring at her, the beginnings of smiles lighting up their faces.

"Darling, please hear me out. Because you two have taken such great risks, both to save the mortals and to fight the curse of the Rhinegold, the White Council has determined that it will, in turn, take a risk on your behalf."

"I don't get it."

"The Council is has given me permission cast a spell of oblivion around the deaths of the mortals."

"What, their families and friends are going to forget them? That's not right!"

"You're misunderstanding me. No one will forget

them. But people are going to soon be forgetting how exactly they died. It's a very complicated process of erasure, which is the reason it is almost never performed. There's not a lot of room for error. It involves going back and restreaming months' worth of media as well as entering the memories of dozens of witnesses to blur the lines. Luckily, the Council trusts me to carry it out. And if I blow it, it's on my head. So I've got my work cut out for me. The real estate deals are on the back burner for the next few weeks. I may not have always been here for you, girls, which no doubt explains a few things. But I watched what you did in that subway station. And now it's my turn to kick in."

"Wow, Dad. I never thought I'd hear you sing the praises of blurred lines. I'm impressed."

"Blurred lines? What are you talking about?"

Molly reached for the phone, and Mardi handed it to her.

"Dad, we have one more question. Maybe you can help us." Molly felt all the eyes of the room fall on her. "Who could have rescued Mardi and me after we were killed on the subway tracks? Who brought us back from the dead?"

There was silence on the other end of the line. A sigh. "I can't be positive," he said. "But I do know there is someone with strong ties to the Underworld who loves you very much and who may have called in a very special favor. Someone who thinks you and your sister should fulfill your destinies here on Earth, to make sure witches use their power for the good, to stay strong against the hatred of certain evil men."

Instantly, although she had never met her mother, Molly was flooded with certainty. "You mean our mother? She's looking out for us?"

"Always," he said. "Your mother is quite a force."

Molly looked straight at her twin. Their smiles locked. They weren't abandoned after all.

41

I'LL BE MISSING YOU

$\mathscr{I}$t was the twins' last evening in town. Labor Day. They were getting ready for their farewell dinner at Goose's Landing, which was opening that night, at long last, to great fanfare. The dock was strewn with fairy lights and ribbons in celebration. There was going to be a lobster bake under a full moon.

Trent would be there, of course, along with Freya, Ingrid, and Matt. Graciella had offered to babysit for Jo and Henry. Jean-Baptiste, his mission accomplished, had already headed home to New Orleans, so they would raise a glass to him as they ate. He had given each girl her own pocket square as a souvenir, suggesting that they carry them as handkerchiefs. Mardi's was jet black. Molly's was hot pink.

"Let me dress both of you tonight," Freya had offered. "That way you can pack all your stuff so you won't have to deal tomorrow."

At first, Molly had been skeptical. She thought she

had made it perfectly clear that she was not so into the vintage.

"Come on, Molly, I have some classic pieces that will look amazing on you." Freya winked a bright green eye. She was irresistible.

Half an hour later, Molly was wearing a pink leather body-hugging jacket and skirt.

"Oh, Fury!" Molly squealed, picking up her little dog and standing on tiptoes to admire herself in one of Freya's many full-length mirrors. "Check us out!"

"You can keep it," said Freya.

Molly didn't know how to thank her.

While Freya worked with Mardi on something more down and dirty to wear, Molly tried on several pairs of strappy sandals, finally settling on a simple white option that looked reassuringly new.

When Ingrid poked her head into the attic wardrobe wonderland to say it was almost time to leave for their reservation, Mardi gave Molly a significant look.

Molly knew it was time to bring up the subject that she and her sister had stayed up half of last night discussing. She had said she would ask, and she was going to be as good as her word. Molly took a deep breath and dove in. "Ingrid, Mardi and I have something we want to ask you, but we don't think we should do it in front of Matt at dinner. Can we have a minute now?"

Ingrid nodded kindly. Freya looked intrigued.

Molly continued. "Do you remember the night of the storm, when we were searching for Mardi on the water, and we found that little drowned boy, and you, well, you called on your mother and you were able to bring him back from the other side?"

"Of course," Ingrid replied softly, understanding now why they would not be able to discuss this matter at the dinner table.

"Well, here's the thing: Mardi and I were hoping you could do something like that again. For our friends. What happened to them was so totally unfair. And even though we didn't do it, our magic was involved. We want to make it right. Please, Ingrid? Can you and Freya please get your mother to help bring them back from the Underworld? They don't belong there yet."

Molly found she was crying. She looked at Mardi, then Freya, then Ingrid. They all had tears welling up in their eyes too.

Ingrid put her arm around Molly, while Freya took both Mardi's hands. The two older witches looked long and searchingly at one another and shook their heads.

"It's a beautiful thought, girls," Ingrid said gently. "But it's impossible. It's much too late. They have been dead too long. There is nothing of their souls left anymore in the mortal realm. If we were, by some miracle, to be able to bring some part of them back, the results would be disastrous."

"They would come back as zombies," sighed Freya. "Or, maybe even worse, as wraiths."

"So," Molly sniffed, "there's nothing at all we can do to show them how much we care?"

"Nothing?" Mardi echoed.

"Well," Ingrid said, "there is one possibility."

Freya gave her sister a questioning look.

"Freya and I could ask Joanna about the possibility of getting a message to them in the Underworld. A message from the two of you. I know it's not what you really want. But would that help?"

"You would do that for us?" Mardi asked.

"On one condition," Ingrid said. "Because getting a missive through the passages is not something we can just do on a whim overnight. If you are serious about this, you girls have to promise to come back to the East End next summer." She smiled, her bright blue eyes alive with mischief. "Think about it. The kids would be over the moon."

Molly and Mardi looked from Ingrid to Freya and back again. Then they all burst out in laughter.

Faintly at first, then progressively louder, a childish cackling mingled with their laughter. They followed the sound to find Henry hiding in a box of lingerie. He had managed to encase his chubby little body in at least seven layers of Freya's clothing, blouses, skirts, dresses, hot pants. It seemed an impossible feat.

"Hey." Matt's voice came from the foot of the stairs. "Sounds like you're having a ball up there, but can you bring it with you? I'm starving."

After dinner, Mardi and Trent took a long walk across

Gardiners Island Bridge to Fair Haven. They were quiet as they strolled arm in arm over the glittering bay, but both were stirred inside by a thousand racing currents. Was this really good-bye?

They barely spoke. Without discussing it, as if by silent agreement, they reached the end of the bridge, crossed the vast lawns of Fair Haven, and found themselves at the greenhouse. They opened its old-fashioned glass door and fell into each other's arms on the wrought-iron bench where they had first gotten acquainted, what seemed like an eternity. ago. The hothouse atmosphere was heavily fragrant.

Mardi focused her dark gaze on Trent, committing his features to memory. It seemed impossible to say good-bye to this face. She would carry it off in her mind's eye and gaze at it forever. It was a crazy feeling. White hot. Had she found her eternal soul mate?

Reading her mind, he whispered, "Mardi, do you feel like hanging out together for a few more centuries?" His smile was radiant and kind. "I promise to age gracefully. You can trust me."

"When you put it like that, the nine months until next summer don't sound so endless."

"Yeah, but just in case you ever even think about trying to forget me, I got you a present that will totally keep my memory alive."

"Where is it?"

He kissed her full on the lips, murmuring, "It's hiding in plain sight."

She looked around the greenhouse for a clue. Freya's herbs were lush and overflowing. The giant ferns glowed in the moonlight. The plant life seemed riper and more beautiful than ever. But she couldn't spot anything specifically different. And within a few seconds, she found her eyes magnetically drawn back to his.

"I used to be scared of your eyes," she said, "of getting lost in them, of drowning."

"I used to be scared of yours too. I guess it's a healthy fear. You know, the fear of eternity."

"Have you shaken it?" She ran her tongue over his lips.

"Have you?"

She pressed herself into the muscles of his chest, willing her body to soften into clay in order to take an impression of him that would last until they met again.

"So, next summer?" His breath was hot in her ear. "You up for another spell in thrilling North Hampton?" He ran his fingers along the snaking curves of her rainbow tattoo.

"Maybe," she teased him. "I mean, this hasn't been nearly as dead a summer as Molly and I thought. But I guess what happens next summer kinda depends."

"On?"

"My present." She beamed gentle mockery at him.

"So that's how it is!" He laughed. Releasing her from his ropy arms, he stood. "This gift of mine is so much cooler than anything your sister will ever own."

"I like the way you talk. Don't stop."

He wandered over to the Venus flytrap. She noticed now that there was more than one. A second plant was flowering behind the original.

He reached beneath the leaves and pulled the plant up from the ground.

Mardi expected to see hanging roots and clumps of dirt. But instead he was holding a sleek black pot, from which the plant grew.

"You're kidding!" She had never been more purely delighted.

"I could tell you coveted one of these from the second you laid on eyes on mine. I can read you, Mardi Overbrook. I know what you want to eat and drink. I know what makes you feel good. I was put in this universe to please you, Goddess of Rage."

She took her exotic plant from him and began to caress it with her gaze.

"You're giving me a carnivorous plant to remember you by? What kind of symbolism is that?" She laughed.

"*Our* kind."

She really loved this this guy.

"Bye, Trent." She kissed him one last time, pulled away, took her flytrap under her arm, and raced off into the night before he could see her cry.

He knew not to come after her. "Good-bye, Mardi."

She could feel his deep blue gaze licking at her back like an undying flame. Through her tears, she smiled. Trent Gardiner wasn't going anywhere. He was the appointed guardian of Fair Haven. He'd be waiting here, beautiful as ever, when she pulled into town next June. Ever after, he'd be waiting.

The next morning, Molly climbed into the Ferrari beside Mardi. Matt had devised an elaborate system for strapping her three large Louis Vuitton suitcases onto the back of the car. Killer and Fury curled up together on a small dog bed at her feet. The Venus flytrap nestled beside them.

Everyone crowded around to say good-bye.

"Hey," Molly said as Mardi shifted the car into gear, "you found a keeper. We're coming back next summer, right?"

Mardi nodded. Her rainbow tattoo shone bright in the morning sun, and a green light twinkled from between her slightly parted lips. She was silent for a long time as they sped through the farms on the outskirts of town toward the foggy field of forgetfulness that they would need to pass through to get back to their real lives.

Finally, Mardi spoke. "You know, Trent took the ring to Fair Haven for us. He went through the passage in the ballroom, and he buried it in the gloaming. I didn't want us to know where exactly it lies. This way, we can never be blackmailed. We're safe now, Molly. The curse can't ever touch us again."

Molly felt a profound relief spread through her

body. But a question lingered. Their mother, the Rhinemaiden. Where was she now? Why had she left them only to miraculously protect them from afar? Molly had always assumed she and Mardi were abandoned. But now it was clear that their mother was watching and protecting them in mysterious ways. Molly furrowed her brow as she burrowed her bare, beautifully manicured feet in between Killer and Fury in their soft bed.

Once the Ferrari had crossed the misty borderline encircling the secretly magical town of North Hampton and the twins were heading west on the Montauk Highway, following signs to New York City, Mardi spotted another Ferrari. A black one. Brand-spanking-new.

Molly watched as her sister shifted gleefully into fifth gear, gunning it, leaving the douchemobile in the dust.

"Nice work," she told Mardi. "Let's crank some tunes."

"Now you're talking. What do you feel like?" Molly asked, realizing she truly no longer felt competitive. The ring's curse of discord was finally lifted.

Molly and Mardi were twin sisters. Identical. Together they could meet anything in their way.

Mardi smiled, her identical dimple deepening in her cheek. "You decide. Anything but opera."

DOUBLE ECLIPSE

SPEAK
An imprint of Penguin Random House LLC
375 Hudson Street
New York, New York 10014

First published in the United States of America by G. P. Putnam's Sons,
an imprint of Penguin Random House LLC, 2016
This omnibus edition published by Speak,
an imprint of Penguin Random House LLC, 2018

THE LIBRARY OF CONGRESS HAS CATALOGED THE G. P. PUTNAM'S SONS EDITION AS FOLLOWS:
Names: De la Cruz, Melissa, 1971– author.
Title: Double eclipse / Melissa de la Cruz.
Description: New York, NY : G. P. Putnam's Sons, [2016]
| Series: Summer on East End ; [2]
Summary: "Trouble continues to bubble and boil for twin witches
(and Norse goddesses) Mardi and Molly Overbrook during their
second summer in North Hampton"—Provided by publisher.
Identifiers: LCCN 2016010052 | ISBN 9780399173561 (hardback)
Subjects: | CYAC: Sisters—Fiction. | Twins—Fiction. | Witches—Fiction.
| Magic—Fiction. | Goddesses, Norse—Fiction. | Mythology,
Norse—Fiction. | Hamptons (N.Y.)—Fiction. | Diaries—Fiction.
Classification: LCC PZ7.D36967 Do 2016 | DDC [Fic]—dc23
LC record available at https://lccn.loc.gov/2016010052

This omnibus edition ISBN 9781984835567

Printed in the United States of America.
Text set in Zapf Intl Light.

1 3 5 7 9 10 8 6 4 2

For the amazing Moretz family:
Teri, Trevor, and Chloë

Thank you for loving the East End coven

LOCKED OUT OF HEAVEN

From the Diary of Molly Overbrook

$\mathcal{D}$ear Diary,

That's how these things usually start, right? "Dear Diary"? I'm only asking because it seems kind of strange to pretend that I'm writing a diary, which should be, you know, *private*, when what I'm really writing is a "therapy assignment" that's going to be read by Dr. Mésomier and my dad and aunts and Odin-knows-who-else. But since right now I'm not really speaking to any of those people, I'm just going to pretend that none of them are going to see this, because if I think of them reading these words, then I'm never going to be able to write down what happened this summer. And although I want to make it clear that I think this is a *totally lame assignment* and it's not really *anybody's business but mine and Mardi's*, I do actually want to write it down. Because, well, it was pretty freaking strange, and maybe writing it down will help me figure out how the Hel, I mean, the Underworld, things could have gotten so messed up between me and my sister.

And since maybe this is going to be read by people who have never met me, I suppose I should catch you up on a few things that happened before summer even started.

So:

Most people know me as Molly Overbrook, but in certain *very* select circles, I'm also known as Mooi, and my twin sister, Mardi, is called Magdi. Most people see us as two fairly normal seventeen-year-olds, albeit ones from privileged backgrounds: Mardi's normal ride is a vintage Ferrari, while I usually go for something with a chauffeur (I like a chauffeured Navigator or Escalade preferably, but a Town Car will do, or even a taxi— although as I learned this summer, nothing beats a Maybach), so I can sip on some bubbly and check my social media feeds while someone else does the driving. Shopping means department stores and individual designers (although in our case, the department stores are Barneys and Jeffrey and the designers are 5:31 Jérôme and Kim Haller). Good hair is an obsession, and we own approximately one hundred different hair care products between us; of course mine gets a little assistance from the Frédéric Fekkai salon. Like everyone our age, we sweated over the SATs, and we'll soon be waiting on pins and needles to see which colleges will let us in.

HOWEVER:

Despite the outward appearance of quasi-normality, we are in fact the daughters of Thor, a.k.a. the god of thunder. No, not the one played by Chris Hemsworth. Our dad doesn't wear a red cape and silver armor, although he *does* have a hammer, which he doesn't swing around as much; he keeps it hanging on a couple of hooks above the mantel in the living room of our Park Avenue penthouse while he jets around the world buying and selling skyscrapers and companies and, I don't know, *islands*. By which I mean that, yes, our father's a genuine Norse god, which makes us goddesses—Mardi's the goddess of rage and I'm the goddess of strength. But we're a little different from our dad and his ex, Ingrid, a.k.a. Erda, the goddess of the earth, and her sister Freya, the goddess of love. They were all born thousands of years ago in Asgard, which is our real home and where we're supposed to live, coming to Midgard (the place humans call Earth) only when they mess things up and need our help.

But Thor (whom we call Troy, when we're not just calling him Dad) and Ingrid and Freya and a few other Aesir and Vanir (which is what the gods call themselves in Asgard) ended up getting trapped here after the rainbow bridge that connected Asgard to the rest of the nine worlds was destroyed almost five hundred years ago, leaving them pretty much stuck here. Like, *forever*.

Literally.

Despite the fact that Thor and Tyr—the god of war (a.k.a. Trent, whom we'll meet later)—and Ingrid and Erda and about a half dozen other gods have been trapped here for so long, none of them ever had any children—that is, until Mardi and I came along seventeen years ago.

To be sure, our births were prophesied a long time ago, but that was before the Bofrir was destroyed, and everyone figured those prophecies had been canceled when the link between the nine worlds was cut—especially because in the legends our mother is supposed to be a Jotun (a giant) from Jotunheim, a world that was also cut off from Midgard by the destruction of the rainbow bridge. And as far as everyone knows, there aren't any giants here on Earth. But then one day our dad showed up with a cute little bundle of joy in each arm (so we're told anyway; we may be goddesses, but you can't expect us to remember things from when we were a couple of months old, let alone a couple of days), and judging by the way glass shattered when we cried for our bottles and the trays on our high chairs would break into a million pieces when we threw temper tantrums, it was pretty clear we were the goddesses from the ancient prophecies. Needless to say, our appearance on the scene raised a lot of questions, but one of them was kind of more important than all the others:

Where was our mother? And who was she?

Well, we'll get to that, but first I want to tell you about this dream I had around the start of the summer. Not once, but every night for more than a week. I know, it's the twenty-first century and no one really cares about dreams anymore besides Jungian analysts—and how can you take someone seriously when their job is to sit on a couch and listen to people talk? Except gods' dreams aren't like humans' dreams—our unconscious is plugged into the magical currents that govern time itself, as in, they're prophetic. (How do you think they came up with the prophecy about Mardi and me all those thousands of years ago? It wasn't from gazing into a crystal ball. It was a dream.)

So:

In the dream, I'm at Fair Haven, which is this beautiful colonial-era mansion on Gardiners Island, just off the East End, where Mardi's boyfriend, Trent, lives. Besides being the Gardiners' ancestral home, Fair Haven also happens to sit on what's called a "seam" between our world and the Land of the Dead, also known as Niflheim, the most fearsome and inhospitable of the nine worlds, with a cold white sun that's not even as bright as the full moon and covered in endless sheets of ice—including Hel, the vast city where dead Vikings are banished if they fail to die a heroic death.

The reason why I'm telling you all this background stuff is because I didn't know it in my waking life—I found it out in the dream. And only after I did a little digging around did I realize it was all true. Which is why I knew this dream was important.

Important, and terrifying.

In the dream, I'm walking toward Fair Haven across the front lawn. In real life, that lawn is as flat and manicured as a croquet pitch or tennis court, every single blade of grass perfectly trimmed to 1.5 inches. But in the dream, the yard is a swampy, cratered mess, alternating puddles of sludge and muddy mounds the size of muskrat nests. Plus, it's raining. Plus, the puddles of water are freezing cold.

Now, I'm a serious shoe girl, and a muddy lawn is not my normal habitat. (Not good for the Zanottis!) Yet in the dream, I'm barefoot and wading right into this vast field of sludge like it's the Mediterranean lapping on the Côte d'Azur, plopping one foot into six inches of ice-cold muck and then the other, as I charge toward Fair Haven. I don't know why, but I have to get to the mansion, and I have to get there soon, or it'll be too late. And so I'm splashing through the mud as fast as I can, slipping every other step and falling on my hands and knees and splashing my face with brown goo. I don't even care what my hair looks like—so you know I must be *completely out of my mind.*

I'm so caught up with just trying to get across the lawn that I'm not really paying attention to my destination. But then, after what seems like hours, I manage to climb onto one of those muddy but still comparatively dry mounds, and when I pause to catch my breath, I look up for the first time, to see how far I am from my destination.

That's when I see the mansion—which just last year was described by *Architectural Digest* as "not only the most beautiful, but the most elegant home on the whole of the East End." Except in my dream it's not beautiful at all, let alone elegant. It's a ruin. Every single pane of glass in every single window has been smashed, and two out of every three of the thousands upon thousands of cedar shingles that normally cover the house have been blown off, and the simple white Ionic pilasters and window frames have been ripped away or hang in splinters from the walls—and that's only what I can see of the house, because the whole enormous building is covered in dark, droopy tangled vines that look more like seaweed than ivy or creeper. The vines cling to the house not like they're growing up its walls but like they're trying to pull them down, and there are big holes in the roof with tree branches growing through them, as if the house had been abandoned for a hundred years or more. Which is impossible. I was there just last summer. The house was in perfect condition. I played croquet with Mardi on this very lawn.

And I mean, I know it was a dream, so the normal rules of reality don't apply. But the thing is, I *knew* I was dreaming, and in the dream I *wasn't surprised* to see Fair Haven looking like this. It was exactly what I expected to see. It was only the part of me that was watching myself dream that was confused. Was I seeing the future? Or maybe some alternate version of the past? And if so, how? Though it was said that the Aesir possessed magical artifacts that allowed them to change time itself, all those were trapped on the other side of the destroyed rainbow bridge. So how was I seeing this vision?

But before the not-dreaming part of my brain could ask the dreaming part of my brain for the answer to this question, I noticed something off to my right, in the east wing of the mansion. The east wing was built in the early seventeenth century, and Trent always said it was the strongest part of the house. Its posts and beams had been cut from solid tree trunks two feet thick and had stood for nearly four hundred years. But now the whole wing swayed like a poorly built tent in a hurricane, and much of the roof had caved in, and some kind of vast . . . mound rose from the hole, like one of those creepy termites' nests in Africa, but a hundred times bigger. But it was only when it flashed a second time that I realized it wasn't the mound that had caught my eye, but a pulse of light somewhere deep within the crumbling walls of the east wing: a thick greenish-yellowish glow that pulsed on and off. And each time it shone on, it cast a shadow that, though monstrously distended, was still recognizable as human, and female.

And even though I didn't know who this woman was, I knew I had to get to her, I had to save her.

✳ 2 ✳

O MOTHER, WHERE ART THOU?

Mardi-Overbrook-Journal.docx

ℒet me guess: the first thing Molly wrote in her diary was "Dear Diary," wasn't it?

Gods, she can be so predictable, not to mention conventional. That's the difference between us. I like to surprise people. When Molly got extensions in fifth grade so she could look like every other Britney-Christina-Beyoncé-Gaga-Katy wannabe, I went all Sinéad (or Amber Rose, if you don't remember Sinéad) and buzzed my long wavy locks down to the skull. And when it grew out, I dyed my hair black to make sure I'd stand out from the basic bimbos of the world even more. I pierced my tongue when I was thirteen and tattooed the rainbow bridge on my neck when I was fifteen. Troy, a.k.a. Thor, a.k.a. Daddykins, says I do these things because I grew up without a strong female presence in my life, but he doesn't know what he's talking about.

I do these things because it's fun.

I do them because I *can*.

No doubt Molly will tell you everything started to go wrong or, I don't know, weird between us, when Janet Steele (yes, *the* Janet Steele) dropped her little bombshell after winning the French Open this past May (yes, *the* French Open), but I don't think that's true. I think everything changed last summer, after Troy booted us off to the East End to get away from a little trouble in Manhattan—trouble that was not actually our fault, as later events made clear. Neither Molly nor I was particularly *thrilled* about spending the summer babysitting for one of Dad's old exes, Ingrid, but Ingrid turned out to be pretty cool, and her sister Freya makes the best cocktail-cum-love-potion you've ever guzzled.

But of course what really made last summer interesting was meeting Trystan Gardiner, a.k.a. Trent, a.k.a. Tyr, the god of war. (Molly mentioned him, right?) Although it wasn't as simple as just meeting him—when you're a goddess masquerading as a witch pretending to be a normal human, nothing ever is.

Molly and I both met Trystan Gardiner in different places, at the same time. If that sounds fishy, that's because it was. See, the Trystan I met—who called himself Trent—was the real Trystan, whereas the Trystan Molly met—who called himself Tris—was really this

evil shape-shifter named Alberich who was just trying to steal our ring, which happens to be made out of
Rhinegold and has all kinds of magical powers.

Anyway, when all was said and done, Alberich had
been defeated and banished, the Rhinegold was safely
locked away in Hel, and Trent and I were the only couple left standing, while poor Molly realized she'd been
dating an absolute troll all along.

But wait, you're asking, isn't Tyr one of the multi-
thousand-year-old gods? What's he doing dating a
seventeen-year-old? Isn't that a little, you know, *ew*?
That's a very good question, and I'm going to get to
it eventually, but for now let me just explain that the
gods trapped here in Midgard are a little different
from the gods who still live in Asgard. See, Asgardians
are immortal. Like, they really live forever and ever,
and pretty much nothing can kill them, and if they
do get killed, then they stay dead. But here in Midgard, the gods' bodies are practically as vulnerable as
human bodies, which means they *can* be destroyed.
But only the flesh: the soul sticks around and migrates
to a newly conceived body. Joanna, Ingrid and Freya's
mother, who was also trapped here in Midgard with
her children, has not only had to watch each of her
children die, in some cases more than once, she's also
had to give birth to each of them two or three times,
which has got to be pretty weird, not to mention kind
of horrible, since when they first come out, they're
like any other baby: crying, breast-feeding, diapers,

the whole nine yards, with no knowledge of who they used to be. It's not until puberty that their powers start to manifest and their memories return to them, a drawn-out and not-particularly-fun process known as the Reawakening—although I imagine it still beats dying.

And so Trent got himself into a little trouble about nineteen years ago, and he ended up burning his mortal body (his second, if I've got the count right). I used to ask him what happened, and he'd go silent. At first, I thought he was trying to hide the fact that he'd done something shady, but then I realized he actually didn't remember—all his memories had died with his old body and haven't returned yet. Or rather, hadn't returned as of the beginning of this summer, although by early June that situation had changed.

In fact, that's when everything changed, but that's getting ahead of the story.

So here we are, in our second summer on the East End. Molly and I ended up liking the place so much that it was pretty much taken for granted that we'd come out and stay with Ingrid and her mortal husband, Matt, and their two kids, Jo and Henry, as soon as school let out. Except this year, only Molly was going to be crashing at Ingrid's cute but kind of small beach house (only 3,000 square feet), while I was going to stay with Trent in Fair Haven, his family's grand home on Gardiners

Island, just off the coast of North Hampton. You could drop Ingrid and Matt's house in Fair Haven's ballroom and still throw a raging party for a hundred of your closest friends in the space left over.

Dad sort of raised his eyebrow at the whole thing, but I raised my own back and that was that. This is the man who used to give us cereal for dinner and left us with a succession of girlfriends over the years.

The day everything began to happen, however, I was over at Ingrid's house to watch the French Open final on TV. I know what you're thinking. *Tennis.* Who watches tennis except for old British people and wannabe Anglophiles? And I'm not even a tennis fan. That's Molly. (Or that was Molly. Something tells me she's not too big on it now.) She'd gotten into it a little during our sophomore year, when she went out for the team, but then Dad made her quit because even though she'd never picked up a racket before, she had this funny way of winning *every single match* she played, and he was pretty sure she was using magic to help her out. Molly claimed she wasn't, and who knows, maybe she wasn't doing it on purpose, but my sister is just about the most competitive person I know—after me—and sometimes when a goddess wants something, she's just going to get it.

So anyway, she quit the team, and destroyed all her gear, including an adorable platinum tennis bracelet that quite frankly looked better when it *wasn't* worn with a tennis skirt. But by then she'd started watching matches on TV—she even made Dad add the Tennis Channel to our cable package—and she'd become obsessed with Janet Steele.

In case you live under a rock, Janet Steele is the number one female tennis player in the world, which is amazing, given that she's something like thirty-seven or thirty-eight years old, which in tennis years is *ancient*. She was once a teenage prodigy, but then something happened when she was twenty or twenty-one and she vanished into the Outback, that big desert in the middle of Australia, which is where she's from. Some kind of "family crisis" was all she'd say—or all her publicist would say, since Janet simply disappeared. She was gone for thirteen or fourteen years, until about two years ago, when she suddenly showed up and started playing again, at around the same age that most tennis players retire. And not just playing: winning. By the end of her first year back, she was in the top ten. By the end of her second year, she was number one. She even almost won the Grand Slam last year (Serena Williams beat her at Wimbledon) and, what with the fact that she's a six-foot-two Glamazon with three feet of lustrous dark hair and legs that would make Giselle jealous, she became the highest-paid female athlete in the world. According to reports, she pulls in more than a $100 million a year in endorsements and prize money. That's Michael Jordan money, people. That's LeBron James money.

So, Janet started the year by winning the Australian Open and cruised right to the French Open final, where she was once again facing Serena Williams. I didn't watch last year's Wimbledon match, but I guess it was a real slugfest, and according to the tabloids, whatever friendship might've existed between Janet and Serena was dead and gone by the time it was over.

"Rumor has it she can be a bit of a bitch," Molly said as she settled onto a couch with a bottomless bowl of Parmesan-dusted popcorn, courtesy of Ingrid's magic and culinary prowess.

The TV was on, but it was just the announcers, droning away about things like "first-serve percentage" and "forehand volleys" and "hitting a clean, flat ball." I would've rather been at the beach, or with Trent, but it was pouring rain outside, and Trent was busy. So I was stuck with the fam.

"Molly, please," Ingrid said. "Little pitchers have big ears." She nodded at Jo, who was sitting a few feet away on an easy chair.

"Oh, Mom, puh-lease!" seven-year-old Jo said, snacking on her own bottomless bowl of crunchy kale chips. "I totally know what a bee-yotch is!"

Ingrid shook her head in defeat.

"Who's the b?" I asked Molly. "Janet or Serena?"

"Puh-lease," she said in her best imitation of Jo. "Janet Steele basically shows up, plays her matches, crushes her opponents, then leaves. Never talks to anyone, doesn't socialize or practice with any of the other players, nothing. Back when she was a teenager, she was supposed to be a real party girl, but now she says all of that is 'beneath her.'"

"Like, literally," I said, pointing to the screen. That woman was tall.

The players were walking out onto the field, or court, or whatever it's called. Serena Williams is like five foot ten or something, with guns like an NBA star, but Janet Steele towered over her by a good four inches. She was more lithe than Serena, but you could see the strength in her shoulders and legs, all three or four feet of them, which were fully on display in a skimpy white tennis dress that barely covered her butt cheeks.

"My Lord," Ingrid said from the other side of the kitchen island. "Is that what they're wearing these days? I have bathing suits that cover more than that!"

"Mo-om!" Jo groaned. "You are em-bar-ras-sing me!"

"Watch it, young lady, or I'll turn those kale chips back into plain old kale, and make you eat till you turn green. Mardi, here are your spicy wasabi peas," she said, proffering an antique earthenware bowl with a bright red stripe around the rim. "I've put a bottomless hex on them, so pace yourself or you're going to end up with a tummy ache."

Tummy ache. Ingrid's fought demons and giants, visited six of the nine worlds, and helped raise people from the dead, but she still talks like a children's librarian (which, btdubs, is what she is in her human guise). You gotta love her.

Just then, Freya burst through the front door. She was rocking a typical Freya look (not that anything Freya wears is "typical"): cutoff denim shorts that were definitely shorter than Janet Steele's tennis dress, and a sleeveless, backless, semi-see-through blouse that showed off her arms, which glittered with bracelets, including an asp coiled high up around her toned left biceps.

"Hey, Molls, what's shaking?" she said before turning to me. "Mardi, I was going through my closet this morning, and I saw something that made me think of you."

She tossed me a little box; inside I found a thick black leather belt. When I uncoiled it, I saw that the chunky silver buckle read *BOY TOY*.

"Oh, my gods, it's awesome!" I practically squealed. "Is it vintage?"

"It's more than vintage," Freya laughed. "It's Madonna's. I borrowed it from her at a club in New York in like 1982, and then when she got famous, I kind of sort of forgot to give it back." She winked mischievously.

Molly tried to hide her disappointment at not getting anything, but you could tell she was upset. This was the third item of clothing Freya had given me since we'd arrived last week, and just the day before, Molly had complained that Freya liked me best and she felt left out. I tried to tell her it was just because Freya and I have the same taste in clothes, not because she liked me better. I mean, Molly's a label queen, and everything she wears has to be right off the runway or she won't even look at it. I don't mean that as a dig or anything. Just stating the facts.

When Molly puts on the same Herve Leger you've seen on a thousand different celebrities, she works it out. But Freya and I are more rock 'n' roll. And besides, I told her, Ingrid clearly preferred Molly to me. This didn't make Molly feel any better, though. "Ingrid dresses more like a librarian than any librarian in the history of libraries," she'd whined.

Now, however, before she could say anything, Freya exclaimed, "Is that *Janet Steele*? She's back?"

Molly immediately perked up. "Do you know her?"

"Know her?" Freya said. "I held that girl's hair out of her face while she puked her guts out. We used to party like it was 1999 when it was only 1995. She used to hang around—"

"Janet's a big tennis star now," Ingrid said in this bland but curiously sharp tone of voice. When I looked over at her, she was frowning at Freya, and her face bore a clear shut-up expression. Like I said, Ingrid's a librarian, so she can make a shut-up face like nobody's business.

"Right, she was always a big tennis star, even then," Freya said, oblivious to her sister's warning. "I always thought it was a little suspicious myself."

"Why?" Molly asked. "I think she's amazing. She's beautiful and talented, and she doesn't care what anyone thinks about her."

"I'm sure Freya's just exaggerating," Ingrid said, coming around the island with a bottle of white wine in one hand, seltzer in the other. "Sis," she said in a not-very-sisterly tone, "why don't you make us some spritzers to drink while we watch the game?"

"It's called a match," Molly said. "A game is, like, I don't know, *baseball*."

"Yes, Mother," Jo echoed drolly. *"Baze-bowl."*

Ingrid and Freya exchanged a significant look, and suddenly Freya's eyes went wide. She opened her mouth, then snapped it shut. With a false smile on her face, she ran to the kitchen, and Ingrid sighed in relief.

I looked back and forth between them, then glanced at the TV. Janet Steele was unzipping her warm-up jacket and shaking out her legs prior to the start of the game, or match, or whatever you call the whole tennis experience. It seemed pretty clear that Freya and Ingrid knew something about her that they weren't saying, and I was determined to get it out of them, if only so I'd have something to talk to Molly about while two grown women spent the next two hours hitting a ball back and forth with giant flyswatters.

But as it turned out, I didn't have to get it out of them. Janet told us herself.

3

YOU DROPPED A BOMB ON ME

From the Diary of Molly Overbrook

$\mathcal{F}$reya came around the counter with a tray of ice-filled glasses and a fat pitcher full of golden liquid.

"Those don't look like spritzers," Ingrid said, frowning in the way that only a woman who knows she's magically immune to frown lines would dare to risk.

Freya laughed. "It's the French Open; I made Pimm's Cups."

"Um, I think that's Wimbledon," Ingrid said.

"Um, what is a Pimm's Cup?" Mardi said.

"Pimm's Cups are traditionally associated with Wimbledon, which starts in three weeks," I added.

"Oh, my gods, this is going to happen *again*?" Mardi said, waving a hand at the screen, where Janet and Serena were warming up. "You've had that TV on twenty-four seven for the *past two weeks*."

"A Pimm's Cup," Freya said before I could inform Mardi that not only was there still Wimbledon to come, but also the US Open at the end of the summer, "is muddled cucumber, lemon, mint, candied ginger, and a liqueur called Pimm's No. 1, which is basically an herb-infused gin. Plus some bubbles to give it fizz. Of course it's me, so I added a little twist of my own—and I don't mean the lemon peel," she said, winking.

I *almost* forgave her for not giving me any presents when we arrived, like she did Mardi.

She handed the first glass to me, and I took an experimental sip. Unsurprisingly, it was delicious—herbal and cooling, becoming warmer as it hit my stomach. It pays to have an aunt who's a world-class mixologist with a sideline in magic potions, even if she gives all her clothes to my sister.

I sniffed at the glass. "Is that elderflower?"

"Nice nose, Molls," Freya said. "I infused the Pimm's with it a few days ago. Gives it a nice mellow finish."

"It's fantastic," I said, taking a longer sip. Then, glancing at Mardi, I added as innocently as I could, "So tell me more about Janet Steele. Where did you guys meet?"

Like Mardi, I had noticed the looks they had exchanged earlier. Freya glanced over at Ingrid, whose frown had gone even deeper. Then she turned back to me, an awkward smile on her face, before her eyes drifted to the TV.

"Whoa, who's the weirdo in her player's box?" Freya asked.

I turned to see the camera focused on a twentysome-
thing guy with pale skin that seemed even whiter next
to his jet-black hair, which was parted in the middle
and fell past his shoulders like Jared Leto used to wear
it. His most striking feature, however, was a Fu Man-
chu mustache that fell a good three inches past his
chin.

A name and caption appeared on the screen below
him:

IVAN
J STEELE HITTING PARTNER

I've seen Ivan a hundred times before, of course, but
as I stared at him this time, I felt a strange chill. In fact,
I've always thought he was a little creepy in a way that
reminded me of vampires I've met—his hair too dark,
his skin too pale, his eyes too, well, empty. But today
was different. Today my dream popped into my head,
so palpably that I could smell the stale salt water and
feel it swirling icily around my ankles. As I looked into
Ivan's dark, empty eyes, I felt as though I was looking
into the broken windows of Fair Haven.

"That's Ivan," I heard Mardi say, shaking me out of
it. "Guess he doesn't have a last name."

"'Hitting partner.'" Freya giggled. "Is that a
euphemism?"

I laughed, shaking off the last images of my dream.
"Some people think so; some people think he's gay.

He's actually kind of a mystery. Even though he's been following Janet to every major tournament for the past two years, no one even knows his last name."

"Ooh, that is mysterious," Freya said, sending another significant look Ingrid's way. I was going to nudge her about Janet again when there was a loud *pop!* from the television, followed by an even louder grunt.

Freya whipped her head toward the TV, almost in relief. "Oh, look. It's starting."

I nodded, even though I was burning with curiosity, and turned to the television. Serena had served one of her trademark 120-mph bombs, but Janet had managed to get it back in play. Now the two were whacking the ball back and forth—two hard-core athletes, and they gave it everything they had. The ball was hurtling across the net, ricocheting from corner to corner, as first one woman and then the other chased down one seemingly ungettable shot after another. Finally, in a move that was half genius, half desperate, Serena walloped a backhand directly into Janet's body. Janet had rushed the net and barely had time to get her racket in front of her. The ball smashed into it and bounced out of the court nearly into the stands, while Serena let loose her trademark "Come on!"

"A twenty-six shot rally on the very first point," the announcer said in an awestruck voice. "If this is any indication of how the match is going to be, we're in for an afternoon of great tennis."

"'Great' is obviously a subjective term," Mardi

muttered. "Pass the Pimm's, please," she added, holding out her already-empty glass.

The announcer's words proved prophetic. For the next three hours, the two women belted bombs at each other. The third and final set went on for an hour and seventeen minutes, until Serena finally made a mistake and Janet fell to the ground in exhaustion and exultation.

"Yes!" someone screamed, and after a second, I realized it was me. I was on my feet and jumping up and down.

"What the Hell?" Mardi said, startling out of her seat. From the bleary-eyed expression on her face, she looked like she'd fallen asleep. Given how many Pimm's Cups she'd downed in the past three hours, I wouldn't have been surprised.

"She won, she won!" I yelled. "Janet won!"

"Okay, okay, settle down," Mardi said, sitting back in her chair. "It's just a tennis game, for crying out loud." She yawned and stretched. "Damn, Freya, those Pimm's Cups are strong. Knocked me right out."

"It's a *match*," I said, "and not just *any* match. It's the *French Open*, and Janet Steele just won it. She's on her way to being the first woman since Steffi Graf to win the Grand Slam!"

"Steffi who?" Mardi said.

I rolled my eyes.

"Hey," Ingrid said, "who wants some tea? I could use a little caffeine after all that alcohol."

"Yes, please!" Mardi said.

"Shhh! They're about to start the trophy presentation."

Serena accepted her runner-up trophy first. She was gracious in defeat, but you could tell she was pissed. That's what I love about Serena. She always keeps it classy, but she doesn't pretend she's happy about losing. "I'll see you at Wimbledon," she finished up, and though she was ostensibly speaking to the audience, it was pretty clear she was really calling out Janet.

"Ladies and gentleman," the announcer boomed, "your French Open women's champion, Janet Steele!"

Thunderous applause shook the stadium as Janet bounded onstage. Though she'd played a grueling three-hour-plus tennis match, she looked like she'd just stepped out of the salon. She'd pulled her long dark hair out of its braid during the commercial break, and it fell in cascading waves around the tight white jacket she'd zipped over the top part of her tennis dress to hide the sweat stains. Her smile was blinding, her skin flawless, and only the tiniest shine on the top of her lip gave any sign of all the effort she'd expended.

"Janet, you first won this tournament an amazing eighteen years ago," the announcer said, pausing to acknowledge the crowd's applause. "At the time, people were talking about you being one of the great champions of all time. But instead of defending your title, you left the game and disappeared for nearly two decades. But now you're back and playing the best tennis of your life. You won three slams last year, and you're halfway to a Grand Slam this year. Tell us what's going through your mind."

Janet waited for the applause to die down. It took nearly a minute, and she milked every second of it with that hundred-million-dollar smile.

"Oh, my God, it's amazing," she said when it was finally quiet enough for her to talk. Her Australian accent was sharp and sporty and not at all posh, which humanized her perfect looks. "I never thought I'd be standing here again after all these years. When I retired back in '97, I thought it was for good. But life has a way of surprising you, and I guess tennis wasn't done with me."

"Looking forward to Wimbledon next month, what kind of shape do you think you'll be in by then?"

Janet smiled and did a little twirl, letting her skirt flip up in the back, "I think I'm in pretty great shape right now." She laughed. The crowd roared with approval, and it was another minute before she could talk again.

"But seriously," she said, "I do have to watch my schedule now. I can't play week in and week out like I did when I was seventeen or eighteen. That's why I've decided to play a limited schedule between now and the US Open."

"But you'll play Wimbledon, of course?" the announcer asked.

In answer, Janet gave the camera her best "say what?" smirk. The audience went wild.

When the applause finally died down, she said, "I'll play Wimbledon definitely, but other than that, I'm going to spend most of the summer relaxing and training at a little house I bought on the East End of Long Island. My daughters are there, and I want to spend more time with them."

There was the sound of something hitting the floor. I realized it was my glass. Fortunately, it was empty, and the carpet kept it from breaking.

"Did she just say—" Mardi began.

"Shhh! She's still talking!" I shushed.

Actually, the announcer was talking. There was a stunned look on his face as he echoed Mardi's question. "Did you say—daughters?"

Janet's smile was beaming. "That's right. I have two gorgeous teenage daughters whom I haven't seen in far too long." She turned from the announcer and looked directly into the camera.

"Molly and Mardi Overbrook, Mummy's on her way. We're going to spend the summer together in the East End."

Just then, Ingrid came around the counter with a tray of tea.

"I made iced instead of hot," she said. "I hope that's—"

She broke off as she saw the stunned looks on all of our faces.

"Did I miss something?"

4

WOMANIZER, WOMANIZER

Mardi-Overbrook-Journal.docx

*M*olly and I looked at each other in silence for what seemed like an eternity. Then we were both on our feet screaming.

"Our *mother*?" Molly screamed at Freya. "Janet Steele is OUR MOTHER?"

"Did you know?" I screamed at Ingrid. "Have you been hiding it from us all these years?"

Ingrid looked desperately at Freya, who suddenly found the top of her left thigh really interesting.

"WILL SOMEBODY PLEASE SAY SOMETHING?" Molly and I screamed at the same time.

Somebody did: Janet Steele.

"I'm really looking forward to getting to know my girls better this summer."

Suddenly, I felt a vibration in my pocket. I pulled my phone out and saw that my feeds were blowing up:

OMG UR MOM!!!!

JANET STEELE???? SRSLY????

DID U KNOW? Y DIDN'T U SAY SMTHNG?

AMAZEBALLS!!!! A-MAZE-BALLS!!!!

Molly had her phone out too, and judging from the way she kept scrolling down—and down, and down, and down—she was being bombarded with tweets, texts, IMs, and notifications from Instagram, Tumblr, Vine, Facebook, and Witchipoo, the by-invitation-only site for teenage witches, vampires, and other magical creatures.

Freya cleared her throat. "Well, I guess the secret's out."

"Freya, wait," Ingrid said. "It's not our place. Troy told us he would talk to the girls when the time was right."

"Daddy *knew*?" Molly said.

I looked over at my twin. Molly has a genius IQ, but sometimes she can be a little spacey.

"Yes, Molly," I said. "Dad knew who he had sex with eighteen years ago."

Molly rolled her eyes. "I *know* that, dummy. But she could've gotten pregnant and not told him."

I rolled my eyes back at her. "And then what? She mailed us to Dad after we were born?"

"Actually," Ingrid said, "she couldn't have kept it

secret. When one of our kind reproduces, we just . . . know."

"What, like a sixth sense or something?" I asked.

"In our case it's more like a sixteenth sense," Freya answered. "But yeah."

Molly was shaking her head, dumbfounded. "So Daddy knew that Janet Steele was our mom all this time and kept it from us?"

"Your dad had his reasons. Being the offspring of the god of thunder comes with a little baggage, you know."

Suddenly, my phone and Molly's rang at the same time.

"Speak of the devil," Molly said, holding her phone up.

A picture of Troy Overbrook—a.k.a. the god of thunder, a.k.a. Thor, a.k.a. our deep-in-the-doghouse dad— shone out from the screen. Molly had snapped the picture at an Italian restaurant one night when we'd gotten Dad a little drunk and dared him to stuff thirty breadsticks in his mouth.

The same picture was lit up on my screen as well. Even with his pale lips distended around what looked like a bundle of firewood, you could still see what a lady-killer he was.

Poor Janet, I thought. *She never stood a chance.*

"He must've conferenced us," I said. "Are you ready for this, sis?"

Molly smiled grimly. "The real question is: is Daddy ready?"

We both pressed our talk buttons at the same time.

"Girls!" Dad said jovially, as though he was calling to wish us happy birthday.

"Um, no," I said.

"Girls—"

"I think she means 'Hel no,'" Molly said.

"Girls—"

"As in, 'Hel no, you don't get to be all "girls!" right now.'"

"Girls—"

"As in, 'Hel no, you've got some *explaining* to do, Troy Overbrook.'"

"Girls—"

"Because if this is true, then it's the lowest, meanest, dirtiest trick you've ever pulled!" I went on. "And on your own *daughters* too."

"GIRLS!"

Dad's voice was so loud it hurt my ear, and I had to jerk the phone away from my head.

"Great Odin," I heard him sigh. "I feel like I've just been double-teamed!"

"Well, you deserve it," Molly said. "I can't believe you kept this from us!"

Dad didn't say anything for a moment. You could practically hear him thinking. "This really isn't the kind of thing you talk about on the phone," he said finally. "Especially not a cell phone. But I'm in a helicopter right now. It's taking me to the seaplane. I'll be in North Hampton soon. Can you wait till then?"

"No!" Molly said sharply.

"But I guess we'll have to," I added glumly. I have to admit, I was impressed that he'd chartered a helicopter and a seaplane to travel a hundred miles. Short of whipping out his hammer and flying—which we had no proof he could actually do—it really was the fastest way for him to get here.

"Okay, then. I'll see you shortly. And, girls," he added, "don't take this out on your aunts, please. They had nothing to do with this."

"Fat chance," Molly said even as the line went dead.

"Right?" I agreed. I turned to Freya and Ingrid. "Spill."

✳ *5* ✳

TELL IT LIKE IT IS

From the Diary of Molly Overbrook

*I*ngrid and Freya stared at each other for so long that I found myself wondering if they were just using telepathy to silently work out a plan. Witches were crafty like that. Then I realized they were just stalling.

"You guys—" I began.

"Okay, okay," Freya cut me off.

"Freya," Ingrid snapped in her worried-mother voice, "it's not our place."

"Troy's on his way here anyway. The secret's out. And it's not like we can tell them much anyway." Freya turned to us. "We don't know that much about Janet either."

"He basically told us nothing, just that she left when we were little," I said, "so I think maybe you know a *little* more than we do."

"So it's true?" Mardi said. "Janet Steele really is . . . our mother?"

Mardi paused before she said *our mother*, like having a mother was something she'd never considered before. And I felt the same way. We were curious, of course, but we'd lived our whole lives without her. Dad once called her a "giantess" (which made sense, now that I knew how tall she was), and Trent Gardiner had suggested to Mardi that our mother was one of the three Rhinemaidens, the guardians of the Rhinegold made famous in Wagner's *Ring* cycle. But when your long-gone mother is described as a fairy tale, it makes it harder to believe in her, not easier, and Mardi and I had long since concluded that we'd never know her. For years, I'd been telling myself that I didn't have any feelings for this woman whom I'd never met, but now, as I looked expectantly at Ingrid and Freya, I knew I'd been kidding myself. What can I say? Even goddesses need a mom.

"Well?" I prompted.

Finally, Ingrid sighed and slumped in defeat. "It's true. Janet Steele is your mother."

Mardi's whoop made the wineglasses rattle on their wire rack. We jumped up and threw our arms around each other and danced around the living room, heedless of Ingrid's beautiful antiques.

"I don't know if I'd get so excited," Freya said when we'd finally quieted down. "There's a reason Troy didn't want Janet in your life, after all."

"Wait, it was Troy who kept us from our mother?" I asked.

"He always said she abandoned us," Mardi threw in. "He was lying about that too?"

Ingrid frowned at Freya. "See, this is why I said we should wait till Troy gets here." She turned to us. "As Freya mentioned, Janet was a bit of a wild girl."

"She was so young when she had us," I said. "It makes sense that she was still figuring things out." I grinned. "So she was more than Dad could handle, huh?"

"In a matter of speaking," Freya said, shrugging.

"I thought we were done with the vague thing," Mardi said. "What did Mom do that was so bad that Dad had to cut her out of our lives?"

"See, that's the thing, Mardi," Ingrid said. "We don't know."

Ingrid is good at a lot of things, like gardening and baking and helping a couple conceive by intricately knotting together two pieces of their hair, but lying is not one of them. I stared her down until she had to look away. She only lasted about five seconds.

"Seriously?" I said. "'We don't know'? You expect us to believe that?"

"It's true," Freya insisted about as convincingly as Ingrid. "Troy never told us. But he made it seem pretty serious. Something to do with—"

She stopped short.

"To do with what?" I insisted.

"Don't torture us!" Mardi said.

Freya sighed helplessly.

"It had something to do with you girls."

"Well, duh," Mardi said sarcastically. "Care to be more specific?"

Now it was Ingrid's turn to sigh. "You were never supposed to be born."

"What?" Mardi and I both exclaimed.

Ingrid made a face like she'd rather be eating worms or walking on hot coals than talking to us about this.

"Normally when you're a god at Thor's level, you get to decide when and if you're going to have children. But Janet tricked him somehow. I don't think even he knows how she did it. If he does, he never told us."

I couldn't believe what I was hearing.

"Are you saying that our own *dad* didn't want us?"

"No, of course not, honey," Freya said. "Your dad loves you very much. You were just . . . unplanned, that's all."

Mardi looked at me. "Can you *believe* this? We're the result of some magical version of a condom breaking."

A little smirk flickered over her face, and despite myself, I chuckled.

"We're Mommy and Daddy's cosmic accidents," I said, getting up to go and grabbing my sweater.

"Don't say that!" Ingrid protested. "You two are practically miracles!"

"Yeah, well, these two *miracles* are gonna go confront their father and find out what's really going on. C'mon, Mardi."

"Way ahead of you," Mardi said, reaching for her leather jacket and her keys, and together we stormed out of the house.

Mardi followed me outside to her car, a vintage 1972 Ferrari convertible whose top was always down (Mardi had cast a rain-repelling hex over the vehicle, which shielded it from unexpected rainstorms). I opened the door and folded myself into the low-slung passenger's seat while Mardi hopped over the closed driver's side door like one of the Dukes of Hazzard and slid her feet beneath the steering wheel. A moment later, the car's old-fashioned engine growled to life and we were peeling out of Ingrid's driveway, a shower of pebbles spraying across her lawn.

"Mardi, come on!" I pleaded. "Just because you're mad at Ingrid doesn't mean you have to ruin her front yard."

Mardi grinned over at me. "Oh, don't be such a Goody Two-shoes. This is just the way I drive."

She shifted—up or down, I have no idea; driving is something I prefer to leave to chauffeurs—and the car squealed onto the asphalt. My head slammed back into the headrest as Mardi accelerated. Fortunately her weather hex deflected most of the wind as well, so all my hair did was bounce a little in the breeze. Believe me when I tell you that there's no crisis so dire that you have to turn an eighty-dollar blowout into a rat's nest.

"What is it with gods and secrets?" I screamed, since

the engine in my sister's vintage automobile didn't come with a muffler. "I mean, what's the point in being *immortal* if you have to hide everything like a common crook?"

"I know," Mardi shouted back. "Sometimes I feel like we're on a cosmic reality show, and somewhere just out of view there's a director giving instructions for everyone to mess with the Overbrook girls—who, apparently, shouldn't even exist anyway."

I shuddered. "What do you think Ingrid meant by that?"

"Who knows? Maybe nothing—she is the goddess of the hearth, after all. She takes things like sex and birth *way* too seriously."

"True. But whatever went down when we were born had to have been pretty serious. I mean, Troy can be a little authoritarian sometimes, but there's no way he would have kept our mother from us unless she'd done something terrible."

Mardi nodded. "Do you think she's really mortal? Or do you think maybe she's like us?"

"She has to be mortal, right? I mean, if nothing else, there's the tennis thing. The Council's super strict when it comes to supernatural beings using their powers to make money. No sports, no gambling, no spell casting during business deals—nothing that would draw attention to our kind and risk another Inquisition or witch hunt. But . . . how could a mortal trick Thor into getting her pregnant?"

Mardi shrugged. "It wouldn't be the first time humans have tricked our kind. Immortality doesn't seem to make the gods any smarter than humans, after all. Just longer-living. But, hey, now that I think about it, Trent said once that she was a Rhinemaiden. Aren't they immortal?"

"I don't think so. I think they're specially selected humans, like the Romans' vestal virgins."

"But why use mortals to guard something so precious?" Mardi countered. "Wouldn't you want the most powerful god you could get?"

"Gods can't do everything, or we'd have done away with humans centuries ago. Maybe guarding the Rhinegold is one of those tasks only humans can do."

"Gods, I hate this!" Mardi said, slamming her fist on the steering wheel and sounding the horn, which sent a flock of seagulls squawking into the sky. "Troy better have some answers, or he's going to discover just what it means to have the goddess of rage as his daughter."

"You know it," I said, grabbing her hand. Mardi squeezed my fingers tightly and flashed me a look of determination, then pressed the accelerator all the way to the floor.

∗6∗

MY HUMPS

Mardi-Overbrook-Journal.docx

I squealed into the lot by the dock at a good sixty miles an hour and fishtailed into a parking space. It was a move I couldn't have pulled off in a hundred years if I'd actually been *trying* to do it, but the truth is I was so distracted by all the thoughts running through my head that I wasn't really paying attention. Fortunately I have what we like to call "witch's insurance," which is to say: Troy had only let me have a car on the condition that he be allowed to put a safety shield on it, which made it almost impossible for me to get into an accident.

I glanced over at Molly, who was gripping the edges of her seat.

"Sorry 'bout that, Moll," I said with a big smile.

"This is why I ride in limos with professional drivers,"

Molly said, slowly relaxing in her seat. She folded the visor down, checked her hair in the mirror—it was perfect as usual, thanks to the hex, of course—then climbed out of the car. We walked across the parking lot toward the pier where the seaplanes docked.

"It's just past five," I said, glancing at my watch. "Dad called around four-thirty, so he should be here any minute."

We scanned the sky to the west, and sure enough, within a few seconds, a tiny speck appeared. It grew rapidly larger, taking on the familiar shape of the seaplane from Manhattan, with its fat yellow pontoons hanging below the wings like a pair of bananas.

"Also?" Molly said. "Can we talk about how Dad always takes the seaplane when he makes us take a car or the train?"

"I know, totally unfair," I agreed. "Although I'd go crazy out here without my car. I don't know how you can stand it."

"I manage to get around just fine," Molly said. "Besides, North Hampton is about half the size of Central Park. You can get around on a bicycle."

I couldn't help but laugh.

"What? I totally rode Ingrid's bike all over town last summer!" Molly protested. "But thank Odin we're goddesses and don't have to work out. Spandex and *headbands* don't appeal to me *at all*." She paused for a moment. Then: "Speaking of working up a sweat . . ."

I knew just what she was talking about, but I

pretended not to. When it was clear I wasn't going to say anything, she prompted, "You've been living in Fair Haven for almost two weeks now. Have you and Trent . . . ?"

I sighed heavily.

"What?" Molly said, turning away from the plane, which was only a mile or two away. "Really? You haven't slept with him? Interesting . . . "

"I mean, I really like him, you know, especially since the end of last summer, after we figured out Trent was the real Trystan Gardiner, and Tris was just—"

"Do NOT remind me," Molly cut me off. "The fact that I made out with that troll is enough to make me heave—even if he did look like a member of One Direction when we were doing the making out."

"Trent doesn't look like a member of One Direction! He's much more Bastille or MGMT, hello."

"Oh, don't be such a snob." Molly laughed. "Looking like Harry Styles isn't exactly the worst thing in the world."

"Okay, first of all, if he looks like anyone from 1D, it's Louis. And second, I'm not a snob. I just don't listen to exactly the same thing as every other seventeen-year-old girl in the world!"

"Sure. Like MGMT or Bastille are *so* radical. Like no one's ever heard of them except Mardi Overbrook and six other super-cool people."

I opened my mouth to protest but thought better of it. This was hardly the time or place to get into a stupid sister fight—not when our dad was about sixty seconds away from landing and explaining the origin of, well, *us*. But more important, I knew that Molly wasn't actually upset about whether Trent looked more like a boy bander or an indie rocker. What upset her was that she'd been duped by an evil dude who came close to stealing our Rhinegold and driving a permanent wedge between us. Ever since we'd managed to chase off Alberich, Molly had been extremely touchy on the subject of boys. In fact, she had deliberately not gone out on a date in *one whole year*. For the average teenage girl, that's like the Siberia of romance. No, it's worse than that. It's the North Korea of romance. But for a girl like my twin sister, who (if I do say so myself) is not only gorgeous but rich, smart, and, oh yeah, *a goddess*, it must be even worse. Seriously, I don't think a day goes by that Molly isn't hit on by some moonstruck Romeo, but she's turned down every single one of them since she discovered that the last boy she'd said yes to was actually a dark elf, and practically a troll. And not an Internet one at that. Like, a *real* troll.

"So," I said, figuring I only had to keep the conversation going for another minute or two before Dad's plane landed, "did you hear that Sal's son is coming to stay on the East End for the summer?"

Sal McLaughlin owned the North Inn, the übercool dive bar/celebrity hot spot where Freya tended bar.

"I might've heard something about that," Molly said in a casual kind of way.

"His name's Rocco," I continued. "Freya told me Sal's ex-wife was Italian, as in Italian-from-Italy. I figured there couldn't be too many Rocco McLaughlins out there, so I looked him up online."

"And?" Molly said, still trying to sound like she wasn't interested, but I could tell her curiosity was piqued.

I held up my phone, where I'd already pulled up Rocco's picture, after first swiping past about two hundred more IMs and alerts about Janet Steele. Seriously, if this kept up, I was going to have to get a new number. A new name even.

"He goes by Rocky," I said. "He just finished his freshman year at Dartmouth."

"Smarty-pants, huh," Molly said, taking a quick glance at my phone. A moment later, however, her eyes strayed back, and this time they stayed. "Huh," she said again, but this time with a totally different inflection.

Based on his looks, Rocky McLaughlin had inherited long inky-black locks and a smooth olive complexion from his Italian mother. From his Irish dad, he'd gotten a pair of piercing pale blue eyes and thin but wide and very pink lips. He had a lean, angular face with high cheekbones and a strong chin with a pronounced dimple. I quickly swiped to the next one, which showed him in just a pair of board shorts, so Molly could see his perfect chest and rippling abs.

"Huh," Molly repeated, except this time she didn't try to hide the fact that she was intrigued. "Well, he doesn't suck to look at, does he?"

"Not. At. All." I had a boyfriend, but there was no harm in looking, was there?

Molly glanced at my phone one more time. "We might have to return to this subject later," she said in her faux-aloof voice. She nodded toward the sky. "Dad's plane is landing. We'd better focus."

"Right," I said, tucking my phone into my pocket. We were at the shore end of the dock, and we started walking out toward the water.

"Looks like a pretty empty flight," Molly said.

"Yeah," I agreed. "Just Dad and the flight attendant and—oh, my gods!"

A dark shape appeared in the water just under Dad's plane, which was only a few feet above the surface of the Sound. It must've been twice as big as a city bus, and as Molly and I watched, horrified, it rose up out of the water like a submarine, torrents of water streaming off its curved shell.

"Is that a . . . *whale*?" Molly screamed.

I was pretty sure it *was* a whale—a humpback whale—but before I could answer, the tip of one of the pontoons on the bottom of Dad's plane caught on its massive steel-gray back. If there was any doubt that the whale's appearance wasn't a coincidence, it disappeared when the leviathan lifted its massive tail out of the water and used it to slap the plane out of the air. The plane slammed propeller-first into the whale's back, then rolled nose over tail, collapsing like a crushed can as it went. As it neared the front of the plane, the whale rolled to its side, and a collosal pectoral fin came out of the water, smashing the plane—and its occupants—in a dozen different directions.

I was about to scream, but I was distracted by a large smooth mound near the front of the whale, a brownish-gray circle with a darker circle inside it. It was only when it blinked that I realized it was the whale's eye. The whale rolled completely over and the eye was gone, but even so, I couldn't shake the thought that the eye had been staring at me. The pectoral fin, which must've been a dozen feet long, slapped the surface of the bay, sending a plume of water up into the air.

Through the mist, I could see things flying every-where—pieces of the fuselage, seats, suitcases, and, worst of all, several spindly shapes that could have only been people. Before I knew it, I was running down the dock.

"Mardi!" Molly screamed, running beside me. "What are you doing?"

"We've got to save them!" I yelled back.

"But the water's freezing! We need to cast some kind of spell."

This was true. Though it was a balmy seventy-five degrees on land, the cool water of the Sound barely tipped the scales at fifty degrees. At that temperature, hypothermia could set in before we reached anyone—and while our souls are immortal, our bodies are made of pretty much the same flesh and blood as everyone else's.

In other words, there was a very real chance that we could die trying to save our father. But we had to do something.

"There's no time for magic!" I screamed even as I kicked my shoes off. "It's Dad!"

I guess on some level Molly felt this too. After all, she was running down the dock every bit as fast as I was, and she'd already lost her shoes. As I launched myself off the dock, I saw a flash of white out of the corner of my eye, and realized she was right behind me.

Then the freezing water closed over me, and all thoughts of Molly or Dad or anything else vanished from my brain. The only thing I wanted to do was get out. I began kicking desperately, frantically, trying to propel myself back out of the water.

But as soon as my head cleared the air, I saw pieces of the airplane fuselage all around me, and remembered why we were there. The water was freezing, but I told myself to ignore it. Dad was in here somewhere. I had to find him.

Just then, Molly's head broke the surface. Her dark hair was plastered across her face and her lips had already gone blue and quivery. There was no hiding the look of determination in her eyes.

"I saw someone that way," she said, pointing to her left. "And I think there's someone over there too." She pointed right, over my shoulder. And then, arcing to her left, she was under again.

I twisted to the right and kicked myself under. The

cold water squeezed me like a giant hand, as if it was trying to crush my bones, but I put it out of my mind, swimming as hard and fast as I could. As I went down, the pressure only grew more intense; my lungs were on fire even as my skin was turning to ice.

And then I saw it. A hand, waving in the current.

For one ghastly second, I thought it had been severed from its body, but then my eyes adjusted to the gloom and I saw the rest of the body dangling below it. I realized the hand wasn't waving in the current—it was actually trying to swim. I squinted, trying to make out the face.

It was Dad!

I kicked harder, all thoughts of exhaustion suddenly gone. In three strokes, I was there. Dad's fingers curled around mine in a vise grip, but even as they did, I noticed his other arm, his left, hanging limply at his side, along with both of his legs. But he was awake and even smiling, albeit grimly. With a nod of his chin, he indicated where we had to go:

Up!

I began frog kicking, doing my best not to hit Dad in the face. His hand clung to mine. The thought of our dad, the god of thunder, in a wheelchair was almost too much to bear.

I told myself not to think such thoughts—not now, when we were still twenty feet below the surface of the water and my lungs were burning and my legs were aching and Dad was hanging off me like a two-hundred-pound anchor. *Just kick, Mardi*, I told my-self. *Kick. Kick. KICK!*

Suddenly, my head burst above the waves, and a second later, Dad's broke through. For a moment, all we could do was breathe, inhaling big ragged breaths of air. Then, faintly, I heard voices.

"There's someone there!"

I looked over my shoulder and saw a man on the dock pointing to me. Then a second man appeared, holding a life preserver. As he tossed it to me, I saw that it was dangling a line.

"Catch!"

The man's aim was good. The preserver landed less than a foot from me, and I grabbed onto it with the hand that wasn't holding Dad. As soon as I had it, I felt the rope tug as the two men began hauling us to shore. Only then did I turn my attention to Dad.

"Are you okay? Dad, can you hear me?"

His eyes had closed, but after a long moment, they fluttered open. He smiled at me weakly.

"I saw you girls on the dock," he said, and though his voice was faint, you could hear the mischief in it.

"Dad, a whale came up underneath your plane! That was what crashed it. A *whale*. That—I mean, that has to be magic, right? Was someone trying to kill you?"

Dad's eyes closed again but not before I could see a flicker of recognition in them.

"Who would try to kill you, Dad? Why?"

"Later," Dad replied, without opening his eyes.

But then they sprang open. "Molly!" he exclaimed. "Where's your sister?"

My head whipped back and forth as I scanned the dark water, but all I saw were pieces of the plane's fuselage scattered over the rippling waves like abandoned beach toys. No matter where I looked, there was no sign of Molly.

* 7 *

DIVER DOWN

From the Diary of Molly Overbrook

As the water closed over my head, I kicked in the opposite direction from Mardi toward the dark shape I'd glimpsed a moment ago. I prayed it was Dad. I prayed he was okay.

Did Mardi tell you about the whale's eye? We talked about it later—how we were sure it was staring at us. There's something especially creepy about an eye the size of your head staring you down. You get the feeling that it's looking right into your brain, reading your thoughts, daring you to do something stupid, like jump in the water and try to save your dad. If it had been anyone else, I don't think I would've had the guts. But it was Dad. We had to do it.

It seemed to take forever before I saw the dark shape I'd seen before: it was falling quickly. I thought bodies were supposed to float? Something about the air in the lungs and the stomach? But then, as I got closer, I saw why it was falling so fast: some kind of cable had coiled around one of the legs, and hanging off the opposite end was the twisted metal framework of a chair.

It wasn't Dad. It was a young woman, only five or six years older than me. Probably the flight attendant, judging from the plain button-down shirt and khakis she was wearing. Her eyes were closed and she wasn't moving, but she couldn't have been in the water for even a minute.

There's still time, I told myself. *I can save her.*

I kicked over to her and grabbed at the cable. It was stiff and heavy, and no matter how much I pulled and twisted, I couldn't get it to unwind from her leg, and all the while I felt it pulling us even farther from the surface.

Damn it! I screamed mentally. *Let go!*

But the cable refused to budge, and so, steeling myself, I grabbed the woman and pulled her to my chest and began kicking for the surface. I could feel the chair hanging off her leg, pulling me down, and for a while, it didn't seem like we were moving. But then momentum finally built, and we began to inch toward the surface. I swam harder and pushed through the water with my free hand.

I looked down at the woman's face. Her eyes were closed but her mouth was gently open, and her loose jaw waved slightly in the current. *Hold on*, I willed her. *We're almost there.*

But that wasn't really true. The surface was still ten feet away, but the chair was so heavy and my legs so tired that we were hardly moving at all. It took every ounce of resolve not to let her go and drag myself to the surface. I kicked, and kicked, and kicked—

—and suddenly I broke through the surface. A strange gasping screaming sound burst from my lungs as I tried to catch my breath. The flight attendant's head sagged backward in the water, and I had to hold it up to keep her from slipping under again. Then I realized it wasn't just her head. It was her whole body. It was both of us, being dragged back down by the weight of that chair.

I tried to kick with my legs, but there was nothing left. They barely moved in the water below me. I was slipping under too. In desperation, I started flailing around with my free arm. My hand smacked against something, and I grabbed it and hung on for dear life. Whatever it was, it floated, and it was enough to keep me and the flight attendant above water. I figured it had to be part of the plane.

In fact, I soon realized it was a big part. Like, half the fuselage. We'd actually come up inside it, I saw now. It tented over us like a giant eggshell.

At first, I was relieved because its buoyancy was holding us up. But very quickly I realized that it was also shielding us from the shore, whichever way it was, and whatever searchers might've joined Mardi and me. I would have to dive under and pull the flight attendant along with me if I wanted someone to find us. And I knew, just knew, I didn't have the strength for that.

"Help!" I yelled, my voice echoing back at me off the warped shell of the plane. "Help! We're over here!"

But I heard nothing in reply.

I looked down at the flight attendant. Her lips and skin had a blue pallor, either because of the cold or because she hadn't taken a breath in a good two minutes. I had taken a mandatory CPR class at school, but I couldn't even do that because of our situation. All I could do was stare helplessly into her face and watch her die.

"No!" I yelled.

And then it came to me: Joanna! Ingrid and Freya's mother. Something had happened to her about ten years ago that caused her to lose her earthly body, but her spirit still hovered over the East End, protecting it and lending aid to her family. She had even once saved a boy who drowned. I'd been there. I watched him come back to life with my own two eyes.

"Joanna Beauchamp!" I called. "Great goddess Skadi! I don't know if you're my grandmother or my aunt or my sister, but whatever you are, I call on you in the name of our family! Do not let this mortal die! Please! I beg you!"

When Ingrid and Freya had called on their mother

that day, there had been a bolt of lightning that pierced the water, and a moment later, the drowned boy had awakened. I braced myself for the electrical current— we had been on a boat last time, and I didn't know if I should expect a shock. I didn't know if I could even survive it.

But as it turned out, I didn't need to brace myself for anything because nothing happened.

"Joanna!" I pleaded with the empty sky. "Please! Save her! She shouldn't have to die because someone was trying to kill Thor!"

Still nothing happened. Nothing except the swirl of the freezing water, numbing my limbs.

I don't know how much later it was before someone found us. Ten minutes? An hour? I couldn't tell you. I barely remember someone prying my fingers off the fuselage, uncurling my arm from the flight attendant's body and hauling us into a dinghy.

"It's okay," someone said to me. "We've got her now."

But I knew they didn't have her. She was dead. She had died in my arms.

8

MODERN GIRLS AND OLD-FASHIONED MEN

Mardi-Overbrook-Journal.docx

So who's the Norse god of the sea anyway? Who's our version of Poseidon, or what's the Roman guy's name, Neptune?"

"Well, there's Norman, of course. Ingrid and Freya's father. But he's in Niflheim now."

"The Land of the Dead."

Dad nodded. "And then there's Aegir," he said, chuckling, then quickly switching to a groan. "I have to stop laughing. The ribs are still tender."

Dad's ribs were the least of the problem. It turned out the crash had, like, *shattered* his pelvis. It was in six or seven pieces, which was why his legs had just hung there when I pulled him out of the ocean two days prior. For a mortal, such a wound would have been catastrophic—he probably would've never walked normally again, and it was a miracle his spinal cord hadn't been injured. Even for a god trapped in Midgard, it was still serious. Because of the risk of internal bleeding, Molly and I had had no choice but to let the ambulance take him to the hospital, where the doctors had done a whole series of X-rays. In addition to his broken pelvis, there were fractures in his left arm and left femur. I guess that was the side the plane had come down on. On top of all that, he also had a pretty serious concussion.

Left to nature, the injuries could have easily taken a year to heal, maybe more, and like I said, there was no guarantee that he would have fully recovered. Ingrid had been forced to whip up a fairly strong magical potion, dragging out her mother's ancient spell books to find one that she thought would work, then hopping on the Internet to get all the things she needed. (Apparently, there are places out in the world that'll FedEx the wings of a hundred Atlas moths—Ingrid only needed the dust, but she had to scrape it off herself—and a vial of venom from the Egyptian cobra, which, FYI, is the snake Cleopatra used to commit suicide.) It took almost two days to gather everything and make the potion.

Dad spent most of that time looped out of his mind on morphine, his entire middle from his sternum to his thighs encased in a plaster cast. Ouch. If Dad had been in his immortal Aesir body, the potion would have healed him completely, but because he was in a mortal body (his seventh, it turned out), the potion could only speed up the process so that what would have taken a year to heal would probably end up taking about a month. Freya had to bewitch the doctor to cut the cast off him, and after that, she and Ingrid administered a forgetting spell to every single person who worked in the hospital so they'd have no memory of how serious Dad's injuries were. That kind of thing is of course totally against Council rules, but it was that or have forty people talking about how Troy Overbrook broke his pelvis at the end of May and was back on the tennis courts by July. The Council likes that kind of talk even less than they like it when magic is used on mortals, so the aunts figured it was worth risking censure.

Finally, we brought Dad back to Ingrid's to finish his recuperation. Like I said, he was probably still going to be down for three or four more weeks, and because Ingrid's potion basically made his metabolism run ten times faster than normal, he was exhausted all the time. Exhausted but starving—Ingrid and her housekeeper were kept busy making him coconut-oil-goji-berry-bee-pollen-whey-powder-flaxseed-wheat-grass-kefir smoothies. (Kefir, by the way, is fermented goat's milk, and the smoothies tasted pretty much exactly like a barn smells.) But Dad, who's much more of a steak-with-a-side-of-steak kind of guy, couldn't seem to get enough of them. He was sipping on one while he rested in Jo's bedroom, which had only that winter been equipped with a full-sized bed. Molly had helped her decorate, so the room was suffused with what can only be described as an *excessive* amount of pink satin and white lace, but it made for some good jokes at Dad's expense. (I have to admit that I took a sadistic pleasure in making Dad squirm. It's rare that you get to turn the tables on your parent when he's a mere mortal, but when your dad is the god of thunder, you have to take every chance you get.)

As you can imagine, all the magic and smoothie making had kept us pretty busy, but once Dad was well on his way to recovery, I couldn't put off my questions any longer. I started with the whale because, well, *a whale tried to kill my dad*. I had to know if he thought it was on purpose. If he had any idea who was behind it.

"Does Aegir rule the sea animals?" I asked.

Another chuckle from Dad, followed by another groan. "What, like Aquaman?" He paused to take a sip of his greenish-grayish stink drink. "I don't really know. I assume he has some kind of influence, but if you're thinking Aegir sent that whale to kill me, you can set your mind at ease. Aegir and I go way back. We once threw a party that was the kind of party people wrote epic poems about."

"Kind of like Truman Capote's masked ball? Or Diddy's end-of-summer white party in East Hampton?"

"Ha!" Dad said, then grabbed his ribs. "No, it was more like the Norse version of a rave. There was this cauldron—you wouldn't believe what Tyr and I had to go through to get it. All I can tell you is that we pissed off a couple of giants." A faraway look came over Dad's face as he remembered the good old days when the gods took whatever they wanted and settled their disputes with swords. "It was the size of a hot tub. Much beer was made in it. Much beer was drunk from it. As I recall, Odin even ended up swimming in it." He shook his head at the memory. "Parents—even gods—should know better than to get naked in front of their kids."

Having never met my grandfather, I was forced to imagine Anthony Hopkins from the Thor movies swimming in a hot tub full of beer. It was an amusing image, although I wondered if Dad was maybe stretching the truth a little.

"Trent used to throw parties with you?" I asked. Sometimes I forgot that my seventeen-year-old boyfriend was also the two-thousand-year-old Norse god of war, and that he'd run around having adventures with my dad for centuries upon centuries before I was even born.

"Why do you think I don't trust him alone with you?" Dad said with a grimace that was only half ironic.

I blushed. "Let's not talk about Trent right now. We were talking about Aegir. You're one hundred percent sure he wouldn't try to kill you?"

Dad nodded, then took another sip of his smoothie.

"Positively. Aside from the fact that we're united in our mutual hatred of Loki, Aegir's been stuck in Utgard since the destruction of the bridge."

I fingered the tattoo on my neck, which commemorated the lost rainbow bridge.

"Is Aegir a giant?"

Dad nodded. "Although technically we're all the same species, you know. Every one of us, even the giants. Whatever the celestial version of DNA is, we all have the same kind. There's no more difference between us than there is between a Norwegian and a Russian or a Nigerian."

"But in all the drawings I've ever seen, giants are, like, twelve feet tall. How can we be related to them?"

Dad nodded again. "Some were a lot taller than that. But look at a Saint Bernard and a Chihuahua. Their DNA is virtually identical. Besides, it's not appearances that divide people—skin color, hair texture, height, things like that. It's the *ideas* people have about appearances. Prejudice isn't just a problem here in Midgard—it's rampant throughout the nine worlds, including Asgard."

"What do you mean?"

"When my father led the Aesir in their revolt against the Jotun, he and Frigg, your grandmother, chose a new form for us, one that more closely resembled the humans of Midgard, because they had already developed a special relationship with them. A little shorter, a little less hair on the shoulders and the top of the feet. As the centuries went on, they started to talk as though we'd always looked the way we do now—as though the Aesir and Vanir really were different species from the

Jotun and the elves and dwarfs. But take my word for it, there's giant blood in your veins, my sweet."

"If Odin led a revolt against the Jotun, how were you friends with Aegir?"

"In the same way the United States and England are allies. Once time passes and tempers cool, you come to realize you have more similarities than differences. Oh, some Jotun definitely held a grudge, as did some Aesir for that matter. Like any other society, it comes down to individuals. Aegir was definitely one of the good giants. I counted some Jotun as my closest friends back in the old days." A far-off look came into his eyes. "Some were very close indeed," he said longingly.

I thought about the stories I'd heard concerning our mother—that she was a giant too. And even though Janet Steele looked human, I couldn't help but wonder if that's who he was thinking about.

"We, um . . ."

I stopped short. Now that I was so close to getting real information about my mother, I found it hard to bring up the subject. Part of the problem was that Molly should have been there with me. It seemed strange—wrong—that I would learn something about our origin without her.

But ever since we'd pulled Molly out of the water, still clutching the lifeless body of that flight attendant, she'd avoided the entire family. She visited the hospital while Dad was there, but she sat apart from us in the waiting room and refused to talk to anyone, and if you actually tried to touch her, she sent out waves of nega-tive energy so intense that cell phones and TVs would go on the fritz, randomly dialing numbers or chang-ing channels. We were afraid that she might short out somebody's life support machine or something, so we had no choice but to leave her alone.

It hadn't gotten better since we'd brought Dad home. Molly had moved out of her guest bedroom and into Ingrid's gardening studio in the backyard. We only saw her when she came in to get food or take a bath. Still, I figured if she was taking the time to wash and comb her hair that things couldn't be too bad, and she just needed time. But this was an important conversation. My sister should have been there with us.

Dad must have sensed the struggle that was going on in me. He put his hand on mine and squeezed, as if he was the one comforting me. "Mardi? Did you want to ask me something?"

I looked at the open door, as if Molly might appear there, but the only thing that came through was the sound of the television downstairs, where Henry and Jo were playing the latest version of Zelda. I turned back to Dad.

"So Janet Steele—she's our mom, right?" I tried not to hold my breath, and watched Dad intently.

He nodded and tried not to squirm.

"And I was just going to ask if . . . I mean, there are legends. That Thor's children were born of a gi-antess. And so I was wondering if Janet Steele . . . ?"

Somehow I couldn't bring myself to voice the question *Is our mom a giantess?* It just sounded too weird.

To my surprise, Dad laughed again and kept on laughing despite the obvious pain it caused him.

"Janet? A giantess?" He reached for his drink and took a long pull. "By Odin, that *is* funny. I mean, she is six foot one, so I can see you might think that. But no, she's as human as they come. A special kind of human, but still human."

My ears immediately perked up when Dad said *special kind of human*, and I felt my heart start to thud in my chest.

"What do you mean, special?" I said, barely able to control my voice.

To my surprise, Dad frowned.

"I'm sorry, this brings up one of the less noble aspects of our history. But I think you're old enough to hear about it now." He took another swig of his smelly smoothie, then continued:

"When the bridge was first destroyed, and those of us who were in Midgard realized we were trapped here for all of eternity, some people didn't take it so well. There have always been some of us who took the whole god thing a little too seriously, basically treating humans like slaves or pets. I guess some people were inspired by the vampires and their human familiars and they basically claimed entire families as their indentured servants—generation after generation raised to do nothing but serve the gods. Janet is descended from one of these families. Her ancestors were forced to serve Loki for several hundred years, until the Council formally abolished the practice after Salem."

As if he'd heard us talking, Fury, Molly's canine familiar, appeared in the doorway. Poor thing: Molly had been so distraught that she hadn't even taken her out to the gardening shed with her. Fury had been wandering the house for two days looking forlorn—forlorn and ridiculous, what with her shaved hindquarters contrasting with the glossy mane that fringed her face.

"Loki!" I couldn't help but exclaim, patting my lap to invite Fury up. She stared at me blankly, then wandered away, her buffed nails clicking on the bare floorboards. "Does that mean our mother is . . . evil?"

Another laugh from Dad. "Calm yourself, daughter. Janet's got a temper on her, but I think it has more to do with being raised in the Australian outback by a bunch of rough-and-tumble cowboys and opal miners. She'd heard stories of her family's history from her grandmother, but had no idea whether they were true or just something the old woman had made up to amuse her."

"Did she know who you were?"

Dad didn't say anything for a moment. His gaze went far away, and I could imagine him conjuring a mental image of when he first met our mother. Judging from the look on his face, however, it was far from the fairytale romance I would have hoped for.

Finally, he nodded. "I wasn't aware of it at first, but later on, I realized she'd known who I was all along."

Suddenly, I remembered Ingrid's comment from the other day, about how Molly and I were never supposed to have been born.

"Did she trick you? Into having kids, I mean."

Another long pause followed by another nod.

"In the old days, when Loki and some of the refugees from the nine worlds still had human familiars, the humans would try to seduce their gods in order to have children by them. As you and your sister and Jo all demonstrate, the offspring of a mortal and an immortal usually take after the immortal parent, and these children, who loved their human parent every bit as much as they loved their celestial one, would often cast longevity spells on their mortal parent to keep him or her alive. Such spells are incredibly difficult to cast—as I recall, one of the ingredients is a dragon scale, and another is the powdered fingernails of one of the undead guardians of Niflheim, which is the only one of the nine worlds those of us trapped in Midgard can still access."

"From the seam under Fair Haven, Trent's family's house, right?"

"That's right," Dad said. "Anyway, your mother had heard these stories, and I guess she got it into her head that she wanted to have a god's child. Specifically, this god's child."

"Hey, give her credit for good taste, right?"

Dad shrugged, but you could tell he was pleased. Modesty is not one of the godly virtues, and Thor was the godliest of them all when it came to loving himself.

Then he turned to me, a nostalgic smile on his face. "She was so beautiful, she didn't need that love potion she gave me."

"She charmed you?"

"Maybe." He winked. Dad was so bad. Growing up, Molly and I had met more Victoria's Secret models, pop princesses, and grade-B starlets than Leonardo DiCaprio and Drake put together.

"You really think she had access to magic?"

"Oh, yeah."

"How do you know?" I said defiantly.

"Well, honestly, because of you. You and Molly."

I stifled a gasp.

"You mean it's true? That we weren't supposed to be born!"

"It's a little more complicated than that."

"Dad!" I almost yelled. "Don't drag this out! I'm dying here."

He smiled and patted me on the knee. "You and your sister were always destined to be born. It's just that we always thought your mother would, in fact, be a Jotun. And . . ." Again his voice fell off.

"Dad! What?"

He grimaced. "It's just, well, we thought you were going to be, well . . . *boys*."

For a moment, I didn't say anything. In the huge silence that followed this surreal announcement, all you could hear was the beeps and whirrs of Jo and Henry's video game coming faintly up the stairs.

"Boys?" I said finally. Then again: *"Boys?"*

Before my dad could answer, the doorbell rang. Simultaneously, I felt a buzz in my pocket. I pulled out my phone and saw a text from Trent.

Ringing ur doorbell. U home?

I don't know why, but I jumped up.

"Mardi?"

"I'll be back!" I said quickly. "I just have to . . ." I didn't finish my sentence, just ran downstairs to answer the door, running right past Jo and Henry, who didn't look up from their game.

As I pulled open the door, I was all ready to confront Trent, a.k.a. Tyr, my dad's old party buddy, to find out if he'd known anything about how his girlfriend and her sister were supposed to have been born male, but the look on his face stopped me in my tracks. His jaw hung open slackly, and his eyes were wide with confusion.

"Trent?" I said, my own confusion overshadowed by concern for him. "What's wrong?"

He shook his head in bewilderment. "We just got thrown out."

"What?" I exclaimed. "From Fair Haven?" The house had been in the Gardiner family for hundreds of years.

He nodded dumbly.

"Your, um, mother bought our house, and she just kicked us out."

✳ 9 ✳

GONNA FLY NOW

From the Diary of Molly Overbrook

$\mathscr{H}$ere, Moll, drink this," Freya said to me, pushing a frothy brown concoction down the bar. "Looks like you need it."

I sniffed at the effervescing foam, inhaling whiffs of chai, cinnamon, honey, and something I couldn't place.

"Is that . . . nutmeg?"

"Close. It's called *shahi jeera*, also known as black cumin. An Indian spice. I infuse it in the rum. It's very centering."

I glanced at the clock. It was three in the afternoon, but I could use some "centering," and although I was usually a vodka girl, rum would do. I bent the tall straw toward me and sipped. The drink had a dark, tealike taste, and I could feel it as it slid all the way down my throat and then—magically, no doubt—spread out through my limbs, making me feel as if I was a bag whose air was being sucked out by a vacuum.

"Wow, that really is"—there was no other word for it—"centering." I took another sip, bigger this time. "Would you call that taste 'umami'?"

Freya laughed. "If you're a foodie, I guess. I prefer something like 'earthy.' Now, go slow," she admonished as I took another sip. "It's got two shots of 120-proof rum in there. It'll knock even a goddess on her butt if she's not careful."

I took another drink. After all, I was already sitting down.

For the next few minutes, Freya continued measuring out her powders, seeds, leaves, and tinctures for the evening shift while I nursed my drink. At first, the surface of my skin felt flushed even as my intestines seemed to be flowing with icy water. But then my skin cooled and my insides warmed up, as if I was an oven turned on full blast, but sitting outside on an iceberg. At one point, I exhaled a long sigh and was surprised when smoke didn't come out of my mouth.

"So," Freya said from down at the other end of the bar. "Want to talk about it?"

"I don't know how to describe it," I said glumly.

"I get it," Freya said. "He's your dad. It's scary to see him like this. I mean, whether he's Thor or Troy Overbrook, you've grown up thinking of him as this invincible figure, and now all of a sudden he looks almost human."

"What?" I asked, trying not to look too guilty. "No, I'm not worried about Dad, although that was really freaky what happened to him."

"Well, we still have to figure out where that whale came from. It's not Loki, since he's made his peace with us. And this has outer worlds magic written all over it. But if it's not your dad that's bothering you, then what is it?"

I shrugged. It felt silly to say it out loud. But I did anyway. "It's that flight attendant. The one who died in my arms."

Freya nodded sympathetically. "I'm so sorry. You know it wasn't your fault."

I shook my head. "It's hard to explain. It's not her death that's bothering me. It's . . . it's that I suddenly realized that I would never die."

For the first time, I was face-to-face with my immortality, and it was overwhelming. It had never bothered me before, but it did now. Our friends, our lovers would one day pass, but we would go on. I felt sickened. "Does it ever get any easier, watching them die?"

In true Freya fashion, she didn't even try to soften the blow. "No," she said bluntly. "But that's a good thing. If it got easier, it would mean that you were detaching yourself. Numbing your feelings. Life is precious. It should be celebrated while it's here and mourned after it's gone."

I was starting to think that Freya was less in aunt mode than in wise-bartender mode, dishing out the secrets of life with each drink. I could appreciate what she was saying, but it was still a lot for the middle of the afternoon. At the same time, I didn't want to leave. Freya and Ingrid were two of the few examples Mardi and I had to show us what it meant to be immortal— goddesses locked out of Asgard, our eternal home, witches here in Midgard, but restricted in the use of our powers, which, in our case, we barely knew the extent of.

I took another sip of my drink.

"I tried to save her," I said.

"You were amazing," Freya said. "You dove into fifty-degree water and dragged a grown woman—and the forty-pound chair she was attached to—up to the surface. I can't tell you how proud we are of you."

"But that's not all I did."

Freya looked up from her apothecary bottles. "You mean magic?"

"Not exactly. Not mine anyway. I called on Joanna."

Freya's eyes went wide. "You called my mom?"

Since this is a diary and I'm doing my best to tell it like it is, I have to admit that I didn't like the way Freya said *my* and left out me and Mardi. I mean, I know Joanna isn't our mom, but still. It was almost like she was saying Joanna was her property, not ours. Her family. Not ours.

"I remembered what you guys did on the boat last summer, with that little boy. I thought maybe she could do the same for that woman."

"Okay." Freya laughed a little, nervously. "Honestly, I'm a bit taken aback."

"I didn't know what else to do," I said, my voice as uneasy as Freya's.

"Honey, you can't just go calling on the goddess Skadi to pull a soul from Niflheim every time a mortal kicks the bucket. For one thing, death is a natural thing. It's part of the cycle—that soul has other things to do, in other realms, and it's not our job to get in the way. For another, Helda, Skadi's sister, is seriously territorial. Believe me when I tell you she does *not* give up her subjects easily."

I nodded glumly.

"I know that," I said, and I could hear the petulance in my voice. "But even so . . ."

"What?" Freya's voice wasn't hostile, but it wasn't nearly as sympathetic as it had been before.

"It shouldn't matter why I called on her. I'm a goddess, for Pete's sake. I'm the newest member of this family. This was the first time I've ever had to confront something like this, and Joanna should have been there for me like she was for you and Ingrid."

For a moment, Freya didn't say anything. Then she shook her head angrily. She began grabbing up her various bottles and beakers and vials and stowing them for the evening shift.

"Look, I know you're new at this. This is your very first incarnation, and in many ways, you're just a typical seventeen-year-old girl. But it's time to face up to who you are and what that means. You're a goddess, Molly, and your father is one of the most powerful gods of them all—one of the most loved, but also one of the most hated. And that means that from time to time you're going to get caught up in plots to kill him, imprison him, or otherwise get him out of the picture so that evil beings can do the evil things they like to do. And the plain truth is that sometimes humans get caught in the cross fire when the gods go after each other, and however sad it may seem, it's not our duty—or even our right—to save every individual life that gets snuffed out too early. Our job is to protect Midgard as a whole."

"Wow," I said, pushing Freya's drink away—a hollow gesture, since it was pretty much empty. "Thanks for the tough love, *Aunt* Freya." I stood up to leave.

"You can call it whatever you want," Freya said, still angrily putting things away. "Sometimes there's no point in sugarcoating the truth."

"It's not like I asked for the dose of reality. You were the one who slipped me the drink and started asking questions. Whatever," I said, ignoring her opened mouth. "I'm taking off. You can save your charms for your customers."

I stalked out of the bar. I'd have slammed the door behind me, but it had a spring-loaded hinge that kept it from banging, so I had to content myself with turning around and flashing Freya a dirty look instead. Then I pivoted on my heel and stormed out—

—and crashed right into the chest of a some guy heading into the bar.

"Whoa, there," he said, and I felt his hands on my arms, steadying me.

Stupid mortal, I thought, shrugging him off. I guess in my anger I must have magicked it up a little because he went flying back about ten feet and would've landed flat on his back if he hadn't been wearing a huge over-stuffed backpack. Only then did I recognize who it was.

Rocco McLaughlin. Rocky. Let's just say that he was even cuter IRL than he was in his pictures. *Way* cuter.

"Holy crap," I said, running to him to help him. "I didn't see you. I'm sorry."

Rocky shook his head a little dazedly, and a fan of bangs swept off his face, revealing a pair of glowing blue eyes. He looked at the door, ten feet away, and then at me.

"Ever thought about playing football? That was some tackle."

"I'm so sorry," I said again, dusting off his shoulders, which weren't actually dusty. I offered him a hand, but he waved it away and stood up on his own. He patted himself clean, and then held a hand out to shake mine. His handshake was strong (and a little gritty). Most guys give girls these weak handshakes as though if they actually squeezed, their fingers might break. I guess Rocky knew better.

"I'm Rocky McLaughlin," he said, "and you are officially the first person I've met during my summer in purgatory, besides my cabdriver, I guess."

"McLaughlin, McLaughlin . . ." I repeated, as if I didn't know who he was. "Like Sal McLaughlin, the owner of the North Inn?" I jerked a finger at the sign behind me, as if I'd only just realized I was standing in front of it.

Rocky frowned at the mention of his dad's name, which surprised me.

"I'm his son," he said in a flat voice. "Although in name only."

"Oh, right!" I said, pretending to remember. "He's mentioned you a couple of times?" I added in a questioning voice, as if I wasn't sure.

"Really?" Rocky said doubtfully. "Because that'd be a couple more times than he's called me in the past eighteen years."

I must've made some kind of grimace because a guilty look flashed over Rocky's face.

"Sorry to dump on you. Sal and my mom were married for a hot minute in the late nineties. Just long enough to make me, and then they went their separate ways. I grew up with her. Sal left when I was a baby. And I'm pretty sure he would have preferred to remain ignorant."

"Oh, Sal's a great guy!" I protested. "I'm sure you two will get along." I pointed at his bag. "Judging from the size of that backpack, I take it you're staying for a while?"

"The whole summer." His voice didn't sound happy at all.

"C'mon, lighten up." I waved my hand, gesturing at the lush greenery, the scattered beach houses and the wide, cloudless blue sky, which felt like an extension of the ocean, just out of view behind the rolling dunes. "A summer at the beach. It can't be so bad."

"No, I guess you're right," Rocky said, though he didn't sound too convinced. "Anyway, I guess I should go in and tell him I'm here." He started toward the front door of the Inn.

An image of Freya popped into my head, standing behind the bar, whipping up her love potions. She was probably still annoyed from our conversation, and if there's one thing I know about Freya, it's how she likes to work off steam.

"The Inn doesn't open till five," I said quickly, stepping in front of Rocky to bar his path. "And Sal doesn't usually come in on weekdays till eight or nine, if at all."

Rocky peered around me, trying to get a glimpse through the window set in the door.

"But doesn't he live, like, upstairs or something?" Even as Rocky said that, he was looking at the roof of the one-story building for an imaginary second floor. "Around back maybe?"

"Um, no, this isn't a Victorian novel. The innkeeper doesn't live with his wife, six children, and three pigs in a barn out back." I laughed to take the sting out of my words. "Sal lives in a very comfortable beach house about a mile, um, yonder," I said, pointing in the distance. I knew where Sal lived, but only by sight.

Rocky looked doubtful, as if I might be trying to trick him. "1762 Dune Road," he said, looking down at his phone again.

"Yup, that's the Inn," I said, pointing to the battered brass numbers nailed to the shingles.

He sighed heavily and shifted the straps of his pack, which suddenly seemed to be biting into his shoulders.

"You wouldn't happen to know his home address?"

As he asked, it popped into my head: 409 Pfenning Road.

"Sorry, no idea," I said. "But if you want, I can walk you there. Like I said, it's only about a mile."

I wasn't sure, but I thought I saw a flicker of a smile cross his face.

"Okay," he said simply.

It was the nicest word I'd heard all day.

"You're lucky I'm wearing flats today, or you'd be on your own," I said as we started out, holding up a leg to show off my espadrilles. "So what made you decide to spend the summer on the East End anyway?"

Rocky sighed again.

"I didn't. Sal did."

There was a hint of warning in his voice—more than a hint—but I chose to ignore it. We had a mile to go, after all. And you know, nothing ventured, nothing gained.

"He thought it was time for some father-son bonding?"

"I guess so."

We trudged on another dozen steps in silence. I was beginning to think that talking was going to be even more painful than not talking.

"I wanted to stay at college this summer," Rocky said finally, "but Sal said he couldn't afford it plus tuition in the fall, so all things considered, I figured I'd better come here."

"Why not stay with your mom?"

We walked another dozen steps before Rocky answered.

"My mom died in March."

"Oh," I said hollowly. "I had no idea." In my head, I yelled at Mardi, who was the one who'd looked Rocky up on social media: *How could you miss that, sis?*

"Cancer," Rocky continued. "I knew she was sick, but she said it wasn't serious. Otherwise I'd never have gone to college in the first place. I would've spent her last months with her. In the end, when she finally told me what was going on, she said she'd kept it from me because she knew I'd lose my scholarship if I deferred for a year, and she was afraid I wouldn't be able to afford college without it. She was right about that anyway. Even after I sold the house, there was barely enough to pay off her medical bills."

"Gods," I said. "That's terrible. I'm so sorry."

"'Gods,'" he repeated with a little bit of a grin. "What are you, some kind of pagan?"

"Oh, you know, just covering all the bases." I laughed. "I'm really sorry about your mom," I said again.

"Yeah, some guys spend spring break in Ft. Lauderdale or the Caribbean. I spent it at my mother's bedside, watching her die. And you want to know the kicker?"

At this point, I was pretty sure I didn't, but since I'd opened the floodgates, I couldn't exactly refuse him.

"I lost my scholarship anyway. It was dependent on my GPA, and after I found out my mom was terminal, I kind of lost all interest in studying. Go figure."

"That really sucks. I'm sorry."

Rocky stopped suddenly, turning to me with a confounded stare. "I didn't mean to dump all that on you."

"It's okay," I said. "You can dump on Molly all you want." Ew. Did I really just say that?

He didn't say anything for a moment. Then: "Molly. Is that your name?"

With a start, I realized I hadn't properly introduced myself. "Molly Overbrook: offensive tackle, shoulder to cry on, and all-around tour guide, at your service."

"I read about you didn't I?" he said. "The girl who pulled the flight attendant out of the water? It was on BuzzFeed."

"That was me," I said. "I tried to save her . . ."

"It's not your fault she died. What you did was pretty freaking brave."

"It didn't *feel* brave," I said. "It felt like I didn't do enough. It felt like—" I cut myself off. There was no way to explain to this mortal I'd just met that it felt like the goddess Skadi, who just happened to be my

grandmother/aunt/sister-in-law/cousin ten times removed, had turned her back on me when I needed her
most.

"Man, it's hot," Rocky said after a minute. "And this
bag is heavy. Hold up a sec." He stopped walking and
dropped his bag to the ground. There were wide lines
of sweat where the straps had cut across his shoulders,
and when he turned, I could see his whole back was
soaked. And with a single smooth motion, he stripped
off the soaked T-shirt, revealing a six-pack and smooth
hard chest plastered with sweat. His jeans hung well below his hips, exposing about two inches of boxer shorts.

It took all my strength to tear my eyes away, and
while I tried not to stare, Rocky hoisted his backpack
again, then tied his wet shirt on one of the many straps
hanging from it.

"That's a little better," he said. "Onward, fearless
leader."

We started walking again.

"So," he said after a moment. "Is it true what that
woman said?"

My heart jumped in my chest.

"Is what true?" I said, trying to keep my voice light.

"Janet Steele? The tennis star? She's your mother?"

I gasped and smacked his upper arm, not too hard,
but hard enough to leave a bit of a red mark. It was
tense beneath its light film of sweat.

"You knew who I was the whole time!"

Rocky's face colored. "Well, not exactly."

"What do you mean, 'not exactly'?"

"When Sal told me I had to stay here this summer, I did a little looking around on social media to see who'd tagged things in the East End, and North Hampton specifically. You and your sister stood out."

"Are you saying that you didn't know if I was Molly or Mardi?" I asked.

He nodded sheepishly.

"But we're so different!"

"Um, you have pretty much the same face."

"That is SO not true! I can't believe you couldn't be bothered to remember which one of us doesn't get strange tattoos in highly visible places and wear torn clothes that haven't been in style since before she was born. I'm almost starting to regret my decision to walk you to Sal's."

Rocky chuckled. "I don't think Mardi's look is so out there—although she does look like she'd be a lot to handle."

"And you think I'm more, what? *Manageable?*"

"If I was ever stupid enough to think that, you have thoroughly disabused me of any such a notion."

"'Disabused'? Trying to show off your college vocabulary?"

The words came out harsher than I'd intended, and I found myself wondering if we were flirting or actually fighting. But the next thing out of Rocky's mouth told me exactly which side of the line we were on.

"What I'm *trying* to say is, I'm glad you're the sister I ran into first."

"You're—oh." I couldn't keep the smile off my face, so I turned and looked over my right shoulder, as if I found the dunes fascinating. I was trying to think what my next line should be. Like "I'm glad you ran into me too" or "Do you have a girlfriend at college?" or "Want to play strip poker?" Before I could make up my mind, however, the sounds of a roaring engine and screeching wheels made themselves heard over the faint wash of the surf.

"Wow," Rocky said. "Someone seriously needs to get a muffler. And learn to slow down."

I nodded but didn't say anything. It's not like I'm an expert on car engine noises or anything, but I was pretty sure whose car I was hearing. The roaring and screeching grew exponentially louder as the still-unseen car raced toward us.

"Sounds like he's coming right this way," Rocky said. "We'd better get off the road."

It's not a he, I wanted to say as Rocky took my hand and led me onto the sandy shoulder of the road. For one moment, I thought about squeezing tightly and pulling him into the dunes and hiding. Then Mardi's Ferrari shot over the crest of the nearest dune. It didn't actually leave the ground or anything, but it might as well have, it was going so fast.

"Holy flying Ferraris, Batman!" Rocky laughed, pulling me back a few feet farther. He opened his mouth to say something else, but whatever it was got lost in the squeal of brakes. I don't know how Mardi managed to stop the car going a thousand miles an hour in ten feet, but she did, right in front of me and Rocky.

The first thing I saw was Trent because the passenger side of the car was closest to us. Second was Mardi, looking at us with a half-amused, half-regretful expression as her eyes flitted between my face and Rocky's, and then down to our hands. That's when we both realized we were still holding hands, and we stepped apart simultaneously.

"Man, I am so sorry to have to do this," Mardi said, "but get in, Molly. We have to deal with something."

"I can't. I'm showing Rocky where Sal lives."

"Up two more dunes, take the first right. You'll see an old junkyard with a beaten-down old trailer in the middle of it. It's not a junkyard. It's Sal's house. 409 Pfenning Road. Now get in, Molls. This is serious."

I turned to Rocky. "You want us to give you a lift?"

Rocky smiled sympathetically. "There's not really a backseat in that thing. And your sister seems like she's in a hurry. I'll see you at the Inn sometime? Or the beach?"

"Beers or bikinis," I said as flirtatiously as I could. "Two of my favorite things." Rocky actually blushed.

I hopped over the edge of the car and squeezed myself into what Rocky had correctly identified as "not really a backseat," even if it was covered with creamy leather.

"Hey!" Trent protested. "You're getting sand all over me!"

"And this is the warrior who's supposed to save us at Ragnarok?" I smirked to Mardi. "We're all doomed." I turned to Rocky as Mardi gunned it.

"Watch out for Freya," I called. "She's incorrigible."

✳ *10* ✳

HOMEWARD BOUND

Mardi-Overbrook-Journal.docx

𝒥 glanced at Molly in the rearview as I sped toward Fair Haven. She was looking out the side of the car with a little smile on her face and her fingers were rubbing together slightly, as if she was remembering the feel of Rocky's hand in hers. I have to say, it was nice to see that smile after days of scowls. I thought about saying it out loud, but figured that would just make her frown again. Instead, I said:

"So that's Rocky McLaughlin, huh?"

Molly met my gaze in the mirror. Her eyes were guarded.

"I guess so."

When we were younger, Beyoncé released *I Am . . . Sasha Fierce*. Molly set her alarm for midnight, when the album went on sale on iTunes, so she could download it to her phone, and by the time everyone in the house woke up the next morning, she'd memorized the lyrics to every single song on the album. She listened to it for three days straight, once going so far as to cast a spell on this poor woman on the subway who tapped Molly on the shoulder and asked her to turn it down because the music was blasting out of her earbuds (Molly turned the woman's gum to glue, which sealed her lips shut for the duration of her subway ride). When she finally took her headphones out to shower, I asked her if she liked the new Beyoncé album and she said, "I guess so."

What I mean is, Rocky didn't know what was about to hit him.

But as fascinating as that was, we didn't have time to talk about it.

I found Molly's eyes in the mirror again. "You're probably wondering why I picked you up."

"Little bit," Molly said.

"You remember how Janet Steele"—I couldn't bring myself to say *our mom*—"said she'd bought a beach house on the East End?"

For the first time since she'd gotten in the car, Molly's expression showed a little bit of interest.

"Yeah. What about it?"

"Well, turns out the house is Fair Haven."

"What?" Molly turned to Trent. "What is she talking about?"

"It's true," Trent said. "Your mo—Janet Steele bought Fair Haven. And she kicked us all out."

"But how? You can't just buy someone's house out from under them, can you?"

"I was kind of wondering the same thing," I said.

"I'm a little vague on the whole thing myself," Trent said. "I guess sometime in the nineteenth century my father transferred ownership of the house to a corporation to dissociate it from the Gardiner family. We'd leave for sixty or seventy years at a time, living in London or Paris or New York, then come back, pretending to be our own grandsons and granddaughters. That way no one would notice that we never aged."

I nodded. Troy had told us about similar schemes he'd used over the centuries. One day, Molly and I would have to do the same thing.

"So anyway," Trent continued, "that first corporation was eventually sold to another corporation, and that corporation was sold to another corporation, and so on and so forth. The whole thing was still supposed to be owned by Gardiner Industries, but after the 2008 stock market crash, the board of directors spun off a few assets to raise some cash."

"Ugh, did you just say 'spun off a few assets'?" I groaned.

"Seriously," Molly agreed from the backseat. "That kind of banker bro talk is just . . . yuck."

"Whatever," Trent said, grinning. "I'm sorry I can't always be all, 'Dude, that dress is radical!' all the time."

"Did you really just say 'Dude, that dress is radical!'?" Molly teased.

"Cowabunga, dude," I chimed in. "Let's go nosh some 'za and kick it at your crib."

Trent rolled his eyes upward. "Odin help me!" He sighed. "Speaking of my *crib*," he persisted, "it turns out the board didn't realize one of the companies they'd sold was the one that owns Fair Haven. But superstar athlete Janet Steele did, and she swooped in and snatched it up—for a song, I have to tell you. She bought the whole place for less than what my stepmother spent on renovations."

"Oh, your stepmother!" I said. "She must be having a fit!"

"Wait a minute," Molly spoke over me. "Are you saying that Janet bought your home on purpose? Like she actually wanted to kick you out?"

"What?" Trent said guiltily. "N-no. I'm sure it was just a coincidence."

"Gods, you're a terrible liar," I said, chucking him under the cheek. "Good thing you're so cute. It's okay," I continued when he started to protest. "Dad told me everything."

"Told you what?" Molly said.

"One sec," I said to Molly, then turned to Trent. "Did you know?"

Trent did something complicated with his face, which I think was meant to be his I'm-so-guilty-I-can't-even-pretend-to-play-innocent expression. "What's the best answer to this question? You tell me what to say, and I'll say it."

"The correct answer is, how in the Hel could you keep something like this from me? We've been dating for a whole year! You should've told me!" I fumed.

"Told you *what*?" Molly practically yelled. "If someone doesn't tell me what in Frigg's name is going on RIGHT NOW," Molly screamed from the backseat, "I'm going to cast a decomposition hex on this Ferrari and you're going to wake up in the morning to a pile of rust!"

I caught Molly's eyes in the rearview mirror.

"Sorry, sorry," I said. "I'm still trying to process all this too."

As quickly as I could, I filled her in on what Dad had told me about the tradition of human familiars among some of the Aesir and Vanir trapped in Midgard, and how some of the familiars would try to trick the gods into having children with them. She absorbed it with an increasingly dumbfounded expression on her face, and when I'd finished, all she said was:

"So Mom's definitely human?"

She didn't look at me when she asked it. She looked at Trent, though it was clear she wasn't looking at a seventeen-year-old boy but at Tyr, Norse god of war.

He held up his hands. "As far as I know, Janet Steele is a perfectly average human being."

In the backseat, Molly looked disappointed.

"Our mother's human," she said in a dejected voice.

"Don't be sad, Molls," I said. "Look at Ingrid and Matt. Humans and witches can get along just fine."

"I know," she said, but if anything, her voice was even sadder. "But we're only just meeting her, and before you know it"—she found my eyes in the mirror—"*we're going to have to watch her die.*"

I held Molly's gaze for a long moment without speaking. I could see it wasn't just our mother's future death she was upset about—it was the flight attendant whose life she hadn't been able to save. I racked my brain for something soothing to say but nothing came, and it was Trent who spoke first.

"Why don't you concentrate on getting to know her first?" He pointed at the sharp outline of Fair Haven, which had just appeared above the horizon. "We're almost there."

No one spoke for the last couple of minutes of the drive. The Ferrari shot over the bridge to Gardiners Island and tore deep ruts in the meticulously combed gravel of their mile-long looping driveway. Trent glanced back at them, then flashed me a look, but didn't say anything.

I pulled up to the front courtyard of the two-hundred-year-old mansion, which wouldn't have looked out of place on the Scottish highlands or in French wine country. The pink bricks glowed softly, and the hundreds of white-framed windowpanes reflected the bright light of the afternoon sun. Ivy grew over the east wing, which was the oldest part of the house, and dozens of rhododendrons bloomed in a dizzying array of purple blossoms.

I tried to remember if rhododendrons bloomed this early in the season or if they were magically enhanced, but horticulture was never my thing.

"It looks so strange," Trent said. "Now that it's not mine anymore."

"It's our mother's," Molly snapped. She pried herself loose from the tiny compartment and jumped out of the car without waiting to see if I was following. She made it almost all the way to the door before she suddenly pivoted on her heel.

"Mardi!" she stage-whispered. "Can you believe we're about to meet *our mother*?"

All I could do was point.

Molly whirled back toward the house. The door had opened just as she'd turned, and there she was:

Janet Steele.

Our mom.

I don't know why, but I'd envisioned her in a tennis dress. I mean, I know why—she's a tennis star, duh—but I also knew that tennis stars are allowed to wear regular clothes when they're not playing, which was what Janet was wearing: a sleeveless sundress with a crisscrossed Greek bodice that loosened into a full skirt flowing softly around her legs. But even so. I'd pictured her in a tennis dress, and it was only when she appeared in civvies that it hit me.

This was our mom!

Molly's brain seemed to be free of such inane

ramblings, however. After a single eternal second during which she stared at Janet, she just ran to her and threw her arms around her.

"Oh, my gods! Mom!" I heard her muffled voice.

Janet's very long, very toned arms folded around Molly's back, and almost regally, she bent her head forward and kissed the top of her head. Since she was so tall, it looked like a normal-heighted woman kissing a little girl.

"My daughter," she whispered, yet I seemed to hear her clearly. "My beautiful Molly."

As she said all this, however, her eyes were still on me. They were piercingly blue and, despite the tenderness of her voice, they bored into me almost aggressively.

"Will you not come to your own mother, Mardi?" I heard her say, although I was so entranced by her stare that I didn't even notice her lips move. Before I knew it, I was out of the car, racing across the gravel to throw my arms around her too.

"Mom!" I cried as she pressed me against her with arms that felt powerful enough to crush bone. "Mom, it's really you!" In answer, I felt the same lips that had kissed my sister press gently against the top of my head.

"Actually, call me Mum" was all she said.

I don't know how long we stood like that, but finally Janet—Mum, I guess I should call her—stood back.

"This calls for champagne."

It was surreal, to say the least. We never had a mother our entire lives and now here she was.

Molly and I looked at each other. In the plus category for having a mum: good hugs and champagne. In the minus: so far nothing. But then:

Mum's gaze hardened as she stared over our heads. I turned and saw she was looking at Trent.

"You should not have brought the Aesir," she said in a voice cold enough to freeze water.

I found myself wondering if Trent was onto something, if "Mum" had a beef with all the gods, and not just Dad. I tried to catch Trent's eye, but he was busy returning Mum's stare. His gaze was cool and guarded. Not quite hostile, but when it comes to ocular interactions between your mum and your boyfriend, I'm pretty sure "not quite hostile" doesn't cut it.

"It's okay; Trent's my boyfriend," I said.

Mum smirked. "Isn't he a little old for you?" I know she didn't mean that he was eighteen.

"Hello, Janet," Trent said now. "It's been a long time."

"Hello, Tyr," Mum answered. "Yes, it has."

They stared at each other defiantly. I guess they knew each other after all.

Mum started to usher us inside, and it was clear Trent was not welcome. I wanted to defend him, but I was too excited to finally meet my mother. I hoped he'd understand.

"It's kind of hot out here," he said.

"As I said before, Aesir, you are not welcome here," she replied.

"This used to be my house, you know," Trent said. "And we mean to take it back."

"The deed is done. Now get off my property before I call the police on you." She looked down at me. "That would be Ingrid's husband, Matthew Noble, wouldn't it? I doubt he'd be too happy arresting his niece's boyfriend, but I'm sure he'd do it. And I'm sorry to be rude to the Aesir, but I really need to talk to you girls alone for now."

Something happened to Trent then. I'm not sure what it was, but even though nothing seemed to change in his outward appearance, he still got bigger somehow. Not bigger, but more substantial, as if his body was sucking in a little more daylight, so that his skin seemed to glow a little, even as he was shrouded in shadow. When he spoke, his voice was deeper than I'd ever heard it, and for the first time, I truly believed my boyfriend was in fact the god of war.

"You overstep your boundaries, mortal. The Council has always treated you with leniency because you are the mother of Magdi and Mooi, the prophesied goddesses of rage and strength. But you can push us too far, and then—"

"It's cool, Trent. Come on, please?" I cut him off before he said something he couldn't take back. "Drive my car to Ingrid's. We'll get a cab to take us home."

"Nonsense," Janet said. "I'll have my driver take you,

of course." She winked at Molly. "I won a Maybach in Monaco last year. It's like riding in a cloud."

"Trent," I said because he was still doing that glowing/shadow thing. "*Go.* Please."

After another long, tense moment, the glow subsided, and Trent was just Trent again.

"I'm not happy about this," he said, sliding over into the driver's seat and starting the car. He pumped the gas, making the Ferrari's engine scream.

"I know it's not ideal, but please don't take it out on the car." My last words were cut off as Trent dropped the car into first without pressing the clutch down all the way, producing a hideous noise from the transmission. Gravel spurted from beneath the tires as the Ferrari lurched into motion.

Trent may be a god, but he sure never mastered the art of driving stick.

* 11 *

IT'S A FAMILY AFFAIR

From the Diary of Molly Overbrook

$\mathcal{I}$t was all I could do to bite my tongue during the whole exchange between Mum and Trent. How dare he speak to her that way. Through hard work and guts and determination, she'd turned herself into the world's best tennis player *and* managed to seduce a god and get a couple of children out of him. Everything Trent had—everything Trent *was*—had been handed to him on a magical silver platter. He needed to climb down off his high horse and admit that a human had outwitted him and his family.

I knew Mardi loved him, but I was upset.

He was rude to our mother.

Our mother. We had a mother. And she was here.

Mum put one arm around my shoulder and one around Mardi's and walked us through the grand central hallway of Fair Haven, beneath the coffered ceiling and enormous spiral staircase, to the rear terrace, which opened onto the estate's formal gardens and the more rustic orchards and coastland of Gardiners Island. As we sat down on a set of white-enameled Venetian grotto chairs, a small man appeared, who looked sort of familiar. Still, it wasn't until Mum said his name that I realized who it was.

"Girls, this is Ivan," Mum announced. "He's my butler-slash-chauffeur-slash-henchman-slash-hitting partner-slash-I-couldn't-get-anything-done-without-him. Ivan, would you bring us a bottle of Jacob's Creek sparkling white wine." She looked down at Mardi and me, a twinkle in her eye. "Have to represent for Australia, you know."

To be promised champagne and then offered sparkling white wine is a bit of a, well, letdown, and it was a struggle to keep the smile on my face, and I could see that Mardi was struggling as well.

But then Mum burst out laughing. "Oh, you girls are terrible actresses. Ivan, break out the Krug for my princesses."

Now I couldn't keep the smile off my face. Krug was so expensive that even a wine snob like our father never bought it, or at least not for family dinners.

"Very good, Ms. Steele," Ivan replied, and bowed. No, really: he bowed, and not like a little nod of the head. He bent all the way over at the waist until he was practically kissing his knees before scurrying away.

"Sit, sit," Mum said, pulling out chairs. "Just look at that view. Isn't it gorgeous?"

It was. Up close there were clipped hedges and multicolored flowerbeds planted in patterns as intricate as Tibetan mandalas, while farther away windswept hills covered in densely green grass and gnarled fruit trees gave way to golden dunes, and the silvery blueness of Long Island Sound. In the misty distance, across twenty-five miles of water, Rhode Island was just visible, looking like a world in another dimension.

Faster than seemed possible, Ivan reappeared with three Baccarat flutes balanced on a silver tray held on one open palm, in the other a silver ice bucket on a three-foot pedestal that must've weighed fifty pounds. He handled everything as deftly as an acrobat, setting the ice bucket down soundlessly, pouring the champagne into the flutes while they were still balanced on the tray resting on his palm, then setting a glass down in front of each of us.

"Will that be all, Ms. Steele?"

"Thank you, Ivan," Mum said. "That will be all, for now." Mum's tone of voice could only be described as imperious. She may have been "new money," but she knew how to act to the manor born. Another bow from Ivan, and he was gone.

Mum raised her glass in a toast, and we raised ours.

"To the new gods of Midgard."

To what? I exchanged a glance with Molly, but it was clear she didn't know what Mum was talking about either. We clinked glasses anyway, and sipped at the Krug.

(I don't want to get anyone jealous, because they only make a few bottles each year, and most of them end up in Russia or the Persian Gulf, but: Krug. Is. Amazing.)

"Why new?" Mardi asked after savoring the Krug.

Mum sort of frowned and smiled at the same time. "Don't you know?"

"No."

Mum laughed. "I guess you wouldn't, even though you two are the first." She paused dramatically, fixing first Mardi in the eye, then me. Then, once again summoning that imperious tone, she proclaimed: "You, my daughters, will be the new gods of Midgard and will propagate an entirely new race of divine beings."

I held her gaze for as long as I could, which was about two seconds, then turned nervously to Mardi, whose expression was somewhere between "Say what?" and "Is she crazy?"

"Whoa there," I said, turning back to Mum. "I know we've just met, and Mardi said she wanted to wait a little before we got into the birds and the bees, but the simple truth is I'm still carrying my V card, and after what happened with Alberich last summer, I'm in no hurry to give it up, let alone start, um, propagating 'an entirely new race of divine beings.'"

Mum's expression didn't change. In fact, her face was totally motionless. Still, I could tell she was disappointed. Disappointed and, well, irritated. I mean, the only thing that happened was that her nostrils flared, but somehow even that tiny gesture was enough to make me blanch a little. It was like, if she sniffed through those flared nostrils, she would suck up me and Mardi through those pink cavities and we'd disappear into her body again. During the French Open match against Serena, I'd seen her shoot that look across the net a couple of times, which Serena, being Serena, shot right back. Since I didn't have Serena's guns, I found myself looking away pretty fast.

But then Mum laughed, and the tense moment was over as fast as it had come.

"I heard about your misadventure with Alberich. The dark elves can be nasty creatures, and he's the worst of them."

"Yeah, Dad was saying something about that too," said Mardi.

"When did you talk to him about this?" I asked, looking over at her. Dad usually only discussed god stuff when both of us were present.

"Um, earlier today," Mardi said, obviously uncomfortable. "We were talking about, um, things," she said, glancing at Mum nervously, and I realized she meant the attack a few days ago, which she obviously didn't want to bring up in front of Mum. "Anyway, I knew I should've waited for you, but you were off, I don't know, sulking—"

"I wasn't sulking!" I cut her off. "I was upset. You'd be upset too, if that happened to you."

I glanced over at Mum as I said this, but she didn't say anything. Just watched both of us keenly, as if she already knew what had happened and was completely not bothered by it.

"Sorry," Mardi said. "Sulking was totally the wrong word. Anyway, I got to talking with Dad, and he told me that all the gods are pretty much the same."

"I wouldn't go that far," Mum snorted. "We are all but pale copies of the great Jotun, whether it's a lowly human like me or a beautiful elf like Ivan."

"Wait," I said incredulously. "Ivan's an . . . elf?"

Mum smiled proudly, as though someone had complimented her on a thoroughbred horse. "Only three in all of Midgard, and just one works for a mortal."

"Wow," Mardi said. "No offense, but how do you rate your own elf?"

Mum's smile grew bigger. "Why, because I'm the mother of the Mimir, after all. My descendants will eradicate the Aesir and Vanir from Midgard, paving the way for the hegemony of the Mimir."

Mardi and I stared at each other for a moment.

"Um, hegemony?" I said finally, although I was pretty sure I knew what the word meant.

"Rule," Mum said simply, confirming my assumption.

"And, um, *eradicate*?" Mardi said.

Mum shrugged. "If you prefer a simpler term: kill."

Mardi set her $250 Baccarat flute down so heavily that about $100 worth of champagne splashed on the table.

"Whoa," she said. "Shit just got real."

No one said anything for what seemed like forever. The only sound was the dripping of Mardi's Krug onto Fair Haven's fieldstone patio and, in the distance, the faint wash of the surf.

Finally, Mum clapped her hands and Ivan appeared as if by magic. (Which, given the circumstances, may very well have been magic.)

"Ivan, Mardi's glass needs refilling."

"Of course, Ms. Steele." Ivan grabbed the bottle from the ice bucket and tilted it over one towel-draped arm, expertly filling Mardi's flute with the maximum amount of liquid and the minimum amount of fizz. The whole operation took maybe thirty seconds, but it was long enough for me to regain some sense of equilibrium.

"M-Mum," I said, stuttering slightly as I realized it was the first time I'd said the word, or at least addressed it to my actual mother. "Are you saying that me and Mardi are supposed to . . . to . . . kill all the old gods here in Midgard? Ingrid and Freya and Trent and, and *Thor*?"

Mum's eyes flitted back and forth between us for a moment. Then, without warning, she threw back her head and laughed.

"Oh, my gods, the look on your face is priceless!" she said when she could talk again. "No, I'm not saying you have to kill your own *father*! That would be unseemly!"

"But didn't you just say we were supposed to kill the older generation of gods?"

"I said the *Mimir* would do it. That doesn't mean it has to be you two! It could be your daughters, or your daughters' daughters!" She smiled brightly as if she'd told us that we'd just run over the last wild panda but it was okay because there were still some in zoos.

"Look, I can see you're a little upset about this, but really, it's nothing you have to think about now. The war is hundreds of years down the road. Maybe thousands. Who knows, maybe by then you'll be so tired of Thor's shenanigans that you'll *want* him dead."

Mardi looked at me with an "are you hearing what I'm hearing?" expression on her face. She was holding her freshly filled flute in her hand like she wanted to break it or throw it or something. And I knew why she was upset and all, but still. This was our mother, whom Thor had hidden from us our whole lives. We'd only just met her, and I wasn't ready to give up on her just yet. So I shot Mardi my best "calm down!" stare, and I don't know if it worked, but at least she put down her glass before she broke it (not to mention wasted all that irreplaceable Krug again). Still, her face was as pink as a breast cancer ribbon, and I spoke up before she could say something she'd regret.

"Are you sure about this?" I said to Mum. "Why can't we just share the space since we're family?"

"Family?" Mum said. "Did you feel like family two days ago, when you called on Skadi for help and she ignored you?"

"Wait, what?" Mardi said, turning to me. "What's she talking about?"

I ignored her. "How did you know I called on Joanna?"

"You think just because I'm human I don't know about magic? But then why wouldn't you think that? You were raised by Thor. He thinks humans are just playthings. All they're good for is pouring his drinks and cleaning his house and sharing his bed. Your call was a noble thing, Mooi. Noble and pure. I felt it all the way on the other side of the world."

"So you know magic?" Mardi said to Mum. "And you called on Joanna to save that flight attendant?" she said to me. "Oh, Moll, why didn't you tell me? I thought you were just upset about the fact that she died, but now I see there was a whole other dimension to it."

"Indeed there was," Mum said. "Mooi was learning that the Aesir care only about themselves."

"But that's not true!" Mardi protested. "Joanna and Freya and Ingrid have saved countless human lives. I've seen it with my own eyes."

"For every life they save, they let a hundred others slip away," Mum said coldly.

"But it would be impossible to save every human life! I mean, you're mortal, after all. You're not meant to live forever."

Mum shook her head back in forth in disappointment. And even though we'd only met her half an hour ago, it was still impossible not to feel a sense of shame.

I mean, she wasn't even shaking her head at me, and I still felt bad, as if I'd let her down.

"Oh, Magdi. Such lies they've filled your head with. You think immortality is something only the gods deserve? What nonsense! Life is not a gift that can be taken back. It belongs to all sentient creatures—forever."

As Mum said this, I felt a warmth fill my body (and it wasn't just the champagne). If I was hearing her right, she was saying that just because she was human she didn't have to die. That I wouldn't have to face the prospect of losing her forty or fifty years down the line, and then have to spend eternity without a mother.

As if she'd sensed my thoughts somehow, Mum whirled toward me, her expression full of tenderness. "Listen to me, my darlings," she said, looking straight at me. "No doubt you know that Gardiners Island sits on a seam between Midgard and Niflheim. But millennia ago, this seam didn't exist, because the nine worlds were all one. Everything existed on the same plane, separated by nothing more than a river or an ocean or a wall or a bit of space.

"But when Odin led the Aesir in his treasonous revolt against the Jotun, he tore the worlds apart and flung them into different dimensions. He wanted to protect the Aesir and Vanir against some future uprising in which the giants and the dark and light elves and humans might unite against Odin and become a tiny band of rebels. This sundering split Midgard from Hel, the great city of Niflheim, which is where the soul goes after its human body has served its purpose, to be born again in a new body free of the weaknesses of this frail shell."

"But, I mean, it's *Hel*," Mardi said. "It doesn't sound like a very pleasant place to spend eternity."

"Indeed it's not, Magdi," Mum said, "but that's your grandfather's doing. Hel is a part of Niflheim, which you know as the land of ice. The sun never shines, and the only plants that grow are pale trees covered in poisonous spikes instead of leaves, and a kind of black moss filled with acid. But once upon a time, before Odin cast it to the farthest edge of the universe, Niflheim was a paradise and Hel was its most beautiful region. Imagine some tropical island, but take away the flies and the snakes and the crocodiles. Every day was like this— high spring, with flowers blooming and birds singing and the fruit of the trees falling at your feet to delight your senses and nourish your body. It was only after Odin split the worlds that it became such a terrible place, which is why it lent its name to the Christian Hell."

"I don't want you to end up there!" I said then. "It's not fair!"

Mum smiled at me. "Don't you worry about me, Mooi. I can take care of myself. But the real question is, why should *anyone* end up there?"

She said *anyone*, but I knew she was talking about the flight attendant who had died in my arms. And she was right: she didn't deserve to be in Hel.

"But what can we do about it?" I said helplessly.

"Why, everything, of course!" Mum said. "Once the Mimir vanquish the Aesir, the barriers holding the nine worlds apart from each other will be destroyed, and they'll finally be reunited. Death as we know it will cease to exist—and it will all be thanks to you!"

12

SAY MY NAME

Mardi-Overbrook-Journal.docx

*O*nce again, another awkward silence took over the patio. One minute, our newfound mum was telling us that it was our job to kill our father and grandparents and aunts and uncles and cousins, the next she was telling us that we were going to save the world.

It was all a bit much, really. Clearly, Mum was insane.

I stood up, a bit unsteadily. The Krug was light on the tongue, but it packed a wallop. "I've got to go."

"Go?" Mum said. "Go where?"

"Home."

"But this is your home now, Magdi!"

"First of all," I said, "I go by Mardi. Not Magdi, which sounds like a food supplement or a website for comic nerds. Secondly, this is *supposed* to be Trent's home and I *was* staying here with him. But since you kicked him out, I guess I'll crash at Ingrid's with Molly, not Mooi—she's not a cow—I mean, until Trent and I can figure something out." I turned to Molly. "You ready?"

Molly looked at me over the lip of her empty champagne flute. I could see that she was a little tipsy too but not so tipsy that she didn't know what was going on. "I . . . think . . . I'm . . . going . . . to . . . *stay*," she said finally, as if she hadn't made up her mind until the last word came out of her mouth.

"You're welcome here as long as you want, Mooi," Mum said, bestowing one of her million-dollar smiles on my sister. "And, Magdi, you are welcome here anytime you wish to return."

The way she said that made me pause. *Anytime you wish to return*, she said. Not *you're welcome here* like she'd said to Molly. It was like she'd already written me off, and it was on me to make it better. We couldn't have been there for an hour, making ours what must have been the shortest mother-daughter relationship in history.

But I didn't know how to express any of that out loud, so all I said was:

"Mardi. *Mardi*."

Mum smiled without showing her teeth, and I had the sense that she was snarling behind her pursed lips. "Changing a few letters does not change your destiny. Remember, I didn't pick this fate out for you. I'm merely destiny's conduit."

"Well, I guess that makes me destiny's child," I

said, "and as an independent woman and a survivor, I, uh . . ." Whatever I was going for got lost in the haze of bubbles that filled my brain. "I'm outta here," I finished lamely.

"Of course," Mum said, the edges of her voice mild but concealing a heart of steel. "I'll have Ivan bring the car around."

"No thanks, I think I'll walk. I need to clear my head."

"Whatever you want, my darling."

Her *my darling* could've cracked a piece of granite in two.

"I, uh . . ." Again my voice faded away. "I'll see you around," I said to both of them, and turned for the door.

As I walked through Fair Haven's wide, empty hallway—Trent had told me that Mum had been "kind" enough to allow the Gardiners to move their furniture out before she took possession, but she hadn't replaced it with anything of her own—I couldn't help but notice how the house seemed indifferent to its change of ownership. Well, Gardiners Island was a magical place, and Fair Haven was where that magic was most heavily concentrated. In a way, the people who lived in Fair Haven belonged to it more than the house—or the island, or the magical portal between worlds—belonged to them. But even so. I had woken up in an upstairs guest bedroom just this morning, a bedroom that had a connecting door to Trent's bedroom (although he had yet to walk through it, or push it open and invite me to the other side). This might not have been the Gardiners' house, but the Gardiners belonged here. And yet they'd been banished by a mortal. A mortal who just happened to be my mother.

It took about ten minutes to walk off the island. The bridge to Gardiners Island wasn't far from the dock where Dad's plane had crashed. I stared at the water, peering for some sign of the accident, but North Hampton is a fastidious kind of place (I've always suspected that Joanna added something to her protection spells to make people more civic-minded, though Ingrid and Freya both deny this), and there was nothing left on the cold gray water to indicate something had happened here. An iridescent sheen was swirling around the dock pilings that might have been oil or gasoline, but also might have been good old-fashioned tide scum.

Nor was there any sign of the whale that had crashed the plane. Matt had told us that it wasn't all that uncommon for humpback whales to feed near the East End, though they usually stayed a few miles offshore. The Sound is pretty deep near North Hampton, however, and it was possible—just barely—that a whale could have strayed in, attracted by food maybe, or the sounds of ships or music, which could sometimes confuse them and lure them off course. Ingrid and Freya had searched through Joanna's spell books for magical detection spells, and late on the evening after the crash, after the docks had cleared, they'd cast the spells over the water. But though they tried three or four different spells, they didn't discover anything incriminating.

If someone *had* sent a whale to kill our father, he or she had used a plain old Midgardian whale and convinced it to attack Dad's plane without the aid of magic. Either that, or the person had managed to scrub any traces of magic from the water and the dock before Ingrid and Freya got there—which suggested that Dad's would-be murderer was living in our midst.

It was hard to say which possibility was more disturbing, and the thought of some evil sorcerer suddenly popping up and deciding to go after Thor's daughter in lieu of the god of thunder sent a chill down my spine. I hurried past the dark pier and the yacht club, from which came the faint sound of late '90s Destiny's Child. I thought it was someone getting the party started a little early, but when I peeked in, I saw it was actually a lone employee, dancing to "Say My Name" while he mopped the floors in preparation for the evening dinner crowd. The guy was lip-synching as he worked, using the handle of the mop as a microphone, and the sight brought a smile to my lips until I remembered the way Mum had refused to say *my* name—kept calling me Magdi, even though no one, not even Dad, ever uses that name. I'd asked Dad why he'd even bothered giving Molly and me Norse names, but all he'd done was roll his eyes and point upward, by which I assumed he meant Asgard. "I didn't have a choice," he'd said.

"Someone is very particular about the names of his grandchildren."

I left quickly, walking past the yacht club and into town proper. North Hampton doesn't have more than a couple thousand year-round residents, but the summer population swells to about five thousand, most of them well-heeled, though not usually as rich as your typical Hamptonite, or as flashy. As a consequence, Main Street is like a cross between a nineteenth-century New England village and something like Beacon Hill in Boston, where they have the same Burberry and Gucci and Louis Vuitton boutiques they have on Rodeo Drive or in the Meatpacking District in Manhattan, but they're housed in quaint old wooden buildings with cedar shingles on the walls as well as the roofs, and slatted shutters that aren't just decorative, but can be closed when a squall or a nor'easter blows in off the Atlantic Ocean. In between the boutiques are the usual assortment of artisanal ice cream and fair trade coffee shops as well as a few shops unique to the area, like a smoky boutique that sells nothing but pipes made from whale bones covered in scrimshaw (Dr. Mésomier put a truth hex on this journal, so you know I'm not making that up—as if I even would) and another store that only sells these ridiculous raincoats made out of some kind of shapeless, colorless waxed cotton that weigh about a hundred pounds but keeps you so dry that you'd think it was magic.

And then there was the Cheesemonger, the store

where Molly had taken a job last summer, mostly because it was run by this cute boy named Marshall, who unfortunately turned out to be Alberich in yet another of his disguises. Last I'd heard, the space was being taken over by Ocean Vines, the fancy wine shop that sold fifty-dollar bottles of Margaux and Montrachet (as opposed to Bob's Booze on the highway, which sells five-dollar airplane-sized bottles of whiskey and rum for people who want a drink on the go). But as I walked past the storefront, I was surprised to see that the CHEESE-MONGER sign was still up, and inside was none other than Sal McLaughlin standing behind the counter, with a crisp white apron pulled over a worn denim shirt rolled up at the sleeves. It was so hard for me to imagine Sal anywhere other than at the North Inn that I had to walk in and see what was going on.

There were three people in the store, and I browsed the shelves of twelve-dollar crackers made of "ancient grains" and jars of things that shouldn't have been pickled but somehow were, including clementines, fiddlehead ferns, and—ugh—snails. I got so caught up in the strange combinations of mouthwatering and disgusting foods that I didn't notice the last customer leave until the bells rang over the door and Sal called out:

"Mardi? Is that you?"

I put down a jar of "postmodern lasagna" made from layers of tripe (the lining of a cow's stomach), pureed breadfruit, and aspic infused with basil oil, and turned toward the counter. Sal was already coming out onto the floor, and he gave me a huge bear hug. Sal is a big man in his late fifties, a good six foot two or six foot three and probably around 250 pounds, a healthy combination of muscles and fat, and I disappeared in his grip, my cheek pressed up against his beard.

"My God, look at you. Where have you been all summer?" he said when he let me go. "Is it possible that you're even more beautiful than you were last year?"

From just about any other man this would have come across as pervy, but Sal was so comfortable in his skin that he made everyone else comfortable too—he hadn't worked behind bars for nearly forty years for nothing.

I waved my hand around the store. "What's going on, Sal? You branching out?"

"Believe me, I'm as surprised as you are. You remember that boy who worked here last summer, Marshall Brighton? Well, we all thought his parents owned the store and he was just working for them. But get this—there were no parents. I mean, I'm sure he had parents somewhere, but he owned the store on his own."

Given the fact that Marshall, a.k.a. Alberich, was around during the dawn of the universe, it wouldn't surprise me to learn that he did not, in fact, have any parents, but I just nodded.

"So anyway, he skipped out at the end of last summer, which is when the Flinzers next door at Ocean Vines decided to move in. But then last October, before they'd even begun renovating, Andy Flinzer checked himself into rehab. Turns out he'd been sampling his own merchandise a little too liberally, if you know what I mean. He's out now, and doing well, knock wood"—here Sal knocked on my head—"but he and Janice have decided to call off the expansion. They don't want any extra stress while Andy's still so new into his recovery."

"Wow, that's crazy. But I still don't get what you're doing here."

"Oh," Sal said, bopping his own forehead. "Didn't I mention? I own the building. I've got three buildings here in town. No wait, four. Five!" he corrected himself. "No wonder my accountant gets so frustrated with me. Anyway, when the Brighton boy took off, he left behind loads of merchandise. The cheese all went bad, of course—you cannot *imagine* the smell when I came in here in March—but there were all these other things, crackers and pickles and, uh, whatever this is." He picked up a jar of something that looked a lot like eyes, grimaced, and set it down hurriedly. "And so anyway, when I found out Rocky was coming, I thought, Why not keep this around for him to run? He's too young to work in the bar and it was too late in the spring to get a tenant in here, so this way I could pay him and it wouldn't look like charity. Rocky's my son, by the way."

"I know," I said. "I met him this morning actually. I guess his cab dropped him at the bar instead of your house, and Molly was walking him there."

"One sec," Sal said because a couple had just walked in. He scooted back behind the counter and whipped

117

up a couple of heroes—thinly sliced speck, shaved Parmesan, and arugula on one, mozzarella and sun-dried tomato pesto on the other. While he was making the sandwiches, the couple also picked up a box of crackers and a jar of pickles—regular pickles—then ordered three different cheeses. Their total came to a whopping seventy-five dollars for what basically amounted to an afternoon snack.

"So how'd he look?" Sal asked as he came back around the counter, his normally smooth brow furrowing with concern. "His mother and I split just after his first birthday, and I've hardly seen him since. Poor Sophia died in March, and I get the sense that he's a little angry at the world."

I shrugged. "I only talked to him for a second, but he seemed okay. You should ask Molly, though. She spent more time with him."

"Actually," Sal said, "I was going to ask Molly if she wanted her old job back. This place is proving busier than I thought, and it's ridiculously lucrative too. I really can't figure out why that boy ran away from such a gold mine."

If only you knew how close you were to the truth, I thought.

"I'll mention it to Molly, but I'm not sure what she'll say. I don't know if you've heard about our own family drama?"

"You mean your father and that freaky accident? How is he doing, by the way?"

"Oh, he's fine; thanks for asking. Ingrid whipped up one of her potions, and he's practically as good as new. But I was referring to our mother." As quickly as I could, I filled him in on the story of Janet Steele and her move to Fair Haven.

"Kicking out the Gardiners!" Sal exclaimed, but you could see he was amused. "I can't say I feel too badly for them. My father always said they were Johnny-come-latelys to the East End—the McLaughlins have been here for four hundred years to their three hundred—but I'm sure they'll land on their feet. People like them always do." He frowned then. "Too bad you girls are all caught up in that, though. I was really hoping to get someone in here with Rocky. I don't want him to feel like he's in solitary confinement."

I shrugged. "I'll talk to Molly, but I dunno. I think she only took the job last year because she kind of liked Marshall, and when he took off, she felt a little burned."

"Well, if she doesn't want it, maybe you do?"

"Maybe," I said noncommittally, although I had a hard time picturing myself in an apron stained with pesto and ketchup. "I'll let you know."

And, after submitting to another bear hug, I headed off to Ingrid's.

13

WALKING ON THE MOON

From the Diary of Molly Overbrook

That night—my first in Fair Haven—I had the dream again.

The ruined mansion. The ice-cold swampy yard. The strobing light in the east wing.

The outline of a female figure, appearing and reappearing with each pulse of the light.

In my dream, I pushed my way toward it across the puddle-filled lawn. Even as I struggled through the mud, I remembered that the east wing was the oldest part of the house, which housed the kitchen and servants' quarters. I'd heard from Trent (and Alberich when he pretended to be Trent) that despite its age, it was by far the sturdiest part of the house: its posts were entire tree trunks, and it had stood through dozens of hurricanes and even one earthquake, and even in the dream I realized how strange it was that this part of the house was in far worse shape than the rest of the mansion. It was almost as if the main part of the mansion had fallen to ruin through natural means, but this part was a complete ruin.

As I grew closer, the outline of the woman grew more distinct. I could see that she was slender, and her hair was long and flowing, but what I couldn't tell was if she was Mum or not. I thought of calling out, but something kept me silent. It wasn't that dream thing where you open your mouth and nothing comes out. My lips were sealed—I didn't want to call out to her. No, that wasn't quite it. I didn't want her to answer.

I didn't want it to be Mum.

By the time I made it to the house, I was covered in mud, grass, leaves. My bare feet were so cold they were numb, but not so numb that they didn't hurt. At least it was easy to get inside—the front door was long gone. But once inside, I had to tread carefully. The hallway floor was destroyed. It looked like someone had taken a hammer—like, say, Thor's hammer—and smashed it to bits. Whatever had happened, it had been done so long ago that trees had had time to grow up through the basement. They reached all the way through the second story and the attic and the holes in the roof, and the light that pushed around their leafless, tangled branches was the only thing that helped me see. I picked my way from one solid foothold to the next, slipping and sliding on my numb, wet feet, until I reached the door to the ballroom. The ballroom was on the east side of the main house. The new wing should be right on the other side.

The ballroom was also where the seam to Niflheim was hidden.

But this is a dream, I told myself. Nothing can actually hurt you here.

But somehow that didn't make me feel better. It was like knowing that I was dreaming somehow made it *more* real. Made me feel more vulnerable rather than safer. But I didn't see that I had a choice. The hallway beyond the ballroom doors had been completely ripped away. There was nothing but shadows disappearing down who knew how far. No way was I going down there.

The ballroom still had its doors, but when I grabbed the one on the right, it turned out it was only leaning against the frame. It was made of solid wood, though, and must've weighed a hundred pounds, and it seemed to be wedged in place, so I had to jerk on it several times before it came away, and then I had to jump back before it fell on me. It clattered and slid across the broken floor before disappearing down a hole. It was a good couple of seconds before I heard it hit bottom—not a crash, but a splash.

I shuddered as I turned back to the . . . well, I was going to say I *turned back to the ballroom*, but the space beyond the opened door wasn't a ballroom anymore. It was more of a . . . a cave, I guess, or a tunnel, really.

In place of the expansive parquetry floors and intricate marquetry walls, there was just dirt and rocks. No, not rocks, I realized. Ice. Great big chunks of dirty, jagged ice, as if they'd been frozen somewhere else, then broken off and dumped here. I remembered what I'd heard about Niflheim. That it orbited a tiny, cold white star and was covered in glaciers the size of continents. Could the seam have been opened somehow? Could Niflheim be pushing into our world? Or was it sucking our world into its own dimension?

My question was answered as soon as I stepped across the threshold. I don't know how, but I knew, somehow, that I was no longer in Midgard. Or no longer just in Midgard. The air felt different. Not smelled different. *Felt* different. Felt like it was made out of thick bolts of velvet that had been soaked in gasoline. Breathing it wasn't hard, exactly, but I could feel it in my lungs. It sat heavy in my chest, like a lungful of dead bees.

As strange as that was, however, what was even weirder was the weight of the room. The gravity, I guess. It was lighter. Like I felt myself weighing less. It seemed like I had to push my foot down to make it touch the ground, or else it was just going to float away. But I stamped my bare foot onto the ground and pushed my way into the room. It took a good, hard push, as if I was walking through water, but as soon as I was all the way in the room, I saw the light. The pulsing green light I'd seen from the lawn. It was at the far end of the tunnel that the ballroom had been turned into, but there was just enough of a curve to the tunnel that I still couldn't see the source. Even so, it was much brighter than it had been outside.

I took a step toward it. The gravity was so light that I half felt like I was going to float off the ground. I threw my hands out to either side of the tunnel, steadying myself on the slippery ice. Suddenly, an old song popped into my head. It was one of Freya's favorites, and she played it all the time at the North Inn, especially when she was closing up.

"Giant steps are what you take, walking on the moon. I hope my legs don't break, walking on the moon . . ."

It wasn't enough to make me feel safe, but it was enough to make me smile. I pushed forward.

But immediately stopped. Something had passed in front of the light up ahead, blocking most of it. It took me a moment to spot the shadow on the wall. The woman's shadow.

Waving at me.

And . . . speaking to me.

"Mooi," it called in a voice I knew I'd heard before, though I couldn't quite place it. "Mooi, is that you?"

It could have been Mum. And yet I wasn't sure—and I felt that if it were Mum, I'd recognize her voice.

"Mooi," it called again. "Mooi? Are you there?"

With a start, I opened my eyes, to the sound of a faint knock on the door.

"Mooi," a voice called. This time, it was really Mum's voice. No one else's. "Are you in there?"

"C-come in," I called, sitting up groggily. The feel of 800-thread-count sheets, lightly scented with lavender, was quickly bringing me back to reality.

The door opened, and there was Mum. She was dressed in a pair of loose gray pants, flats, and a light pink sweater. A Balenciaga purse was slung over one shoulder, a cup of coffee in her hand.

"Are you going somewhere?" I asked.

Mum gave me a regretful smile as she walked across the room and sat on the side of the bed. "This is for you," she said, handing me the coffee. "Hazelnut latte with soy milk."

"How did you know?" I said, taking the cup thankfully.

"Seriously?" Mum laughed. "You've only tweeted about it a thousand times."

"Guilty," I said, taking a sip. "Gods, that's amazing. Did you run into town for this?"

Mum shook her head. "Ivan's a genius in the kitchen."

"Is there anything he can't do?" I asked, laughing. By now I was fully awake. The sun was shining through pale yellow curtains, revealing the polished wood floors and mint-condition French country antiques. My dream felt no more real to me than a bad sci-fi movie I'd scanned past on cable. "So," I said, "loose pants, light sweater, sensible shoes. If I didn't know better, I'd say you were getting on an airplane."

Mum nodded. "England."

"England!" I repeated. And then it came to me. "Oh, my gods, Wimbledon! I completely forgot it comes right after the French Open." I was filled with a strange mixture of excitement and regret. This was the third leg of the Grand Slam, after all, and probably Mum's toughest challenge. "I can't believe you have to take off so fast, though," I said, sounding more like a little girl than I'd intended.

I guess I had stayed at Fair Haven because I was curious about our mother; Daddy and Ingrid didn't much like the idea, but they couldn't stop me either. After all, Janet Steele was our mother. More than curiosity, though, something had drawn me to the house. My dream, I guess.

Mum patted my head. "Believe me, I hate it too. But all of this"—Mum waved a hand at the house—"doesn't pay for itself."

"And there's that Grand Slam to think about too."

"Let's not get ahead of ourselves. One match at a time. I hate to leave you here all by yourself, but, hey, you'll have the whole mansion as your crib, and of course the staff will get you anything you want. Except for those lattes, I'm afraid. I have to take Ivan with me."

An idea popped into my head.

"Maybe I could go?" Once again my voice sounded as eager as a five-year-old's, and I tried to play it down. "I mean, these lattes are pretty addictive."

Mum smiled gently. "I thought about it. But it's the

kind of thing I really should clear with your dad, and given his accident, and the fact that I've only just reappeared, I think we should take it slow."

I resolved to bring it up with Dad when we visited him at Ingrid's as we usually did every few days.

I knew she was right, though I didn't want to say it out loud. I wished Mardi had been here to witness Mum being so reasonable. These weren't the ravings of a snubbed human bent on deicide, but the sound reasoning of a mature co-parent.

"How long will you be gone?" I asked, though I knew the tournament lasted two weeks.

"You never know," Mum said. "I could lose in the first round and be back tomorrow night."

I couldn't help it. I laughed out loud. "We both know it'll be you and Serena in the final. And that you're going to beat her."

"Promise you'll watch me on TV?"

"You know it."

"Come here!"

I threw my arms around her, even though I was still clutching my cup of coffee. Mum's long strong arms wrapped around me, and one of her hands stroked my hair.

"I'm going to miss you," I said. "I mean, I know we've only just met but . . ."

"But I'm your mum," Mum whispered in my ear, "and you're my daughter, and I'm going to miss you too."

She stood up and walked toward the door. Before she went out, though, she stopped. "Oh, I almost forgot." She reached into her purse, pulled out something shiny, and tossed it to me. I snatched it out of the air.

"Nice reflexes," Mum said.

I looked down at my hand. It was a key fob to a car. The logo was a sharply pointed trident. It took me a moment to place it.

"Is this for a *Maserati*?"

Mum smiled mischievously. "Don't think I'm trying to buy your affection or anything. The car's mine. But there's no need for it to languish in the garage while I'm gone. It's a convertible," she added just before she left. "Wear sunscreen."

And then she was gone.

An hour later—one shower, one bagel, and one practice drive on the road that ran around Gardiners Island—I was flying down North Road, which, as the name suggested, ran along the northern edge of the East End, right on the Long Island Sound. I know I've said I prefer a chauffeur, but I do know how to drive, and the Maserati handled like a dream. You could steer it with a single finger. And it was the best accessory ever. It set off my outfit perfectly.

Speaking of which: my initial plan had been to go to Ingrid and Matt's to pick up my clothes, but when I

got out of the shower and glanced at the dresser, I saw
a little note atop it.

I thought it would be easier if Ivan
fetched your things.—Mum

I pulled open one drawer after another and discovered that they were full of all my summer clothes,
plus a few items I didn't recognize, but which went
perfectly with everything I'd brought. How Ivan had
gotten them in there was a whole other question. I was
a pretty sound sleeper, but I had a hard time imagining
he'd been able to unload four suitcases without waking
me. Well, he was an elf. I supposed he was rather light
on his feet.

I pulled on a pair of white denim shorts and a sleeveless printed blouse I didn't recognize. I glanced at the
label. Tom Ford. My mother had the best taste in the
world. Then I made my way downstairs, where an
already sliced bagel sat in the toaster, waiting for me,
then to the garage. As I walked down the hallway, it
occurred to me that this was the part of the mansion
where I'd seen the light in my dream, but everything
was so new and clean and bright that it was hard to
hold on to the image. Even the garage had the pris-
tine feel of a laboratory, with polished concrete floors
and just the faintest tinge of gasoline. There were six
bays, but only one of them was filled. A bright yellow

Maserati, the top already down, sat in the center of the vast space like an exhibit in a museum. It was as shiny as Katy Perry and curvy as Beyoncé, but even so, it exuded a tough, commanding energy. Just looking at it made me feel powerful.

And okay, I know I shouldn't have liked Mum's Maserati as much as I did, but Oh. My. God. What a car. Like seriously, why does Mardi drive that vintage hoopty when she could cruise around in a whip like this? I mean, it's not just that the engine made about a tenth as much noise as Mardi's did, even as it was about twice as fast: it also had a better stereo, a navigation screen that included a DVD player and seats that spooned you so close you felt like an underwear model was standing behind you and kissing the back of your neck. And they'd somehow designed the windshield so that even when the top was down the wind whipped over your head rather than messing up your hair—all without the need of an anti-weather spell.

The car seemed to know where I was going better than I did. North Road to Cross Fork Lane, Cross Fork to Pfenning Road. Pfenning to 409. Sal's house.

Sal and Rocky's.

He came out before I even made it to the porch. He was wearing a pair of low-slung drawstring shorts and a faded T-shirt with a cartoon cat on it.

"Is that Garfield?" I asked as I got out of the car and started toward the front door.

Rocky paused on the narrow porch, looking down at his shirt. "Seriously? This is Azrael. From the Smurfs," he added when my face must've given away that I had no idea who he was talking about. He nodded at the car. "Is that a Lamborghini?"

"A man's got to be secure in his masculinity to admit to watching the Smurfs. The car's a Maserati."

"You say potato, I say *ensalada de papas*." He said the last part in a thick Spanish accent.

"Potato salad?" By now I was at the foot of the steps. I climbed the first and then the second, till I was standing a step below him. There wasn't really room for two people on the top, unless they squeezed together.

Rocky shrugged sheepishly. "*Papa* didn't have quite the ring to it I wanted."

I decided to go for it. I mounted the last step. Rocky had to step back to accommodate me, but we were still only a couple of inches apart. I tapped the cat on his chest.

"And what'd you call him? Azrael?"

Rocky looked down toward my finger, though I'm not sure his eyes made it past my boobs. When he looked up, there was a small, happy grin on his face. His cheeks were dusted with stubble.

"I grew up without a dad. Papa Smurf was my role model."

"Just don't grow the beard, okay? I know it's all the rage right now, but—"

I was going to say that it sucks to kiss a beard, but it seemed a bit premature. I'm pretty sure my blush gave me away, though, because Rocky started blushing too.

"So, do you want to invite me in or something? This porch is architecturally fascinating, but I think I've seen the highlights."

Rocky looked out toward Mum's car. "You drive up in a Maserati and you want to hang out in my dad's trailer? Really?"

"Good point," I said, although from what I could see through the screen door, the interior of the trailer had been completely redone, so that it looked more like something you'd see photographed in *Hamptons* magazine rather than, I don't know, *White Trash Living*, or whatever.

"Oh, and why don't you drive?" I said, tossing the keys up in the air. "I know you want to."

14

TONIGHT'S THE NIGHT

Mardi-Overbrook-Journal.docx

$\mathcal{M}$olly's move to Fair Haven was helpful on one front: Ingrid was able to move Trent off the couch and out to the gardener's shed. She'd denied my request that he sleep in my room when he first moved in, saying that, goddess or no goddess, I was still a teenager. I could sneak around like one. But under her roof, we played by her rules.

"Good lord, Ingrid, she's seventeen," Freya teased her. "Back in our day, she would have been married and had a couple of kids by now."

"Yes, and back in our day, Tyr would have signaled his intentions by clubbing her on the head and dragging her into his hut. Times have changed."

"They certainly have," Freya said drily. "It's not 1950 anymore. Or 1750, for that matter."

"I don't get it," I protested. "You were fine with me staying with him at Fair Haven. And Dad doesn't care where I sleep." I didn't mention that we hadn't actually shared a bedroom at Trent's house, let alone a bed. I guess it would be a little weird since Dad was staying at Ingrid's too, but he was a progressive kind of guy.

"That was your father's decision, not mine. But this is my house and my rules."

"Oh, *Mother*," Jo chimed. "You're such a *prude*." And she took her iPad and stalked up to her room.

"That girl is growing up way too fast," Ingrid said, shaking her head.

But she refused to give in, and so after one of her delicious home-cooked meals and a couple of games of family-friendly Scrabble (no four-letter words allowed, even after I pointed out that they were in the official Scrabble dictionary, so no surprise when the librarian won) Trent headed out to the shed. When he kissed me good night, though, it was on my forehead. I tilted my head up, but all I got was a second kiss on the tip of my nose.

I wasn't surprised that Ingrid didn't let us sleep together, but what surprised me was that Trent didn't put up any kind of resistance at all. In fact, he seemed almost relieved to be able to move out of the house, and so, the next morning, after Ingrid had gone to the library and Matt had driven off in his sheriff's car and Dad was dozing after downing three of Ingrid's buttermilk waffles slathered in homemade raspberry compote, and Graciella, the housekeeper, had arrived to supervise Jo and Henry, I found Trent and announced:

"We're going for a drive."

Trent looked at me with a wary expression. But he followed me out to the car. I, too, was silent, not saying a word until we were through town and out on the highway. I punched it then and felt the satisfying jolt of the engine in the place where my legs met my abdomen.

I knew what I wanted to say to him, but I didn't know how. The thing is, ever since I'd been back, things hadn't been the same between us. It's like we were starting over again. I thought he was my boyfriend, but he hadn't really acted like one. It was so strange because when we were apart, we did nothing but text and talk on the phone and look forward to being together.

"What's wrong?" I asked. "You know what I mean."

"Nothing's wrong," Trent said, running his fingers through his hair and looking everywhere but at me. "Everything's great. I love that we're together again."

"Really? Because you don't act that way. You act like you're nervous to be around me."

Trent unclasped his hands. "Maybe it's because you're totally ambushing me!"

"Uh-uh. Don't make this about me. You've been like this all summer, and it's just gotten worse." I turned to him, despite the fact that I was driving sixty-five in two-way traffic. "Do you not like me anymore?"

"Uh, Mardi," Trent said, nodding at the road, "you want to, uh . . . ?" He nodded at the road again.

In fact, I'd beefed up the protection spells on the car in anticipation of this converstation, and it was practically steering itself, but Trent didn't need to know that. I stepped on the gas, and though I couldn't see the speedometer, I could feel the car's thrust in my gut.

"Answer the question," I demanded, my stomach falling.

Trent looked back and forth between the road and me for several seconds. His eyes were squinted, nervous, though it seemed to me they were more nervous about talking to me than about the possibility of an accident.

"Fine," he said finally. "Just pull over, okay? It's way too soon for me to be starting over again in another body."

The next turnout was for the beach, and I screeched into it. It was a weekday, and early too, so the small parking lot was nearly empty, as was the beach beyond. There was a stiff breeze, and when I killed the engine, the three-foot waves could be heard crashing heavily against the shore.

"Walk with me," Trent said, kicking off his flip-flops and getting out of the car.

This felt like a stalling tactic, but I decided to go along with him. I toed off my sandals and followed him out of the car, where he stood with his hand extended. I curled mine into his gratefully, and he squeezed back, and we made our way out onto the nearly deserted beach. The sand was cool beneath my bare feet, still damp from the tide. The wind almost brought up goose pimples on my legs, but with a moment of concentration, I was able to make them fade away.

"First of all," Trent said, "I like you. I like you a lot."

"I like you too," I said.

Trent shook his head and sighed. "Has anyone ever told you about the Reawakening?" he said finally.

The word rang a bell, but I couldn't remember what it meant.

"It has something to do with our reincarnation, doesn't it? When our Midgardian bodies are destroyed and we're born in new ones?"

"It does," Trent said, "but it doesn't refer to our bodies. It refers to our memories. Our memories and our magic."

"I'm not sure I understand."

"When we're born into a new body, we're not born with all our memories or abilities. We're not infants with the minds of two-thousand-year-old gods. We're not four-year-olds with the ability to blink our eyes and kill our classmates because they spilled our chocolate milk on our finger painting. Those things come later. The magic comes gradually, starting from the time we're born and accelerating during our teenage years before finally finishing up when we're about thirty. But the memories hold off until, ah, juvenescence is almost over."

"'Juvenescence'?" I repeated. "You mean *puberty*?"

Trent's hand squeezed a little in mine, though it felt more like a spasm than something he'd done on purpose.

"So wait," I continued. "Are you saying that this is happening to you now?"

I saw Trent nod out of the corner of my eye. "It started right around the time we met last year. Slowly. Like, really vivid dreams and stuff. But it's kept up the whole time."

"Well, that explains why you speak Norse in your sleep," I said, scratching at the tattoo of the rainbow bridge that coiled around my neck. "But whatever. Keep going with this Reawakening."

"There's not much more to say," Trent said. "I mean, there's two thousand years more, but you don't need to hear the blow-by-blow, do you?"

"I don't get it. So you're just now getting some memories that I thought you already had. What's the big deal?"

Trent sighed heavily and kicked at a seashell in the wet sand, sending it flying.

"It's not 'some memories.' It's century upon century upon century of memories. I'm the god of war, Mardi. I was born in Asgard. I was there when Odin divided the nine worlds and scattered them across the universe. I've been to every one of them, dozens, hundreds, of times. I've—" He broke off, catching his breath.

"I get it!" I said, cutting him off. "You're *old*. You've

done things. But so what? We're both immortal. Age doesn't mean anything to us."

"We're both immortal," Trent said. "But you're only seventeen."

"So what are you saying? I'm too young for you?"

Trent shrugged miserably. "Maybe I'm saying I'm too old for you."

That sounded like a cop-out to me, but I didn't call him on it because I was just starting to figure out what was happening. I stopped walking and turned to him.

"Trent Gardiner! *Are you breaking up with me?*"

Trent turned toward me, catching my other hand in his. But even though he was holding me tightly, I felt him slipping away.

"No. Never. We're meant to be together, Mardi. I feel it."

"But?"

"But maybe not right now. Maybe not for a decade or a century."

I stared at him for what felt like an eternity, dumbfounded. Then I shook his hands off and stepped back.

"I can't believe I'm hearing this!"

"Mardi, please. Don't be angry."

"I'm the goddess of rage, Trent."

"It's not forever. It's just until we're on the same level."

"'The same level'? Condescend much?"

I turned and started running up the beach. But even

as I was running, I was thinking, *Come after me. Catch me. Tell me you were kidding. Tell me you take it all back.*

"Mardi, please!" Trent called. But he didn't come after me.

I kept running.

* 15 *

HEY, GOOD LOOKIN'

From the Diary of Molly Overbrook

*T*he next day, I showed up at Rocky's at seven in the morning. I know, what self-respecting girl shows up *anywhere* at seven in the morning? But it was the first day of Wimbledon, and as defending champ, Mum was scheduled for the first match of the day—it was noon over in London, but the five-hour difference meant that I had to be up at the crack of dawn if I wanted to see her kick some tennis ass.

Of course, I could've just watched it at Fair Haven. Even though all eighteen TVs that had been in the mansion had left with the Gardiners, there was always the screening room with reclining stadium-style seating. But the more time I'd spent driving around with Rocky yesterday, the less I wanted to go back to Gardiners Island.

The bright, burnished mansion I'd woken up in receded further and further and further in my memory, and the haunted house of my dreams loomed larger and larger. I know that was just my mind playing tricks on me, but even if you took the house for what it was, it was still drearily empty. Not just of people (although where the servants Mum spoke of were hiding I could never tell) but of furniture or any other sign of human habitation. Mum had been kind enough to let the Gardiners pack up their belongings when she kicked them out, but she hadn't had the time to do any redecorating herself, so aside from my bedroom, the mansion was freakishly empty. The hallways echoed with the sound of my footsteps, and their doors opened onto one empty room after another, with nothing to show that anyone had ever lived here besides the faded outlines of paintings that had hung on the walls for generations, and similar patches on the floorboards where the carpets had lain. It was hard to shake the impression that the mansion was somehow letting go of its hold on Midgard, as if it was preparing to slide into Niflheim, and the nightmare I'd dreamed about.

Besides all that, there was the fact that Rocky's house—or, well, Sal's—was neutral ground. No matter how empty Fair Haven was, it still felt like Trent's house to me, and even though I knew Mum had acquired it fair and square, I still felt a little guilty walking through its grand, derelict rooms knowing Trent and the rest of the Gardiners were forbidden from doing the same.

. . .

Once again, Rocky met me on the porch. He was wearing another pair of floppy shorts, another holey T-shirt, both relatively unwrinkled, but his thick dark hair looked like he'd just rolled out of bed.

"How do you look so wide awake?" he said in a bleary voice. "I haven't been up this early since, I don't know, seventh grade."

I'm a goddess, I almost said. *I don't actually need to sleep.* But all I said aloud was "I'm a morning person. I've already read fifty pages of *Madame Bovary*, done Pilates, and touched up my nails."

"Why do I get the feeling that none of that is true, and that you're dying for a coffee as much as I am?"

"Coffee!" I screamed. "Oh, gods, yes!" I'd tried to figure out the espresso machine at Fair Haven, but it had more buttons than an airplane cockpit, and the most I'd been able to do was get it to beep angrily and shoot out jets of steam.

Rocky held the door open for me, and I squeezed past him, inhaling a faint, pleasant whiff of clean but unshowered boy, which quickly gave way to the aroma of brewing coffee.

"That smells heavenly."

"Sal does run an upscale bar, after all. He's not going to serve Folgers."

"Anything with caffeine sounds appealing right now."

"Coming right up," Rocky said, shuffling on his bare feet toward the kitchen at the far end of the room.

I looked around the space. It was definitely a bachelor pad, but it was still nothing like I expected. The entire interior of the trailer had been gutted, so the room was one long tube, kind of like a train carriage but even longer and wider and taller. The far end held the kitchen, with gleaming Sub-Zero and Viking appliances, while the middle held a long narrow dining table made out of bleached, battered planks with eight chic mismatched chairs running down the sides, while the near end served as the living area, with a pair of low modern sectionals upholstered pale green flanking a TV that looked like a pool table on its side.

"That is one big TV."

"Sal's single, and he likes his sports. That TV's the wife he doesn't have."

"Well, let's turn his wife on," I said, plopping down on one of the sectionals. "Mum should be walking out on Centre Court right about now."

"Just lemme finish with the coffees," Rocky said. "Hot or iced?"

"Oh, iced! What a good idea!"

"Milk and sugar?"

"As Prince Charming said to Snow White, 'I like my coffee like I like my women: pale and sweet.'"

Rocky laughed so hard he almost spilled the milk he was pouring into a pair of tall glasses. He stirred in some sugar, then hurried down to my end of the trailer.

"Okay, okay," he said, setting the glasses on the coffee table. "Let's see if I can remember how to work this thing." He picked up an iPad. "Sal's got everything networked. Guys and their gadgets," he scoffed, and his voice was a little harsher than it had to be.

"So how's that been, anyway?" I said while he fiddled with the iPad. I had pointedly ignored the subject of family during our time together yesterday.

"Oh, fine, I guess," Rocky said distractedly, his fingers swiping and stabbing over the tablet's screen. "Sal's trying really, really hard. Like when he asked me what I wanted for dinner last night and I said, 'Anything,' and he said, 'If you could have anything in the world for dinner, what would it be?' and I said, 'Filet mignon, I guess,' which is funny because I don't actually like filet mignon. I mean, I don't hate it or anything, but if I'm going to have a steak, I like a good T-bone and—finally!"

The TV glowed to life. It was already tuned to ESPN. There was Mum, still dressed in her warm-up jacket, swatting balls lightly across the court.

"Wow. She is not a small woman, is she?"

"She's listed at six foot two, but when you stand next to her, she feels even bigger. So: filet mignon?"

"Oh, right. So anyway, yeah, Sal doesn't even, like, get the fact that I'm joking; he just called up some place called Michael's and asked them if they delivered."

"Michael's? They're in East Hampton. That's forty-five minutes away."

"Which must be why it took an hour and a half for our dinner to get here, and it was pretty much ice cold by the time it arrived."

"But it was a nice gesture, no? Like you said, he's trying."

"I guess." Rocky shrugged. "I just wish—no, that's not fair."

"What?"

Rocky sighed. "I was just going to say, I wish he'd tried this hard when Mom was alive."

"Ouch," I said. "You're right. Not fair."

Rocky shrugged again. "A lot of things aren't fair. But whatever, let's not be morbid. We've got some tennis to watch. Here's to a speedy victory by Janet Steele."

We clinked glasses and settled in for the match. Mum was playing someone named Svetlana Turkena— or something. I could look it up, but it would take more time than the match did.

"Do we have an official stat on this?" one of the announcers said over nineteen minutes later. "Is this the fastest match in history? Janet Steele just demolished her opponent."

"That poor girl," Rocky said, nodding at Mum's opponent, who was clearly holding back tears as she packed up her rackets and tried to get off court before she started bawling.

"If it makes you feel better, she got paid something like thirty thousand dollars for losing this match."

"I suppose money does soften the blow."

I glanced at my watch. It was past 7:30. Somehow

when I'd suggested that we watch the match today, I'd pictured us hanging out together all morning and into the afternoon, drinking coffee, snacking on chips and popcorn, maybe ordering some burgers from North Inn. At some point around the early afternoon, I was going to suggest casually that we head to the beach for a swim, which would have naturally transitioned to the two of us lying next to each other on towels, at which point I was pretty sure my body in a bikini would push things to their natural next step. I don't mean to sound conceited, but I am a goddess. But 7:30 is a little early to start macking on someone.

Rocky seemed to be similarly at a loss.

"So, uh, did you have breakfast?"

"I haven't actually."

"I think we've got eggs?" He said it with a question mark, although I couldn't tell if he wasn't sure if Sal had eggs, or if he wanted to make them. I decided to put him to the test.

"I would love eggs!" I said with forced brightness. "Poached, please!"

Rocky laughed in my face. "I can do scrambled or burned."

"Scrambled, please."

"Fine. But you have to do the toast."

We got up and made our way to the kitchen.

"Such gallantry," I said. "Do you always make your dates sing for their supper?"

Rocky winked back at me. "Oh, so this is a date?"

I blushed. I couldn't believe I'd let that slip out.

"Hey, I'm not the one who was on social media looking up hot prospects in the East End."

"Really?" Rocky smirked. "That's how you want to play this?"

"What're you talking about, McLaughlin?" I said, grabbing a loaf of bread and twisting it open.

"I'm just saying I don't think I was the only person who was looking around Instagram for, um, what was the term? 'Hot prospects'?"

He handed me his phone, which was open to his social media feed. The header read *Who's been checking me out?* and the first name on the list: *Molly Overbrook.*

"What the Hell," I said, grabbing his phone. I glanced at the time stamp, saw that it was from four days ago, right before Dad's accident.

"Why, that little sneak!" I said.

"What?" Rocky said, opening the fridge and grabbing a carton of eggs.

"Mardi was using my profile when she looked you up!"

Rocky laughed skeptically. "Sure she was."

"Seriously? You don't think I know how to do private viewing?"

"Well, maybe you wanted me to know you'd been checking me out."

"Um, excuse me," I said, taking a step back. I waved my hand down my body like a game-show girl showing off a refrigerator. "Does this look like I have to work that hard?"

Rocky turned pink. But then he recovered enough to say, "Well, even if it was your sister who looked up my profile, you still knew who I was when you met me the other day."

"Yeah? Well, you knew who I was too!" I almost yelled.

"So I guess that makes us even, doesn't it!" Rocky shot back.

"I guess it does!"

"So I guess I'm going to kiss you now!"

"I guess you damn well better!"

Turns out 7:30 in the morning isn't too early for macking at all. Or making out for that matter.

16

WRECKING BALL

Mardi-Overbrook-Journal.docx

$\mathcal{T}$wo miserable days after Trent dumped me on the beach, while I was hanging out with Ingrid's kids, my phone rang. It was a local number, but it wasn't in my phone book.

"No!" Henry screamed at Jo. "First you have to play the *jacks*, then you have to play the queens, and THEN you play the kings. EVERYBODY knows that."

"Whatever," Jo said, slapping down a handful of cards. "I think you're just making the rules up as you go along!"

"Hey!" I yelled. "Keep it down! I've got a phone call!" And a headache, I added silently.

"Hello?" I said guardedly.

"Mardi!" a deep male voice all but yelled into the phone. "Oh, thank God!"

"Sal?" I said. I was pretty sure it was him. "What's the matter?"

"One moment, ma'am," Sal said, although I didn't think he was talking to me. Then, louder: "Herring crème fraîche is the matter!"

"Um . . . sorry?"

"Ma'am, I said I'll be with you in a moment!" Sal repeated in a sharper tone of voice. "Mardi, please, you've got to help me out. I just got an order for six quarts of herring crème fraîche down at the Cheesemonger!"

"Um, okay." I racked my brain for the significance of this factoid. I had vague memories of a sandwich called the Debbie Harry. Molly told me it was one of Marshall's, a.k.a. Alberich's, more inspired creations. Hickory smoked salmon, fermented dill pesto, and herring crème fraîche served on a sourdough and onion brioche. Sounds gross, but somehow it was really good.

"I think it's for the Debbie Harry."

"In my world, Debbie Harry is still the twenty-eight-year-old ex–Playboy Bunny who sang 'Atomic' and 'Heart of Glass.' She is not—thank you!" he interrupted himself in a sarcastic tone. "Please come again! She is not a sandwich. Nevertheless, the East End seems to be full of people who don't know anything about her music career and everything about her reincarnation as one of the most disgusting combinations of flavors I can possibly imagine."

"It's kind of an acquired taste," I admitted. "But what's all this got to do with me?"

"Oh, nothing," Sal said testily. "Except that you said you'd make them for me."

"I . . . huh?"

"The other day? When you wandered into the Cheesemonger? I said I was thinking of asking Molly to work here for the summer, and you said that you wanted to do it?"

"Oh, right!" I'd totally forgotten about it, what with everything that had gone down in the past couple of days. The Gardiners getting kicked out of their house and Molly moving into it and Trent dumping me on the beach, and then just disappearing. Ingrid said something about "Europe," as if that somehow narrowed it down. Trent went all the way to Europe to get away from me? So depressing.

"So I take it Molly turned you down?" I said now.

"Not exactly. She's been too busy letting my son squire her all around the East End in a bright yellow Maserati."

"Rocky has a Maserati?"

"I drive a 1974 Toyota Land Cruiser, Mardi. Do you think my son has a Maserati?"

I didn't bother pointing out that he also owned five buildings in one of the most expensive square miles of real estate east of Rodeo Drive, and that the Land Cruiser, like the refurbished trailer house he lived in, was a total WASP affectation.

"You mean it's Molly's? But where would Molly . . . oh, of course. Janet."

"Who's Janet?"

"Steele? The tennis player. Our mother—never mind. Anyway, I'm sorry Molly's kidnapped Rocky, but I'm not sure—"

"You have to help me out," Sal cut me off. "I can't keep running back and forth between the Inn and the sandwich shop. I'm losing business at both places. Freya's ready to quit, and you know I can't lose her— she's the best bartender on the East Coast."

"I'm only seventeen; I can't help out in the bar."

"The Cheesemonger, Mardi. I need you in the sand-wich shop."

"But I don't know the menu or the merchandise or—"

"You knew about the Debbie Harry. Please, Mardi. I'm begging. I'm begging a kid to save my ass."

An hour later, I was parking in front of the Cheese-monger, when Sal came out of the store in a filthy apron.

"No, no, no," he said. "You can't park right in front of the store. That's for customers."

"Seriously, Sal? I'm doing you a favor here."

"And I'm paying you for it! Now move the car."

I thought about remarking that my dad made in the high eight figures last year, plus he was, you know, a god. But all I did was pull the Ferrari around back, to the small municipal lot there.

"Okay, then," Sal said as I walked in the back door. "So, it turns out that Billy and Bruce's B&B, you know, the one next to the yacht club, has a standing order for a dozen sandwiches every day at eleven-thirty. Just get those ready, and they'll send over their, um, houseboy to pick them up at eleven-fifteen. Then you should go ahead and get ready for the eleven-thirty train from the city. It usually lets off a hungry crowd. I'd just make another dozen assorted sandwiches—making sure you've got at least two veggie, two vegan, and two gluten-free. You know this crowd—they have more dietary restrictions than Catholics during Lent. That'll pretty much wipe out your prepared stocks, so you should probably make some more prep for the afternoon crowd. We've got smoked salmon, cured trout, smoked and herbed turkey, Parma ham, Iberian ham, Smithfield ham, prosciutto, and all the various things that go into the dips and spreads and dressings in the walk-in. Marshall left really detailed instructions on how to make everything—the kid may have been a flake, but he was a wizard in the kitchen. Oh, and I haven't had a chance to get the linen service back in here, so you'll have to wear this for now." And he pulled the stained apron off his sweaty body and draped it unceremoniously over my neck. "Your employee discount is fifty percent," he added, "so feel free to chow down."

And with that, he trotted toward the back door.

"Um, Sal?"

He turned back to me with an impatient look.

"I thought you said Rocky was going to be working here too."

Sal looked at me as though I was speaking Norse.

"Rocky? I told you. He's running around with your sister. They're probably at the beach right now."

And with that, he was gone.

"Holy crap," I said out loud. "What just happened?"

* 17 *

SAIL AWAY SWEET SISTER

From the Diary of Molly Overbrook

So much happened over the course of the next two weeks that I almost forgot about the fact that I hadn't spoken to Mardi once that whole time.

I suppose I could just as easily say that I didn't speak to Dad, Ingrid, Freya, Matt, Jo, or even Henry, but let's face it: as important as all those people were to me, none of them came close to Mardi. Not even Dad, who was still recovering.

Mardi was my twin. She was the most important person in my life. I'd never gone more than two days without seeing her. I'd never gone a single day without talking to her. In fact, I don't think I'd ever gone six hours without talking to her. That's how I knew this fight was serious, even if I didn't know what it was about.

Because really, what had happened to get her so upset?

Mum had repeated some stuff about some old prophecy or something. If I had a dollar for every time someone in our family spouted off about how such-and-such had been foretold or so-and-so was the promised one . . . well, I'm already rich, but I'd be even richer.

Like most old religions, we had prophecies up the wazoo, and the vast majority of them were so vague that you never really knew if they'd actually come true, or if people were just making stuff up. And even if this was one of the real ones, well, what could we do about it? If the fates had decreed that we were supposed to be the end of the old gods, the old gods could hardly blame *us*, could they? And besides, like Mum said, who knew when it would all come to pass? It could be decades. Centuries. Millennia. Couldn't we all just chill and have some fun till then?

Who knew, maybe Mardi was having the time of her life while she was apart from me—I have to say, those two weeks were some of the best of my life.

First of all, Mum was on TV every other day. And she was kicking some serious ass. She won her first three matches 6–0, which if you don't know anything about tennis, that's a total beatdown, and it's pretty much unheard of for it to happen three times in a row. After the third match, Rocky said, "Damn. It's like she's got a magic racket or something." I glanced at him sharply, but he didn't notice. Of course I was wondering the same thing. I mean, she barely broke a sweat when she played—and it was almost ninety degrees on the court. She'd said she was human, and Ingrid and Freya and Dad had confirmed that, but they'd also hinted that it would have taken magic for her to get pregnant by Dad without his consent, or knowledge, for that matter. And if she could pull off something like that, why couldn't she get a nice little hex on her racket, as Rocky had unwittingly suggested, or maybe just on her right arm. It was exactly the kind of thing the Council was likely to miss. They were much more concerned with events like elections or business ventures, or things that left people dead. Tennis was a little under the radar for them.

But then, Mum had been at it for a while now, at two different periods, and she certainly hadn't played down her success, either on or off the court. And as the ex-girlfriend of Thor, she was likely to fall under more scrutiny than most people. No, the more I thought about it, the more unlikely it seemed that she was using magic to win matches. My mother was simply a kick-ass tennis player.

And even better than watching her cruise toward the Wimbledon final was the way she ended each of her on-court interviews: "I just want to say hi to my daughter Molly, who's watching back home in North Hampton. Mum loves you, and she'll be home soon."

And you know, that was great. Really great, except I felt a tiny pang that she didn't mention Mardi. So great that the first time she said it, I actually felt myself tearing up. I didn't realize how much I had missed having a mother. But although the emotions she was bringing up were totally real, Mum was three thousand miles away, and she was still kind of unreal to me.

I mean, I was living in her house and I was driving her car, but I'd only met her once, spent maybe a grand total of four hours talking to her, and it was hard to think of her in the same way I thought of Dad. So mostly I was biding my time, waiting for her to come back to the East End, to figure out if she really was as awesome as she seemed.

But much closer at hand was Rocky. And, well, Rocky really *was* awesome. Like if you ever took one of those quizzes in *Teen Vogue* or *Girls' Life* about the perfect boyfriend, Rocky seemed to have been created right from my answers. He was athletic but not a jock; he was smart but not a nerd; he liked R&B but not gangster rap; he was a great kisser but he didn't pressure me to go too fast. In fact, when we were making out, he was usually the one to break things off first.

I also got the feeling he was always thinking about his mom. It had only been a few months since she'd died, after all. There were times when we'd be doing something—popping popcorn maybe (Rocky liked to make it the old-fashioned way, in a pot on the stove), or flipping past some dumb reality show on TV—and he'd fall silent with this faraway look on his face. I asked him about it a couple times, but he'd always give me this half-happy, half-sad smile and say, "It's nothing."

I hadn't exactly earned the right to his heart's secrets after only a few days of hanging out, and I wasn't even sure I felt ready to carry them, let alone reciprocate them. I mean, it's not like I was going to tell him I was a goddess anytime soon. But it was nice knowing the guy I was hanging out with had some depth to him. The abs didn't hurt either.

And let's not forget: we were both all alone. I mean, Rocky had Sal, and I had Mardi and Dad and Freya and Ingrid and Matt and the kids. But Rocky didn't really know Sal, who was always busy with the North Inn and his other businesses, and I had done a great job of driving a wedge between me and the family by moving into Fair Haven. Not that it would have been hard to avoid them: Dad was laid up in bed, Ingrid had her job at the library as well as two kids to raise, and Mardi, well, Mardi seemed to just disappear, as did Trent for that matter.

I didn't check up on them on social media, but even so, I assumed they hadn't gone off somewhere together or I'd have heard—through Freya if no one else, since she was the one member of my family I still saw, usually in the evenings, after Rocky and I had spent the day watching Wimbledon or lazing on the beach or driving around the North Fork.

In fact, we ended up at the North Inn almost every

night, since neither of us wanted to cook and the chef at Fair Haven didn't know how to make anything less complicated than boeuf en daube, and the North Inn's Kobe beef burger was pretty amazing, plus Freya would give us free drinks.

And on our thirteenth day together, she handed me a box of condoms.

"Freya!" I exclaimed, quickly hiding them in my purse. I glanced around to see if Rocky had noticed, but he was back at our table, staring at his phone. "What are you doing?"

"Better safe than sorry," Freya said as she wiped down the bar. "I can smell the hormones on you two even through all the suntan lotion."

"Nothing has happened! And even if something did, it's not like I'd need these."

"He doesn't know that," Freya said. "First rule of fooling around with mortals: don't give them any reason to suspect that you're different. And secondly, you should be prepared, even though you haven't rounded third."

I blushed. "What makes you think I've never gone to third before?"

"Seriously, Mooi? I'm the goddess of love, in case you've forgotten. I don't miss details like that. If it makes you feel better, he's a virgin too."

"What? You can tell?"

"Goddess of love," Freya said again. "It's not just an honorary title, you know. Also?" Freya paused dramatically.

"Yes?" I prompted.

"He wants you to be his first."

Over at his table, Rocky looked up with a start.

I put my head down on the bar, my heart pounding, while Freya cheerfully made drinks as if she hadn't just blown my mind.

Like I said, this happened on our thirteenth night at the North Inn, which is to say, the night before the Wimbledon final. Although we'd watched the whole tournament at Sal's house, we'd made plans to watch the final at Fair Haven in the home theater. I'd left a note with the cook to prepare a full English breakfast, even though I wasn't quite sure what that was. I woke up to the fragrant smell of bacon and sausage filling the mansion, although when I went downstairs I was, as usual, unable to find any sign of the staff.

A banquet table had been set up in the screening room, laden with warming trays filled with enough food to provision an army. In addition to three different kinds of bacon (regular, Canadian, and maple-glazed) and four different kinds of sausages (bratwurst, chorizo, kielbasa, merguez), there were also scrambled eggs, baked beans, grilled mushrooms, an assortment of scones, enough toast to shingle a barn, and an unappealing black mess that was helpfully labeled "blood pudding," which almost made me not want to eat anything else on the table.

Rocky showed up promptly at seven. I handed him a Bloody Mary, fully loaded with celery stalk, toothpicked olives, and lemon and lime wedges. He made space among all the garnishes for his mouth, took a sip, smiled, and took a longer sip.

"I've gotta say, this is the earliest I've ever showed up for a date in my life."

"Date? Who said anything about a date? Anything before three is just an . . . assignation."

"Hmmm," Rocky said, pursing his lips. "Let me ponder that." But instead of pondering, he leaned in and planted his pursed lips atop mine.

It was 7:05 before he stood up again. Goddesses have an unerring sense of time.

"Nope," he said with a sly grin, "I'm pretty sure this is a date."

"I, uh, I concur," I said hoarsely, then, grabbing his hand, led him toward the screening room.

Rocky lagged behind me like a tourist seeing Venice or New York City for the first time, gawking at the vast rooms as we passed through.

"Wow," he said. "I Google-mapped this place, so I knew it was fancy. But I never realized it was this, well, fancy. Except where's all the furniture?"

"Mum took possession right before Wimbledon. I guess she hasn't had time to decorate."

"Wasn't there furniture from her old house? This place is seriously empty."

"Silly, Rocky. Rich people don't sell one house when

they buy another. They keep adding to their collection, like marbles or baseball cards."

"Okay," Rocky said dubiously. "I just hope you're not sleeping on the floor or anything."

"Wouldn't you like to know?" I teased, and though Rocky didn't answer me, his silence spoke volumes. As did mine, for that matter: the sconces in the hallway, which were off, suddenly flashed on.

"Must be the old wiring," I said before Rocky could ask.

We made it to the screening room without further incident. Once again, Rocky's jaw hit the floor. The screening room at Fair Haven had been done in high Art Deco style, like the movie palaces of the thirties. The walls were covered in heavy red velvet accented with ornate gilded trim. The gilded coffered ceiling was hung with miniature chandeliers whose flickering bulbs imitated gaslight. The plush velvet chairs came in single and love seats, with individual recliners and burled walnut trays for your snacks.

"I don't want to sound like a hick from the sticks, but—wow. I thought only rappers and movie stars had rooms like this. Actually, I never really thought they had them either."

"The truth is, any house or apartment over 10,000 square feet pretty much has to have one, even though the people who own the houses watch their reality shows and pay-per-view on flat-screen TVs just like everyone else. It's a resale thing. You have to have a catering kitchen, and a screening room, and an elevator, even though these things only get used once or twice a year."

Rocky looked at me like I'd just revealed that I could read Egyptian hieroglyphics.

"Sorry, Dad's a Realtor. This stuff is dinner conversation at our house."

Rocky laughed, and we made our way to the buffet.

"How is your dad?" Rocky said as he began heaping a plate with steaming meats and eggs. "You haven't really mentioned him." He tried to keep his tone light, but I could hear the effort in his voice, as if he didn't want to upset me, or seem prying.

"Oh, he's fine," I said as I began filling my own plate. "On the mend? I mean, as far as I know."

"You haven't been to see him?" Rocky said, even though I'd spent every waking hour with him.

"Oh, look at the time!" I said, feeling guilty about not having gone to see Dad. "The prematch chat is just about to start."

Rocky flashed me a look but didn't probe. We took our plates to one of the love seats and sat down next to each other. I could tell he wanted to pry, but decided not to. Good. I picked up the iPad on the side table and turned on the home theater system. It had already been tuned to ESPN. They were talking about my mother and her chances.

"Does it make you nervous?" Rocky asked me. "Your mom being a sports star?"

"I guess?" I said casually. "I mean, it's all so new to me. I'm used to not having a mother, you know? Like I almost forget that the woman they're talking about is actually related to me."

Rocky munched on a piece of bacon before answering. If it's possible to imagine someone eating bacon sadly, that's what Rocky was doing.

"I guess I don't really see myself as ever getting used to not having a mother."

I grabbed the remote and muted the sound.

"Oh, Rocky, I'm sorry. That was insensitive of me."

"Crap," Rocky said. "I didn't mean to sound like I was blaming you or something. You could be talking about, I don't know, bacon or something"—he held up another piece—"and I'd still end up thinking about her."

"It must be so rough," I said.

"You know what's rough? When I *don't* think about her. When I brush my teeth and rinse out the sink afterward, not because my mom will get on my case if I leave toothpaste in it, but because it's just what I do now. I know I just said I can't see myself getting used to not having a mother, but the truth is that I'm afraid that I will get used to it one day. I'll just be another one of those kids who doesn't have a mom and doesn't ever give it a moment's thought."

"I've only known you two weeks, but I already know that's not true. You'll never forget your mom. But that doesn't mean you have to feel sad every single day. She wouldn't want that. She'd want you to be happy."

"I almost hate to say it," Rocky said with a little smile, "but I have been pretty happy lately. And I don't feel like she would mind."

I knew he was talking about me, and willed myself to keep calm. The last thing I needed to do was short out the entertainment system.

Rocky nodded at the screen, where Mum and Serena were finishing their warm-ups. "Turn it up. That's what we're here for."

Before I turned the sound back on, I took his hand.

"Just so you know, I've been pretty happy too."

And that was the last thought I had about Rocky for the next three hours and twenty-seven minutes, because my attention was completely absorbed by the match. I'd barely noticed we were holding hands. I had no idea for how long. And I was so keyed up I couldn't speak—I just squeezed his hand and watched the screen. My heart was beating so hard that I might as well have been out on the court myself.

The women were screaming with each and every shot, and both of them were given fines for "audible obscenity" before the match was over. I couldn't even describe what went on during the last set, it was so intense and I was so overwhelmed. But then suddenly Mum was serving a ball and Serena lobbed it back and Mum pounced on it, firing it past Serena, and then Rocky and I were both on our feet.

"Oh, my gods, she won! She won!" I screamed hoarsely.

"She won!" Rocky screamed just as loud and just as hoarsely. "That was unbelievable!"

On screen, Mum fell down on the ragged grass and lay there for a full thirty seconds, half stunned, half exhausted. When she sat up, she had a dumbfounded smile on her face. The camera flashed to Ivan in her box. He was jumping up and down, screaming.

Rocky and I sat back in our seats as Mum slowly stood up, using her racket as a cane. She walked on heavy feet to the net and shook Serena's hand. Serena's face was stony, but then Mum said something and Serena said something back and offered a flash of her trademark smile, and they walked together to shake the umpire's hands.

"That's class," Rocky said. "I don't know if I could look someone in the eye after they beat me in a match like that, let alone smile at her."

I was still too dazed to reply.

"I can't believe it," I said. "I . . . I just can't believe it."

Mum made her way to her player's box, where she gave Ivan a huge hug.

"That's your mom," Rocky said.

"That's my mum," I said, turning to Rocky. "That's really my mum."

Rocky turned to me. "You must be so—"

"Shhh," I said.

"Huh?"

"Just come here." I pulled him close.

Rocky resisted for a half a second, then fell against me. I put a hand around the back of his head and brought his lips to mine.

"This is a date, remember?"

"I never forgot," Rocky said, and this time his voice didn't sound hoarse as much as husky.

"It's kind of a weird date, but maybe we can give it a more normal ending."

"Are you kidding?" Rocky said after we'd made out for a couple more minutes. "This is the Best. Date. Ever."

He looked up several minutes later. First he said, "Are you sure?" and when I nodded, he smiled and gave me a little nip on my lips. "Turn the TV off," he said then. "I don't want your mom to watch this."

I was so caught up in what was about to happen that all I did was nod and wave a hand at the screen, which went black.

"Wow," Rocky said. "What are you, magic or something?"

"You're about to find out," I said, and I pulled him close again.

18

YOU'VE GOT ME FEELING EMOTIONS

Mardi-Overbrook-Journal.docx

The two weeks after Molly moved into Fair Haven and Trent dumped me and I started working at the Cheese-monger were the worst in my entire life.

Okay, first let me admit that I've led a pretty sheltered life. My family's rich, and, you know, there's a pretty good chance I'm going to live, well, forever. So any complaining I do comes with a pretty big asterisk next to it. And I'm not so self-involved that I don't know that a breakup isn't the end of the world. There'll be other boys. Other Trents even.

Who knows, there might even be Trent again.

But screw that. Screw his *This isn't forever*. Screw

keeping perspective and putting a good face on it and making the best of a bad situation. When Trent told me on the beach that he couldn't be with me, my first thought was that he'd reached inside my chest and ripped out my heart, and my second thought was that the ground had opened up and swallowed me, and my third thought was that if I didn't put as much space between me and Trent as possible, I was going to reach inside his chest and rip out his heart and dig a hole on the beach and bury the body right there.

So I ran. And what made it all a hundred, a million times worse was that the only thing I could think of was running straight to Molly and telling her everything that had happened and crying on her shoulder and eating pint after pint of Ben & Jerry's until even my divine body felt bloated with sugar and cream. But with each step I took away from Trent, I knew I was getting farther and farther away from Molly as well. She'd made it clear: she'd rather be with a mother she didn't know than her own family. And somehow I knew that if I tried to explain any of this to Dad or Ingrid or Freya, they'd end up taking Trent's side. For the first time in my life, I was alone.

Then, one afternoon, Molly walked into the Cheesemonger.

"Mardi!" she said, obviously surprised to find me working there.

I reached out a hand, and the door swung shut. I had never done anything like this before, but I could feel the energy surging through my body.

"Door, lock!" The dead bolt slammed in the door. "Shades, down!" The shades fell with a thump, plunging the store into twilight.

"Okay, sis," I said, turning to Molly. "It's just you and me. We need to talk."

For a long moment, we stood there in semidarkness. Suddenly, the lights snapped on of their own accord. A half second later, they snapped off with a loud pop, and then I heard the motor power down on the refrigerated cases.

"Was that you?" I said.

"I guess." Molly shrugged. "It's been happening a lot lately."

"You know what else has been happening a lot lately? I know things that I didn't know I knew, or I think of something and it just happens?"

"Kind of?" Molly said, in a way that sounded like *all the time.*

"I think it has something to do with the Reawakening."

"The Reaw-what?" Molly said, then waved a hand. "Okay, wait. First things first. What are you doing working here?"

"Covering for you!"

"What do you mean, covering for me? I haven't worked here since Marshall—ugh, Alberich—was here last summer."

I explained to her about my run-in with Sal, and how he'd wanted her to work here with Rocky. "But since you and Rocky seem to have found each other without his help, he decided to ask me to work here instead."

Molly laughed. "No offense, sis, but you're not exactly the vision of a counter girl."

"I figured if you could do it, it can't be that hard."

"Touché. It was kind of fun, but that was mostly because of the flirting."

"Flirting would definitely make this more fun."

"Ha! Trent would murder someone if he even thought you were flirting with him."

I didn't say anything, but suddenly the power kicked back on again.

"Whoa!" Molly said. "Was that you?"

"I guess."

"Oh! Something happened with you and Trent, didn't it? What?"

"Nothing," I murmured.

"Bull! What happened, Molly? Oh no! Did he break up with you?"

"He said we're just on a break."

"Oh, Hel no. You *do not* Ross-and-Rachel my sister. When I see that little punk, I'm going to tear him a new one."

"Before you judge him too harshly, listen." And as briefly as I could, I explained to her about the Reawakening.

"So what?" she said in a bemused voice. "I don't care. No one dumps my sister."

"Too late," I said.

"Okay, whatever, I'll deal with him later. So you think this Reawakening thing is happening to us?"

"I guess you'd have to call it an Awakening, since this is our first time around. But yeah. I mean, how else do you explain all these strange surges of power that have been coming out of our bodies, or, I dunno, dreams and whatever."

"Dreams?" Molly said. "What kind of dreams?"

"I've been having this crazy dream about Fair Haven. Where it's all, like—"

"Ruined?" Molly interjected.

"Yeah! How did you know?"

"And the front yard is like this icy swamp, and there are trees growing through the roof, and this weird light—"

"In the east wing?"

"Yes!"

"You've been having the same dream that I've been having!"

"I have."

I should say this wasn't totally unprecedented. When Molly and I were little girls, three and four, we often had the same dreams, and even sometimes talked to each other in our sleep—from different bedrooms. But it hadn't happened in well over a decade.

"So you saw the silhouette?"

"The what?"

"This woman's silhouette. In the east wing, by the green light."

"Ew, no." I paused, then said cautiously, "Do you think it's Mum?"

"I don't know," Molly said. "Before I can get close to her, I always wake up."

"But you think it's her?"

"I don't know," Molly said again, but I could tell that she thought it was—that she was afraid it was.

"How is she?" I asked now. "How are things between you two?"

Molly frowned at me. "Wait, you don't know?"

"Don't know what?"

"That she's been in England for the past two weeks?"

"No, why would I know that? And why's she there?"

"Seriously?" Molly said. "You don't know?"

"Um, that's why I asked what she's doing there."

"Mardi, she won Wimbledon yesterday!"

"She did?" I asked incredulously. "How do I not know this?"

"I don't know. It's been everywhere. She's even going to be on *Jimmy Kimmel* tonight."

"Oh, my gods, I have got to get out of this sandwich shop! But wait. If she's been in England for the past two weeks, what have you been doing?"

And . . . snap! The lights went off again, and the refrigerator powered down.

"Molly! What—holy crap! No! You—you and Rocky?"

My voice was practically squealing. "And you didn't tell me first? Or call me right after?"

"It just kind of happened," Molly said, blushing.

"I can't believe this. And you didn't call me?"

"Are you mad?"

"At you? No. I mean, I'm still mad about Mum kicking the Gardiners out of Fair Haven, and you taking her side, but of course I want you to be happy."

"I am happy," she said.

I was jealous that she knew something I didn't, but I was glad we were talking again. I missed her.

The power began blinking on and off.

"Is that you?" I said.

"I think it's you," Molly said. "Maybe it's both of us."

I told myself to calm down, and I could see her doing the same. Eventually the lights stopped blinking and everything went dark.

"Wait, do you think we can leave the power on? I have a couple thousand dollars of food that'll go bad otherwise."

"Let's do it together," Molly said. "On three. One. Two. Three."

I willed the power on, and even as I did, I felt a kind of energy moving through me, and realized it was Molly, and the lights popped on.

"Did you feel that?" Molly said.

"That was you, wasn't it?"

"I think I've felt that before," she said. "I just never realized it."

"Maybe it's because we've been apart for the past two weeks."

"Ugh, it was terrible."

I laughed. "You don't sound like you've been having that bad of a time."

"You know what I mean. Rocky's great. But without you it just didn't feel the same."

"I know." I bumped her shoulder. We weren't the sentimental type. For most of our seventeen years, all we did was fight and compete for our father's attention. But we were sisters. Twins. We were each other's closest companion and fiercest enemy.

There was a knock on the door.

"Rocky!" we both said at the same time, and Molly ran to the door, unlocked it, threw it open.

"Hey," he said. "Am I interrupting? I was tired of waiting in the car."

"No," Molly said soothingly, patting him on the back. "We're done. You remember my sister, Mardi."

"Hey, Mardi."

"Hey, Rocky," I said. He wasn't like the preppie monsters Molly often dated, and I immediately decided I liked him.

"So did you get your coffee?" Rocky asked her. He curled his fingers into hers, pulled Molly close to him, and kissed her softly.

"Uh, yeah," Molly said, then kissed him back.

Then he kissed her back.

Then she kissed him back.

Get a room, people!

"So I guess we should be heading out to the Inn," Rocky said. "Dad texted. He said he's got some lunch for us."

"Right," Molly said. She turned to me. "So I'll see you around?" she said, and in that moment, I realized she was going to go back to Fair Haven. To Mum. Somehow I'd just assumed that she was going to come back to Ingrid's with me.

"Sure!" I said with false brightness. "We'll totally see each other around!" I could feel the power surging in me again and had to tamp it down before one of the coolers blew a motor. "Bye!"

But Molly was already out the door. A moment later, a bright yellow Maserati flew down the street, with Molly at the wheel.

"Molly? Driving? The world really is coming to an end."

✳ *19* ✳

CHANDELIER

From the Diary of Molly Overbrook

𝓘 woke up the morning after I saw Mardi to an empty bed. I'd made Rocky go back to Sal's because I wasn't sure when Mum was getting in. She might have been trying to win the Coolest Mom of All Time award, but that didn't mean she wouldn't flip her wig if she came home to find her teenage daughter in bed with a boy.

I had to smile at the thought. Here I was, the goddess of strength, worried about what my mortal mother would do if she caught me in bed with my boyfriend. But I had a lot more experience being a teenager than I did being a goddess, and like every other teenager, I had a pretty good instinct for just how far I could push it.

I hopped in the shower, washed quickly, then pulled on a pair of shorts and a tank top—the AC was cranking inside the mansion, but it looked blisteringly hot outside. Then I headed downstairs. I'd been living there for two weeks, but really, I'd been at Rocky's every day and hung out with him until I went to bed. The only substantial amount of time I'd spent there had been the day before yesterday, and, well, I hadn't been paying too much attention to my surroundings, if you know what I mean. But now as I walked through the wide empty hallways, I was struck anew by the abandoned nature of the place. Not abandoned exactly, but invaded I guess. Even though virtually every trace of the Gardiners had been removed, the place still oozed their presence—in the ghostly outlines of paintings and pictures and rugs, in the paint colors and wallpapers, which reeked of the Georgian aesthetic that Trent's mom favored. Yet swirling around that was a second, more modern presence. The gadgety appliances in the kitchen. The sectional sofa in the drawing room, which had shown up last week and remained the only piece of furniture on the ground floor, aside from a couple of chrome barstools around the kitchen island. The shiny new Maserati. Slowly but surely, Fair Haven was being dragged into the twenty-first century.

And yet, underneath both of these feelings, deeper than them, older than them, was that strange swirling cool energy that emanated from the ballroom. It was almost imperceptible. If the phone rang or I was watching TV, I forgot all about it. But when I first woke up in the morning and my mind was clear, I felt it as clearly as a draft coming in through an open window.

I made my way to the ballroom now, thinking about what Mardi had told me yesterday: that she'd been having the same dream I'd been having. Did that make it more significant? More ominous? She seemed much less bothered by it than I was, but that's Mardi: always putting a brave face on everything. Part of me thought that we'd been sharing the dream just because we missed each other, and this was our minds' way of reaching out for each other. But a bigger part of me told me that was too simple. That we wouldn't be having such a detailed dream over and over again if it wasn't trying to communicate something specific. Something about Fair Haven, and about some kind of danger that it faced, or maybe that came from it. But what?

I found myself at the door of the ballroom. I'd never paid attention to the ornately inlaid panels before, but as I examined them, I realized they corresponded exactly to what I'd seen in my dream. I even recognized one little scratch that I hadn't paid any attention to in the dream—I mean, the door was so damaged that one scratch out of hundreds was hardly noticeable—yet now it popped right out at me, as if to tell me that the doors I'd seen in my dream had really been these doors, and not just something my imagination had made up. Eerie.

Unlike the dream doors, however, these were still mounted on perfectly oiled hinges, and they swung open at a touch. The current of energy grew instantly stronger, so much so that I wondered if perhaps the pattern on the doors wasn't some kind of hex holding it in check, or disguising it from immortal beings who could sense these things. Whatever it was, the sense of . . . something trying to push its way into this room—this world—was so distinct that my skin immediately goose-pimpled, a sensation I'd read about but never actually felt before, since I'm immune to temperatures that fall within the normal range of weather. I rubbed my hands over my arms to warm them, wondering if maybe the Gardiners had been using their magic to keep this energy in check, or if it was just more noticeable with nothing else in the room. The only things left in the tennis court–sized room were its three chandeliers: two good-sized ones at either end, and one massive one in the center.

"I'm gonna swing from the chandelier," I sang. "From the cha-hand-e-lier."

"I don't know if that's such a good idea. That ceiling's older than this country. Who knows how much weight it can support."

I whirled around. Mum was standing in the doorway, dressed in light gray wrap skirt and a skintight midriff-baring top that showed off her toned abs.

"Mum!" I yelled, and ran into her arms.

I hit her so hard that anyone else would have been knocked over, but Janet Steele just threw her arms around me, picked me up, and whirled me around as if I were a five-year-old.

"Welcome back! Congratulations! I'm so glad you're home. And oh, my gods, you won Wimbledon. That match was awesome! I missed you so much!"

"Slow down, slow down," she said. "One thing at a time. First of all, let me get a good look at you." She took a step back and ran her eyes over me, then smiled proudly. "I have to hand it to myself, I gave you some good genes." She pursed her lips. "But there's something different about you."

My mind immediately flashed on my conversation with Freya at the North Inn a few days ago. How she'd been able to tell that Rocky and I were virgins just by looking at us. Could Mum do the same thing?

"Midgard to Mooi," I heard Mum's voice. "Come in, Mooi."

"Sorry, I spaced out there. What did you say?"

"I said it looks like you found the clothes I had Ivan pick out for you. Even so, there's something I've always wanted to do with my daughter."

My heart was still beating over my fears that Mum had figured out I'd had sex, and it was all I could do stammer out, "Wh-what's that?"

Mum flashed her best smile.

"Take her shopping."

I knew I shouldn't let it be so easy to buy my affections, but I couldn't help it. And hey, it's not going to be *that* easy. I have expensive taste.

"If this is your way of making up for lost time," I

said, "you're doing a fantastic job." I gave the chandelier a parting glance, then headed for the door. "Let's go buy my love."

There are a couple of nice shops in North Hampton, but Mum decided to drive us to East Hampton, where there's a Blue & Cream and BCBG and Theory and even Lilly Pulitzer. (Yes, I admit it. I like Lilly Pulitzer. Every girl should have at least one pair of short shorts that looks like it was made from the curtains in *The Sound of Music*.) We grabbed coffee and croissants at a café before we started, and by the time we finished, it was nearly three, and we went to the Clam Bar near Montauk, which is simply *the* 3:00 P.M. place on the East End. Fancy European cars (almost every one of them a convertible) lined the highway for a quarter mile in either direction because, in the classic Hamptons WASPy manner, everything has to be a little bit inconvenient or else it's déclassé or—gasp!—nouveau riche. But luck was with us as we pulled up: a Porsche was backing out of a space right in front of the restaurant.

We hopped out of the car, and even though there was a line of about fifty people, the maître d' took one look at Mum, then called over a couple of busboys.

"Pull out a table for Ms. Steele. Dune view, but make sure she can still see everyone."

I'd gone there a couple of times with Rocky, and I was a little afraid the maître d' was going to say something, but all her attention was focused on Mum—I could've been Mum's assistant for all she noticed me.

Less than a minute later, we were ensconced at a table on the far edge of the terrace, shielded from the sound and smell of the highway but still offering a view of the entire dining area. Mum had said hi to no fewer than six people as the maître d' led us to our table, but when one woman in an East Hampton Tennis Club polo asked for a picture, she just smiled and said, "I've got a starving daughter here. Look for me when I head out."

The woman looked at me with pure envy. "Your mother," she said rapturously, "is a *goddess*."

Janet laughed loudly. "I'm just a tennis player," she said. "It's Molly who's the goddess."

The maître d' asked if she could start us with anything, and Mum looked at me.

"Champagne seemed to go over well the last time I saw you," she said, "but I'm thinking today is more of a mojito kind of day. What do you say, Mooi?"

I blinked a little in surprise. Mum's joke about me being a goddess was one thing, but using my real name? She liked to push the envelope.

"Mojitos sound great."

"Two mojitos, please. Don Q Cristal if you've got it."

"Coming right up."

The maître d' walked away, and Mum turned to me. "What?"

"It's nothing," I said. "It's just that I don't quite believe I'm here. Like I'm going to wake up from this amazing dream where Janet Steele was my mother and she took me shopping and bought me mojitos with premium rum and told autograph hounds to wait until she'd fed her daughter. You're just, well, *fabulous*, aren't you?"

Mum smiled brightly. "I do my best with what nature gave me. And this is no dream. We're really here, and later you're going to use that divine metabolism of yours to sober up and drive your mother home while she sleeps it off in the passenger seat."

I had to shake my head in wonder. It was impossible to believe my mum was this cool, but she really was.

Our drinks came then, and Mum took a sip of the cool minty sweetness before speaking. "I couldn't help noticing that you put nearly five hundred miles on the odometer in the last two weeks. So tell me: what's his name?"

"Wh-what?" I stammered, caught off guard.

"You said yourself that you prefer to be driven than to drive. So I'm assuming you didn't put all those miles on the car yourself, and if you did, it wasn't for your own benefit. Plus I've seen you check your phone about twenty times."

In fact, I'd driven all over the East End with Rocky, showing him the sights, but I had no idea the miles had added up so much—or that I should have worried about them. And I had checked my phone several times that day, but Rocky hadn't texted or called even once. Nor had Mardi, for that matter.

"I, um," I started, then gave up any pretense of lying.

"His name's Rocky—Rocco. His dad owns the North Inn, where Freya works."

Mum frowned. "Rocco. That doesn't sound very Norse."

I knew what she meant by *Norse*.

"He's not a god, if that's what you're asking."

"Mooi!" Mum said, her voice soft but sharp. "A mortal!"

She said it the way some people use racial epithets, which was weird, to say the least, since she didn't know anything about Rocky, not to mention the fact that she was a mortal herself.

"I guess it runs in the family," I said, trying to joke it off.

Mum blinked her eyes in confusion. "What do you mean?"

"You and Dad?" I said. Who else could I have meant?

Mum frowned at the thought of Dad. "What your father and I had was very different," she said. "My family's connection to Aesir goes back generations. But you are a new goddess. You need to set your sights higher."

I really didn't want to get into the whole new gods thing.

"Whatever," I said. "He's just here for the summer. It's not a big deal."

Mum continued to frown for a moment longer, then suddenly smiled. "My first taste of a sulky teenager! How exciting!"

"I said it's nothing—"

"And I trust you," Mum said. "I'm sorry I overreacted. I've got seventeen years of parenting to catch up on. Truce?" she said, raising her glass.

I clinked mine against hers. "Truce," I said, and we drank on it. "So, uh, speaking of Dad," I began.

"Why, what a seamless transition," Mum joked, and we both laughed.

"Sorry," I said. "I know it's totally nosy, but, well, I'm dying to know."

"To know what?" she said, her voice so level that I couldn't tell if she was being coy or serious.

"Everything!" I blurted out. "I mean, mostly about how you met Dad and all that. You didn't just . . . seduce him, did you? You loved him, right? At least a little?"

Mum softened, and had a faraway look in her eyes, and ever so slowly a little, whimsical smile appeared on her face. She reached out and took my hand in one of hers and gave it a squeeze.

"Yes, Mooi, I did love your father. Very much. And it might surprise you to know that *he* seduced *me*."

I laughed. "Don't forget, I've spent the past seventeen years with Troy Overbrook. I've seen all his moves. So what did he do? Send you a drink at a bar, or just saunter up and use that million-dollar smile of his?"

Mum shook her head. "He bought out an entire stadium."

"He *what*?"

"It was 1996. I'd made it to the quarterfinals of the

US Open that year, which had helped get my name out there, but I was still working my way up the rankings. I was playing in a little tournament in Adelaide, Australia, of all places, just to get some practice time before the Australian Open, and when I walked out on court for my first round match, there was no one there except for the umpire and linesmen and four or five people in the players' boxes—and your father. Of course I didn't know then that he was only twenty-two years into a new body. All I knew was that there was this insanely cute boy sitting all by himself in the middle of the stands, and he only clapped when I made a point. My poor opponent was so flustered she could hardly hit the ball, and, well, she was playing me too. I ended beating her 6–0, 6–1 in forty-two minutes. Your dad told me later he spent ninety-eight thousand dollars to buy up all the tickets, plus another twenty grand or so on a private jet from New York, which comes out to almost three thousand dollars a minute. That's a pretty expensive blind date."

"And? Did you go up to him? Did he come up to you?"

"Like I told you, Mooi: I never make the first move. Thor came up to me. He said he'd seen me play at the US Open the year before and he'd decided then and there that he had to meet me."

"But couldn't he have just found you in New York?"

"Oh, that would be too easy, wouldn't it? Especially for a god. He wanted to impress me. And he said he was a little intimidated."

"Dad? I can't believe it! No offense, but he's a straight-up manwhore."

Mum laughed out loud. "Believe me, I had plenty of opportunities to find out. But I wasn't another lingerie model or wannabe starlet. I was an athlete, somebody who had to work her ass off to get anything in life. And then I guess he sensed something about me. Something different. Unique. He wanted to do his research."

"What do you mean?"

"Your father thought I might have been a Rhinemaiden."

I gasped. Alberich had said our mother was a Rhinemaiden! Maybe she wasn't human after all. Maybe she would live forever, with me and Mardi.

"Are you?" I asked eagerly.

"I can tell by the look on your face that you wish the answer was yes, but unfortunately it's no. My ten-times-removed great-grandmother was."

"But weren't the Rhinemaidens goddesses? Or some kind of nature spirit that's basically the same thing as a goddess?"

Mum shook her head. "Legends portray them that way, but they were as mortal as me and the maître d' and everyone else on this terrace—except you. But the bridge was destroyed and Odin was trapped in Asgard; the link between the maidens and the Rhinegold began to weaken. Thor was afraid that they would no longer be able to protect the gold, and so he stole it from them. The maidens died defending it, but my ancestral grandmother, Flosshilde, survived."

"Dad killed the Rhinemaidens? I can't believe it."

"I'm sorry, Mooi, but it's true."

"So what happened then? And why'd Dad spare your grandmother?"

"Why else do men spare women? Because he loved her, of course. But Odin said he had to choose, the gold or the maiden. Thor agreed to let her go only if the gold could be secured with the most powerful spells to his prophesied children, Mooi and Magdi. Odin thought he had won, since the prophecies said that Magdi and Mooi's mother was going to be a Jotun, and since Midgard was cut off from Jotunheim as well as Asgard, he assumed Thor's children would never be born. But prophecies are written in symbolic language, and it seems they misinterpreted what the ancient oracles meant by 'giantess.' And here you are."

"But wait. Did Dad know all this when he saw you?"

Mum shook her head. "He only suspected it. Apparently, I bear more than a passing likeness to my ancestral grandmother."

"And what about you? Did you know it?"

Mum smiled and shook her head. "I suspected it, but I wasn't sure." Another smile, this one rueful and nostalgic and lovelorn all at the same time. "No, all he wanted to do was finally kiss his Rhinemaiden."

I reached for my drink, and was surprised to find

it was empty. I'd hardly noticed drinking it. "So what happened when you met? You won your match, he came up to you, and . . . *what?*"

Mum sipped at her own drink, her lips curled in a demure smile around her straw.

"He shook my hand, and he said, 'My name is Troy Overbrook. I enjoyed watching you play today, Ms. Stahl.'"

"Stahl?"

"German for 'steel.'"

"Oh! He was testing you! What did you say?"

"Your father wasn't finished yet. He said, 'If you win the tournament, would it be okay if I took you out to dinner to celebrate?'"

"Oh, my gods, Dad! Such a smoothie! What did you say?"

Mum smiled wickedly.

"I said, 'My name is Steele, Mr. Overbrook, and I'm going to win this tournament, so you'd better make a reservation now.'"

I clapped my hand over mouth. "And?" I said through my fingers.

"And your father said, 'I already did.'"

* 20 *

HANGING ON THE TELEPHONE

Mardi-Overbrook-Journal.docx

$\mathcal{I}$ thought Molly and I were back on track after we ran into each other in the Cheesemonger, but I guess not. I texted her the next morning when I woke up, and then again after I'd had a cup of coffee, and after I showered, I called her. The texts were unanswered, and the call went straight to voice mail, as if she'd shut her phone off. Which, if you know Molly—or, well, any teenage girl—you know it's something she'd *never* do.

Which meant my sister was ignoring me.

Part of me thought that maybe she was hanging with Rocky, but another part of me knew that Janet was getting back from England today, and that Molly was probably with her. This was all but confirmed when Rocky showed up at the Cheesemonger a half hour after I opened the shop. From the look on his face, he was as happy to be there as I was.

"Hey," I said jokingly. "What can I get you?"

Rocky shrugged unhappily. "An apron, I guess."

"What?" I pretended to be nonchalant, but inside I was thrilled. If I haven't made this clear, making sandwiches is *way* overrated. "You're here to work?"

"Sal's been wanting me to work here since I got to North Hampton, but I was hanging with Molly and I guess he let it go. But when she didn't come over this morning, he was all like, Why don't you head down to the Cheesemonger?"

"So where is Molly? I thought you two were joined at the hip by this point."

Another shrug, even more dejected. "Dunno. I texted her a couple of times this morning and tried calling her too, but it went straight to voice mail. I guess she's hanging with her mom or something?"

"Janet's back?" I said, as if I didn't know.

I could tell that Rocky had noticed I said *Janet* instead of *Mum*, just as he'd said *Sal* instead of *Dad*, but he didn't ask me about it.

"Molly thought she was getting back today, or maybe last night. She had some talk shows to do—*The View*, Seth Meyers, one of those ESPN roundtable things where people talk really fast at the top of their lungs— so she told Molly she wasn't a hundred percent sure when she'd manage to get out here. I guess she made it."

"Well, don't worry. I'm sure she'll call you in a bit. So," I continued, grabbing an apron from beneath the counter and tossing it to him, "you want to help me get Billy and Bruce's order ready?"

"I guess," Rocky said, draping the apron over his head. "If you tell me what that means."

I nodded. "If you head to the walk-in and bring out the parsley–pine nut pesto, arugula-walnut pesto, habanero–black bean tapenade, chipotle mayonnaise, red pepper hummus, gefilte fish, smoked brisket, and blood pudding, I'll get out the cured meats, cheeses, and pickled products, and we'll assembly line this production together in no time."

Rocky looked at me slack-jawed, as if waiting to see if I was joking.

"It's not as overwhelming as it sounds. Just bring out everything from the middle two shelves left of the door."

With two people working, we got the order together before their errand boy arrived.

After that, we got the sandwiches ready for the 11:30 train, then passed the rest of the day in near silence, both of us on our phones when we weren't helping customers or dealing with the occasional delivery. I resisted texting or calling Molly, but I couldn't stop myself from looking in on her various social media accounts. She wasn't posting anywhere, not even a single like on

Facebook or Instagram or one raving Tweet about the latest celebrity breakup or shoe trend. Was it possible she really had turned her phone off? Was Ragnarok upon us?

It was busy enough that we never really got bored, however, and soon enough it was five o'clock. There was one last mini-rush from the afternoon train, and then we closed.

"Don't worry" was the last thing I said to Rocky on his first day at the Cheesemonger. "I'm sure she'll call you later."

That night, after we closed up shop, I decided to head over to the North Inn. I'd heard through Ingrid that Molly and Rocky were spending a lot of time there, and so I'd avoided it out of respect. I'd figured if they hadn't invited me, they wanted some alone time, and the North Inn was the one surefire place where Molly and Rocky would get served. Who was I to stand in the way of young love? But now that I knew Molly had put Rocky (and me) on hold, I figured the Inn was fair game, and I hadn't seen Freya in a while. And I could have used a good stiff drink, preferably something magicked up enough so that even my divine body would feel it.

When I walked into the bar, Freya took one look at me, shook her head, and pointed to a barstool. I slumped into it gratefully as Freya began pulling out unlabeled bottles and lining them up on the bar.

"I'm a good aunt, aren't I?" she said as she began pouring transparent, brown, and red liquids together.

"What do you mean?" I said confusedly. "Of course you are."

"I serve you drinks even though you're underage. I give you the run of my closet, which contains the best items of clothing between here and Madison Avenue. Or, let's face it, between here and Rodeo Drive."

"You're awesome, Freya. Getting to know you has been one of the best things about this past year."

"And I'm pretty good with the advice, if I do say so myself. Not too many people know how to negotiate the fine line between being an immortal goddess and a teenager, but I don't think I've ever steered you in the wrong direction, have I?"

"Of course not. You're like a big sister–best friend–super-cool aunt all rolled into one."

Freya nodded as she poured her concoction into a cocktail shaker filled with ice, capped it, and shook it vigorously. She set the shaker aside, grabbed a chilled martini glass and a bottle of absinthe, poured a splash of the green, anise-smelling liquid into the glass and swirled it around, coating the inside of the glass, then poured the residue out and strained the liquid from the shaker into the glass. It had a beautiful golden-brown color, just touched by red, and smelled of licorice and cinnamon, and the tangy bite of some kind of sharp whiskey. My mouth immediately began to water.

I reached for the drink, but Freya pulled it away.

"Then why, dear Mardi," she said in a tone that was half hurt, half theatrical, "would you not tell me that you broke up with Trent Gardiner *two weeks ago?*"

It was still early, and there were only a half dozen people in the bar, all coupled off at individual tables, but still I winced at Freya's words. It made it seem so final.

I looked up at Freya, who was eyeing me with an expression that was half reproachful, half sorrowful.

"I'm always here for you and your sister, Mardi. Always." She pushed the drink toward me. "Now. Dish. What did that dirty SOB do?"

One hour and three drinks later, I raised my hand and waved it around.

"And why should I even care if he thinks I'm too young?" I said in a voice just this side of a shout. "No offense," I said to Freya. "You look great for your age."

"None taken," said Freya, who was busily pouring a round of shots for a group of investment bankers who were doing their best imitation of weekend rockers. She winked at the banker-rockers with a look that said, "Kids. They can't handle their alcohol."

"What's in these things anyway?" I said, holding up my empty glass. "I don't usually get drunk, but I am feeling *all right.*"

"A magician never tells," Freya said, pushing the drinks toward the banker-rockers and slipping the stack of twenties they gave her into the register. She turned toward me.

"So enough about him," she said. "Here's the real question: do you want him back?"

"Oh, gods," I said, pushing my glass toward her. "That requires another drink."

"Give me your car keys, and I'll think about it."

I pulled my car keys from my pocket and handed them over. It was worth it.

"So?" Freya said as she began lining up her bottled potions and tonics. "Forget about Tyr for a moment. What is it that Mardi wants?"

Freya's use of Trent's Norse name made me think about what he had said that terrible day on the beach—how as the memories of his millennia-long past came back to him, he felt further and further away from me. And though I'd never thought about it much, I'd always felt it. Despite the fact that Trent looked and dressed and generally acted like a hot eighteen-year-old, there was always something older lurking inside of that. A kind of amused distance in his eyes when he watched me and Molly shopping or bickering or doing the "Single Ladies" dance. And now that I thought about it, I realized that detachment had always kept me from committing to him 100 percent. I gave him 90 percent maybe, 95 percent even, but there was always a part of myself I held back. A part of me knew Trent would always be different from me, and maybe that difference would never be bridged.

From out of nowhere, a thought popped into my head: *He's Aesir. You're Mimir. You don't belong together.* I could even hear it in Janet Steele's Australian accent.

I shook my head to make the words go away. Just because I didn't know what I wanted, like every other teenage girl in her first relationship, didn't mean I was ready to sign on to some cosmic war between the generations of gods. It sucked to be dumped, but I didn't actually want to kill Trent. But all I said to Freya's question was:

"Have you met Sal's son? Rocky?"

Freya smiled, but it quickly turned into a frown when she saw the look on my face.

"You mean the cute boy who's been following Molly around like a puppy dog for the past two weeks? The one Molly seems to be equally smitten by?"

"If she's so smitten with him, why didn't she return any of his texts or calls today?"

Freya pushed a fresh drink toward me. "Because she's a woman, and it's her prerogative. And how do you know this?"

"Because Sal made him work at the Cheesemonger with me today?"

"Back up. You're working at the Cheesemonger? That's why you smell ever so faintly of speck and Gruyère?"

The last sandwich I'd made that night had been the Italo Calvino: speck (an Italian ham that's somewhere between pancetta and prosciutto), Gruyère, rosemary-infused olive oil, twenty-five-year-old balsamic vinegar, served open-faced atop a chewy piece of focaccia.

"Wow. That's some nose you've got on you."

"Never mind my nose. You're not really thinking about making a play for your sister's boyfriend, are you? Are you that mad at her?"

"I would never make a play for Rocky if Molly was with him. But let's face it: this was her pattern before Alberich messed with her head last summer. She crushes on a boy, attaches herself to him at the hip for two weeks, then abruptly severs the connection and runs for the hills. I would never go against girl code or twin code, but still . . . "

"Huh," Freya said, in this way that was supposed to be blasé but was clearly just a stalling tactic. She whipped up a couple of drinks, then made her way back to me.

"How many men do you think I've been with?" she said in a casual voice.

"What?" I said, taken aback. "How should I—"

"A *lot*," Freya said sharply. "You live three thousand years in a body like this, you see plenty of action, especially when you're the goddess of love. And how many of those men do you think I met because Ingrid had dated them first?"

"Um, I don't know—"

"None! Zero, zilch, *null*. You don't go for your sister's castoffs, Mardi. It just never, ever, ever turns out well!"

"How do you know if you've never tried it?" I asked, annoyed at Freya for reading my mind.

"Seriously?" Freya said. "Our kind have started wars over this kind of thing. Promise me that you won't go after this poor boy."

"Fine," I said. "I won't go after him." *But what if he comes after me?*

"Don't think I don't know what you're thinking," Freya said. "I invented the it's-not-my-fault-if-he-makes-the-first-move excuse. Literally."

"Look, I promised not to go after him. But I can't promise to be a saint."

"Well, don't call me when this explodes in your face. And by explodes, I mean literally explodes. I don't care if Molly's dumped him or not. She is not going to look kindly on you taking sloppy seconds on her ex."

The way she said *sloppy seconds* made me look at Freya sharply. Of course she was right. I was being crazy even entertaining this. I had to stop thinking of Rocky. He was totally off-limits. To change the subject, I said, "Have you ever heard about the Mimir?"

Freya pursed her lips. "That's not what you were going to ask me about."

"What makes you say that?" I said as innocently as I could.

"Because whatever you were thinking about had something to do with love." She jerked a thumb into her chest. "Goddess of love, remember?"

"I'll say!" one of the investment bankers called out from down the bar.

"Easy, slugger," Freya called, but it seemed to break

her line of thought. "What did you ask me about? The Mimir."

I nodded.

"Definitely rings a bell," Freya said, "but I can't put my finger on it."

"It refers to the gods of Midgard. As distinct from the Aesir and Vanir."

Freya laughed. "Hate to break it to you, but the Aesir and Vanir *are* the only gods."

"Well, yeah," I said. "Right now they are. But according to Janet, prophecies have been predicting the Mimir since the beginning of time. Supposedly they're the offspring of the Aesir and humans, and they'll overthrow the Aesir and the Vanir in the same way the Aesir overthrew the giants and took control of Asgard."

For a moment, Freya continued mixing up a couple of East End Manhattans, but then she suddenly put her shaker down and turned to me.

"Hold on a sec," she said. "Janet thinks that you and Molly are these Mimir peeps?"

I nodded my head. It sounded kind of silly when I heard it aloud.

Freya quickly grabbed her shaker, poured the two Manhattans, and shooed her customers away.

"On me," she said when they tried to pay. "Okay, first of all," she continued to me, "it's not like the Jotun and the Aesir were all buddy-buddy and then the Aesir just got it in their heads to take down their friends. The Jotun were a violent, oppressive bunch, subjugating any kingdom or country they could find, killing people pretty much at random, and enslaving the rest. Including the Aesir. What Odin and the others did was no different from what the European settlers did to the Native Americans."

Freya's tone had been forceful enough that a few people had turned to look at her, but she glared at them so hard that they all quickly glanced away. One clueless fellow approached the bar with an empty glass in hand, but Freya snapped, "Can't you see I'm busy?" and he went scurrying back to his table.

"Secondly," Freya continued, turning back to me, "these Mimir that Janet told you about. I'm starting to remember the stories. But they're not the children of Aesir and humans, like you and Molly. They're the children of Aesir and Jotun. And given how much the Aesir and the Jotun hate each other, the chances of two of them hooking up are looking a lot worse than the chances of you and Tyr getting back together."

"Ouch!" I said. "It's not like I *believe* anything she told us," I continued defensively. "It's just why I haven't been all up her skirt the way Molly has. I don't think she should be telling those kinds of stories any more than you do—and especially if they're not true."

"Sorry," Freya said. "But that kind of nonsense makes me angry. I've got half a mind to head out to Fair Haven tomorrow and give Janet a piece of my mind. That said, I think you shouldn't avoid her."

"Really?"

"She's your mom. Sounds like she's got a chip on her shoulder, which, given the way our kind treated her ancestors, seems understandable. But the only thing that's going to get rid of it is if someone starts telling her the truth."

"That makes sense, I guess. Though I'm not exactly known for my tact."

"News flash, Mardi: none of the Overbrooks are. Nor are the Beauchamps, for that matter. Even Ingrid's got a temper. But like I said. She's your mom. You deserve to have a relationship with her. If it's a bit strained some-times, well, welcome to the rest of the world. Moms are complicated." She glanced up at the sky. "Sorry, Jo-anna," she mouthed with a grin.

I took a moment to finish my drink. "Okay, then," I said as I put it down. "Maybe I'll give her a second chance." I slid my empty glass toward Freya and stood up. "You want to call me a cab?"

"Nah," Freya said, tossing me back my keys. "You're not drunk anymore."

"What?" I said, then realized that I did in fact feel totally sober. "How did you . . . ?" I glanced at my empty glass, which Freya was whisking away.

"Helps when the bartender's a witch." She winked, then hurried down the bar to a fresh round of customers.

* 21 *

TONIGHT'S THE NIGHT

From the Diary of Molly Overbrook

$\mathcal{I}$t was over a week before I spoke to Mardi again. I have to admit, I was surprised when she didn't respond to my texts or answer any of my calls. As the goddess of rage, Mardi is, not surprisingly, hot-tempered, but she's not petty or vindictive.

I was more surprised, though, that Rocky didn't reach out to me either or respond to my texts. He'd seemed totally cool about what happened on Saturday. So why freak out now? Part of me thought that maybe it was because I didn't call him on the Monday when Mum came home until late that night, when I went up to bed. But we'd been running around constantly and there hadn't been a chance. For some reason, I knew Mum wouldn't like it if I was on my phone while I was with her, and I was also learning about her life, and her time with Dad, and that was so fascinating that I barely gave my phone a thought the whole day.

And Janet Steele, I was learning, was a busy woman. By the time I rolled out of bed in the morning, she'd already been up for hours. She would have gone for a five-mile run on the beach or a two-mile swim in the ocean, or worked out in the state-of-the-art gym she'd set up in the basement. She also spent at least an hour on social media, making a point to respond personally to fifteen or twenty of her Twitter followers as well as posting a few pics on Instagram and her official Facebook page. A lot of the recent pictures featured me, which on the one hand was kind of amazing because there I was: Molly Overbrook, eating barbecued shrimp with Janet Steele (with a tamarind-sesame glaze courtesy of Ivan); Molly Overbrook, trying on bikinis with Janet Steele (a Lolli one-piece with cutouts in all the right places for her, a Stone Fox cheeky bikini with a string bow over the bottom for me); Molly Overbrook, picking out bedroom furniture with Janet Steele (an Art Deco white lacquered suite whose six-foot-tall wedding cake headboard looked like something right out of a Golden Age of Hollywood black-and-white movie, probably because it had been used in Jean Harlow's bedroom in *Dinner at Eight*).

But on the other hand, well, it was only me, and aside from selfies I snapped in the bathroom to get my makeup approved by my friends at school, I'd never really been photographed alone.

Sure, we had our ups and downs, but it was always me and Mardi because, you know, we were twins. A package deal. We were always photographed together, one punky, the other a little more princess. It was just how it had always been, and looking at pictures of myself without Mardi made me feel lonely. But when I shot her a cute little text, nothing came back. It was like my messages were going out into a black hole.

After her morning workout and fan stuff, Mum practiced tennis. Fair Haven was from "that generation of mansions," as Mum put it, that had a clay tennis court, which is a perfectly fine kind of tennis court, but it's more European than American, and besides, the clay court season was over, and it was time for hard courts, so Mum drove to the North Hampton Tennis Club to practice there. I didn't even know there was a North Hampton Tennis Club, although it made sense—there was a North Hampton Yacht Club, a North Hampton Polo Club, and a North Hampton *Water* Polo Club, so of course there would be a tennis club too. It wasn't big, only twelve courts, but even so, Mum didn't want anyone watching her practice, so she made arrangements for the club to close each day between 10:00 and 1:00 so she could practice in private, which is to say, she basically rented all twelve courts at a premium fee, because the just-before lunch slot was by far the most popular time for the North Hampton set to get their game in, since their hour on court was really just an excuse for them to spend another hour in the day spa getting a massage and pedicure and facial, followed by another two hours dining on a liquid lunch. I assumed it must be costing Mum a fortune to get the club to turn away so much business, but it turned out Mum's apparel sponsor was this cool Australian sportswear brand called Lorna Jane, which was trying to break into the American market. LJ of course had a Janet Steele line of tennis clothes, and in exchange for allowing a photographer to snap pics of Mum working out in her own line, the company picked up the bill for her practices. This is why the rich get richer: because half the time, they don't actually pay for anything.

So anyway, 10:00–1:00 tennis practice, and of course I went with Mum the first couple of times because, one, I loved tennis, and she was Janet Steele, and of course I was going to watch her at a private practice, and two, she was my mum, and I wanted to spend every minute with her to make up for lost time.

What I didn't realize I'd be doing, though, was not just watching, but *playing* tennis with her.

"Uh-uh," she said the first day we went to the club. "No daughter of Janet Steele's is going to sit on the sidelines while Mum's on the court."

I think I mentioned that I'd played tennis a little. I mean, you're a girl growing up on the Upper East Side, you're going to take tennis lessons, along with ballet, piano, conversational French, dressage, and cotillion. (Seriously. People still do that.) So yeah, I could swing a racket. But with Janet Steele?

"Uh, that's okay, Mum. I'm happy to just watch and tweet a few pictures for you."

Mum didn't say anything. All she did was toss me a racket. Since her Wilson Pro Staff rackets cost $2,000 each (they stopped making them in the 1980s, but Mum swears by them), I figured I'd better catch it before it clattered to the ground, and more on reflex than anything, my right hand shot out and snatched it from the air. My palm stung from the impact. Turned out Mum threw a racket just like she hit a tennis ball: hard.

"Nice reflexes," she said. "Let's see how you serve."

I tossed the ball up in the air a couple of times to see how the breeze affected it. Then I held the ball up.

"Ready?"

I tossed the ball in the air. I smashed the racket into it. It shot away from me, skimming a half inch over the top of the net and slicing deep into the service box. Mum actually had to jump the get the ball, and for one brief moment, I thought she might actually miss. Then the ball was whizzing back at me faster than I would have believed possible. I was still unwinding from my serve as the ball bounced off the baseline and smashed into the fence behind me.

I turned and saw that Mum had hit it so hard that the ball stuck in the chain link. When I turned back to Mum, a broad smile was plastered on her face.

"Mooi," she said proudly, "that was one hell of a serve." Her face set in a determined line. "Again."

. . .

And that's how the next ten days passed. Mum dragged me to the club every morning (although dragged makes it sound like she forced me when I wanted to go), and we played for two, three, sometimes four hours a day, then lunched on tuna niçoise salads or ostrich burgers. When word got out that Janet Steele was playing tennis with her daughter every morning at the North Hampton Tennis Club, people began to show up to watch. Since Mum had rented the place out, the club left it up to her to let the spectators in or not. At first, she said no, thinking the crowd would make me self-conscious, but when I told her I didn't mind, she gave the okay. By the end of the week, it was all over the Twitterverse and the blogosphere and the gossip mill, there were more than a hundred people in the tiny bleachers each morning. And the crazy thing was, most of them were there for me. I mean, don't get me wrong, they never would have come if Janet Steele hadn't been on the court. But everyone knew who Janet was, and how she played. I was the unknown commodity, and they all wanted to see what I could do. And it turned out what I could do is play tennis.

Even today I couldn't tell you if magic was involved. I mean, I know objectively that it had to be. I only ever played tennis in seventh and eighth grade, and here I was holding my own with the number one tennis player in the world. That couldn't just be good genes, right?

But I certainly never thought about magic when I was on the court. There were a dozen pretty simple spells I could have cast that would have improved my performance and made Mum's worse—hexes I could have cast on my racket or the balls or, say, Mum's shoes (I will admit that the idea of making each of her shoes weigh ten pounds appealed to the practical joker in me), but once I stepped on the court, all those fantasies disappeared and all I wanted was to hit a tennis ball with my mum. Never mind that she was Janet Steele. Never mind that I was the goddess of strength. I was a teenage girl with a mother, and we had this interest in common. I wanted to milk it as much as possible, as long as possible.

But each night as I made my way through my social media feeds, checking out what people had to say about me, I knew that wasn't all that was going on. I scanned through the thousands of comments, always looking for one name that never showed up. Mardi's. I knew she had to be seeing the pictures—despite the obscurity spells Joanna had cast around North Hampton, they were still showing up everywhere, from TMZ to Dlisted to Radar. I thought that if she could see how much fun Mum was, how normal she was, she would realize that we weren't sitting around scheming about killing Dad or casting Ingrid and Freya into some dark corner of Hel. But if Mardi was indeed seeing all the pictures and stories about me and Mum, she gave no indication.

And of course there was Rocky too. The couple of

weeks I'd spent with him had been like a dream, and after a day of missing him, and another day of being pissed at him, and then a third day of being pissed at myself for missing him, he started to fade away from my mind. *Screw him,* I told myself (no pun intended). *If he can't take a modern woman, it's his loss.* Of course a part of me knew I was just covering up my real feelings with anger, it was easier to be mad than to be hurt. Between Rocky this summer and Alberich last summer, I was starting to think that boys weren't worth the trouble.

Almost two weeks had gone by and I felt like a junkie desperate for a fix. I needed to see my sister—to talk to her, punch her, fight with her, make up with her, gossip with her, steal clothes from her, get makeup tips from her. (Okay, not that last thing. If I want raccoon eyes, I'll walk into a door or something. But everything else.) And so anyway, Mum must've read my mind, because on Friday afternoon, as we were munching on Caprese salads made from heirloom tomatoes, buffalo mozzarella, and olive oil infused with Thai basil, she said:

"So you know tomorrow I have to fly down to the Bahamas for the Nassau Open. It's one of the mandatory tournaments on the pro tour, and as much as I'd like to skip it and hang out here with my daughter, I'm the defending champion, and my ranking will take a big hit if I don't play."

Of course I knew the tournament was coming up and that Mum was the defending champion. I'd watched on TV last year as she beat Aga Radwanska for the title. But I wasn't expecting what came out of her mouth next.

"I'm hoping you'll come and sit in my player's box. And I'm hoping you can talk Magdi into coming too."

My heart flipped in my chest when she said that she was hoping I'd come, and then it did a backflip with a triple twist and, I don't know, a half gainer, when she said she was hoping Mardi would come too.

"Oh, it's perfect!" I said. "There's no way she could say no to an invitation like that!" Which didn't really make sense, since Mardi cared about tennis about as much as she cared about, oh, Ariana Grande, which is to say: not at all.

"My fingers are crossed," Mum said. "But even so, I think it'd be better if you asked her. Phrase it as a sister-sister thing, not a mother-daughter thing."

There was something about the way Mum said this. It seemed a little dishonest. A little sneaky. But I also suspected she was right.

"I'll do it!"

"Marvy," Mum said. She reached into her bag and tossed me the car keys. "Take the Maserati. I'll have Ivan pick me up in the Maybach."

After almost two weeks of being driven around, it was fun to be back behind the wheel, especially of a

Maserati. That seat—I mean I know it was the same shape as the one on the passenger side, but somehow, with one hand curled around the gear stick and the other dangling off the leather-clad steering wheel, the fit just seemed so much tighter.

This feeling of rightness was amplified by, like, a hundred when I pressed the ignition and the car roared into life. The sound was so full of adrenaline that I didn't even think about turning the stereo on. The engine was its own music, and I thrilled along to it for the twenty minutes it took me to drive from the tennis club to the Cheesemonger. I had a brief flash of Marshall/Alberich, but pushed it out of my mind and marched up to the door of the shop.

I stopped just before I pushed it open, however, because when I looked through the glass and past the ten-dollar stone-ground ancient-grain flatbreads and fifteen-dollar mochi cookies, I saw that Mardi wasn't working alone.

She was with Rocky McLaughlin.

There they were, in matching seersucker aprons with the Cheesemonger logo embroidered on the chest (say what you want about Alberich, he had surprisingly good taste in food and clothes for a dark elf), hanging out behind the counter. Rocky was making a sandwich for a short, portly man while Mardi sat on the counter sipping some kind of boutique soda in a bottle shaped like a brandy snifter, and both were laughing at something with a kind of private look on their faces—as though they'd developed a special code so they could crack each other up without upsetting their customers. That look told me that this arrangement wasn't a new thing. That they'd been working together for a while.

Then it happened.

Rocky turned around to get something. He leaned over Mardi, deliberately getting in her space, and she was smiling up at him. Nothing was happening, it looked innocent, but something about it seemed a little too intimate, a little too close for my comfort.

I shoved the door open hard enough that all three of the store's occupants jumped, but my voice was all sweetness and light.

"Hey! So this is where you've been keeping each other!"

Mardi's eyes shifted nervously between me and Rocky.

"Hey, Molly," she said uncertainly. "Yeah, I'm working here, just like I said I was."

"And you too!" I said, turning toward Rocky with what I could tell was an insane smile on my face. "Who would've guessed you'd end up here too, working with my sister!"

Rocky's expression was a little confused, a lot more guilty. "Uh, yeah. I mean, Sal owns the shop and everything, and he'd been wanting me to work here. Keeps me off the streets and all that," he said to the customer as he handed him his sandwich. "Will there be anything else?"

The man shook his head, and Rocky rang him

up while Mardi and I glared at each other without speaking.

"How lucky for you!" I said too loudly as soon as the man had walked out the door. "How lucky for both of you!"

"Molly, please," Mardi said. "It's not what you think."

The truth is, I don't know what I'd been thinking. Only that it was really strange my sister and my boy-friend had both dropped off the face of the planet (or at least my planet). But here they were together, smiling and laughing; I felt sick.

I took a deep breath, concentrating on controlling my emotions. I wasn't going to give Mardi the satisfac-tion of knowing I was jealous, plus it wouldn't do to put on another display of errant magic in front of Rocky or I might have to kill him.

"So," I said when I was sure I could speak without screaming. "Mum's having a party this evening, and she needs some finger food. I was just going to go to Dispirito's, but of course I should totally be loyal to Sal, shouldn't I?

"I was thinking the Orson Welles," I said to Rocky, ignoring Mardi. The Orson Welles was a sandwich Marshall (when I still thought he was Marshall) and I had come up with one day last summer to pass the time. We tried to think of the grossest, most-impossible-to-eat sandwich possible—pesto, anchovies, and gor-gonzola served between two slices of inch-thick pumpernickel slathered in pickled bitter melon–aji mayonnaise—which, for reasons that are more mysterious than the origin of magic, turned out to be a hit. What can I say? WASPs will eat, wear, or drive anything, as long as it's expensive enough.

The Orson Welles was also a particularly difficult sandwich to make, what with the number of ingredients and the generally disgusting odor most of them gave off, and Rocky made a bit of a face as he contemplated making them.

"Uh, sure," he said. "How many did you—"

"I think fifty would do it." I cut him off.

"Wow, fifty. Not sure we have enough, uh, bitter melon–aji mayo on hand."

"It's okay," I said. "I don't need them right now. You can make up a new batch of mayo and deliver the sandwiches to Fair Haven tomorrow. You know where Fair Haven is, right? It's where Mardi's boyfriend Trent used to live," I said pointedly. "Where you and I watched the Wimbledon final together? And then hung out together after."

Rocky's eyes dropped. "I don't know why you're mad at *me*," he said under his breath. Then, shaking it off, he said, "I'm going down in the basement to see if we have any more pickled bitter melon."

"There's a whole barrel of it in the back corner," I said, waving my hand. "It's the one with the Chinese writing on it."

I waited until Rocky had disappeared to confront my sister.

"What is going on between you two?" I demanded.

"Molly, nothing is going on. I swear. Come on."

We stared at each other. I believed her. She would never do this to me. "Fine, Mum has a message for you," I said.

"What message?" Mardi asked. She tried to sound nonchalant, but I could tell she was interested.

"Mum's playing in the Nassau Open starting tomorrow. She thought we could fly down with her and watch her play and do some of the touristy stuff afterward."

"Nassau?" Mardi said. "Like Nassau County, Long Island?"

"No, you ignoramus. Like Nassau, the capital of the *Bahamas*."

"Oh!" Mardi's eyes lit up. "When are you leaving?"

"Tomorrow."

"What time?"

"Whenever. Mum chartered a plane."

Mardi's eyes went wider. "For real?"

I shrugged. "Janet Steele has some baller moves."

I could see Mardi fantasizing about the trip. On the plus side: champagne in the plane, chilling on the beach where the weather and the water would both be a good twenty degrees warmer than the still-tepid East End. On the minus side: hanging out with the sister whose boyfriend she'd apparently stolen.

"I dunno," she said finally. "I kind of committed to helping Sal out."

"Whatever," I said in the most blasé tone I could

muster. "The limo heads to the airport at ten tomorrow. Be at Fair Haven if you want to go," I added as I walked out the door.

I heard Mardi sigh, and then the door swung closed between us.

✳ 22 ✳

LEAVING ON A JET PLANE

Mardi-Overbrook-Journal.docx

𝓘van answered the door the next morning before I'd even rung the doorbell.

"Good morning, Magdi," he said, bowing deeply. "If you want to wait in the breakfast room, Ms. Steele and Mooi will be with you shortly."

"It's Mardi," I said, rolling my eyes. "Mar-dy."

"As you wish, my lady," Ivan said, and scurried away. It was only after he'd left that I realized he'd never said where the "breakfast room" was. The Gardiners were fancy people, but not quite so fancy that they'd ever set aside one of the twenty-five or thirty rooms in Fair Haven specifically for breakfast. If they took breakfast as a family, they ate in the dining room. Otherwise they scarfed down a bowl of cereal or some eggs in the kitchen, like normal people. I peeked into the dining room first, but not only was there nobody in there, there wasn't any furniture either: just faded spots on the parquet and on the wallpaper where rugs and pictures used to be. Dust bunnies swirled in the corners, suggesting that Janet had no use for this room at all.

I made my way to the kitchen then, but it was empty too, though filled with an intoxicating smell of fresh-baked pastries and coffee. Ingrid had of course made me breakfast before I left—you have to understand that that kind of thing is, like, part of her DNA—but whatever Ivan (or whoever cooked in Fair Haven) had made smelled so delicious that I was ready for round two.

I raised my head and sniffed, as if I could track breakfast like a dog on the trail of a rabbit, but whatever other abilities I have, the power of supersmell is not one of them. I had no idea where breakfast had gone, so I just pushed through the door closest to me.

I was pretty sure the hallway beyond the door was the one that led to the servants' quarters: in place of the elaborate parquet of the main hallways, there was simple wood, and the walls were plain white instead of covered in hand-blocked wallpaper, and the trim was unadorned instead of elaborately carved. But what made me pause was the dirt. I don't mean dust like I'd seen in the corners of the dining room. I mean mud, trampled into the floor and pushing up against the walls, where it had dried and crumpled and been trampled down again until the floor looked more like a tunnel than a hallway in a three-hundred-year-old mansion, with only a few glimpses of the floorboards visible where the inch-thick coating of dirt had accumulated. The walls were filthy too, with trails of dirt and food and other stuff I couldn't identify lining them in long streaks, as if someone had dipped their hands into muddy puddles or jars of peanut butter or molasses and deliberately dragged them along the walls. And when I stood next to the streaks, I couldn't help but notice that nearly all of them were either about five feet above the floor—which is to say, Ivan's shoulder height—or about six feet, which is to say, Janet's shoulder height. I mean, I knew she hated the Gardiners, but did she hate them so much that she had to defile the house she'd stolen from them?

And I knew I should probably turn around and go back into the, you know, not-crazy part of the house, but I couldn't help myself. This hallway was obviously in heavy use, and I wanted to see where it led. And so, doing my best to put my new Miu Miu studded patent-leather sneaks into the least dirty parts of the floor, I began to make my way down its length. It got darker the farther I went. There were only a few windows, but they'd been plastered with mud and let in almost no light. But I was still able to see that there were bits of green and brown things scattered about as I went, leaves and sticks they looked like, piling up more and more toward the end of the hall, which made it look even more like a tunnel or a path in a forest. There were also a few feathers and things that looked a bit like fur and bones, all of which made it feel like I was walking into an animal's lair, just like in my dream.

I came to the end of the hall and turned. There was only a little passageway left. It was darker than the long corridor I'd just walked through, not to mention about ten times dirtier, and there was a bit of a smell too, something not-so-fresh, maybe a little fishy. Here and there among the leaves and sticks, I thought I saw the glint of a bone.

From what I could see, the floor was wetter too, and I hesitated. Before I could decide whether or not to continue, a door burst open at the other end of the hall and Janet Steele appeared.

"Magdi!" she almost shouted, her face startled, guarded.

I caught a glimpse of the room behind her. It was dark but seemed quite large, and even filthier than the hallway. Then she hurriedly pulled it closed and locked it.

"Can you believe this mess?" she said as she turned toward me and began picking her way down the muddy hall in a pair of high-waisted flowy gold pants tucked into stiletto calf boots in black snakeskin.

"Are those Haider Ackermann?" I said. "They're so chic I want to die!"

"I know," Janet said. "And I have to walk through this mess in them. Can you believe it?" she said. "A staff of eight, a gazillion dollars in the bank, and yet they let this happen."

"What did happen?" I said as Janet put her arm

on my shoulder and steered us back toward the main house.

"Ivan said a family of weasels was camped out here. Living, breeding, eating, and—" She sniffed, made a face. "Everything else too, from the smell of it."

"But I thought you said the servants live here?" I said as we walked toward the kitchen.

"Did I?" Janet said, but didn't explain further.

We were walking past some of the streaks of finger- and handprints on the wall.

"Weasels?" I said. "Really?"

"That's what Ivan said. He cleared them out before I got here." She glanced at the stains on the wall and shook her head. "You know Fair Haven sits on a seam between Midgard and Hel?"

"I heard something about that," I said vaguely.

"Tyr sealed it all up hundreds of years ago, of course, but still, a little energy can't help but leak through. It attracts all kinds of weirdness," she said, waving a hand at the dirty floor and walls. "This is the newest part of the house, but I'm guessing we must be pretty close to the seam."

I knew that in fact the seam was located in the ball-room, which, if I had my bearings (and I wasn't sure I did), wasn't far from here. But I didn't point that out to Janet. If she was serious about this war-between-the-gods thing, I wasn't going to give her any ammunition.

"I'm tempted to have Ivan bulldoze it." Janet was still speaking. "Build something nice and modern. Glass and steel. Impregnable," she added as she pushed the door to the kitchen open. "But I don't know. These old places have their charms—literally, in the case of Fair Haven."

"Ha!" I laughed as we stepped into the kitchen.

"Mardi! There you are!" Molly's voice rang out. "Ivan told me you were here, but I was beginning to think he was having a joke at my expense."

I was a bit taken aback at Molly's seeming good cheer, after the frosty invitation she'd given me in the Cheesemonger yesterday. I guess she'd believed me when I said that nothing had happened between me and Rocky. Seeing her again made me realize nothing could happen between me and Rocky. Even if I was attracted to him, I couldn't do anything about it, and I wouldn't.

"Sorry, I just took a bit of a wrong turn, but here I am, ready and raring to go."

"Woo-hoo, Bahamas!" Molly said.

Now, I know I'm the dark, jaded sister and Molly's the bright, happy-go-lucky one. But not even she had ever said "woo-hoo" in her life. I found myself wondering who had kidnapped my real sister and sent this Stepford clone in her place. But all I said was:

"Woo-hoo." I couldn't bring myself to shout it, though, which didn't matter, since Molly had already turned to Janet.

"What were you doing in the servants' quarters, Mum?"

"Ivan told me the skunks were back. Thought I'd better check myself."

"Skunks?" I said. "I thought you said—"

"I'm going to get one of those humane pest removal services in here while we're in the Bahamas. Hopefully they can trap the little critters and cart them over to Hither Hills State Park on the big island. Well, is everyone packed? We don't want to be late."

"Late for what?" Molly laughed. "We're flying charter."

"Yes, and I'm paying for it. You miss a commercial flight and you pay a hundred bucks to change your ticket. You show up late for a charter and they charge you five thousand for the inconvenience. And I don't know about you girls, but I would much rather spend that money on boots," she finished up, lifting up one of her feet and flicking off a piece of mud with one golden-lacquered nail. "Not to mention bikinis!"

Molly and I looked at each other and smiled, and this time her joy didn't seem forced. "Yes, please!"

At the sight of the two of us looking all sisters-in-love, a big grin spread across Janet's face.

"Look at the two of you! My girls, together again." She extended her long strong arms and pulled us into a three-way hug. I felt Molly's arms snake around us as well, and after a moment's hesitation, I gave in and joined in the hug.

"We're going to have so much fun!" Janet breathed into my ear.

Mum climbed into the Maybach and I went to follow, but before I could, Molly's hand closed around my arm like a clamp.

"I know you want to sleep with Rocky, you little slut. I've got my eye on you."

"Molly, what the—"

But before I could even finish my question, she'd shoved me out of the way and climbed in next to Mum.

"Hurry up, slowpoke," Mum called to me. "We really don't want to be late."

I got in warily, trying not to make eye contact with Molly. Her rage filled up the back of the car like a toxic gas, although Mum seemed oblivious to it. I just hoped Molly wouldn't crash the plane.

* 23 *

CARIBBEAN QUEENS

From the Diary of Molly Overbrook

About a half hour after we took off from the East Hampton airport in Mum's chartered plane, a funny thing happened. Both my phone and Mardi's started buzzing like crazy. Voice mails, text messages, alerts from Twitter and Instagram and Facebook and a half dozen other social media feeds. At first, we thought something terrible had happened, and we started scrolling through them in alarm, trying to find out what it was. Then Mardi looked up, anxiety replaced by confusion.

"These are all old. Like two, three weeks old."

I hadn't been paying attention to the time stamps, but then I checked and saw that she was right. The most recent message was from yesterday; the oldest dated back almost a month to—

"The day I moved into Fair Haven."

Mardi shot me a look when I said that. We hadn't spoken a word to each other since I'd hissed into her ear outside Mum's Maybach, and I could tell she was biting her tongue so we didn't get into a fight.

"Look at that," I said sarcastically. "There are all the messages you said I didn't send you. *So good to see you yesterday. Let's hang out at the North Inn with F. Maybe you can come out to FH and show me where everything is.*"

"And all the messages you said I didn't send you!" Mardi protested. "*So glad we finally talked. I missed you! It's Jo's birthday tomorrow. Are you coming to the party?*"

"I missed Jo's birthday?"

"She wasn't happy," Mardi said. "Neither was Ingrid."

"Oh, look," I said, changing the subject. "Here are all the messages I sent Rocky. You remember Rocky? My boyfriend? *Yesterday was amazing. I miss you already. Where are you? Is something wrong? Are you mad at me? WTF?!*"

"Molly, please," Mardi said in a placating tone. "He didn't get them. Neither of us did. How were we supposed to know that you weren't having another one of your freak-outs?"

"'Another one'? Because freaking out is apparently something I do all the time?" I huffed.

"Come on. Even you have to admit you've been a little gun-shy ever since Alberich."

"I might use the word *cautious*. But I wasn't being cautious with Rocky. *As you know.*"

"Nothing happened! And I didn't know what was going on," Mardi said. "You have to believe me."

"Well, you should have tried harder to find out. You should have driven out to Fair Haven."

"You don't think I did? Three times! You were never there!"

"Well, then I was probably at the tennis club with Mum. All you had to do was look online."

"How?" Mardi said. "None of those pictures and posts went up."

"Bull," I said. "Look," I continued, holding up my phone to her. "Here's a picture from the club—that's the day after Mum got back from England. And there are more than three thousand likes from that day alone."

"But look at my phone," Mardi said, showing me her screen. "The alert from the picture didn't come until just now."

I was so mad that it was hard for me to focus, but when I'd stared at the picture and the responses below it, I saw that she was telling the truth. Somehow the picture had gone out into the Twitterverse—to everyone's phone in the world, except Mardi's.

"This smells like magic," I said.

Mardi nodded. "Like someone was playing a trick on us."

"Who was playing a trick on whom?" Mum said, emerging from the front of the plane, where she'd been hanging out with the pilot, who apparently gave her lessons.

Mardi glanced at me warily, discreetly shaking her head. "No one. Just this dumb Internet prank."

"Ugh," Mum said. "I try not to know anything about it. Ivan handles all my accounts, and I'm pretty sure he uses some kind of magic script to keep them going. Speaking of which." She clapped her hands twice. "Ivan!"

Ivan appeared from the galley at the back of the jet.

"Yes, Ms. Steele?"

"My daughters' glasses are empty."

"Begging your pardon, Ms. Steele. Mooi, Magdi, can I refill your champagne, or would you prefer something else?"

"Uh, champagne's fine for me," Mardi said, clearly uncomfortable at the way Mum was ordering Ivan around like a servant. I still found it a little off-putting, but it seemed to be their dynamic.

"Me too," I said.

"And my throat is dry," Mum added as Ivan collected our glasses. "Bring me a juice. Nothing too tart."

"As you wish, Ms. Steele," Ivan said, bowing low and backing out of the cabin.

With Mum present, Mardi clearly didn't want to talk about the situation with Rocky or the weird, possibly magical glitch in our electronic communications, and I decided to let it go—for now. Even if some magical force had hidden my texts and phone calls and social media posts from her and Rocky, and vice versa, she still should have tried harder to track me down before making a move on the guy I'd been seeing. But I didn't need to have a knock-down, drag-out fight with my sister the first time we hung out with Mum. Better to break her in easy.

Instead, we spent the rest of the flight sipping champagne and eating caviar, and before I knew it, we were landing in the Bahamas—or the BH as everyone called it—and then heading off in a waiting limo to the hotel.

The hotel was a bit like the Chateau Marmont in LA, with a large main building and a dozen or so "bungalows" scattered around it. "Bungalow" makes me think of a little building, but ours was bigger than Ingrid's house in the East End, a single-story U-shaped building that wrapped around a private pool, with bedrooms that opened right onto a private beach. I mean, my old room at Ingrid's looked out on the beach too, but it was on the second floor, and, well, as nice as the beach is in North Hampton, it's hard to compete with the tropics' perfect eighty-five-degree weather and seventy-five-degree water.

Seconds after we arrived, all three of us were in our bikinis (four if you count Ivan, whose Speedo was almost as tiny as our swimsuit bottoms—I guess he's European?) and splashing into the water. It was heavenly, and afterward, when Mum and Ivan went off to the tennis club to get in an hour of practice, it just seemed too peaceful to start fighting with Molly. And so it went for the next six days: every morning a pitcher of fresh-squeezed peach nectar appeared outside our door, served with a selection of croissants and fresh Caribbean fruits (gri gri, papaya, and chironja were my faves). They were so good they actually made me look forward to breakfast (and that's saying something).

But as good as breakfast was, dinners were even better. Normally, Mum said, she would've wined and dined us at the best restaurants in Nassau, but since she was playing a tournament, she had to be super careful about what she ate. So instead of going out, she'd arranged for a personal chef to come to our bungalow every night and cook for us. It was one of the few times I thought about the fact that Mum wasn't like me and Mardi and Dad—that she was human. We never worried about how healthy our food was, only if it tasted good. But Mum was mortal, and she had to be extremely conscious about what she put in her body to keep it not just looking as good as it could, but working as well as it could, and for as long as it could. Her chef, however, put any of those thoughts out of my brain because he served up an unbelievable array of grilled fishes that had been caught that same day in the Florida Straits— swordfish and octopus and shrimp and several things that came in shells that kind of grossed me out a little, but tasted *divine*. It didn't hurt that Sebastien, the chef, was gorgeous and spoke with a beautiful French accent (he was from Martinique).

Meanwhile, though, there was the tennis tournament itself. This was the first time we'd been seen in public together as Janet Steele's daughters. I started the week with 846 followers on Twitter. By the time Mum won the tournament the following Sunday, I had 13,351. Mardi scored almost as many. But of course the real star was Mum. There were paparazzi stationed outside the gates of our hotel to snap her picture in the morning, and sport photographers stationed at the practice courts to watch her warm up each day, and TV cameras at the matches themselves, to catch her in all her glory.

Crazily enough, even though our hotel was right on the beach, we never actually put on our swimsuits after that first day until our last day in the BH, the day after Mum won the tournament. Mum had scheduled an extra day at the hotel so we could all chill out and actually spend some time together without Mum being "distracted" by the tournament (although I have to say, when she wasn't playing tennis, she didn't talk about it at all, and seemed not to think about it either). And so, after another breakfast of croissants and guanabana (it tastes like the perfect marriage of a strawberry and a pineapple), we slipped on our bikinis and made our way to the beach, which in our case just meant walking out the door. Although just as we were finishing breakfast the phone rang, and Mum ended up getting called off to do an interview with ESPN Australia, who happened to have a correspondent in the Bahamas.

"They've promised to let me shill for my clothing line and my vodka, so I kind of can't say no. It pays the bills, you know."

"You have your own vodka?" Mardi and I exclaimed at the same time.

"Only in Australia and Asia at this point. But we sold a hundred thousand bottles last year, and we're getting ready to move into Europe and the US. It's called Fe, after the atomic symbol for iron. That's okay," she said to Ivan, who'd appeared in the room with the keys to the rented car. "I've called a cab. You stay here and look after the girls." She kissed us both and swooshed out the door.

Ivan stared glumly after her for a moment, then shook his head and turned to us brightly.

"So what're we starting the day with? Mojitos or margaritas?"

"Mojitos!" Mardi and I said without looking at each other.

"One pitcher of mojitos coming right up," Ivan said. "Go get your sun on, and I'll be out in two shakes of a fish's tail."

We've been to the tropics before—Dad's a big fan of Turks and Caicos, and took us there every January for four years in a row when we were in grade school, and we've also been to Anguilla and Cozumel and the Canary Islands—but every time I go to one of these fabulous beautiful places, I ask myself why I don't live there year-round. But I know the answer: it's because

I'd never do anything again. I'd just camp out in a lounge chair and have cute cabana boys bring me cold drinks all day long, basking in the sun (I'm a goddess, remember—no need to worry about skin cancer) and getting up once an hour or so to take a dip in the water. If there is a heaven, I can't imagine it looking like anything other than a Caribbean beach. And if that's not what it looks like, well, maybe I'll take Mum up on that whole Mimir revolt-against-the-gods thing after all.

"This is heaven, isn't it?" Mardi said to me at one point.

"Oh, my gods, that's eerie. I was thinking exactly the same thing. I want to die right here," I said. I couldn't really be that mad at Mardi for long. And I believed her that nothing had happened between her and Rocky. Of course nothing had happened. No matter what, we're sisters.

"Geez, morbid much?" Mardi laughed. "But I wasn't just talking about the beach. I was talking about being here with you. With you and . . . Mum."

"Really?" I said. "You're coming around to her?"

"How can I resist? She's been nothing but fabulous."

"Oh, I'm so glad! I knew you'd change your mind!"

Mardi took another sip of her mojito. "I'm not saying I'm ready to move in yet, but she's definitely winning me over. But really, I'm much more happy hanging out with you."

For six days, we'd hung out, taking all our meals together, shopping and watching tennis together, even sleeping in the same room like we had when we were little girls. But even though everything had seemed peaceful on the surface, underneath I had been seething with jealousy. No matter how much fun we were having, I couldn't get over the idea that she'd betrayed me with Rocky. And even though I believed her, I couldn't shake the thought. I still didn't want to shatter the peace, especially since it involved Mum, and so I kept on biting my tongue.

But suddenly, I realized that I didn't want to fight about it. Chances are something like this would happen again—and again and again—over the course of the hundreds or thousands of years that Mardi and I would be alive. If we got in a fight over every single boy or every single betrayal, whether real or accidental or purely imagined, we'd be fighting to the end of time.

I turned to her on her lounge chair. She was looking at me nervously, and I knew she'd been picking up on my mood.

"I'm happy we're hanging out too," I said, reaching out for her hand and giving it a squeeze.

We sat there like that for one more moment, and then Mardi grabbed her glass and drained it.

"Okay, enough schmaltz. Let's go swim!"

24

LEFT SHARK, RIGHT WHALE

Mardi-Overbrook-Journal.docx

I can't tell you how happy I was as Molly and I leapt off our lounge chairs and ran across the sparkling white sands toward the softly rolling blue water. I mean, I knew that at some point we were going to have to have it out about Rocky, but now I knew that we'd get through it one way or another. Sparks would fly, favorite items of clothing might mysteriously disappear, hair might even get pulled, but we'd survive this and get back on track.

We ran all the way to the water and splashed in without slowing. The Caribbean is amazing—warm but not balmy, so you don't have to take that minute or two to adjust before you dive in. We ran in until we were up to our waists and then dove straight in. The water was so clear that you saw every grain of sand on the bottom, every little brightly colored fish that flitted by. We swam and splashed each other and dove down to the bottom, pretending we were looking for pearls or gold doubloons from long-ago Spanish galleons, and generally behaved like seven-year-olds, for a good twenty minutes. When we were finally sated, we were a couple hundred feet offshore, where the water was still only eight or twelve feet deep, lazily treading water. And then I had to go and ruin it.

"It's true," I said.

Molly had been staring at the beach, and she used her hands to turn her body toward mine, rather than just look over at me.

"What is?" The look on her face was totally calm and trusting, and I could hear my brain scream, *Don't do it!* But I had to come clean. She was my sister.

"I liked Rocky."

Molly's face didn't change, didn't seem to move, but it hardened somehow, and I could've sworn the water got five degrees colder.

"I know," she said finally.

"I know you know. But I still had to tell you."

"How could you?" she asked, and what made her question so hard was that it wasn't angry. It was hurt, and I knew I'd put that hurt there.

"I don't know," I said. "I was just so confused after Trent dumped me, and there was the whole Mum situation, and you weren't responding to my texts, and—and he was just there. It was like he was as close to you as I was going to get. Like if I couldn't hang out with you, I could hang out with him."

"Okay, ew," Molly said, and I was relieved that she could make a little joke.

"I know! Although on some level, it didn't feel like it had anything to do with poor Rocky at all. It didn't matter what he looked like or said. It just mattered that he had this connection to you. I didn't mean to. I would never hurt you. I just needed to flirt with someone. He likes you."

"If he liked me so much, why was he spending all his time with you?" Molly said coldly.

"Maybe because I didn't give him a choice."

"What do you mean?" Molly said, looking at me sharply. "Did you use magic?"

"I mean, not consciously. But our powers are really acting up lately. Maybe I did something without realizing it."

"No offense, sis, but that sounds like a bit of a cop-out."

"I know it does, and I don't mean to duck responsibility. What I did was totally wrong. But as I float here in this beautiful, seventy-five-degree water and look back at it, it doesn't seem like it had anything to do with me. It was like something was acting through me. Making me do something I wouldn't normally do."

"What, like magic? You think someone didn't just hex our phones? They hexed you too?"

"Honestly, no. It feels . . . bigger than that. Deeper. I'm wondering if it has something to do with the Re-awakening. If it's not just our powers that are being affected. If our emotions are being changed too."

"The divine version of adolescence?"

"I guess so."

Molly was silent for a long time.

"I dunno, Mardi," she said eventually. "Part of me thinks you're just trying to get a pass for a low blow. But part of me knows what you're describing. This feeling of not being a hundred percent in control of what I do or say or even feel. Something weird is going on inside us right now. And who knows, maybe that did cause you to do what you did with Rocky. But, well, you did, and now things can never be the same between him and me again. Whatever Rocky and I might've had, it's gone now. And at least part of the blame for that is on you."

"Molly, come on. You know I'd never do anything to hurt you."

"But you did, Mardi. You hurt me. A lot."

Her voice was so quiet. So reasonable. She could have been explaining the rules of a card game to Jo. It terrified me.

"Molly, please. Don't be like this. Yell at me, trash my car, tell Dad to ground me for the next hundred years. But don't shut me out like this."

"I'm not shutting you out. I'm just not . . ." She paused, searching for a word. "I'm just not ready to trust you. I still love you, but I'm not sure I can ever trust you again. I know nothing happened, but liking the same guy as me still feels like a betrayal."

"Molly!" I said. "No!"

"The nice thing is, we're immortal," Molly said in a sad voice. "We've got eternity to figure it out. But I guess the bad thing is that if we don't work through it, we've got a really long time to feel awkward around each other."

She turned then and started swimming toward the shore.

"Mooi!" I called, using her Norse name. "Please don't leave it like that."

I wanted to swim after her, but I knew I couldn't. That if I did, it would just make it worse.

"Mooi!"

Something brushed against me then. At first, I thought I kicked myself with my own leg, but even before that thought was over, I felt a long scraping sensation and realized that whatever it was, it was way bigger than my own leg. And then I was being smacked aside by something that hit me like a baseball bat, sending me flying out of the water. But as I was soaring over the waves, I saw a dark shape beneath and a dark fin that was at least as tall as me piercing the water. The fin angled away from me then, and I saw the long black back and the gleaming white belly, the unmistakable markings of a killer whale.

"Whale!" I screamed just before I splashed beneath the surface.

As the water closed over me, I struggled to keep my body turned toward the whale. I wasn't sure how one fought off a killer whale attack, but I figured I had a better chance if I at least saw it coming. It was swimming at an angle away from me, and I saw the length of its body, from its rounded snout to its thick body with its wide pectoral fins spinning like a propeller to the muscular action of its fluke, which pumped through the water heavily. Within seconds, it had disappeared in the depths, and for a moment, I allowed myself to think that it was leaving. Then a dark shadow reappeared and grew quickly larger as the whale sped back for round two.

I kicked myself to the surface to grab some air, and for the brief second I was above water, I whipped my head in Molly's direction and called out to her. I was back under the water so quickly, however, that I couldn't tell if she heard.

Then the cool blue water closed around my ears, and I turned my attention back to the whale. I was trying to think of some magic that I could use to fight it, but before I could even gather my thoughts, it was on me. I couldn't believe how big it was. I'd always imagined killer whales to be only a little bigger than dolphins, but this monster's body was as tall as I was, and its gaping jaws looked like they could swallow a Saint Bernard whole. I paddled helplessly as it raced in my direction. At the last second, it turned on its side but continued heading straight for me. I started to ask myself why, but then it hit me: as big as it was, I was still too tall to fit in its mouth. It had to come at me sideways to take a chunk out of me. But if it could turn sideways, so could I.

I beat the water furiously to spin my body. The whale lunged for me, its jaws aimed squarely for my midsection. It turned, but I was able to grab its snout and turn with it, and then the whale's own momentum carried it past me. I rolled along the length of its body, one of its flukes smashing against one of my ankles as I propelled myself toward the surface to grab another breath of air.

As the whale sped past me, I thought I had time for a quick breather. Its body was too big for it to simply whirl around like a seal. But I didn't think about the tail. My head was just breaking the surface when I felt a push from beneath me. The next thing I knew I was flying through the air again. The whale had literally picked me up and thrown me with its massive flukes—in the same direction it was swimming! It was actually throwing me in front of its mouth!

"Molly!" I screamed. "Molly, help!" I was so disoriented I couldn't tell which way to look.

Then I was under again. I whirled around. The whale was right there, turning to take a bite out of me. I didn't even have time to spin. I just stuck out my hands and pushed at the big snout to keep my body out of the gaping mouth. I expected to roll along the side again, but this time, the whale was perfectly centered, and I felt myself being driven backward through the water as the whale swam. The pressure of the water against my back was so great that it took all my strength to keep from buckling and slipping into its mouth.

For the first time, I glimpsed the creature's eyes. I stared at it, and it stared back with pure hatred. If there'd been any doubt that this was a magic attack, that look completely erased it. This wasn't a wild animal hunting. It was here to kill me. Which meant one of two things: either it had been hexed to come after me, or it wasn't actually a killer whale at all, but some kind of shape-shifter that had taken this form. If that was the case, it was probably the same creature that had attacked Dad's plane.

The whale held my gaze for a moment, then suddenly its snout jerked downward to the sandy bottom of the sea. I knew what it was doing immediately: it was going to pin me to the ground. If it couldn't squirm around until it managed to get its jaws around me, it would just pin me underwater until I drowned. But it was moving so fast I couldn't see how to get out of its way without getting one of my legs snapped. And so, helplessly, I let myself be pushed toward the ground. As a goddess, I knew I could hold my breath two or three times longer than a mortal, but that was it. I just prayed something would happen before I ran out of air.

As if reading my thoughts, a pale form appeared in my peripheral vision. I looked over: it was Molly! She must have heard my call!

She swam up to the whale broadside, one hand curled into a fist. Before I knew what was happening, she struck it in the only vulnerable place on its body: the eye that was staring at me so malevolently.

It wasn't a hard blow, but a whale's eye is every bit as tender as a person's. And just like a person, it jerked away from the assault. The twist of its neck was enough to dislodge me, and I rolled safely out of the way. The whale arced off in the opposite direction. It smacked at me with its tail again, but this time I was ready, and all it did was push me a few feet closer to the surface.

I kicked upward to where Molly was already treading water and through to the surface.

"You came back!"

"No time!" Molly said grimly. "That thing's going to be on us again in seconds."

I nodded. "Let's link arms. If we can make ourselves too big for its mouth, it can't get us."

"Got it," Molly said. We grabbed each other's arms and dove under.

Just in time: the whale was barreling straight for us. Molly's elbow was crooked tightly around mine, and I could feel her legs swirling through the water. The sight of our conjoined bodies obviously confused the whale because it slowed down. I thought it might swim past us, when suddenly it rolled in for a bite. But we were too wide for its mouth, and with our two free arms and four legs, we managed to kick ourselves out of the way. The whale shot past us, and we kicked ourselves toward the surface.

"Start for the shore," Molly said as soon as we were in the air. "No way we can dodge this thing forever. But if we get into shallow-enough water, it won't be able to follow."

"Good plan!" I said, mostly because I wanted to be encouraging. The shore was still hundreds of feet away. It seemed to me that we'd be exhausted long before we managed to reach it.

"Back under," Molly said then, nodding toward the dark fin that was knifing our way. "Here it comes again."

We dove under and faced off another charge. The whale tried spinning this time and slapping us with its tail. But as agile as it was, it was still so large that it couldn't move in for the kill fast enough. It was able to send us rolling through the water, but by the time it had managed to turn around and charge us again, we'd regained control and were able to kick and push ourselves out of its mouth, then kick up to the surface again and snatch a breath.

Over and over again, it charged us. Over and over again, we managed to elude its grasping mouth. I kept thinking someone would see us, but that's the one drawback to a private beach: no gawkers or paparazzi, but no one to rescue you when a magical orca comes after you. The only person at the bungalow was Ivan, but he was apparently busy inside.

But with each attack, we managed to swim a few feet closer to the shore. I could feel my arms and legs tiring and could hear in Molly's ragged breaths that she was exhausted too, but if we could just keep this up for a while longer, we'd be out of the whale's reach. The water was only eight feet or so deep where we were. It wouldn't be long now until we could get to safety.

But as soon as I realized this, the whale did too, because it suddenly changed tactics. Before, it had been swimming out to the deeper water to turn around and charge us, essentially driving us toward the shore. But after its next attack, it swam toward the shallow water instead. When it turned around, its entire back rose out of the water, and its tail churned up clouds of sand. And then, when it came for us again, it swam slowly instead of charging. It didn't ram into us but managed to lodge its snout between our arms. Suddenly, its tail started churning: it was driving us back out to sea!

I looked at Molly. We had no choice: we had to let go of each other to get out of its way, and hope that we could rejoin our arms before the whale turned around and charged us. I nodded at her, hoping she understood. She nodded back, flashing me a grim smile.

I slackened my arm and felt hers slide away. We kicked off the whale's body, and it went speeding by us. It pivoted quickly, though, and swam back toward the shore to turn around.

"It knows we're trying to get to land!" I said as we broke the surface. "It's pushing us back to sea!"

"I can't keep this up much longer," Molly panted. "What are we going to do?"

"We have to keep fighting," I said. "Just a little longer. I think help is on the way." I could feel it.

"What do you mean?" Molly asked frantically, but there was no time to explain. We could see the whale's dorsal fin straightening out and beginning its charge. We linked arms and dove under to meet it.

But when we were up again, I pointed to the sky.

"Look!" I said.

"At what?" Molly said confusedly.

"Clouds!" I yelled just before I grabbed Molly and pulled her under to face another attack.

Molly's face was still confused as we dove under, but then I saw comprehension come into her eyes. She understood.

The sky had been crystal blue for the seven days we'd been here. But in the last ten minutes, it had begun to turn gray: thick dark clouds came rushing in, which seemed to form out of nothing. That wasn't normal weather. That was magic.

That was Thor.

Or at least that's what I told myself as, holding tight to Molly, my exhausted arms and legs fended off the twentieth or thirtieth lunge from our attacker. Because if it wasn't, we were done for.

"It's Dad!" Molly screamed when we broke the surface.

"It has to be!" I answered.

"What's he doing?" she said. "And why's it taking him so long to do it?"

I didn't have time to respond before we had to dive under again. I had no idea what the answer to Molly's first question was, but I was pretty sure the answer to her second had something to do with the huge distance involved. Dad was a thousand miles away. I'd never heard of anyone casting a spell from that distance. But Dad was the god of thunder. If anyone could do it, he could.

The whale came at us and I readied myself to fight it off. My legs felt like jelly. My free arm was numb, my palm scraped raw. *One more time*, I told myself. *I can do this one more time.*

The mouth was there, gaping open. I pushed at the side of the head weakly, barely keeping myself out of its jaws as I glimpsed one of Molly's kicking legs. It actually struck the whale right in the lip. The jaws snapped shut, missing her foot by a fraction of an inch. The whale snapped its head up, almost ripping Molly from my grasp. We rolled down the length of its back until our arms caught the dorsal fin, which we wrapped around like a piece of ribbon. The whale rolled, pulling us lower in the water, then jerked the other way. I felt Molly's hand slip down my arm, then pull free. I clutched futilely at her writhing fingers. I even opened my mouth and called her name, my voice sounding like a zombie groan beneath ten feet of water. As I watched helplessly, the whale's massive tail struck Molly full in the chest and stomach and sent her flying.

"Molly!" I screamed again, then choked as water rushed into my mouth. I barely managed to keep one eye on Molly and the other on the whale's dark form as it rocketed through the water. I clawed my way to the surface, whirling my head around, trying to find Molly. The glowering clouds cast dark shadows, and I could barely see anything.

Then I saw a flat form about fifteen feet to my left. It was Molly! Floating facedown in the water!

I began swimming toward her, screaming at my exhausted limbs to *move, dammit, get me to my sister!*

But even as I was heading toward her, a dark fin shot up out of the water and began racing toward her. It was farther away from her than I was but moving ten times faster than me.

"No!" I screamed. It was all I could think of. "No! No!" Like the whale was a bad dog I was trying to frighten away from a kitten.

But it ignored me and raced onward, its dark form cutting the water like a torpedo. Forty feet. Thirty. Twenty.

Suddenly, the sky exploded in light and everything disappeared. I heard a tremendous crash, but all I could see was pure whiteness, even behind my squeezed-together eyelids. And then: silence, as sudden and complete as the flash of light.

I pried my eyelids open. Everything was blurry and

suffused with a golden aura, but I could just make out Molly a few feet ahead of me, and another dark shape floating a few feet past her. It was far too small to be the whale, but I could smell the distinct aroma of charred flesh.

I raced to Molly with the last of my strength. Even as I got to her, her head jerked up, and she began coughing and choking.

"It's okay, Molly. I've got you. It's okay, it's okay."

"What—what happened?" Molly said. "Where's the whale?"

"I think Dad zapped it with lightning," I said. I smoothed her matted hair out of her face. "It's okay. It's gone."

"But what's that?" She was looking toward the dark mass floating about ten feet away. It had the unmoving quality of a dead thing, and it was completely flat in the water, but even so, we could tell it was human. Or at least human-shaped.

We pulled ourselves slowly toward it, but my eyes were still so singed from the lightning blast that it wasn't until we were right next to it that I noticed the stripe of red at its midsection, the distinct cut of a Speedo on a muscular man's body.

It was Ivan, and he was dead.

25

LOVE IS A BATTLEFIELD

From the Diary of Molly Overbrook

It took all my powers of persuasion to convince Mardi to get on the plane back to North Hampton. At first, she told me that she didn't want to go anywhere near a plane that Ivan had touched—she was convinced that he'd booby-trapped it or something. Mum told her that it was unlikely we'd be in the same plane on the way back, since the charter company had been using it throughout the week, and Mardi reluctantly agreed. Later, though, when we were in our bedroom packing, she confessed to me the real reason she didn't want to get on the plane.

"It's not Ivan I'm worried about," she told me. "It's Mum."

It was about six in the evening. Seven hours had passed

since Ivan had attacked us. Mum raced back from her interview as soon as I called her. The first thing she did was make sure we were both unhurt, but aside from a few scrapes and bruises and being generally exhausted, we were fine. Then she stripped down to her swimsuit, grabbed one of those lightweight plastic kayaks that the hotel had provided, and set out to find Ivan's body. At that point, less than an hour had passed since the attack, but there was no sign of it. Still, neither Mardi nor I thought there was any chance he was still alive—not in that body, anyway. There had been a hole in his chest the size of a basketball. You could've put your head through it and looked out the other side.

"Sharks probably got 'im," Mum said, her accent coming out more strongly than ever with her anger. "And good riddance."

Mardi and I were still in too much shock to ask her the questions that were burning in our both our minds. Had Mum known Ivan was a shape-shifter? And if so, did she know if he was the one who had attacked our father's plane?

"When I think of the trust I placed in him," Mum growled. "My daughters' lives! I want to resurrect him just so I can kill him myself!"

We'd been due to fly out the next morning, but Mum called the charter company and told them she wanted to leave that day. There wasn't a plane on the island, which was why we had to wait till the evening. Mum told us that we should both lie down, and I reluctantly agreed. I was exhausted, but I was also so keyed up that I wanted to go for a run or pick up an ax and chop down a tree. I could tell Mardi felt the same way I did, but it was equally clear that she didn't want to be separated from me, and so when I trudged down the hall, she shuffled after me, and when I climbed into bed, she slipped in behind me and curled her arms around me.

"I can't believe how close I came to losing you today," she whispered in my ear.

I wrapped my arms around hers, interlacing our fingers together. "There was no chance of that happening," I said with a bravery I tried hard to feel, even retroactively. "Not when we work together."

Mardi pulled me even closer.

"Remember we used to sleep like this when we were little girls?"

I nodded. "Why'd we ever stop?"

"I dunno," Mardi said, and I could feel her shrug. I heard her open her mouth to say something, but all that came out was a yawn. It was infectious: my jaw fell open and a long, achy yawn sighed from my mouth.

"I've never felt this tired in my life," I said.

Mardi nodded but didn't say anything, and a moment later, I felt her breath come softly and evenly against the back of my neck. I thought about asking her if she was sleeping, but before I could get the words out, my eyes dropped closed, and I was asleep too.

. . .

The next thing we knew, Mum was shaking us awake.

"Come on, girls, let's get you packed and get to the airport. The sooner we're off this island, the better."

My body felt stiff as a board, as though I'd been in a fight—which I guess I had been. Mardi was stretching awkwardly, and I could tell she was sore too. She voiced her reservations about the plane, and Mum reassured her, then left us to go pack her own things. That's when Mardi dropped her bombshell:

"It's not Ivan I'm worried about. It's Mum."

I looked at her, first in confusion, then in disbelief.

"You think . . ." I found it hard to say the words aloud. "You think *Mum* was behind this?"

"Think about it, Mardi. Ivan was practically Mum's slave. He would never do anything against her will, let alone something as drastic as try to kill her daughters."

"But, but," I stuttered. "It's *Mum.*"

"What does that even mean? We barely know her. About the only thing we know about her is that she wants us to kill our own father. So why shouldn't she want to kill her own children?"

"But it's Mum! Our mother!"

Mardi just looked at me for a moment. Then she shrugged helplessly. "Have it your way. But I'm not getting on a plane with her."

She grabbed her phone and, while I watched in disbelief, pulled up a number and pressed call. She held the phone to her ear for a moment, then pulled it away. "Huh."

"What is it?" I asked.

"I'm trying to call Ingrid's, but it's not going through."

It hit me then: Dad! We'd never reached out to him, to thank or tell him we were still alive, or just find out if it was him who'd saved us. I pulled my phone from my pocket and immediately called Ingrid's, but I got the same result as Mardi: nothing. No ringing, no busy signal, nothing. I tried her cell then, and Matt's, and Freya's, and the North Inn, and Mardi did the same. But none of the calls went through.

"Weird," I said.

"Weird?" Mardi said. "Or magic?"

"You think it's part of the same thing that stopped all our text messages and phone calls from going to each other?"

As an experiment, I called Mardi's phone, just to make sure we weren't in some kind of dead zone. The call went through immediately.

She turned to the bedside table then and picked up the hotel phone. It took some doing, but she finally figured out how to call the US. Once again, the phone on the other end refused to respond.

"If someone did cast a spell preventing us from communicating electronically," she said as she hung up the phone, "it wasn't just on our phones. It's on us."

"Or on the East End," I said. "Remember how all those

old messages came through about a half hour after we took off? Maybe someone cast some kind of perimeter spell that keeps us from communicating electronically."

"That's a very specific spell," Mardi said. "I have no idea how you'd cast it, but I suspect it's not easy. It'd take a seriously powerful magic-user to pull it off."

"That rules out Mum, then," I couldn't stop myself from saying. "As a mortal, there's no way she could cast a spell that powerful."

"Yeah, but Ivan probably could have. He was an elf, remember. And as his shape-shifting shows, he had some serious power."

"Which makes it that much harder to believe that he was following Mum's orders when he attacked us. If he had all the power, why would he demean himself by following a human's commands?"

"I don't know," Mardi said. "But he certainly didn't seem to have a problem with washing her clothes and fetching her drinks and all that."

"Whatever," I said. "We can talk about this more later. For now, let's just get home." Mardi opened her mouth to protest, but I spoke over her. "For the gods' sakes, Mardi. Mum's going to be on the plane with us. She couldn't hurt us without hurting herself."

Mardi just grimaced at me for a long moment.

"Fine," she said finally. "But I am not going to be happy about it."

Angrily, she began stuffing things in her suitcases.

. . .

The trip to the airport and taking off all went smoothly. Mardi might have been angry still, but she didn't seem to want to pick a fight, with me or with Mum. At least not yet.

Mum opened a bottle of champagne even before the plane took off. By the time we were at cruising altitude, we were already on our second bottle. We were drinking quickly enough that Mardi and I were feeling the effects of the alcohol, which, frankly, was a relief, because even though I'd told Mardi I didn't believe Mum was behind Ivan's attacks, I was still nervous about being thirty thousand feet in the air so soon after someone had tried to kill us. Just because I didn't think Mum was helping him didn't mean that he didn't have some other partner out there. At least this wasn't a seaplane—there'd be no whale rising out of the waves to smash us to bits.

As we were settling into the third bottle, Mum sighed heavily. "Well, I suppose I owe you girls an explanation."

My heart did a somersault in my chest. I looked over at Mardi to find her staring at me, looking equally startled.

"An explanation," I managed to spit out. "About what?"

"Well, about Ivan, of course," Mum said.

This time I didn't look at Mardi. I was afraid that she might flash me one of her I-told-you-so looks and I might short out the plane's electrical system.

"Well, I guess, sure," I stammered, "if you think you

have to, but, I mean, you could've hardly known he was going to do something like that. Right?" I added desperately.

Mum laughed. "Believe me, girls, I'm as surprised as you at what happened. But that doesn't mean I shouldn't have seen it coming. Ivan has always been jealous of my attention. He often professed to love me, not in a platonic way, but in a romantic way. It sometimes made our relationship . . . tense."

It took me a moment to get it.

"He wanted you to be his wife!"

Mum nodded, a modest smile on her face, but you could tell she also felt she deserved it.

"But Ivan was an elf!" said Mardi.

"Not just an elf, he was an elf prince," Mum corrected.

"And he still wanted to marry a human?" asked Mardi.

"You make it sound so degrading, Magdi!" Mum laughed. "And lest you forget, I'm not any just any human—I'm the mother of the Mimir. Elves have long awaited the coming of the new gods and the opportunity to restore the balance of power between the nine worlds."

"But," I cut in, "if being the mother of the Mimir made you so special, why would Ivan try to kill us?"

"I don't think he was trying to kill you, Mooi," Mum said. Before I could protest that if he hadn't been trying to kill me, he had a funny way of showing it, she continued: "He was trying to kill Magdi."

"What?" Mardi and I said at the same time, even as the lights in the cabin flickered on and off.

"Girls, please," Mum said calmly but firmly. "Control your emotions, or you're going to do Ivan's work for him."

I looked at Mardi and nodded. I took a couple of deep breaths and saw her do the same. I wasn't sure which one of us was sending out the energy that was messing with the plane's electrical system, but the lights stopped flickering, and we both breathed a sigh of relief.

"Thank you," Mum said. "I'd hate to go down in history as the woman who missed the Grand Slam because she died in a plane crash."

"You were saying that Ivan was trying to kill me, not Molly," Mardi prompted.

"He never told me this, but that's my suspicion. We had talked about your obvious discomfort with the information I gave you, and that Mooi seemed a little more receptive. When you two made up, we hoped that Mooi would bring you around, but Ivan was afraid that you were actually going to persuade her to distance yourself from me and the prophecies about the Mimir."

"'Bring her around'?" I repeated. "For the record, I don't remember ever signing on to the whole 'kill Dad' plan."

"Speaking of killing Dad," Mardi said coldly. "Was it Ivan who attacked Dad's plane? And did you know about it?"

Mum's face stiffened at Mardi's words. She turned slowly to her.

"Yes, Magdi," she said in a soft and somehow disappointed tone, "I knew Ivan attacked your father's plane."

Mardi shifted to me, but before we made eye contact, I shifted my gaze to Mum. Like I said, I had no need to see my twin gloat.

"Did you know before or after the attack?"

Mum took a long moment before speaking.

"I know you probably think I hate your father," she said finally, "especially after what I told you about the coming war against the old gods. But I want you to know that what your father and I had was real. It was love. And when you love someone once, you never stop loving them."

"With all due respect," Mardi said, in a voice that wasn't respectful at all, "that wasn't an answer to my question."

"Wasn't it?" Mum said. "Thor wasn't just the love of my life. The universe picked us out to be together. To conceive you. Don't think my spells to give birth to his children would have worked if we hadn't been destined to be together. If we hadn't been chosen to bring something wonderful into being. Something that could raise Midgard from the weakest of the nine worlds to the equal of Asgard or Jotunheim or Ljosalfheim. When you share that kind of bond with someone, you could never wish them dead. Never."

"And yet you said that it was our destiny to kill our own father, and Ingrid and Freya and all the old gods."

"I said it was the new gods' destiny," Mum said. Her

tone didn't really change but you could hear the scolding in it, and Mardi's eyes dropped to the floor of the cabin. "You two are the first. You will be the most powerful, and their queens, but that doesn't mean that the sword or the wand that finally strikes down Thor in a decade or a century or a millennium will be held in one of your hands."

Mum shrugged, as if to say these things weren't worth worrying about, and who knew, maybe for a mortal a hundred or a thousand years was such an overwhelming amount of time that it was inconceivable for her.

"Prophecies are a slippery business," she continued. "Much of their language is deeply symbolic, which means they're open to interpretation, and even then they often get some details wrong. According to all the legends, you two were supposed to be male, yet here you are, as beautiful and feminine as any two goddesses who ever lived. And yet the Council itself decreed that you were the foretold deities of strength and rage, and even your father agreed that you were the new gods that had been prophesied."

"Wait, Dad knows?" I turned to Mardi. "Did he say anything to you?"

"Nope," Mardi said in a closed-off tone. I wasn't sure if she was trying to suggest that Mum's statement wasn't to be trusted, or if she was trying to cover up the fact that she had had intimate conversations with Dad about our divine nature, which is something we'd never done on our own. I wanted to tell her it wasn't her fault. I was the one who'd run away, after all, at exactly the moment when there were all kinds of things we needed to learn from Dad. I could hardly expect her to wait for me.

"No doubt he didn't want to burden you, especially during the Reawakening."

"So Dad knows that Mardi and I, or our descendants, are supposed to kill him?"

Mum laughed. "I doubt he finds it quite as dramatic as the two of you did. Your father once told me that if he had a dollar for every prophecy about his demise at the hands of his father, his brother, his children, or some other of his relatives, he'd be a rich man."

"He already is a rich man," I joked.

"That's what I told him." Mum laughed. "At any rate, if he really was worried about the two of you killing him, he wouldn't have saved you this morning. Have you heard from him?"

"We can't get through," Mardi said. "We think someone—well, Ivan, I guess—cast some kind of spell that keeps us from communicating with other immortal beings, or at least the ones in the East End. Would a spell like that still work even with Ivan dead?"

"If he used an energy source like a lodestar or a moonstone to power it, it would. If he relied on his own energy, the spell should have died with him." At the last words, Mum's voice cracked. "I still can't believe he would do such a thing to my daughters. He served my family for so long—ever since the Council liberated us from our vassalage. In many ways, I knew him better than my own parents. I never once questioned his loyalty. But I guess the hearts of immortal beings are different." She looked up with a startled expression, as if just remembering that her daughters were also immortal. "Just promise me that when you come into your full powers, you won't forget about your poor old mum."

I felt a knot in my stomach. The lights flickered again, and I was sure it was me until I glanced over and saw Mardi's white knuckles gripping the arm of her seat.

I took a moment to calm myself, then I said, "Will he come back? Like we do, if our Midgardian bodies are destroyed?"

"I don't know," Mum said, a strange mixture of loss and anger and fear in her voice. "I know it's never happened before. But elves manifest differently. Their bodies are much more powerful, their magic more concentrated in them, and less dependent on material aids like wands and powders and all that. But to the best of my knowledge, he probably is really, truly gone . . ."

Her voice trailed off, and for a moment, she just sat there, her face sad at first, then angry again, and then she shook her head and smiled brightly.

"So you haven't spoken to your father at all?" she asked, clearly changing the subject.

I shook my head. "I told you. We tried calling . . . but if Ivan was behind this, his hex still seems to be in effect, even though we're not in the East End."

"It's probably because Troy's there," Mum said. "Hold on," she added, and got up and walked to the small table at the far end of the cabin. There was a set of cabinets behind it, and she opened one and pulled out a phone.

"What's Ingrid's number?"

Mardi and I looked at each other, then laughed. We may be goddesses, but neither of us had memorized her number, and I had to pull it out of my phone.

Mum dialed and a moment later sang out, "Ingrid Beauchamp. It's been years since I've heard your voice."

She grimaced then and held the phone away from her ear.

"They're fine," she said loudly, obviously speaking over Ingrid. "They're fine," she repeated. "They're sitting right here in front of me. I'm afraid they can't come to the phone. Ivan seems to have cast some kind of spell interfering with their ability to use electronic devices—no doubt he was piggybacking on Joanna's hexes around the East End." She sighed. "Girls, yell something so Ingrid knows you're all right."

"Hi, Ingrid!" we both yelled at the same.

"We're fine!" I added, grinning at the mental image of Ingrid's disapproving-librarian frown.

"Satisfied?" Mum said. "Anyway, we were calling to say we're on the way home, and to thank Troy for—what?" she interrupted herself, or, I guess, responded to an interruption from Ingrid. "Oh, my gods. Is he—"

I flashed an alarmed look at Mardi. Was Mum talking about Dad? Had something happened?

"I see," Mum said. "I'll tell the girls. We should be back in North Hampton in about three hours. I'll send them straight over."

She hung up the phone.

"What happened?" Mardi almost yelled.

"I want you to calm yourselves, girls. No need to bring the plane down."

"What happened?" I said, doing my best to keep my emotions under control.

"It's your dad," Mum said. "I'm afraid the spell he cast against Ivan was too much for his body to handle in its weakened state. He's fallen into a coma. Ingrid doesn't know if he's going to wake up."

* 26 *

GOD OF THUNDER

Mardi-Overbrook-Journal.docx

$\mathcal{G}$irls!" Ingrid yelled in a voice louder than I'd ever heard her use before. "Oh, thank gods, you're home!"

She threw her arms around us in a bear hug that would have crushed a mortal's ribs and moved her lips back and forth from one of our cheeks to the other, kissing us over and over.

"I knew something was terribly wrong," she said when she finally let us go. "I just had this feeling. A pit in my stomach as though I'd swallowed poison. I called Freya and she felt it too, but when we tried to get ahold of you, all our calls went straight to voice mail. And then your dad—" She broke off. Her eyes dropped to the floor. "Your dad just screamed, 'Not my daughters!' The whole house shook. I mean *shook*." She pointed, showing us dozens of cracks in the plaster, as well as a half dozen broken vases and pots that had sat on shelves and on top of credenzas and sideboards. "I ran upstairs and he was in some kind . . . some kind of trance. His lips were moving, but I only caught the occasional word. 'Storm Caller' and 'Lightning Bearer,' which are some of your father's names in Old Norse. It sounded like he was summoning a storm, but the sky remained perfectly clear. It was where you were, wasn't it? He called a storm to save you, from whatever was threatening you."

"A killer whale," I said.

"A killer elf," Molly said at the same time.

"A shape-shifter!" Ingrid said. "One of the Fallen Elves!"

"The what now?" I said.

"Millennia ago, during the war between the Aesir and the Jotun, Odin called for allies among the nine worlds. The dwarfs took the side of the giants, but the elves took our side. All save a few, led by Johan, the king's son, who had the power of shape-shifting."

"Johan?" Molly said doubtfully. "Ivan maybe?"

Ingrid nodded her head. "After the Jotun and their allies were defeated, Johan was said to have taken refuge among the tribes of the east, which meant the Russians. Ivan is the Slavic word for Johan—John."

"Well, John or Johan or Ivan or whatever you want to call him is pretty dead right now," I said. "Dad's lightning bolt ripped a hole in his chest the size of . . . well, does it matter how big it was? It was a hole."

"Do you know if he'll come back?" Molly asked. "Are the elves like us?"

"I'm afraid so," Ingrid said. "Somewhere out there, he's invaded some poor woman's womb. He'll colonize a newly fertilized embryo before it has time to form a soul, and the parents will end up raising a demon as their own child. There are ways to find it, though. We can kill him before he's ever born. We'll kill him over and over again if we have to!"

Ingrid's eyes were so wide they were ringed by white. Her nostrils flared, and her lips were practically frothing. I'd never seen her like this. Who knew the goddess of the hearth had the heart of a warrior?

"Let's worry about that later," Molly said. "How's Dad?"

And all at once, the bravado was gone. Ingrid's whole body bowed as if someone had dropped a hay bale on her shoulders. I reached out to her, half afraid she was going to sink to the floor. But beneath my hand, Ingrid's arm was as hard as steel.

"I don't know," she said in a muted voice. "After he cast his spell, he never came out of his trance. He seemed conscious at first, though delirious, but then his eyes closed. I'd say he's in a coma, but that's a human term. Dr. Mésomier says it's more like a state of suspended animation. He's breathing about once per minute, and his temperature's barely seventy degrees."

"Is there some kind of magic that can help him?" I asked.

Ingrid shook her head. "It's not his body. His body's fine. Weak, but uninjured. Still he expended so much of his magical essence on that spell that he's . . . lost, is how Jean-Baptiste put it."

"Lost?" Molly repeated in a terrified tone. "What does that mean?"

Ingrid shrugged helplessly. "Jean-Baptiste says that your father's soul is wandering between planes right now. If everything works out, he'll find his way back to his Midgardian body. But if he takes a wrong turn or gets confused, he could end up in Niflheim."

"In Hel," I said.

"Wait," Molly interjected. "Do you mean *forever*? Do you mean Dad could . . . could actually *die*?"

Ingrid just stared at us miserably. "Oh, girls. I'm so sorry."

Molly and I didn't say anything, but I felt her fingers curl around mine and we took off for the stairs. Molly's hatred of exercise is boundless, but she ran so fast, Usain Bolt would have been left in her dust. It was all I could do to keep up.

But as soon as we burst into Jo's room, we came to a full stop as though we'd run into a wall. Dad's body on the bed just looked so . . . so . . .

"Is he dead?" Molly asked in a horrified voice.

"No!" I said harshly. "We'd know. We'd feel it."

Molly nodded, but she moved slowly as she approached the bed, as if she was afraid that I was wrong. Jo had a miniature peacock chair woven from white rattan with a tufted pink cushion on it, and Molly pulled this up to the bed and sat in it gingerly. Ingrid or someone had pulled the pink blanket up to Dad's chest, and his arms lay atop it. Tentatively, Molly picked up one of his hands.

Of course I wanted to run to Dad too, but I held back to give Molly her moment. It was the first time she'd seen him in a full month. As much as I needed to feel my father's hand in mine, she needed it more. Unlike me, Molly had gone off to live with Mum, but I'd stayed at Ingrid's with Dad.

"It's cold," Molly said in a hushed voice. She looked up at me with a small, determined smile on her face. "But it still feels like Dad."

I took that as my cue and grabbed a small silver gilded stool with yet another pink cushion and crossed to the other side of the bed. I sat down tentatively, not sure if the stool's thin, curly metal legs would hold my weight. When it didn't buckle beneath me, I relaxed into it and grabbed Dad's other hand.

Molly was right. It was cold. Not frigid, but chilly, as if he'd been walking outside in the winter with no gloves. But it was supple, and even though it didn't respond to my touch, you could still feel the strength in the muscles. This was the same hand that had once punched a hole through a brick wall and thrown a baseball a full mile. It was the hand that had held Thor's hammer.

"It definitely feels like Dad," I said.

For a long time, we sat there like that, Molly holding Dad's right hand, me holding his left, inhaling and exhaling in unison, as though we could fill his lungs with our breath. Then I had to ruin it all by speaking.

"This is what a real parent does."

Molly started at the sound of my voice, and I wondered if she'd dozed off.

"What are you talking about?"

"A real parent loves you so much he knows when you're in danger. He risks his own life to save yours."

Molly looked at me warily. "I don't get it. Are you saying Mum wouldn't do this for us?"

"Well, where was she when Ivan was trying to have us for dinner?"

"Have you for dinner, you mean? And you know where she was—she was giving an interview to ESPN Australia."

"Listen to yourself. 'Giving an interview to ESPN Australia.' She said on the plane that she knew Ivan wanted me dead. She should have never left us alone with him."

Molly looked shocked. "It's not like she thought he would actually try anything. He'd served her family for generations. Hundreds of years. Why would she think he'd betray her now?"

"Why?" I repeated incredulously. "Why? Because he *said* he would, that's why!"

"I can't believe this! After everything that's happened,

you still think Mum was in on it. You think—you think your own mother wanted you dead."

"That's not all I think," I shot back. "I think she wanted Dad dead too. I think she was trying to jump-start this whole god war thing, maybe get it out of the way in her lifetime."

Molly's knuckles went white around Dad's, and I was surprised I didn't hear bones crack.

"What are you even *talking* about?"

"Think about it," I said. "Mum knew Dad was weak. She knew he would sense that we were in danger, and that it would take an extra-strength spell for him to summon a storm from a thousand miles away. So she conveniently makes herself scarce, gets Ivan to take his killer whale form and attack us, and waits for Dad to do himself in. It's the perfect plan—no one can link it to her."

"That's because there's no link!" Molly almost yelled. "You just made the whole thing up! Mum told us—she still loves Dad. Maybe not in an I-want-to-get-back-with-him kind of way, but certainly not in an I-want-to-kill-him way either."

"My gods, Molly. It's staring you in the face, and you refuse to see it. When are you going to stop taking her side, and remember who your real family is? She tried to kill me! She tried to kill Dad!"

Molly's jaw dropped open. "How dare you suggest that I don't love Dad as much as you do! That I don't love you!"

"Well, if you do, you've sure got a funny way of showing it!"

"Oh, my gods! You're jealous! That's what it is. For once in my life, I have something that you don't have, and you can't stand it! You get the Ferrari, you get the rad tattoos, you get Freya, you get Tyr. You always get everything! Well, guess what? Mum likes me better than you, and you know why? Because I'm not a selfish brat like you!"

"Selfish!" I screamed, jumping up so fast that the stool rolled away across the room. "Selfish!" I screamed again. "All my life I've carried you, and you call me selfish! Talk about the pot calling the kettle black!"

"Really!" Molly said contemptuously, standing up so that she was on my level. She leaned over Dad's prostrate body and shoved her face in mine. "Were you carrying me when you tried to steal Rocky?"

"Ha!" I screamed back, leaning toward her so that our noses were practically touching and I could feel her hot breath on my face. "You can't steal the willing!"

"WHAT?" Molly yelled, and at the same time, I heard a tiny, sharp *pop!* followed by a little tinkle, and realized that she'd exploded all the lightbulbs in the room.

"You heard me!" I yelled back as a whiff of smoke filled my nostrils. Out of the corner of my eye, I could see thin tendrils of smoke curling out of the electrical sockets in the wall. "I didn't have to steal him because he liked me better!"

"OH!" Molly screamed, and stamped her foot so hard

that every single stuffed animal and book fell off the shelves in Jo's room. "HOW! DARE! YOU!"

"Girls, please," a faint voice said somewhere below us. "It would be terribly rude to burn down Ingrid's house after all she's done for us."

"I'll burn it down if I want to!" I yelled, and only after the words were out of my mouth did I realize who I was yelling at.

"Dad!" Molly screamed. "Dad, you're awake!"

"Girls, what's going on up here?" Ingrid's voice came from the hall. "I was using my brand-new KitchenAid mixer, and the motor just—Thor!" she interrupted herself as her flour-covered form appeared in the door. "Oh, thank Odin!"

She ran toward the bed, but there was no room for her to get in, because Molly and I had both thrown ourselves on Dad.

"Girls, please," Dad said, laughing weakly. "I just managed to get myself out of the astral plane. Please don't smother me and send me back there."

"You're okay!" I yelled. "Oh, Dad, you're okay."

"I'm fine," Dad said. "Or I will be, once I get one of Ingrid's smoothies in me. That storm took a lot out of me."

"You're going to get more than a smoothie," Ingrid said, beaming. "I've got a wild boar in the freezer downstairs. We're eating Valhalla style tonight! Assuming any of my appliances still work," she added, casting a baleful look at me and Molly.

"I'm sorry," I said. I tried to catch Molly's eye, but she refused to look at me. "I guess I was just overwrought and got carried away."

"It's okay," Dad said. "It was your voices that brought me back. The dulcet tones of home," he added, laughing.

"Overwrought?" Molly said, her eyes suddenly boring into me. "That sounds like a typical Mardi excuse."

"Molly," Ingrid said in a warning voice. "This isn't the time for fighting. Your father's very weak."

"Her father will be fine," Dad said. "But he wouldn't mind a slight reduction in volume."

"Things'll get a whole lot quieter when I go back to Fair Haven," Molly said.

"Molly, no!" Ingrid said. "You've only just gotten home. And I'm making a big dinner to celebrate your father's recovery."

"I'm sure it'll be delicious, Ingrid. Maybe I can have some leftovers tomorrow. But there's no way I'm sitting down at the same table with this traitor who calls herself my sister."

"Are you serious?" I said. "Dad, tell her she can't go!"

But Dad just looked at Molly with sad but respectful eyes.

"I'm afraid this is Molly's call. If she feels like she needs to stand by your mother, I'm not going to stand in the way of that."

"But she tried to kill you!"

"Maybe," Dad said. "It wouldn't be the first time

someone's tried to kill me. Hel, it's not even the first time this summer. But she's still your mother."

Molly looked as confused as I felt, as if she'd been expecting Dad to order her to stay.

"You're not mad at her?" she asked Dad.

"Whatever beef your mom and I have, it's between us, and you shouldn't let it affect your relationship with her. I hid her from you for seventeen years. I'm not going to keep making the same mistake."

My eyes flashed back and forth between Dad and Molly.

"Molly," I said in an urgent whisper, "get over yourself."

Molly's eyes jerked up to meet mine. I could see her brain searching for something to say.

"You get over yourself," she said finally, in a half-defeated voice, as if she knew how lame her comeback was.

And then she ran from the room.

✳ 27 ✳

SAVE THE BEST FOR LAST

From the Diary of Molly Overbrook

$\mathscr{B}$y ten o'clock the next morning I was at the Cheese-monger. It had been a miserable night. In the first place, when I ran out of Ingrid's house, I found myself standing in her front yard with no way to get anywhere. Ingrid lives a couple of miles outside of North Hampton, and a good ten miles from Gardiners Island, so I was not about to walk. I'm not Mardi. I could always call a cab, but I didn't want to just stand around in Ingrid's front yard for twenty minutes waiting for it to get there. So I ended up having to walk something like a half mile down the road to the next house, where I called a cab, and then I stood around like some crazy stalker until it arrived to pick me up.

Then, when I got back to Fair Haven, I discovered that Mum wasn't there. I went through the whole house looking for her. That probably doesn't sound strange to you, but Fair Haven is a really big house, and I'd never actually gone through the whole thing before, even though I'd lived there for more than a month now. I discovered that Mum's room was the only other furnished room in the house, although all the furniture was brand-new and looked like it had never been used. And who knew, maybe it hadn't? Or, like, only one or two times—she'd been on the road almost every day since she'd bought the place. What surprised me was that her suitcases weren't there. Ivan had left the Maybach at the East Hampton airport when we'd gone to the BH, and she drove me and Mardi to Ingrid's and told us she was coming back here. But even if the car was in the garage and its trunk was empty, and my suitcases were in my bedroom, there was no sign of Mum or her luggage anywhere. I looked in all twenty-seven rooms of the mansion. I even poked my head into the east wing. The part of the house that had been featured in my dream, which held the kitchen and the servants' quarters. I'd been in the kitchen, of course, many times, but I'd never ventured beyond it. Even though it was the servants' wing, I expected something pretty grand because once upon a time, it had actually been the original house.

But to my surprise, it was run-down and filthy. Not, like, dirty, but filled with dirt—and leaves and twigs and branches and a lot of little white things that looked like animal bones. And that was just the hallway. The rooms off it were even worse. The glass had been broken out of the windows and, judging by the piles of poop and fur and feathers, it looked like raccoons and crows and whatever else had been going in and out for who knew how long. But way before Mum had taken over the place. This surprised me, to say the least. It was hard to imagine Trent's mother allowing this kind of squalor in her house, even if it was a part she wasn't using. These were supposed to be servants' quarters. The Gardiners had employed a dozen people, and Mum had said she'd kept a few of them. Yet clearly they weren't living here, and after poking my nose in three or four rooms, I finally gave up and headed back to the normal part of the house.

Somehow I got turned around, though, and instead of coming out into the kitchen where I went in, I ended up in the ballroom. I guess I knew that the ballroom abutted the east wing, but I'd never realized the servants' wing actually "communicated" with it, as they used to say. But there I was, and as I stared at the doors on the opposite side of the room, the ones that opened onto the front hall, I realized that the last time I'd been in this room had been in my dream, and I had a sudden creepy chill that I'd somehow crossed into that other dimension, the one I'd felt in my dream. I made my way gingerly across the room, as if at any moment I might slip back into that strange place.

I got there without incident, closed the doors behind me and made my way back toward the kitchen. It was dinnertime, and the only thing I'd had all day was a few berries for breakfast and the champagne on the plane, so I was pretty ravenous.

When I walked into the kitchen, I got an answer to at least one of my questions. Because there, on the counter, was my favorite meal: a sushi platter with a small garden salad and a bowl of miso soup on the side. The food was laid out on the same china I'd been eating from since I'd moved into Fair Haven, and there were no take-out containers in the trash. The soup was piping hot, and the shrimp and unagi (that's eel, if you're not a big sushi eater) were fully cooked, but the stove and the oven were both ice cold. The food hadn't been delivered, in other words, but it hadn't been made here either. So Mum hadn't employed a staff, after all. She'd used magic. That explained why the servants' wing had been allowed to fall into disrepair, although I was curious why Mum had tried to cover up the fact that she was running the house with magic rather than with people. Maybe it contravened some Council ruling I didn't know about? Yet another thing I wanted to talk to my mother about, but unfortunately, she was nowhere to be found.

And, though I waited till two in the morning, she never showed up. Or at least I think she never showed up—Fair Haven is easily big enough that a whole crew of people could come and go without being heard. But I waited in Mum's room, picking at my sushi off and on and going through a couple of bottles of sake, until I finally fell asleep in the middle of a *Gilmore Girls* marathon.

Needless to say, I had the dream again. I mean, between the scare with Dad, the fight with Mardi, Mum's disappearance, and actually going into the east wing, it was bound to happen. I made it across the puddle-filled yard and negotiated the ruined floorboards in the hallway as before, pulled off the door to the ballroom and found myself faced with the same strange dimensional shift as before. This time I forced myself to go all the way into the ballroom, where once again it morphed into that strange curving tunnel. The light was burning at the end of it. The woman's shadow was visible, projected on the wall. Her voice echoed to me.

"Mooi, is that you? Mooi? Are you there?"

"Mum?" I called back. "Mum, is that you?"

"Mooi," the voice called to me. "Go back. It's not safe here."

I still couldn't tell if the voice was Mum's, but something about the way it said *go back* had the opposite effect on me. Whoever was saying it was in distress, was in danger, and for some reason, I felt like I had to help her. I went barreling down the hallway.

"I'm coming! Hold on, I'll be right there!"

"Mooi, no! Go back! You shouldn't have to see this!"

By then I was almost at the end of the hall, and I didn't bother answering. Just charged forward around the last bit of curve. The light was stronger there, but I still couldn't see the source. The shadow on the wall was at least twelve feet tall, but I couldn't see what was casting it. As I ran the last couple of steps, I could see bits of doorframe poking through the mud and roots, I knew from my experience earlier in the evening that I was running out of the ballroom and into the oldest part of the house. *This is it!* I told myself. *I'm finally going to figure out what this dream is trying to tell me.*

But instead of seeing the light source or whoever was casting that shadow and warning me away, all I saw was . . .

Mum's bedroom.

I was wide awake, standing in the middle of the room as if I'd been sleepwalking. But then, when I looked down at my feet, I saw it was more than that.

My feet were covered with mud and leaves, and when I scraped them off, I realized they were ice cold— my feet and ankles were so numb that I could barely even feel them.

I was so freaked out that I ran into Mum's bathroom and hopped in the shower and turned on the water even before I had my clothes off. I stripped and scrubbed myself with lavender-scented soap under the steaming water until even my Asgardian skin was tinted bright pink. Then I toweled myself off with one of Mum's six-foot-long bath sheets until I was bone dry, wrapped the sheet around myself and skipped back through the eerily empty hallways to my room. It was almost nine, I saw when I checked my phone, and I decided to head into town for a cup of coffee and a croissant. I dressed and headed downstairs to the garage, but I had to go through the kitchen to get there, and there, on the counter, was the cup of coffee I'd been craving.

"Uh-uh," I said to the steaming cup. "No magical food today."

The key to the Maserati was hanging on a peg in the garage, and I grabbed it and hopped in, pressed the garage door opener, and backed out so fast I almost ripped the top of my head off on the bottom of the door, which had only raised itself halfway up. I spun out on the gravel parking lot and shot down the mile-long driveway at a hundred miles an hour—or, if not exactly a hundred miles an hour, then fast enough that Mardi would've been impressed—and didn't slow down until I was back on the North Fork.

And it's not like I was heading to the Cheesemonger. The Cheesemonger just happened to be between me and the Last Cup Before Europe (which claimed to be the easternmost coffee shop on Long Island), the only place in North Hampton that can make a soy hazelnut latte that doesn't taste like a cross between a McDonald's milk shake and a Styrofoam peanut. But when I saw the Cheesemonger's awning, something made me stop. I don't know, maybe it was the empty angle-in parking spot right in front. In the past month, I'd gotten pretty good at driving forward and, you know, turning left and turning right, but reverse was like a whole other language. What I mean is, I can't parallel-park worth a damn, and when I saw the spot, I grabbed it.

As I marched up to the front door, I saw that it was

still dark inside the shop. I glanced at my watch. It was a few minutes before ten. When I was running the shop with Marshall, we always got here a half hour early so that we'd be good to go at ten. But I guess Mardi and Rocky ran a looser shop.

Well, screw that, I said to myself.

I pushed on the door. The lock held for a moment, but a teenage goddess in need of her first cup of java of the day isn't going to be put off for long. I felt a thump beneath my fingers as the dead bolt dropped out of its slot and the door fell open. The morning's bread delivery—baguettes and bagels and croissants and, if they were still getting them, the best apricot-ricotta Danish you've ever tasted—sat in a bag beside the door, just waiting for someone to come along for it. I grabbed it and made my way inside, past the shadowed tables covered with pine-scented crackers and jars of kohlrabi pickled in ginger, caraway, and pomegranate brine, straight to the counter. Though I'd only been in the shop once in the past year—and that just to fight with Mardi—I still remembered where everything was. I measured the beans, ground them, fired up the La Marzocco espresso machine and, while my double shot was dripping, poured some soy milk into a pitcher and frothed it into a fluffy cloud. Five minutes after I'd entered the store, I had a steaming latte in my hand. The first coffee I'd brewed in a year.

Nervously, I took a sip.

"Girl, you still got it," I said out loud. I took another sip. "Damn, that's good."

And of course I could've just grabbed a Danish from the bag and taken off, let Mardi and Rocky try to figure out why the door was open and the espresso machine was warm. Instead, I walked over to the light switches and flipped them on, and then I unloaded the bag of bread into its various baskets and fluffed some gingham napkins over them to keep them fresh, and then I wandered back to the walk-in and grabbed the spreads—a dozen different kinds of butters and cream cheeses and honeys, a dozen more kinds of jams and jellies and preserves—and set them in their slots on the cooler table. Somewhere in there, I must've grabbed an apron out of habit, and by the time I'd done that, I knew I was there for the day. Coffee in hand, I made my way around the shop, refamiliarizing myself with the store's exotic and esoteric comestibles and generally making things pretty.

Thank the gods I wore flats today.

My first customer came in at 10:05. I was halfway through his order—a toasted pumpernickel-raisin bagel with a cranberry cream cheese schmear—when the bell over the front door tinkled, followed a moment later by a hushed but still distinct gasp.

"M-Molly?"

I didn't look up, but I knew it was Rocky. In fact, I think I'd known Rocky was coming when he was halfway down the block because the bagel in my hand was smoking, and I hadn't yet run it through the toaster.

"Miss," my customer said, "that bagel seems to be burnt."

Just the way he said *burnt* annoyed me. Move to England if you want to say *burnt*. We're American. We say *burned*.

I looked up at the customer. He was a middle-aged man wearing a green pencil-striped button-down tucked over his huge belly into a pair of pleated khaki shorts. He only had about eight strands of hair, but he had at least as much product on them as I use, and his bronzer was sweating off his neck and staining his collar brown. In other words: a banker.

I hate bankers.

"Something tells me you like burned bagels," I said to him in a flat voice.

"I . . . like burned bagels?" he repeated in a confused voice.

"In fact, you probably wish this bagel was more burned. You probably wish it was on fire." I held up the bagel on its plate and it obligingly burst into flame.

"I like my bagels burnt," the man said.

"*Burned.* You like them *burned.*"

"I like them *burned,*" he repeated, nodding his jowly chin like a deflating air puppet.

I clapped the two halves of the charred bagel closed. The flames went out in a puff of acrid smoke, and I handed it over to him like that. No bag, no schmear.

"That'll be twenty—no, fifty—bucks," I said.

The man pulled out his wallet and dropped three twenties on the counter.

"I assume the ten is my tip," I said in my sweetest, snidest voice.

"I like my bagel burned!" the man sang out, and all but skipped out of the store.

Throughout all this, Rocky hadn't said another word, and I hadn't acknowledged his presence. But once the customer was out of the store, he turned to me incredulously and said, "What—?"

"Just happened?" I finished for him, even as he said, "—are you doing here?"

He added, "And yeah, what just happened?"

What just happened was that I'd broken at least half a dozen Council rules about using magic in front of mortals—and using magic on mortals—in a non-life-threatening situation, but all I said to Rocky was "Must've turned the toaster up too high. You know those banker pervs. They're all masochists—they love it when a pretty girl abuses them."

Rocky just looked at me for a minute, clearly disbelieving what he'd just seen, and I found myself contemplating putting a hex on him to make him forget what had just happened. I could do it gently, whispering a few words over some valerian leaves and dropping them in a glass of iced tea, or I could do it roughly, literally pushing the thoughts out of his brain with an image of my own making. But though one would leave a little psychic scar and the other would give him nothing more than a headache, both felt wrong to me for some reason. I had cared for Rocky. You didn't treat people you liked this way. Before I had to choose between two equally unpleasant options, however, he shook his head.

"Okay, then, that's one question. And question two?"

"The what-am-I-doing-here question?" I stalled. He nodded. "Didn't you get the memo? I work here."

Another long stare, followed eventually by another shake of the head. Without another word, he headed to the back room to drop off his backpack and came out wearing a Cheesemonger apron. You know the old saying about the tension being so thick you could cut it with a knife? Well, we were in a cheese shop. I'd say it was somewhere between a firm feta and a hard Havarti. But all Rocky said was:

"You started on Billy and Bruce's order yet?"

"Are they still getting all those Anthony Weiners?"

"A dozen. Plus a dozen Marilyn Monroes."

"How gay men can eat so much red meat and mayo and stay so thin is beyond me," I said, pulling out a platter of pepper-crusted roast beef and a tub of dill-infused aioli.

Rocky didn't say anything, but the corner of his mouth twitched.

"Was that a smile?" I teased.

Rocky's mouth twitched again. His lips actually curled this time, and I caught a glimpse of teeth.

He laid out twenty-four slices of rye bread and began

spreading horseradish mustard on every other slice. I followed along behind him with the aioli.

Rocky started to slice the roast beef into wafer-thin shavings, and I laid on the red and brown slices of prepared bread like a maid in a boutique hotel making the bed with Yves Delorme sheets. I tried to imagine what the name of this color would be. Lipstick-and-Tobacco, I thought, or Cranberry Iced Tea. Or who knows: Rare Roast Beef.

I laughed again.

"What's so funny?" Rocky said.

"I couldn't even explain it if I wanted to. Let's just say that if I can't build a career out of making sammies and coffee, I can always try to come up with product names for bedsheets."

Rocky looked at me like I was crazy, but crazy in a good way. He stared at me with a confused but gleeful, goofy grin on his face, framed by crescent moon dimples. And then the smile faded and his dimples disappeared, like a crazy double eclipse.

A line from that old Vanessa Williams song popped into my head. *Sometimes the sun goes 'round the moon . . .*

"Molly," Rocky said, "what happened to us?"

I knew he didn't mean the customer from ten minutes ago.

He meant what had happened to us after we'd watched the Wimbledon final and celebrated by losing our virginity to each other, and then I'd disappeared.

What had happened? I thought to myself.

I thought about telling him that what had happened was that he and I had met right when my mother had resurfaced in my life, and as great as he was, he couldn't really compete with her. Couldn't compete with any mother, but the fact that my mother just happened to be Janet Steele made it that much harder for him to stand out.

But I knew that wasn't true.

I thought about telling him that my mother's major-domo was so jealous of her daughters that he cast a spell on their phones so they couldn't contact anyone. Just to screw with them. But aside from the fact that I knew I couldn't tell Rocky that, I knew it wasn't true either.

I thought about telling him the truth: that I'd fallen in love with the sweetest, funniest, sexiest, good-hair-having boy I'd ever met, but he was mortal. A mortal who I knew was going to die one day, while I'd still go on living year after year, and no matter how powerful my magic grew, the only thing I'd have left of him was a memory.

All of a sudden, I was filled with incredible respect for Ingrid. Respect, and sympathy. Because I knew that as much as I loved Rocky, she loved Matt a thousand times more, and she was still going to lose him and keep on living.

"Molly?" Rocky said in a nervous voice. "The look on your face is scaring me."

I looked up at him. Wide jaw. Full lips. Stubbled cheeks. Hair that any member of One Direction would kill for. And right then I knew that if I spent all my time worrying about the future, I'd never be able to enjoy my present. Eternity was going to be really freakin' miserable if I lived it that way.

"Nothing happened," I said. "I freaked out a little bit, I guess. It was my first time, you know."

He nodded goofily. "I remember," he said in a hushed voice.

"You damn well better," I said, and gave him a little shove.

"It was my first time too," he said, his voice even more hushed—husky—now.

"I remember," I said.

"You better," he said, and gave me a little shove. But he didn't let go when he pushed and ended up pulling me closer than I'd been a moment ago, until the fronts of our jeans were just touching. His hands were resting on my hips, and I could feel them trembling slightly, as he fought off the desire to crush my body against his.

"If you don't kiss me, I'm afraid your hair's going to catch fire like that bagel did."

"What?" he said confusedly. Then: "Oh, never mind," and his mouth closed over mine.

Because I'm a goddess, I can tell you that our kiss lasted exactly ninety-eight seconds. It would have gone on a lot longer than that, but then three things happened.

First, the bells over the door rang.

Then the toaster exploded.

And then a familiar voice rang out:

"Oops."

✳ 28 ✳

WAKE ME UP INSIDE

Mardi-Overbrook-Journal.docx

𝓐t the sound of my voice, Molly and Rocky had broken their lip-lock. They both stared at me in shock for a moment. Then Rocky whipped his head around toward the flaming toaster.

"Holy crap!" He jumped toward the fire, whose flames were racing toward a shelf of boxed teas. His hand darted out and pulled the plug on the toaster. Then he reached under the counter and pulled out a box of . . . baking soda, it turned out, which surprised me, to say the least. But when he vigorously shook the box over the flames, they began to sputter. Within a few seconds, the fire was out, nothing but a thick white smoke emanating from the counter like the aftermath of a stage magician's trick.

I saw all this out of the corner of my eye. My gaze

was focused on Molly, and her eyes never left mine. She watched me warily.

"Mardi, what are you talking about? What's wrong?"

I didn't know what to say, but something about seeing them together made me want to summon my father's lightning and hurl it somewhere.

"Mardi, calm down, you're not really jealous," Molly said. "You were just into him to get back at me over Mum."

"That's ridic—"

I was cut off by the piercing shriek of the smoke detector. My hand jumped up of its own accord, my fingers curled into a claw. The smoke detector exploded off the ceiling in a dozen pieces.

"What the Hell?" Rocky exclaimed into the sudden silence. "What is going on with this place today?"

A look of concern replaced the anger on Molly's face. "Mardi, what are you doing? You're going to get yourself busted by the Council!"

"What council?" Rocky asked. "Like, the city council?"

"Uh, not exactly," I said. "The White Council, which oversees supernatural beings and the use of magic."

"Mardi!" Molly said, darting a look at Rocky. There was a confused expression on his face, but then he let out a little nervous snort.

"Okay, this is going from uncomfortable to just weird. Maybe I should take off for a while, let you two work this out?"

"Stay where you are!" Molly barked.

Rocky froze in his tracks, and his eyes glazed over as though he was hypnotized. He wavered back and forth slightly, as if a breath of wind could knock him over. Molly looked startled. I don't think she'd intended to use magic, let alone turn Rocky into a zombie.

"Now who's trying to bring down the Council's wrath?" I smirked.

"Oh, crap," Molly said, ignoring me. She hurried over to Rocky and walked him backward a few steps until he was leaning against a counter. "Rocky? Babe, wake up."

It was the *babe* that got me. Even as Rocky started to blink rapidly, I said in a deep, powerful voice:

"Yes, Rocky, wake up. Wake up and let Molly explain to you how she used her powers to make you fall in love with her, then kicked you to the curb as soon as she got what she wanted!"

"Wh-what?" Rocky said, his eyes clear now, but still dazed.

"Are you *kidding* me?" Molly said. "If anyone used magic to seduce Rocky, it was *you*."

"Magic?" Rocky said, his face rotating from Molly to me and back again. "Babe, what are talking about?"

There it was again. *Babe.* In that one word, I knew I'd lost and Molly had won.

I opened my mouth, but Molly spoke first.

"Mardi, think about what you're about to say," she implored, nodding at Rocky. "We can still roll this back without having to resort to . . . other means."

"What, like wiping Rocky's memory?"

Rocky looked completely at sea now. "I must've inhaled too much smoke. What the Hell are you two talking about?"

And of course what really pissed me off was that I knew I should have lost. Knew I shouldn't have been fighting for Rocky in the first place. I was the one who'd used Rocky as a toy, a stand-in, not Molly. But I was overcome by a rage that felt like it had been building in me all my life. Not just seventeen years, but seventeen hundred. Seventeen thousand. And now, finally, I was going to let it out.

I whirled on Rocky.

"Don't know how to break it to you, *babe*, but the pair of sisters standing in front of you are witches. And not your garden-variety, sold-my-soul-to-Satan bubble-bubble-toil-and-trouble witches, but card-carrying goddesses of the Asgardian variety. Your *babe* beside you is really called Mooi, the goddess of strength, and I'm Magdi, the goddess of rage."

Molly's jaw dropped. I could see Rocky fighting to disbelieve me, but I'd put just enough magic in my voice that it was impossible. As surreal as my words were, he had no choice but to accept the truth behind them.

"Witches," he said, the way the character in *Jurassic Park* says *dinosaurs* the first time he sees a living, breathing one. "Goddesses."

Suddenly, Molly raised her hand and pointed it at him. "Sleep," she commanded.

Rocky's eyes rolled back in his head, and his knees buckled. Molly must've been accessing some of her goddess of strength power, however, because she caught him as if he was as light and precious as a Balenciaga gown slipping off its hanger. As if he were no bigger than a sleeping infant, she kneeled and laid him on the floor behind the counter.

"I think I know what's going on here," she said as she stood up again. "I think this is the Reawakening! Our powers are manifesting."

"Really?" I said skeptically, not because I didn't believe her but because I felt like being a bitch. "Whatever it is, it feels good." I waved my hand at a shelf and watched as jars and boxes flew across the room and shattered against the walls and floor.

"I'm serious, Mardi. You've got to get yourself under control. It's like the magical equivalent of hormones. It's not you who's doing this; it's chemicals, or energy or something. And every time you use your power, I can feel it triggering mine too."

"I don't know why you're complaining. Isn't this what Mum wants? For us to embrace our identity as goddesses? The Mimir? The saviors of Midgard?"

"Look around you. Does this like you're saving anything?"

Molly waved a hand at the store, which was in shambles. As she did, I could feel a wave of . . . something . . . an energy . . . a force . . . a pulse away from her, and still more items went sailing through the air. A horrified expression took over her face, and she snatched her hand back as if it had been shocked.

"What's happening?"

I threw back my head and laughed, and was rewarded with the sight of the pressed-tin ceiling buckling and tearing like wet paper.

"You called it, sister. It's the Reawakening." I threw out my arms and felt the whole store shudder. "Embrace it. It feels wonderful!"

"Mardi!" Molly screamed. "Stop!"

Another wave of power hit me, hard enough to send me reeling backward. I managed to stay on my feet, but the overstocked table beside me wasn't so lucky. It went flying *Real Housewives*-style across the room, nearly going through the plate glass window at the front of the store.

"That's how you want to play it?" I said. "Okay, let's do this!"

I flung out my hands. Molly was still on the far side of the counter, which shuddered and lurched and then rolled toward her, sending bowls and buckets and knives and forks clattering to the floor. Molly screamed in fear and jumped forward to catch it. She ignored all the little things, throwing herself at the counter itself, catching it with both hands before it tipped all the way over. It must've weighed twenty or thirty times what she did, though, and she was clearly struggling to hold it upright—especially since I was still using my power to push it forward.

"Goddess of strength, huh?" I said. "What do you say we put that to the test?" Squinting my eyes, I concentrated all my anger at the counter. The glass sneeze-guard shattered, and the tubular metal frame began bending like licorice.

"Mardi, stop!" Molly grunted. "You're going to hurt Rocky!"

"What?" I said, confused, but not so confused that I stopped pushing at the lopsided counter. "Rocky?" I'd completely forgotten about him. "Where's—?"

I was cut off by a loud *crack!* The marble slab on top of the counter had shattered into half a dozen pieces and begun falling to the floor on the far side of the counter. *Crash! Crash! Crash! Thud!*

Thud?

I figured it out a half second before Molly screamed.

"Rocky!"

Thud.

29

HIGHWAY TO "HEL"

From the Diary of Molly Overbrook

*C*rack!

The marble countertop broke into pieces and began falling to the floor, directly over Rocky's body. I wanted to swat them away, but I couldn't let go of the counter or it would fall on him and crush him. I tried pushing with my mind the way Mardi was, but I had to see the pieces clearly to affect them and there were too many and they were falling too fast. I managed to keep three of them from smashing into Rocky's chest and stomach and legs, but then there was a sickening thud at the other end of Rocky's body, and I whipped my face around just in time to see a massive piece of marble—at least a hundred pounds worth—falling off Rocky's head. His body twitched once, and then it settled into an eerie stillness.

"Rocky!"

I felt something move through me like a chill. My whole body shuddered, and the next thing I knew, the entire counter was flying through the air toward Mardi. I didn't see if it hit her, though, because I'd fallen to my knees next to Rocky.

"Rocky!" I screamed. "Rocky! Wake up!"

I could feel the magical force behind my words, but it didn't matter. Rocky didn't move. I snatched his wrist to feel for a pulse, but even as I did, I saw the . . . the dent in his forehead oozing with blood, and I realized it was hopeless. It was at least an inch deep, and bleeding profusely.

I whirled toward Mardi, who was extracting herself from the wreckage of the counter with a dazed expression on her face.

"What—what happened?" She seemed genuinely mystified.

"What happened?" I screamed. "YOU! KILLED! ROCKY!"

My voice was so loud that the windows at the front of the store shattered outward. Some part of my brain heard the squeal of brakes and a few startled shouts, but my rage was still focused on Mardi—who seemed to have no idea what she'd done.

"What? No. No!"

But the answer was lying dead at my feet.

Mardi stood up as if to run toward us, but one look at my face stopped her.

"Stay back!" I yelled, grabbing Rocky in my arms.

"What's going on in here?" a voice said behind Mardi. A sixtysomething woman in rubber boots and gardening gloves had appeared in the glassless window. "Is everyone okay?"

Mardi spun around.

"Fire!" she yelled.

I heard the magic in her voice and felt static electricity prickling the air around my skin. For a moment, I thought the whole store was going to burst into flame, but instead, it burst into smoke—thick, blinding bolts of black smoke that filled the entire space.

Suddenly, I heard Mardi's voice at my side.

"Out the back," she hissed. *"Now."*

Part of me wanted to hurl her away, but another part knew she was right. Rocky's body was still in my arms, and I turned and ran into the back room and then out the back door, Mardi hard on my heels.

The first thing I saw when I was outside was her Ferrari. I ran to it and propped up Rocky's body in the passenger seat.

"We've got to get him to Ingrid," Mardi was saying. "She might be able—"

"Haven't you done enough?" I snapped.

"Molly, please," Mardi begged, her eyes brimming with tears. "You have to let me fix this!"

"Fix this?" I sneered. "It's way too late to fix anything." I was already running to the driver's side of the car, but even as I reached for the door handle, I remembered: Mardi's car was a stick, and I had no idea how to drive it. I kicked the door in frustration, knocking a massive dent in the metal.

"What are you doing? Where are you going?"

"We've got to get to Fair Haven," I said.

"What? Why?"

"Because that's where Rocky's headed. Are you going to drive me, or do I have to destroy your transmission?"

"What are you talking about?" Mardi said, her face a mask of bewilderment. And then her eyes bulged. "Wait, you mean—"

I nodded. "The seam. Niflheim."

Mardi shook her head in terror and disbelief.

"What are you planning to do?"

"I'm going after him," I said. "I'm going to the Underworld."

I don't remember the drive to Fair Haven. I just remember squatting in the back of Mardi's car and reaching around the passenger seat to hold Rocky in place so that he didn't hit his head when Mardi screeched around a corner or stomped on the brakes. There's something really ridiculous about that, I know, given the size of the dent in his forehead. Given the fact that he was already dead. But although I didn't know if I'd be able to follow his soul through the seam into Niflheim—let alone drag it back—the one thing I could do was keep any further damage from happening to his body.

Then we were sliding to a stop on the gravel path. The first thing I saw when I got out of the car was the skid marks I'd left when I headed out that morning, less than two hours before. It seemed amazing to me that so much had changed in such a short time.

I swept up Rocky in my arms and ran for the door.

"Molly," Mardi said, running along after. "I'm sorry. I'm so—"

"Don't talk," I said. "Just—don't talk."

"I have to talk," Mardi said. "I have to apologize. I have to help. You have to let me make this right."

"You want to help? Open the door."

Mardi just stared at me helplessly for a moment, then turned and grabbed the door handle. I half expected it to fly off its hinges, but either Fair Haven was more sturdy than the Cheesemonger or Mardi was getting herself under control, because all that happened was that the door flew open and banged against the interior wall.

I ran in, heading straight for the ballroom. Mardi ran ahead of me and threw the door open.

"Do you even know where the entrance to the seam is?" she asked as I laid Rocky's body on the floor as gently as I could.

"I think we've already gone in it," I said.

"What do you mean?" Mardi asked, her head whipping from side to side as if the ornate walls of the ballroom might suddenly disappear, replaced by the ice sheets of Niflheim.

"You've seen it in the dream. I know you have."

A frightened look came over Mardi's face. "You mean the tunnel? With the light at the end."

I nodded. "I don't think it's a question of finding the seam. It's a question of knowing how to use it."

"And how do you do that?"

"Not me. Us."

"Us?" I could hear the confusion in Mardi's voice, the fear. But underneath that, I knew she understood.

"We've been having the same dream," I said. "We see the house, ruined. We come into the ballroom and find ourselves in a tunnel. We see the light at the end. But every time we go toward it, we wake up. I think it's because we can't go through it alone. We have to go together."

"Our power," Mardi said, nodding. "It's stronger when we're together." She glanced down at Rocky's body. I could tell she didn't want to, but she couldn't stop herself. "It's too strong."

"That's a risk we have to take. If we're going to save Rocky, we're only going to do it together."

I stared at her, a question on my face that I couldn't put into words. Finally, Mardi nodded.

"Okay," she said. She held out her hand, and I took it. I could feel an electrical charge run through my body.

"Now what?" Mardi said.

"Now we dream," I said.

Mardi nodded again and closed her eyes. I closed mine.

"I can see the tunnel," I said.

For a moment, there was nothing. And then I felt a cold puff of air on my skin. The ground seemed to soften beneath my feet, and then it went hard again, but it was a different kind of hardness. Before, it had been smooth, polished wood, and now it was slightly uneven, like rough-hewn stone or chopped ice. An odor came to my nostrils. It wasn't stinky or anything like that. It wasn't even unpleasant. It was just . . . cold.

I opened my eyes. The frozen mud walls of the tunnel were all around me.

"Mardi."

She opened her eyes.

"You did it," she breathed in awe.

We did it, I thought, but I didn't say it out loud because I was still too furious at her. But then I realized that if this was going to work, we would have to put aside our anger. For now at least.

"We did it," I said.

"We haven't done anything yet," she said, nodding at the far end of the tunnel. "We still have to go through."

Only then did I realize there was light at the far end of the tunnel, but no shadow. No woman. For some reason that felt wrong to me. Off. She should be here.

And suddenly it hit me. The female shadow I'd seen. It hadn't been Mum. It had been Mardi!

I could see the same thought occur to Mardi.

"Of course!"

We started forward. The floor grew colder and icier

with each and every step, and we slipped back and forth but pressed on.

"I don't know why I ever thought it was Mum," she said. "It was you, the whole time."

"Or you," I said. "In my dream. But . . . ?"

"What?"

"But if it was you, why were you warning me away?"

"I don't . . ." Mardi's voice broke off. "I don't understand. Was it you?"

That's when we heard the voice.

"Mooi? Magdi?"

There was no mistaking the voice this time, or the shadow that appeared on the wall.

"Magdi? Mooi?" Mum's voice called. "You shouldn't be here."

We rounded the corner, and there it was.

Niflheim. An endless, almost featureless plain of frozen snow lit by a pale, massive sun that cast almost no light. Yet that light was reflected by a billion crystallized snowflakes. A brightness relieved by only a single shadow.

Mardi's hand squeezed in mine. We were so in sync that I could feel her eyes slide with mine up the length of that shadow, until it reached a pair of delicate feet. Feet as white as the snow they stood on, and shod only in a pair of open sandals, and at least a foot and a half long.

Our eyes traveled up the endless length of ankle,

of thigh, up the short tunic that fell from her narrow waist and hung from one shoulder until finally we came to the face.

Mum's face. But it was at least twelve feet off the ground.

✳ 30 ✳

SEE YOU
ON THE OTHER SIDE

Mardi-Overbrook-Journal.docx

Girls, what are you—no, *how* are you here?"

I opened my mouth to answer, but Molly was faster.

"There's no time. Mardi kill—" She stopped and gulped. "Rocky was killed. Accidentally. We've got to grab his soul before it reaches Hel. He shouldn't be here."

Mum frowned. "Rocky? The human boy you had a crush on? How did he die?"

"It doesn't *matter!*" Molly pleaded. "We just have to—"

"I killed him," I cut Molly off.

This is not a sentence I ever imagined saying to anyone, least of all my own mother. Nor was her reaction anything like I might have expected. She didn't appear shocked, or angry, or scared. All she did was purse her lips for a moment, as if she was still trying to picture Rocky's face. Then: "Why did you kill him?"

Molly stamped her foot into the frozen ground. "Can we stop talking about this and start going after him? *Please!*"

Mum reached down and used one of her massive fingers to stroke Molly's hair.

"My darling Mooi. I know you're upset. But this is a serious matter you're talking about, and before we can even think about trying to intercept your friend, we first have to ascertain whether we have the right. So I ask again," she said, turning to me, "why did you kill Rocky?"

Mum had spoken gently, nonjudgmentally, but her words fell on me like hammer blows.

"It was an accident," I blurted. "I didn't mean to. I couldn't even see him."

But even as the words left my lips, I knew they were inadequate. Technically they were true. I hadn't been able to see him behind the counter, and I hadn't been thinking of hurting him when I pushed the counter over. I was thinking only of hurting Molly.

But we were fighting over him, and I knew there was a part of me that had been thinking, *If I can't have him, Molly can't have him either.* It was just like the time we were four years old, when we had talked Dad into buying us a one-of-a-kind Victorian doll we saw in an antiques store in Paris. We had promised to share, but inevitably we disagreed about what to do with it (as I recall, I had wanted the doll to go for a horseback ride, while Molly wanted it to serve high tea to its doll companions). The disagreement escalated into a screaming match, and the screaming match came to blows. Soon enough, we'd each grabbed hold of the doll, and seconds after that, the doll was in pieces, its cloth body ripped to shreds, its porcelain head shattered. And I still remember screaming, "If I can't have it, you can't have it either!"

"I wanted him, but he liked Molly more than me. So I guess I decided to hurt him. I mean, I wasn't thinking about it, but on some level, I must have wanted to do it. And then my powers just kind of took me over."

"It was both of us," Molly said now. "It didn't feel like we were in control of them. It felt like they were in control of us."

Mum nodded. "It's as I feared. The Reawakening is upon you."

I shot a glance at Molly.

"You knew this was going to happen?"

"I suspected it would. Your births are unprecedented, so no one could say for sure what was going to happen, but if my calculations were correct and you were going to turn out to be the goddesses of strength and rage, then your powers were going to descend upon you in one fell swoop. Your bodies and minds are still more mortal than immortal, which means that you are going to have a harder time assimilating your power than the Aesir or Vanir when they reincarnate. That's why I chose to reenter your life now," Mum finished. "I wanted to be able to help you through the process."

"I don't want to sound ungrateful, but can we finish the explanation later? After we've saved Rocky?" Molly stared at Mum hopefully. "We are going to save Rocky, aren't we?"

Mum shook her head, and Molly gasped, but Mum put a hand up.

"Not you. Me."

"What do you mean?"

"Rocky's soul is loosened from his body. As a consequence, it is traveling at a far greater speed than you could hope to reach without magical assistance, and we don't have time to prepare the necessary spells. Plus, someone needs to stay here to keep the portal open. Given how inconsistent your powers are, it's safer if both of you stay. For one thing, your powers tend to manifest more when you're together. They're also stronger that way."

"But I want to come," Molly said. "He's my boyfriend. I love him."

"Mooi," Mum said firmly. "Arguing is pointless, and juvenile. If you came, you would only hurt our chances of saving your friend. You and your sister need to stay here and keep the portal open."

"How do we do that?" I asked.

"Simply by standing in it," Mum said. "The energy that powers the Reawakening doesn't come from Midgard—it comes from the farthest reaches of the universe, in the infinite wastes beyond the nine worlds, and it enters Midgard through whichever seam happens to be closest to the two of you. In this case, that's the seam in Fair Haven. As long as you stand within it, or just on the other side of it, it will stay open."

Mum paused, looking at both of us sternly.

"I want to be clear on this," she said. "Under no circumstances should you come after me. If you step through the portal and I'm not there to reopen it, you'll be trapped on this side. And though there are other ways back, they are difficult and dangerous, even for goddesses—and there's no way a mortal would survive them. Do you understand?"

Molly and I nodded.

"Okay, then," Mum said, waving a hand at the darkened tunnel entrance behind us. "Go back in the tunnel, and wait for my return. It shouldn't take long."

She bent down and grabbed Molly, wrapping her in an enormous hug, and did the same to me. Her arms felt the same as they had when she was human-sized. Just bigger. So much bigger.

She kissed me on the top of my head.

"Go," she said.

She turned then, and started running. She looked

just like a normal person running, yet somehow the ground seemed to melt beneath her feet. The plain of ice was miles and miles long, but within seconds, she was out of sight.

"Wow," Molly said as we ducked back into the tunnel. "That was fast."

"That was insanely fast," I said, joining her inside the tunnel.

Molly stared across the ice field, as if Mum might suddenly reappear. After a long moment, she turned away, taking another step into the tunnel.

"So I guess now we wait."

"I guess," I said. "And try not to kill each other."

I heard it as soon as the words left my mouth.

"Sorry," I said. "Poor choice of words."

"Ya think?" Molly said sarcastically, before waving her words away. "I'm sorry. That was stupid of me. I know you didn't mean anything by it. Gods," she continued, "why is it we always feel the need to escalate things? Everything always turns into World War III between us."

"I know. Goddess hormones, I guess. They're like human hormones on steroids. Supersteroids."

To my surprise, Molly shook her head. "I don't think so. I mean, sure, we're wrestling with our new powers, so our fights are more destructive, but we've always argued, for as long as I can remember."

Somehow, I knew what she was getting it.

"You think it's because of our divine nature? I mean, I'm the goddess of rage. You're the goddess of strength. These aren't exactly gentle callings."

"I wonder," Molly said. "Do you think our whole lives are going to be one big struggle to hold them back? To keep from killing or destroying everything that crosses our path?"

"What if we can't control them? What if our powers win and we become something like Loki—agents of chaos, of destruction?"

"No!" Molly said forcefully. "I refuse to believe it. You're a good person. I'm a good person. I know that."

I nodded, but I wasn't as convinced as Molly. But then, she hadn't just killed someone. I had.

"Look at Freya, at Ingrid," Molly continued. "They have very specific callings like we do. Freya's the goddess of love, Ingrid the goddess of the hearth. And you can see how their divine natures influence their personalities, but they're way more complex than that. It's not like Freya's just a slut or Ingrid sits around knitting all the time. They do other things—lots of other things."

Despite myself, I snickered. "Freya is a bit of a slut," I said.

Molly laughed too, just a little, but it was so good to hear it in that cold dark place, especially after what had just happened between us.

"Rage, strength, they're not such terrible things," I said. "Especially when they work with each other rather than against each other. Look at Joan of Arc. She was full of righteous fury, and she used it to lead an army."

"Or the Rhinemaidens," Molly said. "And we're descended from them. I mean, assuming that Mum was telling the truth."

"Maybe not," I said. "The Rhinemaidens were human, and, well"—I waved a hand at the field into which Mum had disappeared—"the evidence is starting to look like maybe Mum's not actually human, after all."

Molly stared across the vast field, but the only thing that appeared was a small spray of snow and ice flakes, kicked up by a distant breeze.

"Maybe she's part human," she said after a while. "Or I don't know, maybe she's managed to acquire magical powers somehow. The Rhinemaidens were some of the most blessed humans of them all. Odin was supposed to have given them all kinds of gifts to help them defend the Rhinegold. Maybe some of those gifts were magical talismans or . . ." Her voice trailed off.

"I know," I said. "There are so many questions. I feel like I want to grill Mum for—" I broke off. I thought I'd seen movement on the horizon. A small shadow appeared above flat fields of ice, wavering but distinct. "Is that—?"

"They're coming back!" Molly cut me off, stepping to the edge of the tunnel.

"Careful," I said, taking her arm. "I don't know if the portal will just snap closed if we step across the threshold, but we shouldn't risk it."

I could see that it was taking all of Molly's willpower not to run across the field to the tiny form that was coming toward us swiftly, though not at the supersonic speed at which it had left.

"I only see one person," I said. "Where's Rocky?"

"She's carrying him!" Molly said, and then I saw it, the smaller body tossed across Mum's shoulders like a stole. "Oh, thank the gods, she's got him!"

Molly gasped then, and I was about to ask what was wrong when I saw it too.

A kind of wave or shadow crested the horizon behind Mum, stretching out on both sides of the field almost as far as the eye could see. At first, I thought it was a wall of snow tumbling toward Mum like an avalanche, but then I heard the faint growls and snarls floating across the field.

"Is that . . . barking?" I said.

Molly didn't say anything at first. Just nodded. Until: "It's the Hounds of Hel."

Mum raced across the field with Rocky's inert body draped over her shoulders. From somewhere, she'd procured a sword, as thin and pale as an icicle, and she swung it fiercely with her free hand, skewering any hound that dared to get too close to her.

"There must be thousands of them," I said.

Molly nodded. "Freya wasn't kidding when she said Helda doesn't like to lose one of her subjects." She winced as one of the hounds detached itself from the pack and launched itself at Mum, only to find itself impaled on the flashing ice sword and tossed away like a canapé.

"Holy crap, that was close!"

"I want to go to her," Molly said. "I want to help."

"Molly, no," I said, grabbing her arm again. "You can't. We have to keep this portal open. If it closes and we're stuck on the far side with that . . ." I let the image speak for itself.

"Damn it," Molly said, stamping her foot. "This is frustrating. Run, Mum!" she called. "Run!"

If Mum heard, she didn't answer. Just kept running and slicing and stabbing at any hound that approached.

My hand had slipped from Molly's arm to her hand, and we gripped each other tightly.

"Run, Mum!" I yelled. "You can make it."

Still no answer, but she was getting closer, barreling toward us like a wide receiver racing toward the end zone with the other team hard at his heels.

We could hear her footsteps now, each heavy tread smacking into the crystallized snow with a sound like breaking glass. Her breath sounded ragged like a wheezing car, and over that came the horrible barks of the hounds.

Suddenly, the dogs' barking changed. Before it had been just this cacophony, but now I heard little yips and growls in the middle of it all. It was like they were—

"They're talking to each other!" Molly said.

But they weren't just talking. They were giving directions. Because all at once, the two wings of the pack surged forward and began to fold around Mum and Rocky.

"They're trying to cut her off!" I yelled.

"No!" Molly screamed.

Before I knew what was happening, she'd pulled her hand from mine and shoved me backward, into the tunnel. Then she was off, racing across the field toward the pack.

"Molly!" I screamed. "Molly, come back!"

She ignored me, racing toward Mum and Rocky and the hounds. I took a step toward her, but as I did, I felt the walls of the tunnel shake. No, not shake: squeeze. It was like they were threatening to close in on me.

"No!" I screamed as Molly had. I threw my hands against the walls and pressed back. "You are not going to close," I yelled at the tunnel. "Stay . . . open!"

I could feel the walls vibrating against my hands. Showers of dirt and ice fell from them, but they didn't collapse.

And now Molly was reaching the horde. To my surprise, she ran not for Mum but for the dogs. Her fist raised above her head. A moment later, one of the hounds was flying through the air. Then another, and another, and another. Molly was beating them back with her bare hands.

"Do it, Molly!" I yelled. "Kick their asses!"

Molly and Mum made their way toward us, Molly clearing a path, Mum keeping the dogs behind them at bay. But the dogs were swirling around like water. It was impossible to get them all.

Suddenly, the dogs were on me, and before I knew it, a dark shape was lunging at me. My hands were practically buried in the wall. I reacted by instinct, lifting a foot and kicking the snarling beast right in the jaw. It went flying over the pack and disappeared in their midst.

But as quickly as the first dog was gone, another followed after it. Molly managed to grab this one by his tail, swinging him in a wide arc and tossing him away.

"There's too many!" Mum said, her sword slicing right and left. "I can't keep them all back!"

They were nearly at the entrance now, but there were at least a dozen dogs between them and me. Luckily for me, most of them were focused on Mum and Molly, and I only had to kick the occasional one away. But I couldn't see how they were going to get through. For every hound they held back, three more took its place.

"Mooi, go first!" Mum yelled. "I've got them."

"I'm not leaving you!" Molly yelled.

"Go!" Mum commanded in a voice that had to be obeyed. "Or we're all going to die!"

Molly turned from Mum and began beating a path toward me. As she got closer, I could feel the walls of the tunnel start to stabilize, and as soon as I thought it was safe, I let go of them and helped her clear the last of the dogs. A minute later, she was standing beside me.

I wanted to throw my arms around her, but there were still hundreds of dogs, snarling and snapping at us.

"I'm here, Mum," Molly called. "Just a few feet farther. You can make it."

"There are too many," Mum called back. "They'll come through after us. We're going to have to close the portal."

"What?" I yelled. "How?"

"I'll worry about how," Mum said. "You just worry about catching Rocky."

"Wha—" Molly yelled, then broke off as a dark form soared through the air toward us. She grunted as Rocky's body slammed into her, barely managing to avoid dropping him. Fortunately, he seemed to be unconscious.

"Now run!" Mum yelled, striking away the dogs with her sword and fists.

"Mum, no!" Molly yelled. "We're not leaving you!"

"Run!" Mum commanded, even as the walls of the tunnel started to shake more violently than ever.

"Molly, come on! The tunnel's coming down."

I grabbed her hand and yanked. I didn't want to leave Mum, but if the tunnel collapsed on us—on Rocky—then everything she had done would have been for nothing.

We ran across the shaking ground, dodging huge chunks of ice and frozen mud that fell from the ceilings. At the far end of the tunnel, I could see the hallway of Fair Haven, the bright light of Midgard shining on its polished floor.

We dashed for it, leaping over gaps that opened in the ground beneath us as the floor of the tunnel split apart. In the end, we had to jump across five feet of black nothingness, and we tumbled roughly into the hallway. But the ground was still shaking, and we heard the creaks and snaps of breaking timber and shattering plaster.

"What's happening?" Molly said, cradling Rocky in her arms.

"It seems like the whole house is coming down! We've got to get outside!"

"But Mum!"

"We can't help her, Molly. We've got to save Rocky!"

Before Molly could answer, the floor cracked and split in two, tipping up like the *Titanic* in the big final scene. We tumbled down the slope toward the front door, which obligingly cracked and fell off its hinges. We rolled across the steps and onto the lawn.

All of this couldn't have taken more than a few seconds. But when I looked back, I saw that the house had just broken apart.

"It's our dream," Molly said.

"Did Mum do that?" I whispered.

"I don't—" Molly broke off. "Where's Rocky?"

"What? I thought you had him!"

"I did. Then we rolled down the hallway and he was knocked loose."

She jumped up and started to run toward the house, but I grabbed her hand.

"Molly, no. It's still shaking. The whole thing could fall down."

"Mardi, let go of me or I'll—"

A weak voice to our left cut her off.

"M-Molly? Mardi?" We whipped our heads over to see Rocky sitting up in my car where we'd left his body earlier. He was rubbing a bruise on his head, but other than that looked fine.

"What in God's name just happened?"

RHIANNON

From the Diary of Molly Overbrook

$\mathcal{D}$ad sat propped up by pink pillows in Jo's bed, staring at the laptop resting on his thighs, which was open to the *New York Times*'s homepage.

> *Massive Earthquake Strikes Gardiners Island.*
> *350-Year-Old Mansion Destroyed. Janet Steele*
> *Feared Lost Among the Wreckage.*

"Girls, girls, girls," he said, snapping the laptop closed. "What kind of trouble have you gotten yourselves into?"

Twenty-four hours had passed since our trip to Niflheim. Rocky was recuperating from a minor concussion at Sal's house, and Mardi and I had both spent the night at Ingrid's. But there had been no sign of Mum. We had told him and Ingrid and Freya everything that had happened, and as far as I was concerned, he should have been the one answering our questions, not the other way around.

"Is there no way we can get through the seam to see if Mum's okay?"

Dad shook his head. "You heard Freya and Ingrid. It looks like your mother closed it from the other side. Unless someone opens it from that side, it's closed for good."

"That seems like a lot for a mortal to pull off," Mardi said from her perch across the room.

"It certainly does," Dad said, sighing heavily.

That sounded like a cop-out to me.

"Dad, come on," I pushed him. "Was Mum—is Mum really mortal? Or is she really a Jotun, like the legends say."

"Jarnsaxa," Mardi prompted. She glanced at me. "I looked it up last night."

"Jarnsaxa," I repeated. "Janet Steele. Sounds a bit like Mooi/Molly or Magdi/Mardi to me."

"Jarnsaxa," Dad repeated, a little smile playing over his lips, a mischievous twinkle coming into his eye.

"Dad! Spill it!"

"Sorry, girls. You're going to have to ask her yourself."

My heart started pounding in my chest. "Then you think she's okay! You think she's coming back!"

"Oh, I wouldn't worry too much about her. She's a resourceful woman. And she has a way of turning up when you least expect her. Now go find your aunt and ask her to whip me up one of her smoothies," he said, waving away any more questions. "I'm famished!"

ACKNOWLEDGMENTS

Thank you again to the wonderful team at Penguin, especially my editor Jennifer Besser and my publicist Elyse Marshall, as well as Kate Meltzer and Jacqueline Hornberger. Thank you to Richard Abate and Rachel Kim at 3 Arts. Thank you to my family and my friends. Thank you to all the loyal WitchEEs out there who have followed this story.

Turn the page for a sneak peek of

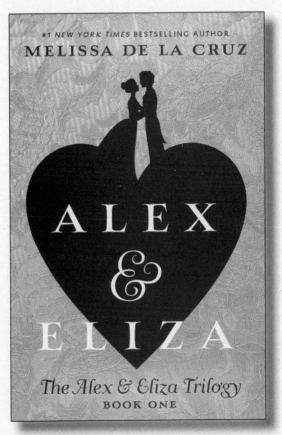

Copyright © 2017 by Melissa de la Cruz

"*Hamilton* fans obsessed with Alexander Hamilton and Eliza Schuyler's Revolution-era romance need this deep dive into the romance that changed American history."
—*Seventeen*

PROLOGUE

⌐◦⊕◦¬

Mansion on the Hill

Albany, New York
November 1777

*L*ike a latter-day Greek temple, the Schuyler family mansion sat atop a softly rounded hill outside Albany. Just over a decade old, the magnificent estate, called the Pastures, was already known as one of the finest houses of the New York state capital by dint of its exquisite furnishings and trimmings. The *pièce de résistance* was The Ruins of Rome, a set of hand-painted grisaille wallpapers decorating the home's second-floor ballroom, which Philip Schuyler had brought back from a year-long trip to England in 1762.

The local gentry was impressed by the mansion's square footage and elegant appointments, but they were more taken with the general's and Mrs. Schuyler's impressive pedigrees: Philip was descended from the Schuylers and the Van Cortlandts, two of the oldest and most prestigious families in New York, while his wife, Catherine, was a Van Rensselaer, the single most prominent family in the northern half of the state, *whose tenure stretched all the way back to the Dutch days of the early 1600s. Rensselaerswyck, as their estate was known, encompassed more than half a million acres, an unimaginably vast parcel, rivaled only by that of the Livingston family, who controlled what Catherine derisively referred to as "the bottom half" of the state. As a married woman, Catherine wasn't entitled to any claim on the Van Rensselaer properties (or, for that matter, her husband's), but rumor had it that her sizable dowry had paid for construction of their Albany mansion, as well as the Schuylers' country estate outside Saratoga.*

Just shy of his forty-fourth birthday, General Philip Schuyler was a handsome man, tall and fit, with a military bearing and a full head of hair that, like George Washington, he wore powdered and softly curled, rarely resorting to the elegant (but rather itchy) affectation of a periwig. As a commander in Washington's Continental army, Schuyler had organized a brilliant campaign against the British forces at Québec in 1775, only to be forced to resign his commission in June of this year, after Fort Ticonderoga fell while under his command. The defeat had been a double tragedy for Philip. Not only had the British taken the fort, they'd also seized his aforementioned Saratoga estate. Though not as grand as the Albany property, the Schuylers' second home was still sumptuous enough that John Burgoyne, commander of the British forces, chose it for his personal residence. But the coup de grâce came when the Continental army retook Saratoga in October, and a spiteful Burgoyne set fire to the house and fields during his retreat. General Schuyler had all but depleted his wife's inheritance building the house and bringing the land under tillage, which was expected to provide much of the family's income. The loss put a serious dent in the family's finances and cast an ominous shadow over their future.

Not that an observer would know it. Unused to idleness, General Schuyler had spent the past four months striding about the Pastures, laying out new beds in the formal gardens, regimenting the orchard harvest with military precision, supervising the construction of gazebos and guest houses and servant cottages, and generally getting in everyone's way, servant and family member alike. In a magnanimous gesture that indicated just how chivalrous he was—and how bored—Schuyler had even offered to put up the captured John Burgoyne before the British general was shipped back to England. Thus, did Schuyler's one-time rival and his entourage, some twenty strong, "occupy" the Albany mansion for a full month, and even if they didn't burn it down when they left, they still managed to eat a good-size hole into the family's provisions, comestible and otherwise.

Catherine Schuyler, one year younger than her husband, had been known as a "handsome woman" in her youth, but thirteen pregnancies in twenty years had taken their toll on her waistline. Practical, strong-willed, and stoic, she had buried no fewer than six of her children, including a set of triplets who hadn't lived long enough to be baptized. If the pregnancies had stolen her figure, the deaths had taken her smile, and watching her husband fritter away her financial assets had done little to improve her spirits.

Mrs. Schuyler's love for the seven children who remained to her was evident in the care she took of them, from the wet nurses and nannies she handpicked to raise them, to the tutors she hired to educate them, to the cooks she employed to keep them well fed. And somehow in the midst of the numbing cycle of births and deaths, declarations and proclamations, sieges and seasons, the Schuylers' three eldest girls had all reached marrying age.

Angelica, the oldest, was a whip-smart, mischievous brunette, with glittering eyes, her pretty lips set in a perpetual smirk. Peggy, the youngest, was a waifish beauty, with a waist so tiny that she rarely bothered with a corset, and alabaster skin set off by a mass of lustrous dark hair that was simply too gorgeous to powder or bury under a wig (no matter what Marie Antoinette was covering her head with at Versailles).

Eliza, the middle daughter, was as clever as Angelica and as beautiful as Peggy. She was also the most sensible, more interested in books than fashion, and, much to her mother's consternation, more devoted to the revolutionary cause and the mantle of abolition than to marrying one of its well-off colonels.

Her mother really didn't know what she was going to do with her.

Three daughters, each a prize in her own way (though Eliza would need a strong man to match her spirit). Under normal circumstances, marrying them off would be a feat of sustained diplomacy in which the first families of New York bound their blood and fortunes together like European aristocracy. But

New York's respectable families were few in number, and word traveled quickly. It would be only a matter of time before people found out just how much the Schuylers had lost at Saratoga, at which point the girls would become damaged goods. It was imperative, then—both to their futures and the family's—that they married well.

But it was even more important that they married fast.

And so, Mrs. Schuyler resorted to a strategy that had served her own mother well in times of need.

She was throwing a ball.